Paul Finch is a former cop and journalist, now turned full-time writer. He cut his literary teeth penning episodes of the British TV crime drama, *The Bill*, and has written extensively in the field of children's animation. However, he is probably best known for his work in thrillers, dark fantasy and horror.

Paul lives in Lancashire, UK, with his wife Cathy and his children, Eleanor and Harry. His website can be found at: www.paulfinch-writer.blogspot.com.

By the same author:

Stalkers
Sacrifice
The Chase: an ebook short story

PAUL FINCH

The Killing Club

AVON

AVON

A division of HarperCollins*Publishers*
77–85 Fulham Palace Road,
London W6 8JB

www.harpercollins.co.uk

A Paperback Original 2014
1

A catalogue record for this book is
available from the British Library

ISBN 978-0-00-755125-5

Set in Sabon LT Std

Printed and bound in Great Britain by
Clays Ltd, St Ives plc

For my children, Eleanor and Harry, with whom I shared many a chilling tale when they were tots, but whose enthusiasm is as strong now as it ever was

Chapter 1

Gull Rock was just about the last place on Earth.

Situated on a bleak headland south of that vast tidal inlet called 'the Wash', it was far removed from any kind of civilisation, and battered constantly by furious elements. Even on England's east coast, no place was lonelier, drearier, nor more intimidating in terms of its sheer isolation. Though ultimately this was a good thing, for Gull Rock Prison (aka HM Prison Brancaster) held the very worst of the worst. And this was no exaggeration, even by the standards of 'Category A'. None of Gull Rock's inmates was serving less than ten years, and they included in their number some of the most depraved murderers, most violent robbers and most relentless rapists in Britain, not to mention gangsters, terrorists and urban street-hoodlums for whom the word 'deranged' could have been invented.

When Detective Superintendent Gemma Piper drove onto its visitor car park that dull morning, her aquamarine Mercedes E-class was the only vehicle there, but this was no surprise. Visits to inmates at Gull Rock were strictly limited.

She climbed out and regarded the distant concrete edifice. It was early September, but this was an exposed location; a stiff breeze gusted in across the North Sea, driving uncountable whitecaps ahead of it, lofting hundreds of raucous seabirds skyward, and ruffling her tangle of ash-blonde hair. She buttoned up her raincoat and adjusted the bundle of plastic-wrapped folders under her arm.

Another vehicle now rumbled off the approach road, and pulled into a parking bay alongside her: a white Toyota GT. She ignored it, staring at the outline of the prison. In keeping with its 'special security' status, it was noticeably lacking in windows. The grey walls of its various residential blocks were faceless and sheer, any connecting passages between them running underground. A towering outer wall, topped with barbed wire, encircled these soulless inner structures, the only gate in it a massive slab of reinforced steel, while outside it lay concentric rings of electrified fencing.

The occupant of the Toyota climbed out. His tall, athletic form was fitted snugly into a tailored Armani suit. A head of close-cropped white curls revealed his advancing years – he was close on fifty – but he had a lean, bronzed visage on which his semi-permanent frown was at once both dangerous and attractive. He was Commander Frank Tasker of Scotland Yard, and he too had a heap of paperwork with him, zipped into plastic folders.

'I don't mean to tell you how to do your job, Gemma,' Tasker said, pulling on his waterproof. 'But we've got to start making headway on this soon.'

Gemma nodded. 'I understand that, sir. But everything's on schedule.'

'I wish I was as sure about that as you. We've interviewed him six times now. Is he going to crack, or isn't he?'

'Guys like Peter Rochester don't crack, sir,' she replied. 'It's a case of wearing them down, slowly but surely.'

'The time factor . . .'

'Has been taken into consideration. I promise you, sir . . . we're getting there.'

Tasker sniffed. 'I don't know who he thinks he's being loyal to. I mean, they didn't give a shit about him . . . why should he give a shit about them?'

'Probably a military thing,' she said. 'Rochester reached the rank of Adjudant-Chef. You don't manage that in the Foreign Legion if you're a non-French national . . . not without really impressing people. Plus they say he commanded total loyalty from his men. And that continued when he was a merc. You don't carry that off either unless you give a bit back.'

'You're saying Rochester's lot like each other?'

'Yes, but that's only one of several differences between them and the run-of-the-mill mobs we usually have to deal with.'

He shrugged. 'I'm not going to argue with that. You've done most of the homework on this case. The original question stands, though . . . how long?'

'Couple more sessions. I think we're almost there.'

'And you've borne in mind what I told you about DS Heckenburg?'

She half-smiled. 'Yes, sir.'

'We don't want him anywhere near this, Gemma.'

'He isn't.'

'He's a loose cannon at the best of times, but he could really screw this up for us.'

'It's alright, sir.'

'I'm surprised he hasn't at least been asking questions.'

'Well . . . he has.'

Tasker looked distracted by that. 'And?'

'I'm his guv'nor. When I tell him it's off-limits, he accepts it.'

'Does he know how many times you've interviewed Rochester?'

'He's been too busy recently. I've made sure of it.'

Tasker assessed their surroundings as he pondered this. Continents of storm clouds approached over the sea, drawing palls of misty gloom beneath them. Plumes of colourless sand blew up around the car park's edges. The hard net fencing droned in the wind. In the midst of it all, the prison stood stark and silent, an eternal rock on this windswept point, nothing beyond it but rolling, breaking waves.

'Hellhole, that place,' Tasker said with a shudder. 'I mean, it's clean enough . . . even sterile. But you really feel you've reached the end of the line when you're in there. Particularly that Special Supervision Unit. Talk about a box inside a box.'

He glanced uneasily over his shoulder.

'Something wrong, sir?' Gemma asked.

'Call me paranoid, but I keep expecting Heckenburg to show up.'

'I've told you, Heck's busy.'

'How busy?'

'Up-to-his-eyebrows busy,' she said. 'In one of the nastiest cases I've seen for quite some time. Don't worry . . . we've got Mad Mike Silver and whatever's left of the Nice Guys Club all to ourselves.'

Chapter 2

In a strange way, Greg Matthews looked the way his name seemed to imply he should. Detective Sergeant Mark Heckenburg, or 'Heck', as his colleagues knew him, couldn't quite put his finger on it, but there was something forceful and energetic about that name – *Greg Matthews*. As if this was a guy who didn't waste time dilly-dallying. There was also something 'Middle England' about it, something educated, something well-heeled. And these were definitely the combined impressions Heck had of the man himself, as he watched the video-feed from the interview room at Gillbridge Avenue police station in Sunderland.

Matthews was somewhere in his early thirties, stockily built, with ashen features and wiry, copper-coloured hair. When first arrested he'd been clad in designer 'urban combat' gear: a padded green flak-jacket and a grey hoodie, stone-washed jeans and bovver boots, as they'd once been known. All of that had now been taken away from him, of course, as he was clad for custody in clean white paper, though he'd been allowed to retain his round-lensed 'John Lennon' spectacles, as apparently he was blind as a mole without them.

None of this had dampened the prisoner's passion.

Three hours into his interview, he was still as full of his own foul-mouthed righteousness as he had been on first getting his collar felt. 'It's not my problem if someone thinks they've had it up to here with these neo-Nazi pigs!' he said in a cultured accent, far removed from the distinctive Mackem normally found in these parts. 'The only thing that actually doesn't surprise me about this is that another bunch of Nazi pigs, i.e. you people, are in a mad rush to find out who's responsible.'

'The question stands, Mr Matthews,' Detective Inspector Jane Higginson replied. She was a smooth, very cool customer. Her dark hair was cut short but neatly styled; her accent was much more local than Matthews's, betraying solid blue-collar origins. 'Why aren't you able to tell us what you were doing on the night of August 15?'

'Because it was five fucking weeks ago! And unlike you and your little wind-up clockwork toy friends, I don't have to keep a careful account of everything I get up to in an officious little pocket-book. Not that I think *you* do, by the way. We could look through your notes now, and I doubt we'll find any reference to harassment of ethnic or sexual minorities, intimidation of protest groups, illegal searches of private premises, brutality against ordinary working-class people, or general, casual misuse of authority in any of the other ways you no doubt indulge in on a daily basis . . .'

Matthews was articulate, Heck had to concede that, which was probably par for the course. He was leader of a self-styled 'action group' loosely affiliated to various militant student societies. He and his cronies were political firebrands, anarchists by their own admission . . . but did that make them killers?

'What about August 15?' Higginson persisted. 'Let me jog your memory . . . it was a Saturday. That must help a bit.'

'I do lots of different things on Saturdays.'

'You don't keep a record or diary? An industrious man like you.'

That was a sensible question, Heck thought. He'd been present when Matthews was arrested that morning inside his so-called HQ, which was basically a bike shed, though it had been packed with leaflets and pamphlets, and its walls were covered with posters and action-planners. Two state-of-the-art computers had also been seized. Matthews didn't just talk the talk.

'The only reason you can be refusing to cooperate on this, Mr Matthews, is because you've got something to hide,' the Detective Constable acting as Higginson's bagman said.

'Or because you're so deluded that you're more concerned about your street-cred than your personal liberty,' Higginson suggested.

Matthews bared his teeth. 'You really are a prissy, smarty-pants bitch, aren't you?'

'Moderate your language and tone, Mr Matthews,' the DC warned him.

'Or what? You'll beat me up?' Matthews laughed. 'I'm surprised you haven't already. Go on. There's nothing to stop you. I think you'll find I can take it.'

That depressed Heck, at least with regard to any chance these arrests might lead to a conviction. The guy didn't even realise the films and tapes made of interviews in custody were carefully audited; they couldn't just disappear. Along with Matthews's refusal to ask for legal advice, not to mention the 'no result' search they'd placed on him and his group with Special Branch, it all combined to suggest they were dealing with a pretender rather than an actual player.

'If only beating was where you lot drew the line,' the DC said. 'When did you decide you were actually going to murder Nathan Crabtree?'

'This is such bollocks.'

'Before or after the twentieth time you threatened to kill him online?' Higginson asked.

Matthews feigned amusement. 'If that's the best you've got, I pity you.'

Online, Matthews had regularly visited a number of rough and ready social-networking sites, usually hosted overseas, which catered for extremist ideologies. Their stock-in-trade were bitter, rancour-filled exchanges between anonymous individuals with ridiculous monikers. In normal times, any political forum would have been a strange place for an uncouth bunch like Nathan Crabtree and the other two victims, John Selleck and Simon Dean – quasi-political boot-boys with scarcely an educated brain-cell between them – to finish up, but from what Heck could see, the internet was increasingly allowing crazy activists to find an audible voice.

Heck turned from the video monitor, and ambled across the 'Operation Bulldog' Incident Room to the display boards bearing images of the crime scenes. There were three in total, and each one was located in a different corner of Hendon, Sunderland's old dockland.

The first, where Selleck had died, was inside a derelict garage; the second, the site of Dean's death, on a canal bank; and the third – the death-scene of Nathan Crabtree himself – under a railway arch. From the close-up glossies, it ought to have been easy to distinguish the victims as white males in their mid-to-late twenties, but it wasn't. So much blood had streamed down the faces and upper bodies from the multiple contusions to their crania, and had virtually exploded from the yawning, crimson chasms where their throats had once been, that no facial features were visible. Even distinguishing marks like tattoos, scars and piercings had been obliterated – at least until such time as the medical examiners had been able to move the bodies and wash them down.

The murders had happened over a three-week period the previous August, and though they'd raised a few eyebrows among the police, that had been more through surprise than dismay – because Crabtree and his crew had been well-known scumbags. Members of a semi-organised group called the National Socialist Elite, they were basically skinheads without the haircuts, but also football hooligans and small-time drug dealers. They'd spent most of the last few years menacing local householders, drinking, brawling and alternately bullying or trying to indoctrinate younger residents with their unique brand of hard-line British 'patriotism'. They'd been against Muslims, queers, lefties and – taking a break from the political stuff, just to win some brownie points with the common man – nonces. They were believed to be responsible for the brutal beating of an OAP in his own home after the rumour had got around that he was listed on the Sex Offenders' Register. The rumour had later turned out to be incorrect, but either way, the case against them was unproved.

'No, he was a paedo, for sure . . . and the lads knew it,' Crabtree was reported to have said, after the revelation the victim was innocent. 'Someone needed to sort him.'

The problem was, someone had now sorted the lads.

And in spectacular fashion.

The first victim had simply been dragged into a garage, and there beaten unconscious before having his throat cut with a sharp, heavy blade. At the time it could have been anything from a mugging gone wrong to a personal score. But then the other two had been nabbed over the following two weeks, and it became apparent that something more sinister was going on. The second victim, after being hammered with a blunt instrument, had been bound to a fence on the side of a canal, and had his throat cut with the same blade as before. In Nathan Crabtree's case, the perpetrators had gone even further. Though his body had been found under a

9

railway bridge, it had first been bound upright to a brick pillar with barbed wire, before his throat was slashed.

Heck appraised this scene the longest.

The wire was a nasty touch. Not just a sadistic measure designed to inflict maximum pain and distress, but indicative of enjoyment on the part of the killer. Whoever the perpetrator was – Heck wasn't convinced they were dealing with more than one, but then he wasn't in charge here – he'd displayed an aggressive loathing of his three targets, particularly Crabtree. Okay, that put Greg Matthews back into the picture – he'd clashed online with these right-wing apes more times than Heck could count, but there was still nothing in his past to suggest he was capable of such violence.

And then there was that damned barbed wire.

Heck couldn't help thinking the use of such material was trying to spark a dim and distant memory – but it was proving elusive.

'You're not convinced we've got the right people, are you?' someone said.

Heck turned. Detective Sergeant Barry Grant stood to his left, wearing his usual sardonic smile. Often, when Heck was posted out to Counties in his capacity as SCU consultant – or rather, a specialist investigator from the Serial Crimes Unit – he encountered a degree of resistance, though not in the case of DS Grant, the taskforce's File Preparation Officer, and a chap who had so far proved very amenable.

Grant was a shortish, older guy but rather dapper, given to matching blazers and ties, buttoned collars and pressed slacks. He had a well-groomed mop of chalk-grey hair and horn-rimmed glasses, the net effect of which was to make him look a little old to be a serving copper – not an inaccurate impression, as he was well into his fifties. But as Heck had already discovered, Grant was here for his brain, not his brawn.

Heck shrugged. 'I'm not saying there wasn't enough for

us to pull Matthews in . . . but whoever carved these ignoramuses up was seriously *driven*. I mean, they were on a mission . . . which they planned and executed to the letter.'

They assessed the gruesome imagery together. Alongside Grant, Heck looked even taller than his six feet. He had a lean but solid build, rugged 'lived-in' features and unruly dark hair, which never seemed neat even when he combed it. As usual, his suit already appeared worn and crumpled, even though it was clean on that day.

'I hear you think we should be looking for a single suspect?' Grant said. 'Rather than a group like Matthews and his people.'

Heck pursed his lips. He'd made the comment a couple of times during the post-arrest debrief, but had thought no one was listening.

'I know it doesn't look likely on the face of it,' he said. 'But here's my thinking. Crabtree and his gang lived and breathed urban violence, and they were usually team-handed. There's at least five or six of them still at large. They're also connected with various football factories, which means they can call an army into the field if they need one. On top of that, they have local credentials. They know every alley and subway. The whole East End of Sunderland is their turf.'

'All of which makes it less likely that one bod could do this on his own,' Grant said.

'Not if he knows the ground too,' Heck argued. 'In all three cases, the vics were skilfully entrapped. Witnesses say Crabtree chased someone half a mile before he was killed – in other words he was lured. Course, they didn't say who by. They didn't get a proper look.'

'They never do, do they.'

'And apparently he was led a merry dance . . . all over the housing estates.'

A different display board featured a large, very detailed street map of the Hendon district. Trails of red felt pen, constructed from the fleeting glimpses witnesses had admitted to, indicated the zigzagging routes taken by the three victims, each one of whom – for reasons not yet known – had suddenly taken off in pursuit of someone in the midst of their everyday activities, the subsequent footrace leading each man directly to the spot where he was murdered. All three had been on their own at the time, which suggested they'd been observed beforehand, and stalked like prey.

'We're talking careful preplanning here and good local knowledge,' Heck said. 'Greg Matthews and his mates aren't urban guerrillas . . . they're student gobshites. On top of that, none of them are Sunderland natives.'

'I'm not sold on Matthews either,' Grant said, 'but another crew could easily be responsible. I don't see why it needs to be one man.'

'Call it a hunch, but I keep thinking . . . Rambo.'

'Rambo?'

'First of all, we've canvassed all the main gangs on the east side of town. None of them are a fit. Secondly, none of your team's grasses are talking, which more or less rules out the rest of the local underworld. That knocks it back into the political court – Matthews and his like. Except that no . . . they may *say* they're fighting a war, they may dress like commandos, but whatever else they are, they aren't *that*. Not for real.' Heck rubbed his chin. 'We're looking for someone below the radar. Someone who knows every nook and cranny, but who's a loner, a misfit . . .'

'Could it be you've forgotten we're in the Northeast?' Grant chuckled. 'A violent misfit? Won't be a piece of piss singling him out.'

Heck pondered the question in the station canteen.

It was lunchtime so the place was crowded: uniforms and plain clothes, as well as traffic wardens and civvie admin staff. Heck had only been up here in the Northeast five weeks thus far, and aside from Grant, hadn't made friends with anyone locally, so he sat alone in a corner, sipping tea and hoping the DSU in charge of the enquiry would eventually bail the suspect downstairs. It didn't help that there were no alternative faces in the frame, but even if there had been Heck hadn't made enough of a mark on the enquiry yet to expect his opinion to carry any weight. His SCU status, while politely acknowledged, didn't cut much ice on its own – which in some ways he understood. The Serial Crimes Unit might be good at what they did, but they were based in London, which as far as many northern coppers were concerned was a different world. It didn't matter that SCU had a remit to cover all the police force areas of England and Wales, and subsequently could send out 'consultant officers', like Heck, who had experience of investigating various types of serial cases in numerous different environments – there were still plenty of local lads who'd view it as interference rather than assistance.

'Mind my whips and fucking stottie!' a voice boomed in his ear.

A chair grated as it was pulled back from the table alongside Heck.

'Oh . . . sorry,' the uniform responsible said, noticing he'd nudged Heck's arm and slopped his tea – though he didn't particularly look sorry.

Heck nodded, implying it didn't matter.

The uniform in question was one of a group of three, all loaded down with trays of food. The other two were younger, somewhere in their mid-to-late twenties, but this one was older, paunchier and of a vaguely brutish aspect: sloped forehead, flat nose, a wide mouth filled with yellowing, misaligned teeth. When he took off his hi-viz waterproof and hung it over the back of his chair, he was barrel-shaped, with flabby, hairy arms protruding from his stab-vest; when he removed his hat, he revealed a balding cranium with a thin, greasy comb-over. He ignored Heck further, exchanging more quips with his mates as they too sat down to eat.

Uniform refreshment breaks wouldn't normally coincide with lunchtime, which on Division was reserved for the nine-till-five crowd, so this presumably meant the noisy trio had been seconded off-relief for some reason, most likely to assist with Operation Bulldog. Heck relapsed into thought, though at shoulder-to-shoulder proximity it was difficult for their gabbled conversation not to intrude on him, despite the strength of their accents. Heck was a northerner himself. He'd initially served in Manchester before transferring to the Metropolitan Police in London. Even though he'd now been based in the capital for the last decade and a half, there were many ways in which the north still felt more familiar than the south, though the north was hardly small – and Sunderland was a long way from Manchester.

The PC who'd nudged his arm was still holding the floor. Heck could just about work out what he was saying. 'Aye t'was. Weirdest lad I've ever seen, this one.'

'Ernie Cooper, you say?' a younger colleague with a straight blond fringe replied.

'Aye. Bit of an oddball.'

'You were H2H off Wear Street?' asked the other colleague, who was Asian.

'Aye.'

'Bet you didn't get much change there?'

'Wouldn't think you'd find Ernie Cooper there,' the older PC added. 'Two-up-two-down. Bit of a shithole outside. Aren't they fucking all, but that's by the by. He answers the door – suit, tie, cardy. Like he's ready to go to church or something.'

14

'I know what you're gonna say,' the blond said. 'It's inside his house, isn't it?'

'Aye.'

'Was in there last year. Reporting damage to his windows. Bairns chucking stones.'

'Thought he was off to work, or something,' the older PC explained, 'so I says "Caught you at a bad time?" He says, "no, come in." What a fucking place.'

'Shrine to World War Two, isn't it?' the blond agreed.

Heck's ears pricked up.

'Everywhere,' the older PC said. 'Never seen as much wartime stuff. And it's neat as a new pin, you know. It's orderly. Like it matters to him.'

The blond mused. 'Bit of an obsessive, I think. His dad, Bert, was a commando or something. Got decorated for bravery.'

It was a simple association of ideas, but Heck had been brooding on his own comments from earlier and the thought processes behind them – *they may dress like commandos, but whatever else they are, they aren't that.*

'And then there's that bloody big knife on his living-room wall,' the older PC added. 'Enough to scare the crap out of you.'

Heck turned on his chair. 'Say that again?'

At first the three PCs didn't realise he was talking to them. When they did, they gazed at him blankly.

'Sorry . . . DS Heckenburg. I'm on Bulldog too.'

'Aye?' the older PC said, none the wiser.

'I've been attached from the Serial Crimes Unit in London.'

'Oh aye?' This was Blondie. He sounded less than impressed.

'It's what you were saying about this bloke . . . Something Cooper?'

'Ernie Cooper.'

15

'His father was a veteran, yeah?' Heck asked.

'Was, aye,' Blondie said. 'Been dead five years.'

'How old is the younger Cooper?'

The older PC, who wasn't bothering to conceal how irked he felt that his meal had been interrupted, shrugged. 'Late fifties . . . more.'

'You know him?'

'Not well.'

'Has he got form?'

The older PC frowned. 'Bit. From way back.'

'Violence?'

'Nothing serious.'

'But now you say he's got a big knife?'

'Aye, but it's not what you think. It's a wartime memento . . . something his dad brought home. A kukri knife, you know. Antique now.'

Heck's thoughts raced. The kukri knife – or khukuri, to be accurate – was that sharp, heavy, expertly curved weapon still used by Gurkha battalions in the British Army. It was infamously well designed to deliver a fatal stab wound, but was also known as a powerful chopping tool. And what was it one of the medical officers who'd examined the three murder victims had recently said? Something like: 'The lacerations are deep – they've gone clean through the muscles of the oesophagus in a single incision. We're talking a finely honed, but very heavy blade . . .'

'Was Ernie Cooper a military man himself?' Heck asked. The older guy shrugged. 'Not that I know of.'

'Factory worker,' the Asian PC said. 'Retired early.'

'Is he fit?' Heck wondered. They exchanged glances, now more bewildered than irritated by the protracted nature of the interrogation. 'What I mean is . . . can he run? Seriously fellas, this could be important.'

Blondie shrugged. 'Seen him jogging. Used to be part of

16

the Osprey Running Club, I think . . . ultra-distance. Probably knocking on a bit for that now.'

'Nah, I still see him running,' the Asian PC said. 'On his own, like. Don't see him running with anyone else. Never have, to be honest.'

'And you say his dad was a commando?'

'Aye . . .' Blondie confirmed. 'Bert Cooper. Well-known character up the East End. War hero like.'

'Commando?' Heck said. 'Don't suppose you can be any more specific?'

'He wasn't a commando,' the Asian replied. 'I read his obit in the paper. He was a para. He was in the desert and at Pegasus Bridge.'

'Aye, Pegasus Bridge,' Blondie said. 'That was where he won his medals. Remember my dad saying.'

Heck sat back. 'I'd like to meet Ernie Cooper, if you don't mind.'

The older PC shrugged. 'We don't mind. Why should we?' He rummaged in his jacket pocket. 'Can give you his addy right now.'

'Might be easier if you were to introduce me to him,' Heck said. 'Help break the ice maybe.'

The older PC glanced at his mates as if he couldn't believe the audacity of such a request. 'Before or after I've had my nosh?'

Heck stood up. 'I'll probably need an hour actually. Can you meet me downstairs at two?'

'Well . . . suppose I can put this lot away in an hour.' The older PC indicated his plate, which was piled with chips, eggs, sausage, beans and buttered bread. In less charitable mode, Heck might have commented that considering his bulk, which, now he was seated, bulged over his waistband and utility belt like a stack of tyres, the guy would be lucky to live through the next hour, but that would hardly help.

Besides, his thoughts were now on other things.

Like the Leibstandarte.

'What?' Jerry Farthing said – that was the older PC's name. 'The Leibstan-what?'

'Full title . . . 1st SS Division Leibstandarte,' Heck said from the front passenger seat of Farthing's patrol car.

Farthing drove thoughtfully on. 'Nazis, yeah?'

'Frontline shock-troops. Total fanatics. Most of them had been recruited from the Hitler Youth when they were still too young to see through the Führer's bullshit.'

Farthing looked puzzled. Up close, he gave off a faintly sour odour – sweat, unwashed armpits. He hadn't shaved particularly well that morning; his leathery, pockmarked cheeks were covered with nicks. 'I'm sure this is leading somewhere . . . I just hope it's worth it.'

'There was one place where we saw the Leibstandarte at their best.' Heck checked a mass of notes he'd recently scribbled in his notebook. 'Wormhoudt. A farming area near Dunkirk. That's where they murdered a bunch of British POWs with machine guns and grenades. Eighty men died . . . *after* they'd surrendered.'

'Nasty.' But Farthing still looked baffled as to how this concerned him.

'That was in 1940,' Heck said. 'In 1945 it was the other way around. Then, the 1st SS Division were in the rear-guard as Hitler's forces fell back into Germany. That April, quite a few of them got captured by British airborne forces at Luneburg. Ever heard of Luneburg, Jerry?'

'Can't say I have.'

'Well . . . if someone else had won the war, it would have gone down as a place of infamy. It'd be regarded as the scene of a notorious war-crime.'

'I'm guessing we got payback for Wormhoudt?'

18

'At least forty members of the Leibstandarte were executed on the spot.'

'What goes around comes around.'

'Yeah. It was war. What's interesting to us, though, is the method of the execution.'

'Okay . . .?'

This train of thought hadn't occurred to Heck straight away on hearing that Ernie Cooper's father had been a commando in World War Two, or that Cooper himself was a World War Two obsessive. But then the word 'para' had been mentioned, and it had jogged Heck's memory again – this time significantly.

The other thing, of course, was the wire.

'The British paratroopers who grabbed those SS men made them run the gauntlet,' Heck said. 'You know what that means?'

'Aye. Blokes line up on either side and hit them with rifle butts while they run down the middle.'

'Rifle butts, spades, trenching tools, anything,' Heck said. 'After that – and this is something I knew I'd read about once before – they tied them to posts . . . according to some accounts, with barbed wire.'

'Jesus,' Farthing said. Then the parallel seemed to dawn on him. '*Jesus!* . . . Are you serious?'

'Then they cut their throats.'

'Throats . . .' Briefly, Farthing was almost distracted from driving. 'Okay, there's a similarity with the way Nathan Crabtree copped it . . .'

'More or less with the way they *all* copped it . . .'

'Yeah, but that was probably nothing to do with Bert Cooper.'

'On the contrary . . .' Heck flipped a page in his notebook. 'Bert Cooper's unit, the 15th Air Pathfinder Brigade, were implicated. In fact, our Corporal Cooper was one of ten men arrested by the Special Investigation Branch. It was even suggested he did the throat-cutting. He was held for six days while the evidence against him was assessed.'

Farthing had turned a slight shade of pale. 'And?'

'He was released on grounds of "battlefield trauma". Instead of being charged and sent to the glasshouse, he received four months "psychotherapeutic counselling".'

'And . . . where've you learned all this?'

'It's all in the public domain, Jerry . . . you have heard of the internet?'

Farthing shrugged. 'Aye, but . . . even so.' He clearly wasn't enjoying hearing these revelations. 'What's it got to do with his son? I mean it's seventy bloody years ago.'

'Well for one thing, his son's still got the knife. Or so you said.'

'Hang on . . . we don't know it's the same knife. It probably isn't.'

Heck glanced sidelong at him. 'Seriously? Why else keep it in a place of honour?'

'He told me his dad took that knife off a dead Gurkha at Medenine in 1943.'

'Even if that's true, doesn't mean it wasn't the weapon used two years later on those SS prisoners. Might even have been a kind of poetic justice in that.'

Farthing shook his head. 'I'm sorry . . . this is a stretch.'

'Well, let's look at Ernie Cooper himself. You told me he's got form for violence.'

'Nothing serious.'

Heck flipped another page. 'Wounding his wife?'

'That was quite a while ago, wasn't it?'

Heck read on. '1977, to be precise. He actually assaulted her twice that year. On the second occasion, which was so serious that she subsequently left him, he received a two-month prison sentence. In 1979, he served time again, this time six months for threatening to kill members of a local Irish family. Apparently the Irish dad had been mouthing off down the pub about the Warrenpoint massacre of eighteen paratroopers by the IRA, saying it was justice for Bloody Sunday. Ernie Cooper went round that night, banging on their door and windows, threatening to burn the place down while they were all asleep. Two years later, he got locked up again . . . drew a suspended sentence for assaulting a bunch of CND members who'd tried to lay white poppies at the Cenotaph on Remembrance Sunday.'

Farthing shrugged. 'Aye, but if that was his last offence . . . I mean, 1981. It's no wonder he's not on our radar.'

'That was the last time he got *arrested*,' Heck said. 'It wasn't his last offence. Seems our Ernie's a bit of a letter-writer. He's had stuff in all the local rags, having a pop at drug addicts, prostitutes, child molesters and "bad families", as he calls them. Saying they should all be wiped out, quote, "to make the streets decent again".'

'Alright, so he's a right-wing nutter . . .'

'He got cautioned only five years ago for forcibly confiscating some kid's skateboard because he said it was annoying the whole street. He was also advised after another bunch of kids said he'd called them "dope dealers" and threatened them with a baseball bat.'

'Okay, I get it. He's got a temper.'

'He's also got a big bloody knife that was once used to murder a number of SS men,' Heck said. 'So what do you reckon, Jerry?'

Farthing nodded resignedly. 'I suppose we can have another chat with him.'

Chapter 3

Time hadn't made much impact on the Hendon district of east Sunderland.

It mainly comprised rows of age-old terraced housing, scruffy high-rise apartment blocks and the odd derelict industrial unit. A notorious area in law and order terms even during its docklands heyday, now it was largely unemployed, which made things even worse. The street they pulled up in was typical; a single row of houses facing onto a low-lying stretch of overgrown spoil-land cordoned off by a rickety old fence. The house fronts were black with grime, many of their doors dented and battered. It boasted ten dwellings in total and was bookended by two corner shops, which, as far as Heck could see, contained nothing but rubbish.

They parked Farthing's Vauxhall Astra patrol car opposite number three, alongside the only gate in the fence. As soon as they climbed out, the September breeze took hold of them. There had been squalling rain that morning and the road was still damp, its gutters lined with puddles. Now the sun had emerged, but rags of grey, wind-tossed cloud were strewn across it, absorbing any warmth. There was no one else in sight. No curtains twitched either in the house directly facing them, or in those next to it. No lights were on.

PC Farthing knocked on the front door and waited, while Heck stood behind him. There was no response. The interior lights remained off. Farthing knocked again. Still there was nothing; not a sound from inside.

He glanced at Heck and shrugged. 'Well . . . we tried.'

Heck ignored that, crouching at the letter flap and pushing it open. 'Mr Cooper!' he shouted. 'This is the police. Can you open up please?'

Still there was no sound from inside. Heck tried again twice, to no avail, before straightening up.

'Satisfied?' Farthing asked.

'Far from it. If you were under suspicion of murdering three gang members, and the police came round before you'd got a chance to do the rest of them, would you open the door voluntarily?'

'You can't be bloody serious . . . I only spoke to this fella as part of a house-to-house. To ask if he'd seen anything the day Crabtree got chased.'

Heck dug under his jacket and produced a folded document, scanning quickly through it. 'We'll never know how much he saw until we check him out properly.'

Farthing's eyes bugged. 'Is that . . . is that a warrant?'

'No, it's a beautician's appointment. Course it's a bloody warrant.' Heck tested the front door with both hands, but found it unyielding. 'This is pretty solid. Let's try round the back.' He set off along the pavement.

'You've had a busy lunchtime, haven't you?' Farthing said, hurrying to follow.

'Couldn't have done it without you, Jerry. Told the beak about Cooper's track record of political violence.'

'Political?'

'Picking on hippies and IRA supporters. Told him about

23

that nasty knife you saw too. I'll need a statement about that, of course.'

'Jesus H . . . I told you that knife was an antique.'

'A combat knife's a combat knife, Jerry.' They turned the corner at the end of the row, and entered a squalid backstreet. 'Anyway, we've got the warrant now . . . and this is more like it.'

The rear gate to number three was missing from its hinges, revealing a tiny paved yard. Unlike the surrounding environment, this area was cleared and well-swept. A clothes prop was leaning against the coal bunker, with a basket of pegs next to it.

'I'm not sure about this,' Farthing said as they entered. There was a rear ground-floor window to the house and a rear door. Both looked to be closed and locked. 'I don't like forcing entry, even with a search warrant.'

In response, Heck rapped loudly on the rear door and shouted at the top of his voice. 'Mr Cooper . . . we are police officers! This is really quite important! Could you open up please!' They waited for half a minute. Heck tried again. A further wait brought no reply. Heck glanced at Farthing. 'The occupier was definitely at home when you called this morning?'

'Aye . . . he let me in, gave us a brew.'

'Okay . . . well he's pretty clearly absent now. Would you agree?'

'Suppose so.'

'Good.' Heck put his shoulder to the rear door, and it crashed inward, its rusted lock flying off with the first impact. Inside, the house stood in sepulchral dimness.

'Mr Cooper, it's the police!' Farthing called as they shuffled through a narrow scullery into a small, tidy kitchen. 'We have a warrant to search these premises!'

There was no reply, but Heck glanced around. 'Place is immaculate,' he observed.

'He's always a well-turned-out bloke.'

'Bit like a soldier, eh?'

In the hall, a shoe rack stood close to the door, on which Heck noted two pairs of muddy trainers. A raincoat was draped over the foot of the banister. Aside from these mundane items, this part of the house also looked neat. Its linoleum floor shone, as if mopped regularly. But the real surprise came when they moved sideways into the lounge, which in the past had been knocked through into the dining room to create one large living space, the walls of which had since been completely covered with sepia-toned news cuttings.

Fascinated, Heck's attention flitted from one headline to the next.

Soviets launch winter offensive

British triumph in desert battle

As he'd heard in the station canteen, this was World War Two. Every aspect of it. But it wasn't like a temporary display. The thousands of carefully interlocked cuttings here had literally been turned into wallpaper, incorporated into the fabric of the house's interior. And it was a professional job; there wasn't a square inch of plasterboard exposed. Heck glanced into what had once been the dining room.

Mussolini snatched from mountain redoubt

Royal Navy enters Pacific

Grainy images had been mounted to create maximum impact: frostbitten German troops surrendering in Russia; British tanks rolling over the sunburned plains of Alamein; U-boat survivors bobbing like driftwood in an oil-filled sea.

In addition, there were four framed black and white snap-shots on the mantelpiece, each one depicting the same toothily grinning face: a young squaddie, usually with tousled hair and dust on his cheeks. In one, he'd been photographed in what looked like a desert graveyard, and had a small mongrel dog sitting on his left shoulder. In another he was hefting a Bren gun.

'I've heard about living in the past,' Heck said. 'But this . . .'

'Fuck!' Farthing interrupted. 'The knife's gone.'

He was standing by the lounge sideboard, where other items of memorabilia were arranged. Two of these were cruciform medals done in black metal with white edging, attached to black, white and red ribbons – Heck recognised them as Iron Crosses, second class. In a glass case on the wall there was a faded red beret, with a silver badge attachment depicting an eagle clutching crossed daggers. Also fixed on the wall, as Farthing now indicated, there was a bent wooden scabbard, bound with black leather and clad at its sharpened tip with slivers of plate metal.

Heck didn't need to be an expert to recognise the sheath for a khukuri. Though the knife itself was absent, its two smaller cousins – the chakmak and karda, utilised for sharpening the main blade, were still in place.

'He might just have taken it to get it cleaned, or something,' Farthing said.

'That in itself would be a tad suspicious, don't you think?'

Before Farthing could reply, a shudder passed through the house, and then another, and another. Heavy feet were descending the stairs, and at speed. Heck and Farthing both lurched to the lounge door at the same time, briefly hampering each other. When they finally burst into the hall, they caught a fleeting glimpse of a tall shape in a fawn tracksuit vanishing out through the front door, slamming it closed behind him.

Heck reached the door first, but was briefly foxed by its special security lock. He twisted and turned the handle and hit the button repeatedly, all without consequence.

'Here,' Farthing said, pushing past.

He managed to get the door open, and they blundered outside.

The street was empty again, but two things struck them simultaneously: the front nearside tyre of the police Astra had been slashed to the ply-cord – as though someone had dealt it a passing blow with a heavy blade; and the gate in the fence opposite was now open and swinging.

'Shit!' Farthing shouted, heading across the road to his car.

'What's on the other side of that fence?' Heck replied, going for the gate.

Farthing was now busy filching his radio from its harness. 'What . . . oh, wasteland. Industrial wasteland . . .'

'Can you get the car round there?'

'Not without changing the tyre, obviously . . .'

'Sod the bleeding tyre!' Heck ran through the gate. 'And get us some support!'

On the other side, a beaten earth path wove crazily down a shallow slope, looping between dense stands of Indian Balsam, their September seedpods now loaded to capacity and exploding as Heck barged against them. The path unfurled ahead of him for dozens of yards, but there was no sign of Cooper, which was disconcerting, given that he was in his fifties. Though what was it they'd said about him – that he'd formerly been an athlete? Heck swore under his breath. He'd known fitness fanatic coppers who were still ripped and energetic in their mid-sixties.

He fished his own radio from his pocket as he circled a thicket of hogweed and found himself following a rusty wrought-iron fence. Thirty yards ahead, there was a gap in this; on the other side of that, a muddy lane led beneath a dripping black railway arch. Heck kept running, doing his damnedest not to slip and slide in his leather lace-up shoes.

'Alpha-Echo control from DS Heckenburg, Operation Bulldog, over?'

'DS Heckenburg?'

'I'm pursuing a suspect in the neo-Nazi murders. I could use some back-up, and some geographical guidance, over?'

It was several seconds before he received a response, which was no surprise as the passage under the arch ran forty yards at least. When he re-emerged into the open, Heck found himself on a dirt track strewn with bricks and twists of wire, which led past a broken-down gate onto the forecourt of a nondescript derelict building.

'Excuse me, sarge . . . can you confirm that you're pursuing a suspect in the Hendon murders, over?'

'That's affirmative. His name is Ernest Cooper, male IC1, tall, six-two or six-three, late fifties, over.'

'Whereabouts are you, over?'

'That's the problem. I don't bloody know.' Heck could have beaten himself up at that moment. He hadn't even memorised Ernest Cooper's address, and he'd dropped the warrant back in the house, so he had no point of reference at all. All he knew was that he was somewhere in Sunderland's East End.

'Can you contact PC Jerry Farthing?' Heck hadn't memorised Farthing's collar number either, which was another black mark against him. 'He'll tell you where we are, over.'

'Affirmative. Stand by.'

'I can hardly stand by,' Heck said under his breath, as he jogged through the gate onto a broad, cindery parking area. About thirty yards ahead, the scabrous edifice of the main building was visible. Its upper windows were yawning cavities. A protruding lattice of rusted metalwork ran along the front, about fifteen feet up; the relic of a canopy, beneath which wagons would have idled. Fragments of mildewed signage remained, but were unreadable.

Heck hesitated to go further. Was it feasible that Cooper, fit as he was, could have got this far ahead? The problem was there didn't seem to have been anywhere else he could run to. It was all a bit worrying, of course, because if Cooper was the perp, and it now seemed highly likely he was, there were only three reasons why he'd run like this: either there was somewhere else he could go, some bolthole where he could lie low; his personal liberty was less important to him than finishing off the work he'd set himself, eliminating Nathan Crabtree's gang; or both of the above.

In no doubt that he needed to catch this guy right now, Heck advanced towards the building, scanning it for any identifying marks he could pass to Comms. Most of its ground-floor entrances were covered by wooden hoardings, but the most central one had collapsed, exposing black emptiness.

He stepped through this, ultra-warily.

Total darkness enclosed him – but only for a second. Very rapidly, dimmer light sources became apparent, and his eyes attuned to an area that was like a small lobby, half-flooded with water, crammed with broken bricks and masonry. Anyone attempting to dash through here would likely have fractured an ankle. Instead, Heck tip-toed through it, balancing on planks and fallen joists. A secondary door led into a cavernous inner chamber, the entrance to which was only accessible at the end of sixty yards of cage-like corridor, lagging and bits of cable hanging down through its mesh ceiling.

Again, Heck halted. Going further on his own was asking for trouble. Cooper had the khukuri knife – and he was clearly a dab hand at using it. With a single blow, he'd disabled a police car. Speaking of which – Heck gritted his teeth with fury at Jerry Farthing. Any bobby with his experience ought to have known that checking damage to a company vehicle was of less importance than apprehending a suspect. In fact, he *would* have known it. The reason Jerry had refused to join the chase was a lack of motivation. Whether that was down to fear or laziness, Heck wasn't entirely sure, but the bastard was clearly past his best.

Then, to his surprise, he heard the chugging of an engine outside.

He scrambled back through the brick-strewn lobby, and felt a vague pang of guilt at the sight of Farthing's Astra wallowing to an unsteady halt on the forecourt, its front nearside tyre hanging in ribbons. He walked quickly over there. 'Have you put Comms in the picture? I wasn't able to . . .' His words petered out.

Farthing, white-faced and sweating, climbed slowly from the driver's side, while someone else climbed from the passenger side. The newcomer was slim but tall, about six-foot-three. He was in his late fifties, with lean, angular features and pale blue eyes. He had grey hair cut so short that it was really no more than a circular patch on top of his head, and a clipped grey moustache. He wore a fawn tracksuit, and a khaki belt, into the left-hand side of which the khukuri knife was tucked. This was a truly admirable object – its blade shone wickedly and there was a carved steel lion's head at its pommel. But he also wielded a firearm: a Luger nine-millimetre, that most iconic weapon of the Third Reich, which he now trained squarely on Farthing's head.

They'd been fooled, Heck realised. He'd gone straight through that gate in the fence without considering that their quarry might be somewhere closer to home – hiding under the police car perhaps, or squatting around the back of it.

'Please tell me you managed to get a call out first?' Heck said to Farthing.

But Farthing was too busy jabbering to his captor. 'Mr Cooper . . . this is ridiculous. You're not going to shoot us. I mean, come on, you can't . . .'

'Shut up,' Cooper said, quietly but curtly.

'Look, we were only here to ask you a couple of questions . . .'

'I said shut up!'

'Jesus, man . . . you can't just fucking shoot us!'

'Don't do anything rash, Mr Cooper,' Heck advised.

'Rash implies unnecessary, pointless, futile.' Cooper's accent was noticeably Sunderland, but more refined than most. He waggled with his pistol, indicating that Farthing should walk over and stand alongside Heck, which he duly did. 'I assure you, Sergeant Heckenburg . . . the action I take here today will be none of those things. Now empty your pockets, please. Every weapon you're carrying, every communication device. I want them placed on the ground. When you've done that, put your hands up.'

Heck stooped, laying down his radio, mobile phone and handcuffs. Cooper watched him intently and yet unemotionally. His pale blue eyes were like teddy bear buttons; it was quite the most unnatural colour Heck had ever seen.

'That looks like an original 1940s Luger to me, Mr Cooper,' Heck said. 'Another spoil of war?'

'Inside!' Cooper indicated the yawning doorway behind them.

Heck held his ground, fingers flexing. He glanced around. There wasn't a building overlooking them. The only high points in sight were the towering hulks of disused cranes. Directly overhead, the sun had gone in, tumbleweeds of cloud scudding through a colourless sky.

Cooper pointed the Luger directly at Heck's face. 'I said move.'

Heck turned, hands raised. Farthing did the same, half-stumbling, the eyes bulging in his sweaty, froglike face.

'I'm guessing you haven't tried to fire that before?' Heck said over his shoulder.

'It's fully loaded, I assure you,' Cooper replied.

'Yeah, but what do you think'll happen if you fire it now . . . for the first time in seventy years?'

'Keep walking,' Cooper instructed.

Farthing whimpered as the dark entrance loomed in front of them. Heck glanced sideways; tears had appeared on the chubby cop's milk-pale cheeks.

'You still need a way out of this, Mr Cooper,' Heck said. 'Shoot us now, and what happens next?'

'That hardly matters to *you*.'

'But what about you? Won't be much chance of getting the rest of Crabtree's gang if you're sitting in jail. It might be the other way around. Crabtree's lot will have friends on the inside . . .' Bricks and other rubble clattered under their feet as they stumbled into the mildew-scented interior.

'If I feared retaliation, I'd never have embarked on this course,' Cooper said.

'And what course was that?' Heck wondered. 'Bumping off some Nazis? Carrying on your father's good work?'

'Father was the finest of the fine. During this nation's darkest hour, fighting men like him shone.'

'Pity he didn't restrict himself to the fighting, eh? Pity he became a war criminal.'

'It's no crime to execute those responsible for heinous deeds.' Cooper's voice had imperceptibly tautened. 'Father was always an honest man. He believed in justice and a firm response to wickedness. Along *there* . . . all the way to the end.'

They now faced the meshwork corridor with its hanging cables and rags of lagging. The open spaces beyond it were hidden in funereal gloom.

Farthing all but sobbed aloud.

'And what wickedness were Nathan Crabtree and his

cronies committing?' Heck asked, starting forward, eyes darting right and left.

'The mere fact you have to ask that condemns you . . . but their main fault is simply being who they are.'

'You don't share their views? I'm surprised.'

'Which again shows how little you know, sergeant. Animals like that . . . they call themselves British. And yet they terrorise the weak, punish the innocent. They call themselves patriots . . . even though they defame our flag, besmirch our name . . .'

'So how'd you do it?' Heck asked. 'Lure them to their doom. I'm guessing they didn't know they had a runner on their hands?'

'What are you doing?' Farthing blurted, suddenly jerking out of his tearful reverie. 'We don't want to *know*, okay Mr Cooper? We don't want to know anything.'

Cooper appeared not to have heard the outburst. 'I propositioned the two henchmen. Made sexual remarks to them. One while he was using a public lavatory. The other while he was crossing a public park.'

'As easy as that, eh?' Heck said.

'Dumb animals follow their instincts. As for Crabtree, I presented him with certain photographs I'd discovered on the internet. Offered them for sale to him in a pub. I knew he would pursue me for as long as was necessary.'

'And in each case, when you got to the pre-prepared spot, you just turned around and pulled your Luger?'

'The brutes are so easy. They were even easier to render unconscious. If your forensics people were ever to examine my khukuri, they'd find as many blood flecks lodged in its lion head hilt as they would in the grooves or bevels of its blade.'

'They aren't going to find it, Mr Cooper,' Farthing said in an attempted manlier tone. 'You have my word on that.

33

Look . . . *we* couldn't stand Crabtree and his Nazi pals either! We're *glad* they're dead. We weren't investigating this case very hard . . .'

'I'd like to believe you, PC Farthing,' Cooper said, 'I really would. But in modern Britain, the establishment – an amoral, drug-addled band born of the 1960s and 1970s, of whom you are the willing servants – have proved numerous times how uninterested they are in finding justice for the oppressed, and in fact have expended much more energy defending the rights of the vile. So no, I don't believe you.'

Heck said nothing. They were now approaching the end of the meshwork passage, though just before that a sheet of grimy polythene part-hung down overhead.

'Okay . . . you don't like us.' Farthing's voice turned whiney again. 'But what good is killing two bobbies? Look . . . I've got a wife and three daughters! What's it going to do to them if they never see me again? How will they cope?'

'Widows and fatherless children were left equally bereft in the years following the war,' Cooper replied. 'They managed.'

'Oh, cut the crap!' the PC snapped in a strangled tone. He swung sharply round, the eyes bulging like wet marbles in his pallid, frightened face. 'If you're going to do it, do it! Don't bore us with your good old stiff-upper-lip "who-d'you-think-you're-kidding-Mr-Hitler" bullshit!'

Heck spun around too, taking advantage of the distraction to grab the edge of the hanging polythene and yank the entire thing down; a crumpled mass of water-laden sheeting, which covered their startled captor head to foot.

Cooper didn't fall beneath the weight of it, but it hampered him and blinded him. He never even saw the rocketing punch that Heck threw at his face, but grunted on impact. There was a splat of scarlet on the other side of the sheeting, and yet he remained upright. Already he was fighting the encumbrance off, levelling his Luger.

'Leg it!' Heck shouted, snatching Farthing by the sleeve.

'What . . . where to?'

'Anywhere! Just bloody leg it!'

Chapter 4

They ran together, but in no particular direction. The wilderness of the shop floor lay all around them, littered with rubble – but it was wide open. There was nowhere to duck or hide. Heck glanced back. Cooper was stumbling out from the mesh corridor.

'Down here!' Farthing squawked. To the left, a steel stairway dropped through an aperture into dimness.

They descended without thinking. Some ten feet down, it deposited them in a concrete corridor with numerous doors leading off it, though at its farthest end, maybe eighty yards away, there was a smudge of light. They ran towards this, but only seconds later heard the heavy *clunking* of feet on the stair behind.

'Oh Christ!' Farthing gasped.

Passing door after door, they saw nothing but mould-streaked walls, rotted pipe-work. Heck glanced back again. The tall, rangy form of Cooper was pursuing them along the passage, silhouetted on the light seeping down the stair. He was walking rather than running, but with long, loping strides. Heck was confused as to why, in this narrow field of vision, he hadn't already opened fire. Possibly, just maybe, it was his eyes. Cooper was nearly sixty, and perhaps didn't have his glasses with him. It was certainly the case that he'd had to get close to his other victims. This gave them a chance, of sorts.

Heck bundled Farthing around the corner onto another shop floor. This one was dimmer than the first, and strewn with further rubble, but still there was nowhere to hide.

'Oh . . . shit!' Farthing stammered.

Heck pushed him towards a double-sized doorway, and beyond this into a tall timber passage that was broad enough for forklift trucks to drive down it. Their footfalls echoed as they hammered along, emerging fifty yards later in what had once been an internal loading bay, a series of concrete platforms abutting into a hangar-like space where HGVs were once accommodated. It was filled with litter and old leaves, and stank of oil.

There was no further access from here. Panting, Heck could only gaze at the huge folding steel doors that separated them from the outside. Again, they heard feet reverberating along the service passage behind.

'*Fuck!*' Farthing hissed.

They scrambled through a smaller-sized doorway on the right, entering a confused sprawl of interconnecting offices and corridors. Again, all were cluttered with rubbish and cross-cut by shafts of light penetrating from various external windows, though most of these had been closed off with corrugated metal. They turned several corners, before blundering into a final room, and finding there was nowhere else to run.

They slid to a halt, sparkling with sweat. Farthing made to double back, but Heck motioned for silence.

Seconds passed as they listened.

Suddenly, there was no other sound.

'Let's kick our way out,' Farthing said, lurching towards

the window, which no longer sported glass beneath its metal cladding.

'Wait!' Heck whispered.

They froze again. Still there was no sound. Had the maniac lost them? Or was he creeping up even now?

'*Fuck this!*' Farthing said, but Heck grabbed his arm.

'Just wait! He's had a couple of chances to pop us, and he hasn't taken them. It may be he needs to get close.'

'So?'

'So hang on! We don't know how solid that shutter is. It could take us five minutes, and if we make a racket it'll bring him right to us.'

Farthing licked his lips. 'You go see where he is . . . I'll try and get it loose quietly.'

Heck padded back to the door, stopping alongside a low shelf, on which someone had left a wrench. It was old and rusty, but still satisfyingly heavy. He grabbed it, and peered out into the half-lit corridor. To his left it right-angled out of sight; to his right it ran straight for forty yards before vanishing into shadow. He glanced back, to where Farthing was feeling around the edges of the corrugated metal. With a slight creak, it shifted. The PC gazed at Heck.

'Couple of kicks and this is gone, I'm telling you!'

Heck motioned to him to wait just a second, and slipped out into the corridor, walking to the nearby corner. Around it, the passage led twenty yards to what looked like a fire-exit. He hurried up there and shoved down on the escape-bar, but there was no budge in it. As he pondered this, there came a series of thundering blows from behind. He knew that it was Farthing – hammering on metal.

He darted back to the corner and around into the main corridor, just in time to see the tall shape of Cooper loom out of the shadows at the far end, gun levelled.

'You total prat!' Heck shouted, barging back into the office.

Farthing was still working on the corrugated metal, half of which had been bashed through, though the rest of it wouldn't shift. 'Didn't know where you were!' he wailed. 'I thought he'd nabbed you!'

'Fucking idiot!' Heck grabbed up an office chair, hurling it through the air.

The impact was cacophonous, and the rest of the corrugated shutter fell away, more dim light spilling inward. Farthing vaulted out through the empty frame first. Heck followed, sensing the figure appear in the office door behind.

'*Oh shit!*' Farthing screamed.

They weren't outside.

They were in another enclosed space; some kind of garage, empty except for dust and debris. Farthing staggered across it towards a set of double doors, the central cleft of which promised daylight. Heck twirled back to the window. Cooper was framed on the other side, bloody-chinned, gazing along his pistol barrel.

Heck threw the wrench.

It flashed through the air, a spinning blur, and struck its target in the middle of his chest. Cooper went down with a choked gasp and Heck tensed, ready to pounce back through the empty frame and overpower him, but there was no clatter of a firearm dropping loose. So he turned and hurtled across the garage, to where Farthing was throwing his shoulder at the double doors. Heck joined him, left foot first. With a splintering *crash*, the bolt on the other side gave way. The doors swung open, and fresh air poured in. They tottered out into a yard which seemed to run along the back of the main building and was dotted with the relics of cars and trucks. Another brick wall, maybe twelve feet high, hemmed them in.

'That way,' Heck said, pointing left.

About seventy yards in that direction stood a pair of tall wrought-iron gates. They were closed and chained, but there was a gap between the top of the gates and the overarching brickwork. It was a climb, but it wouldn't be impossible.

Farthing shook his head. 'N— no . . . *that* way!'

He pointed right, where only thirty yards away, beyond the gutted shell of a van, stood a single gate – this one wide open. Some instinct told Heck this was a mistake – but Farthing was already stumbling towards it. Heck followed, glancing over his shoulder. There was still no sign of Cooper. The wrench had caught him a good one; there was even a chance it had done the job for them, but that would be a hell of a gamble.

'*Bloody hell, no!*' Farthing cried. Now that he'd circled the van, he could see through the narrow gate – into a cul-de-sac; a smaller yard encircled by yet another high wall, this one surmounted with shards of glass.

With a creak of hinges, the garage door opened behind them.

Heck snatched Farthing's collar and dragged him down to his knees, so the wrecked van would fleetingly screen them. He flattened himself on the concrete to gaze underneath it. Cooper's feet limped into view on the other side. The guy was obviously hurt, limping and breathing heavily; he moved away from the garage slowly, warily – scanning for his prey.

'Doesn't give up, like, does he?' Farthing breathed. He slumped alongside Heck, shoulders pressed back against the crumpled bodywork. His face was pasty-white, and dabbled with beads of hanging sweat. 'Really . . . really wants to kill us.'

'Got no choice,' Heck mumbled, still watching.

Cooper had advanced about ten yards, and now appeared to be pivoting around. If he ventured right, he'd locate them

40

almost immediately. But if he went left, towards the double-gate, there was a possibility they could sneak into the garage and double back.

Only after several torturous seconds did the gunman make his choice, cautiously edging left. Heck held his breath, though Farthing appeared to be struggling with his. He gave a slow, sharp gasp.

'Shhh!' Heck said.

Cooper progressed into the wider yard, checking every nook and cranny.

'Can you make it back through the building?' Heck asked, glancing up.

Farthing looked dismayed. 'All that . . . all that way again?'

'I'm guessing he already knows that smaller gate leads nowhere. So he's covering the other one. He's got us bottled up in here. All he needs to do now is find us. We've *got* to make a run for it.'

'I don't know . . .' Farthing shook his head, clutching the side of his chest. 'I don't know if it's my heart, but . . .'

'Your heart?'

Fresh sweat streamed down the older PC's face; he wasn't so much white now, as green. 'Something's wrong. I'm not in shape . . . as you've probably seen.'

Heck glanced back under the vehicle. Cooper's legs were a considerable distance away – maybe sixty yards. If he *was* short-sighted, that might be an adequate distance for them to chance it. But now Farthing had a problem with his heart . . .?

'It never bloody rains,' Heck said under his breath. He glanced back up. 'And you've got a wife and three daughters, haven't you?'

Farthing nodded and swallowed, his brow tightly furrowed.

Heck sighed and made his decision. 'If I can get back inside and leg it through the interior, it may draw him away.

41

If I manage that, can you at least make it to that double-gate over there?'

'Don't know if I'll be able to climb over it . . .'

'Jerry . . . rough as you may feel, you're going to have to do something. The SAS aren't going to turn up!'

Farthing looked agonised by the choice he was facing, but finally nodded. 'Suppose I've . . . more chance getting over that gate than of making it all the way back through this place . . . especially if you've drawn him off. But . . . what if you get lost in there? He knows his way around!'

Heck shrugged. 'Chance I'll have to take.'

'A bloody hell of a chance!'

'Least there's no one at home who's going to miss me.'

Heck glanced under the van again – Cooper had reached the far end of the yard. It was now or never. He turned to Farthing and offered his hand. Farthing at first looked surprised, but then nodded and gripped it, his palm moist, clammy.

Heck got up and ran, bombing the short distance towards the garage.

It hadn't been so complex a route through the old factory, he was sure – but he couldn't picture it easily. All he could do was keep going – and yet that resolve faltered when he was halfway over and spied the tall shape of Cooper sprinting back towards him. Heck had the brief, crazy notion to swerve away from the garage and barrel straight at the nutter, taking him down with a head-on rugby tackle. But no . . . all the bastard needed was proximity. The second he got Heck in range, he'd shoot.

So thinking, Heck veered into the garage. The window yawned ahead of him, and he was so pumped with adrenaline that he felt he could dive straight through it. Maybe get hold of the wrench again, maybe peg it at Cooper a second time, wind him even more badly . . .

He tripped.

His toe caught on the corrugated sheet when he was ten feet short of his goal. He went sprawling forward, landing hard, the palms of his hands grinding over the glass-strewn concrete, his jaw striking it with dizzying force.

Struggling against grogginess, Heck rolled over onto his back – only to see the rangy form of Cooper come ghosting through the gloom of the garage and stop about three feet away. Despite his exertions, the oldster looked remarkably cool; aside from the sweat on his brow and dabs of dried blood on his chin, he was amazingly unflustered. He'd drawn the khukuri, and now raised it aloft with one hand. With the other, he pointed his Luger down at Heck.

'For all the trouble you've put me to, sergeant,' he said, 'I still regret this. You were a worthier opponent than the others. Please take that as a compliment.'

And he fired.

Or tried to. It was the aged, internally rusted mechanism that betrayed him. It detonated in his fist with a blinding blot of flame and a *clung* of rending metal.

Heck blinked and flinched as hot fragments scattered over him: splinters of scalding metal, and flecks of softer, wetter material. His heart almost skipped a beat as he lay there, but he was unhurt. Warily, he opened his eyes again – to find that Cooper was still on his feet, but white-faced, and glassy-eyed. Only slowly did he twist his head around to survey the smouldering lump of meat where his right hand had once been. Ironically, what remained of the gun was still present, dangling from his sole remaining finger, though that was more bone than flesh.

The knife fell to the floor with a clatter, but the shriek of agony rising in Cooper's chest didn't get a chance to erupt before Heck had sprung upright and rammed two heavy punches into his lower body. The third caught Cooper in the mouth, and knocked his head spinning.

'I don't often hit the afflicted,' Heck said, circling as the guy tottered, and then firing in a fourth and a fifth blow, the latter hurling the gunman senseless to the ground. 'But at least it's the kind of *firm response* your dad would have appreciated.'

'I guess I'm somewhat diminished in your eyes,' Farthing said.

Heck glanced around. He stood by the garage door, sipping coffee from a paper beaker. His clothes were still damp, the palms of his hands stinging where they'd been skinned, though a couple of light dressings had since been applied. The factory yard was alive with radio static and filled with police vehicles, their blues and twos swirling in slow, lazy patterns. The ambulance carrying Ernest Cooper, now cuffed safely to one of DI Higginson's oppos, pulled slowly away through the open double-gate. The DI herself followed in an unmarked car.

Farthing, still pale around the gills, clutched his hat to his belly – a vaguely sheepish gesture. His expression was tense, worried.

'Diminished?' Heck still had half an eye on the garage interior, where the firearms team, who, having made safe the bloody tangle of metal that had once been the Luger, had picked it up with a pair of forceps and were feeding it into a sterile sack.

'Well if I'm not, I should be. I was shit scared.'

'You think I wasn't?' Heck replied.

'Aye . . . but you kept it together. Me . . . I just sat there, like.' Farthing's cheeks reddened. 'Didn't know what to do. Just sat there, waiting for it.'

Heck shrugged. 'You were tired . . . and you weren't feeling so good.'

'That's another thing. There was nothing wrong with me.'

He let that point hang, waiting nervously for Heck's response – which, when it came, was no more than a raised eyebrow.

'I know I'm not fit,' Farthing said. 'Let's face it, I'm a fat bastard . . . I couldn't have run much longer. But I wasn't having a heart attack. I was just paralysed with fear. I'd have done anything to get you to take the risk . . . while I sat it out.'

Heck shrugged again. 'My head was scrambled too. I'd already figured he couldn't see very well. I mentioned that his gun was probably kaput . . . the odds would likely have been better if I'd just taken him on.'

'What a thought.' Farthing shuddered – he'd already vomited once, not long after support units had arrived; briefly, Heck thought he was going to do it again. 'Taken him on? A madman like him?'

'It's about survival,' Heck said. 'If you're worried you let me down, Jerry, you didn't. Your wife and daughters are more important to you than I am . . . course they are. No one would argue with that.'

'That's the other thing.' Now Farthing really did avert his gaze. 'I haven't got a wife and daughters. Haven't even got a girlfriend. I mean, face it . . . who'd have *me*?'

Heck regarded him long and hard, too tired to voice the brief, fierce annoyance he suddenly felt.

Farthing shrugged as he watched the ground, shuffling his feet. 'Might as well own up to it now. We'll be living in each other's pockets for the next few days, getting the story straight. Bulldog'll be all over us . . .'

'And I'd learn the truth from someone else?' Heck said. 'And as a result, I might inadvertently let it slip how you behaved back there? So even though you're coming clean now, you're not exactly doing it for honourable reasons, are you?'

But just as quickly as his anger had risen, it subsided again. Shouting and kicking-off would serve no purpose now. Plus he had no energy for it.

'It was just chat,' the PC added unnecessarily. 'I was trying to save my own arse.'

'Well . . . it worked. In a roundabout sort of way. Don't knock it.'

'I'm sorry, like.'

'Let's just say you owe me one.'

'I'm sorry about something else too.' Farthing blew out a long, weary breath. 'Sorry that I *don't* have anyone to go home to. First time I've ever thought that . . . just about now, that little house of mine is going to feel a bit empty.'

'We've got our lives, haven't we?' Heck grunted. 'Bloody hell, Jerry, we can't expect *everything*.'

Chapter 5

It was another of those mid-September nights that left you in no doubt autumn had arrived. Darkness came early, and with the darkness an unseasonal chill. The trees were still in plumage, but strengthening winds rattled their dank branches, whipping their leaves, sending black, cavorting shadows along rain-damp city streets.

Heck saw none of this as he drove his white Citroën DS4 into the personnel car park at New Scotland Yard. He'd travelled all the way from Sunderland that afternoon without taking a break: nearly two hundred and fifty miles.

Sallow-faced and unshaved, wearing jeans, trainers and a sweatshirt, he made his way upstairs to the Serial Crimes Unit offices, which, as he'd expected at nine o'clock in the evening, were largely unmanned.

The first person he met was DCI Ben Kane, who, having recently been promoted from DI, was now second-in-command at SCU. While overall boss, DSU Gemma Piper, was engaged on other matters, he was currently running all day-to-day operations, including the delegation and supervision of routine assignments. He was a squat, bespectacled forty-year-old, whose sensible short hair, tweed jacket and chequered bow-tie gave him a nerdish air. Heck had always regarded Kane sceptically, thinking he seemed more like a teacher than a senior investigator in one of the Yard's front-line units – his unofficial nickname in SCU was 'Schoolmaster Ben' – but on the upside, as deputy-gaffer, Kane's role here was now mainly administrative, which meant he'd be out of their hair a lot more.

Kane was closing up his briefcase when he spotted Heck approaching along the central corridor. He regarded him quizzically. 'You back already?'

Heck shrugged. 'Cooper's on remand, guv, awaiting trial . . . all my arrest papers are in. Job done.'

'Yeah, I've read the file. Not your most straightforward arrest.'

'No . . . got there in the end, though.'

'This lad, Jerry Farthing. You'll be on the witness stand with him. He up to it?'

In his arrest report, Heck had downplayed PC Farthing's loss of control on the day in question, but there'd been no way to hide the Sunderland bobby's ineptitude when it came to the cat-and-mouse game they'd been forced to play with Ernest Cooper, not to mention the actual arrest.

Heck shrugged again. 'He's a bit of a headcase, if I'm honest. Not sure he's long for this job. But I've had a couple of sessions with him . . . to get the facts straight. Think he'll be okay.'

Kane shoved his briefcase under his arm. 'Do you always have to do things the hard way?' It wasn't as harsh a question as it sounded. Kane seemed genuinely fascinated to know.

'We pull them in any way we can, guv. You know that.'

'Well . . . Northumbria are happy. These are the results we want, I suppose. Well done.'

Kane nodded and continued down the corridor to the lifts.

Heck slouched on through the department. One or two individuals were around, finishing paperwork, waiting on phone calls and such, but the Detectives' Office, or 'DO' as SCU members preferred to call it, was deserted.

He humped his sports bag, currently stuffed with miscellaneous toiletries and unwashed clothing, over to his desk, dumped it in the aisle and slumped into his swivel chair, which, having moulded itself neatly to his buttocks over so many years, was such a relief that it induced an audible sigh.

Heck stretched, switched on his anglepoise lamp, then unlocked one of his lower drawers and rummaged through the bric-a-brac for the half-full bottle of Chivas Regal he usually kept in there. Grabbing a mug from the tea-making table behind, he was about to pour himself a couple of fingers when he noticed Gemma Piper leaning in the doorway.

'Ma'am . . .' he said, making to stand up.

Gemma gestured for him to sit. She looked as tired as he felt, which was not her normal form. Her top two buttons were undone, her sleeves rolled back to her elbows, one blouse flap hanging over the waistband of her skirt. She still looked good of course, but then she always looked good to Heck.

'Dare I ask what you're doing here?' she said.

'Well . . . I'm not needed back in the Northeast until the trial, so I thought I'd come home for a bit.'

She arched a pencil-thin eyebrow. 'Heck . . . you consider this place home?'

'It's a bit functional, but SCU are the only family I've got, so . . . yeah.'

'Bloody drama queen.' She entered, suppressing a yawn. 'Unfortunately, there's only me here at present.'

'Don't worry, ma'am . . . *you'll* do.'

'You've already got a big sister, Heck.'

49

'Who's talking about a sister?'

She regarded him coolly, until he refocused on the whisky bottle, carefully unscrewing its lid.

He glanced up. 'You mind?'

'You're off duty . . . why should I?'

'Fancy one?'

'I'm *on* duty, I'm afraid.' Gemma leaned back against the facing desk, while he poured the golden spirit. 'Sounds like we almost lost you?'

'Nah, you're not that lucky.'

She paused for a lengthy moment. 'Want to talk about it?'

'It's okay. It's just the streets.' He sipped, unable to conceal the pleasure it gave him. 'They get dicey.'

She nodded, respecting that. 'So . . . Cooper's banged to rights?'

'Sure is, but I'll be amazed if he doesn't go down for diminished capacity.'

'They're already making that call, are they?'

'No, but he's evidently three sheets to the wind.'

'You think?'

'Do you want to know what I *really* think, ma'am?' Heck sat back, puffed out his cheeks. 'For the first time, I think it's shades of grey.'

She frowned. 'This case?'

'This job. It happens more than we may realise. Some things about Ernie Cooper made him okay. He believed in decency, justice. He had that wartime generation attitude off pat . . .'

'Except that he wasn't of that generation. He just wished he was.'

'Those guys he murdered were out-and-out scumbags.'

'They were sadistic crimes, Heck. Cooper *enjoyed* killing those men . . . I read that in your own progress report. Plus it was premeditated. *Plus* he was going to kill you.'

50

'I could have been the last casualty of World War Two,' Heck mused, smiling at the curious thought.

Gemma smiled too – which was a rarity and a treat.

She was famous in the job for her good looks, but also for her efficient and authoritative manner. As head of SCU, Gemma didn't tolerate fools or slackers. She ran an elite department, which alternately made her proud and frustrated. They were only as good as their worst failure, she would say. She didn't like loose ends or open cases. She demanded regular results and hard work, but in return would defend her staff to the death if she felt they were in the right. All over Scotland Yard, they called her 'the Lioness' – as much for her willingness to scrap as for her wild blonde mane. Gemma didn't mind that, so long as it was never to her face.

In the past, when they'd been junior detectives working together at Bethnal Green, she and Heck had been lovers. It seemed an age ago from his perspective, but he'd been in her proximity ever since, and it never ceased to enthuse him – in various ways. She drove him mad on occasion and their former relationship had never meant that she wouldn't severely discipline him if necessary; but she set the standards he aspired to, and yet would still tolerate the instinct and imagination he brought to his investigations, because she also knew the value of those who thought outside the box.

In the words of Gemma's own mother: 'They were two peas in a pod; who on earth had thought it a good idea to shell them?'

'You say you're on duty,' Heck said. 'At this time?'

'Rochester paperwork,' she replied. 'Interpol don't keep the same hours we do.'

Heck tried not to let the mere mention of the name Peter Rochester – or Mad Mike Silver as he was more often known – ruffle his feathers. He poured more whisky, drank it in a

51

gulp. 'He may be in Gull Rock, but they say the lifers there get it easy these days.'

'That isn't true.'

'I hear they've even given him a Malacca cane to walk around with. Like he's some kind of plantation owner.'

'He's crippled,' she said. 'So he needs a stick. To deny him that would be to deny him his basic human rights.'

Heck snorted as he drained his mug. 'Human rights . . . he's lucky he wasn't in Gull Rock fifty years ago, when it was all treadmills and whipping-posts.'

'Take it from me, Heck, there isn't much happens around Mad Mike Silver that has anything to do with luck.'

'Is he still stonewalling you?'

'What else?'

'So he hasn't even dropped any of the bit-players our way yet . . . like Jim Laycock for instance?'

'Even if he had, which he hasn't – because the Laycock link is a total non-starter, Heck – I wouldn't tell *you*.'

'And no leads on Nice Guys' underbosses overseas? Nice Guys' operational bases? Dumping grounds for Nice Guys' victims in the Baltic, the Med, the Caspian . . .?'

'Heck, stop . . . okay!'

'Well, you know my feelings on Mad Mike . . .'

'Course I do. Which is why *you're* going nowhere near him. Ever again.'

Heck put his bottle away, took his mug to the sink and washed it. 'We're all law-abiding people in here, ma'am.' He grabbed up the few bits of paperwork he'd actually come in for, and crammed them into his sports bag. 'We have a system, and we stick to it. We respect all human life – that's why we do what we do.' He headed for the DO door, turning once before leaving. 'But there are definitely times when a lamppost and a good piece of rope wouldn't go amiss.'

Gemma let that pass, nodding as he waved goodbye and listening to his footfalls recede down the corridor. Eventually, after the lift doors had slid shut, she walked back to her own office, where she closed the door behind her and stood staring at the mobile phone on her desk. Waiting tensely for a call which, in all honesty, she hoped would never come.

Chapter 6

It was just before midnight on September 19 when alarm sirens began sounding through the concrete corridors of the medical wing at HM Prison Brancaster, amber lights flashing at each electronically sealed checkpoint, the wards going into lockdown as the officers' hobnailed boots hammered up and down stairs and gangways.

Medical emergencies were not uncommon in a jail where the inmates were exclusively the most volatile and unstable in the penal system. Despite Gull Rock's tough but on-the-whole progressive regime, violent assaults among prisoners were a daily event, suicides occurred with regularity, and homicides were not infrequent. On top of that, there was grave ill-health: STDs were transmitted widely, while drugs were still smuggled in and often led to ODs; there were also a number of older men housed there – full-term lifers now in their seventies and eighties.

The upshot was that, though medical staff responded swiftly and efficiently if they thought someone might die, staff from other parts of the prison almost never came running.

Until now.

Until word got around that the casualty on this occasion was Inmate 87156544, real name Peter Rochester, also known as 'Mad Mike Silver'.

For quite some time, Peter Rochester had been Britain's unofficial Public Enemy Number One, and where the tabloids were concerned, a hate-figure on a par with Osama bin Laden. Even the chattering classes, those who habitually attempted to grapple with the psychology of ultra-dangerous offenders rather than condemn them outright, had difficulty finding anything positive to say about him. The problem was Rochester's intellect. He wasn't some drooling madman; he wasn't bipolar; he wasn't schizophrenic; he didn't have mummy issues. He was quite clearly a psychopath – but of the most organised and calculating variety. To start with he was aloof and confident, unfazed by the extreme emotions he aroused among his fellow inmates, amused by the frustrations of his captors. He could withstand the fiercest interrogations; he didn't respond to threats, bribes or trickery, never giving anything away unless it served his purpose. As such, any information the authorities had accrued on Rochester was paper-thin. Even his basic background remained sketchy; his full list of criminal activities was incomplete, his catalogue of known associates empty. It was some considerable time after he was first incarcerated before the British police were even able to establish his true identity.

Rochester, it was now known, was a British national, a native of the Home Counties, who, having been rejected by the British Army on medical grounds when he was still only seventeen, joined the French Foreign Legion, later seeing action in Bosnia, Kosovo and Ivory Coast, and impressing in almost every theatre. It was only afterwards, when he felt he'd risen as far as he could in one of the world's official military elites, that he became a mercenary soldier and in due course an international criminal, peddling drugs, guns and even human cargo, and finally forming the so-called 'Nice Guys Club'.

The subsequent British investigation into this previously unknown organisation uncovered evidence that was almost too horrific for words. The Nice Guys' *modus operandi* was alarmingly simple: for seventy-five thousand pounds a shot, they would abduct any woman a paying client nominated, and provide a safe, private space where said client could rape and abuse her to his heart's desire. The Club would provide the necessary security, and undertook to dispose of all the evidence afterwards, including the woman – none of their victims were known to have survived.

The case was finally broken by one Scotland Yard detective in particular, DS Mark Heckenburg of the Serial Crimes Unit, though he was shot and almost killed in the process. The Nice Guys also suffered fatalities – five died in total, but despite this, and despite the conviction of Peter Rochester, there was dissatisfaction at various levels: the Club's numerous British-based clients got away scot-free thanks to the untimely disappearance of some very vital evidence, whilst Heck himself was never convinced the Nice Guys had all been accounted for, especially those he suspected of running parallel operations overseas. A series of internal investigations at Scotland Yard attempted to ascertain the reason why a general police response to the crisis had been so slow to emerge, and finally punished those senior officers deemed culpable for this – but that didn't make anyone especially happy.

The key to everything, of course, was Peter Rochester – now serving a full-life term in Britain's toughest high-security prison, and yet increasingly a man with leverage. Heck's comments about the possible existence of foreign Nice Guys Clubs hadn't gone unnoticed, and Interpol and Europol were now handling daily communiqués from police forces across the world concerned about their own extensive lists of inexplicably vanished women. It was anyone's guess whether Rochester would eventually play ball, so when he'd gone into apparent cardiac arrest without warning, Gull Rock had suffered a collective nervous breakdown.

Though medical staff managed to stabilise him, he'd now slipped into a coma, and the next response was to have him transferred to the Queen Elizabeth Hospital, King's Lynn, where there was a fully equipped cardiology unit.

Transfer of any prisoner beyond prison walls when he was deemed as high-risk as Peter Rochester was a complex task, and would almost always fall to SOCAR, Scotland Yard's specialised Serious Offenders Control and Retrieval division. By pure good fortune, an armed SOCAR unit was on-site at the time, having just returned several members of a notorious gang of London blaggers to Gull Rock, after supervising a day out for them at the Old Bailey.

Chief Inspector Andy Braithwaite had tactical command. He was a rugged Yorkshireman with lean, pitted features, a shaven head and a huge handlebar moustache. A former Royal Marine, even at forty-seven he was wiry and fit, and suited his Kevlar body armour with POLICE plastered across the back of it. If he ever drew the Glock nine-millimetre that he wore at his hip, you'd have no doubt – and you'd be right – that he was ready, willing and able to use it.

Braithwaite listened intently, chewing gum, while Maxine Mulgrave, Security Governor at Gull Rock, outlined the circumstances to him in the outside corridor connecting to the prison infirmary. 'The ambulance has got here already, but obviously we need an escort urgently,' she said, palefaced. 'You couldn't have come at a better time.'

'We're ready to go now,' Braithwaite said, affecting his usual nonchalant air when taking custody of an offender whose potential for wreaking havoc registered on the seismic scale. 'I've got two gunships, containing six men each. We're all kitted out for a spin.'

'Good. There's no time to waste.'

And within less than ten minutes, just after midnight, an armoured cavalcade left HM Prison Brancaster, bound for King's Lynn, a journey of just under thirty miles. Two motor-cyclists from the Norfolk and Suffolk Road Traffic Unit, who'd accompanied the SOCAR team on their initial journey to the prison with the blaggers, now rode at the point. Next came the SOCAR command car, a sleek high-performance BMW, white but covered with bright orange flashes, asterisks and other insignia to enable friendly forces to identify it quickly. The two gunships came next – heavily armoured troop-carriers bearing similar markings to their command vehicle, both filled with highly trained, heavily armed men, though an ordinary civilian ambulance, containing prison staff as well as two medics and the actual casualty, was sandwiched between them.

'Road should be clear enough at this time of night,' Braithwaite said to his number two, Sergeant Ray Mulligan, a burly, bull-necked former rugby player with a battered face and a blond crew-cut, who was wedged behind the BMW's wheel.

Mulligan merely grunted.

The coastal road from Gull Rock wasn't a coastal road as such – it curved inland around the edge of the North Norfolk coast, but it was hemmed in from the north and east by mile upon mile of barren saltmarsh. It was a desolate enough scene by day, but now, in the pitch dark, there was an awesome blackness broken only occasionally by sentinel streetlamps, these usually located at sharp turns or unex-pected bends. To the right, where the marshes lay, was a solid void with only tiny pips of light to denote the fishing boats out on the Wash. At least the road was high speed. Sightseers almost never had cause to drive along here, so though it was narrow and inclined to weave, the cavalcade proceeded at a steady fifty miles an hour.

'How's he doing?' Braithwaite asked his mobile phone.

'No change,' came the tinny voice of the prison officer riding in the ambulance. 'We need to get there soon.'

'ETA twenty-five,' Braithwaite said.

Mulligan grunted and continued driving, the reddish glow of the motorcyclists' tail-lights reflecting on his tough but solemn features.

Braithwaite checked his watch. Everything was going to plan so far.

They'd proceeded about ten miles, but were still in the midst of marshy desolation, when the motorcyclists flashed their hazard lights and started slowing down.

Braithwaite's eyes narrowed. He felt for his Glock, but then reached for his radio instead, passing a quick message to the team in the first gunship. 'Possible hold-up ahead. Everyone stay loose . . . looks like an RTA.'

Mulligan worked down through the gears. 'See something, guv?'

Braithwaite pointed. A wrecked vehicle emerged into view on the road ahead, framed in the glare of the motorcyclists' headlamps: a white Peugeot 106, lying skewwhiff across both carriageways, upside down. Its front end had caved in, and a column of steam rose from its exposed engine. Braithwaite checked his wing mirror as, one by one, the other vehicles in the cavalcade slowed to a halt.

In front, the two motorcyclists pulled one to either side of the road, and quickly dismounted. It was now evident that a body lay on the blacktop alongside the upended wreck. It wore jeans and a tracksuit top, but by its slim form and mass of splayed-out golden hair, it was a young woman. The immediate signs weren't good – she lay motionless and face-down in a spreading pool of blood.

'Shit!' Mulligan said, grabbing for his radio. 'This has only just happened . . .'

'Wait!' Braithwaite signalled for caution, before opening the front passenger door and climbing out.

'Guv, what're you . . .?'

'Don't touch her!' Braithwaite hollered at the two motorcyclists.

Both had removed their helmets and knelt down alongside the casualty, checking for vital signs. The first glanced around at the commander, startled. But the second had seen something else. 'Oh Christ . . .'

Braithwaite walked forward, his gaze riveted on the arm of a second casualty, broken and bloodstained, protruding through the Peugeot's imploded windscreen. He halted, before swivelling around and peering back down the length of the cavalcade. SOCAR Sergeant Alan Montgomery was climbing from the cab of the first gunship. Unlike his gaffer, he was helmeted, but his visor was raised. He evidently couldn't see what had happened, and was seeking an explanation.

But Braithwaite was too bewildered to offer one. 'This . . . for real?' he muttered, glancing to the front again, and noting with a deep chill the trickles of blood coagulating on the tarmac.

Mulligan, who'd also climbed from the command car, joined him. 'Guv?'

'I thought . . .' Braithwaite stuttered. 'I mean . . .'

'Sir . . .?' one of the motorcyclists interrupted. 'We need to . . .'

Which was when the roadside explosive concealed near the rear of the cavalcade detonated with a volcano-like *BOOM*.

They spun around, eyes bugged, faces lit brightly by the searing, fiery flash.

The noise alone was agony on the ears – a devastating roar accentuated by a twisting and rending of steel as the second gunship was flung over on the blacktop, reduced in less than a second to a smoking mass of blistered scrap. They tottered where they stood, red-hot shards raining down around them, too stunned to respond.

At a single guttural command, the darkness came alive, spangled with blistering, cruciform gun-flashes. An echoing din of automatic gunfire accompanied it.

Sergeant Montgomery was the first to go down, flopping to his knees, both hands clutched on his groin, jack-knifing backwards as more rounds struck his face and upper body. But only as the first gunship began jerking and shuddering to repeated high-velocity impacts did it actually strike Braithwaite they were under attack.

He and his men had been through all the specialist training programmes. They were tough and experienced, routinely armed; an elite cadre within the British police. High-risk prisoner transport was their forte; pursuit and capture of fugitives and escaped convicts their bread and butter.

But anyone can be taken by surprise.

The first gunship's immediate reaction was to get the hell out, but its cab was already so peppered with lead that its supposedly bulletproof windshield collapsed inward, and it skidded and slammed into the back of the command car, which, as it was also armoured, wasn't shunted sufficiently to allow it through.

And still Braithwaite and Mulligan could only stand there, rounds whining past them like a swarm of rocket-propelled hornets.

With a dull metallic *clinking*, two small objects came dancing out of the darkness and across the road surface. Braithwaite watched them incredulously as they rolled to a halt by the front offside of the first gunship.

Hand grenades.

They detonated simultaneously.

Their combined explosion was not adequate to throw the heavy troop-carrier over onto its side. It was a smidgen of the power applied by the IED that had done for the second gunship, but it mangled the driving cab, in which Montgomery's sidekick was still taking shelter, blowing out all its windows, shredding the guy in a hailstorm of glass and metal. The rearmost section buckled with the force, the blazing gunfire increasingly ripping through its reinforced bodywork.

Braithwaite was still helpless, still frozen – unable to comprehend the unfolding events. When a brutal implement smashed without warning into the back of his unguarded skull, sending him reeling to the floor, it might almost have been expected. There was a resounding *thud* as Mulligan suffered the same fate.

The blacktop backhanded the side of the chief inspector's face, yet somehow he retained consciousness, and despite the hot red glue dripping through his vision, found himself staring again down the length of the cavalcade, against which numerous figures were now moving, having emerged from the darkness on the right. Some were attacking the ambulance by hand, working with tools on its battered doors, prying them open. Others were still shooting – particularly down at the far end, Braithwaite realised, which meant they were drilling bullets through the burning, blasted scrap remaining of the second gunship, finishing off any poor devils who hadn't yet been turned to a mess of meat and bone. Though dazed, Braithwaite was struck with wonderment at the variety of reports issuing from the weapons on view. But one was louder than the others: a repeated deafening clatter, as though a dozen men were beating iron frames with hammers.

He craned his neck up, blinking through the crimson stickiness. And he saw it.

A Hotchkiss Portable Mark 1 machine gun, already fixed on its tripod and with a two-man crew operating it – one to fire, one to feed the belt. It was on the road to the rear of the first gunship. Stupefied as Braithwaite was, a terrible understanding struck him. With no other choice, the surviving SOCAR team – so well armoured, so expertly trained – would have extracted their MP5 assault rifles from the safe in the troop-carrier's floor, and would now be disembarking from their vehicle in 'stick' fashion, as they'd rehearsed so many times – straight into that focused fusillade, the stream of red-hot .303 slugs cutting through them like a buzzsaw.

'No . . . pleeease . . .' screamed a shrill voice behind.

Though it required a heart-straining effort, Braithwaite managed to roll over and look the other way. His eyes alighted on Sergeant Mulligan, lying face-down, a wound like an axe-chop in the middle of his stiff blond crew-cut. But he also saw their assailants, for the first time up close: ski-masked, gloved, wearing dark combat clothing. They stood around on the road in no particular formation, talking idly, dressing their smouldering weapons down.

'Tavor TAR-21 . . . Beretta MX4 . . .' he mumbled, eyes flickering from one gun to the next. 'Chang Feng . . . SR-2 Veresk . . . SIG-Sauer MPX . . . Mini-Uzi . . .'

No doubt it was the stock of one of these that had crashed against his cranium, and Mulligan's too . . . but in Christ's name, this was a devil's brew of hardware! Where had the necessity arisen to pack such firepower?

Behind him, meanwhile, the heavy machine gun had ceased to discharge. One by one, the other, lesser arms also fell silent . . . so now he could hear additional voices. These too sounded relaxed, some were even chuckling. It was over, the fight was won – and they were enjoying the moment.

'Pleeease . . .' the frantic voice cried again.

Ahead, a small clutch of gunmen pushed and kicked the

two Norfolk motorcyclists across the road. The motorbike cops hadn't been armed to begin with, and had now been stripped of their helmets and hi-viz jackets; their faces were badly bloodied.

'Into the ditch,' said a casual voice.

The ambushers did as instructed, shoving the motorcyclists down into a muddy hollow running along the verge, where they were told to sit and keep their hands behind their heads. None of this made sense, Braithwaite tried to tell himself. This was ridiculous, insane . . .

One man in particular emerged from the ambushers' ranks. He too wore gloves and dark khaki, while an assault rifle – an L85 – was suspended over his shoulder by a strap. But he was more noticeable than the others, because if he'd been wearing a woollen balaclava before, he had now removed it – which was never a good sign. He was somewhere in his late thirties, with smooth, clean-shaved features and a head of tousled sandy hair.

Braithwaite tried to swallow a spreading nausea as the man strode up to him and peered down, almost boyishly handsome and yet with an ugly right-angled scar on his left cheek. 'Who are you?' he asked. His accent was vaguely Scandinavian.

'B . . . Braithwaite . . .'

'You command here?'

Braithwaite tried to nod, but the pain in his head was turning feverish and the vision in his right eye blurring. He had a horrible suspicion his skull was fractured. 'My . . . my sergeant,' he stammered, indicating Mulligan's body, though another of the ambushers was already kneeling beside it.

The kneeling man glanced up and shook his head with casual indifference.

'Make sure,' the Scandinavian said.

A pistol appeared – an Arcus 94, and three quick shots

rang out, each one directed into the back of Mulligan's already shattered skull.

'What . . .' Braithwaite tried to speak, but phlegm-filled vomit frothed from his mouth. 'What the . . . the fuck do you think you're . . . what the fuck . . .?'

'Put him with the others.' There was no anger in the Scandinavian's voice, but it was firm. It brooked no resistance.

Braithwaite was taken by the elbow and yanked to his feet. He went dizzy, pain arcing down his spine, and had to be forcibly held upright while they patted him down. His Glock, the only weapon he was carrying, was confiscated and he was walked – though it was all he could do to stumble – across the road, and dumped down into the ditch alongside the motorcycle cops, both sitting hunched forward, hands behind their heads. There were others there as well: the two prison staff and the two medics from the ambulance. Perhaps unsurprisingly, but no less horribly, there was no one from either complement of men who'd been riding in the gunships.

Fleetingly it seemed as if the hostages were forgotten, some of their captors keeping half an eye on them, but the rest moving back and forth along the cavalcade, which was now a scene of unprecedented carnage, the police vehicles reduced virtually to wreckage. There was still fire and smoke, and a stench of burning flesh. The crew from the first gunship lay in shapeless bundles, rivers of blood crisscrossing the road on all sides of them. The ambushers stepped into and around this without any concern.

Braithwaite, who thought he'd been about to faint as they'd steered him towards the ditch, had now recovered his composure a little. He eyed the ambushers as closely as he could. For the most part they were nondescript even in their urban terror gear, the masks rendering them indistinguishable from one another. They seemed fit and organised, and something else was now clear – they were multinational. They openly conversed, and though it was all in English, he heard various accents – one was Cockney, another sounded Russian, another Australian; in another case, he detected a twang of the USA.

The thing was, they were so calm. The men they'd just mowed down were on-duty cops – at least some of them might have got radio messages out, and yet these guys were walking around as if they had all the time in the world. But then, maybe they did. The nearest place was still the prison, but that was ten miles away, and no help could be expected from there anyway. It was easily another twenty miles before the next area of conurbation, but what use was that? This prison transport had been kept well under wraps. The best they could hope for was a response by routine unarmed patrols – but how could they cope with a situation like this? With such overwhelming firepower?

A sudden clanking of gears drew his attention elsewhere. A monstrous vehicle, previously hidden in the darkness beyond the smashed Peugeot, rumbled to life, a battery of brilliant headlights glaring out from it. Slowly and noisily, a bulldozer came shuddering into view, its huge steel digging-blade canted downward. It briefly halted, but when orders were shouted by the Scandinavian, it altered direction and continued apace, connecting with the Peugeot, and with a clangour of grinding metal, shoving it sideways across the road. Braithwaite's injured scalp tightened as he watched the massive mud-caked tracks pass over the body of the fair-haired girl, crushing her flat, pulped organs splurging outward.

When the wreck had been thrust across the ditch and into the marshy blackness on the other side, the dozer straightened up and halted on the verge, its engine chugging. A second vehicle emerged from the darkness behind it, this one reversing. It was an everyday high-sided van, but its sliding rear door was already open and inside Braithwaite glimpsed the sterile whiteness of an improvised medical chamber. It bypassed the prisoners and continued down the bullet-riddled ruins of the cavalcade, finally stopping next to the ambulance.

With great care, several of the ambushers lifted the prone shape of Peter Rochester, now on a wheeled gurney, neck-deep in woollen blankets, from the back of the ambulance, and placed him into the van. One of them climbed in after him, carrying his drip. With a clang, the sliding door was closed, and the prisoner's new transport jerked away, accelerating up the road and vanishing into the night. About fifty yards ahead, on either side of the tarmac, other vehicles now throbbed to life, their headlight beams cross-cutting the dark in a shimmering lattice.

The ambushers sloped idly in that direction, guns at their shoulders, chatting. There was no triumphalism, no urgency – they'd got what they came for, and the job was done. The sandy-haired Scandinavian strode among them.

'Are you . . . are you maniacs out of your minds?' Braithwaite couldn't resist shouting. 'What the hell do you think you've done here? Do you really think you'll get away with this?'

Almost casually, the Scandinavian diverted towards the ditch side, a couple of his comrades accompanying him. 'A timely intervention, Mr Braithwaite . . . I almost left without saying goodbye.'

He and his compatriots cocked their guns and levelled them.

Braithwaite could only stare, goggle-eyed.

The rest of the captives begged, wept, whimpered.

All came to nothing in the ensuing hail of fire.

Chapter 7

Heck was seated in his favourite breakfast bar at the bottom end of Fulham Palace Road, waiting for eggs Benedict, when his eyes strayed from his morning paper and happened to catch a breaking-news bulletin on the portable TV at the end of the counter.

Thanks to the twisted metal coat-hanger serving as the TV's aerial, the image continually flickered, but Heck, slumped at the nearest table, was too close to avoid the photographic mug-shot that suddenly appeared on the screen. It portrayed a man in his late thirties or early forties. He was handsome, with a square jaw, a straight, patrician nose and a mop of what looked like prematurely greying hair. Even though the shot had clearly been taken in custody, he wore a sly but subtle grin.

Heck sat bolt upright.

'Rochester,' the newscaster intoned, 'who was convicted of abducting and murdering thirty-eight women across the whole of England and Wales, was serving life at Brancaster Prison when he developed chest pains late yesterday afternoon. It was during his subsequent transfer to hospital when the incident occurred . . .'

The scene switched to an isolated road, possibly on the coast somewhere, though a barricade of police vehicles with beacons swirling prevented further access to the camera crew. Beyond them, police, forensics and medical personnel were glimpsed moving around in Tyvek coveralls. In front of the barricade stood two firearms response officers, MP5 rifles across their chests.

The gorgeous Jamaican lady behind the counter leaned over to switch the channel.

'Whoa, no Tamara . . . please, I was watching that!' Heck shouted.

She relented, sticking her tongue out at him as she moved away.

Heck remained transfixed on the screen.

'There are reports of at least sixteen fatalities,' the newscaster added, 'though that number is yet to be confirmed, and of course it may increase. None of those listed, or so we're told, is Peter Rochester . . . better known to the public of course as Mad Mike Silver. Rob Kent is on site with the latest . . .'

Rob Kent appeared on screen, a plump reporter with a balding head and wire-framed glasses. He looked pale and harassed. 'It's . . . well, it's a terrible scene here,' he began. 'As you can see, the place is flooded with security personnel. Not to mention ambulances, though I have to say . . . I've yet to see any ambulances leave, though I have seen several undertakers' hearses moving away, carrying what looked like closed caskets. This obviously means they're moving, or have started to move, some of the dead . . .'

'Do we have a clearer picture of the circumstances, Rob?'

The reporter raised his mike. 'Well . . . no one's saying very much yet, but it seems pretty clear to me. To start with, this is an incredibly bleak spot. We're over twenty miles from King's Lynn, nearer thirty miles from Fakenham. There is literally no other habitation anywhere near . . .'

He walked to his right, the camera panning with him, catching open grassland, ripples of wind blowing across it towards a flat but hazy horizon.

'So this is the ideal spot to launch an ambush . . . if indeed an ambush it was. From what we can gather, the security detail taking Rochester to hospital was subjected to a highly disciplined assault. I haven't had this confirmed by any senior members of the police yet, but those are the words I'm hearing: "a highly disciplined assault".'

Kent shook his head; doubtless he was a seasoned reporter, a man who'd witnessed the aftermath of many atrocities, but he looked genuinely shaken by what he'd witnessed on the lonely road from Brancaster to King's Lynn.

'Can you confirm whether or not Peter Rochester is on the casualty list, Rob?'

'The official line is that we have no word about Rochester's location or condition at this time. Of course, he was being transferred to hospital because he was thought to have suffered a heart attack yesterday afternoon, so what state he's likely to be in now is anyone's guess . . .'

Heck stood up, his chair scraping back so loudly that other customers jumped. 'Tamara, love!' he shouted. 'You're going to have to cancel those Benedicts.'

She turned from the range, dismayed. 'They're almost done!'

'Sorry darling . . . I've got to go. I'm sure someone else'll appreciate them.' He hurled the requisite money onto the counter and dashed from the café.

'Heck . . . you're flaming murder!'

Various SCU detectives were present in the DO when Heck barged in, still in his day-off gear of jeans, sweatshirt and trainers. The first one to see him came hurriedly across the office. It was DC Shawna McCluskey. Originally, like Heck, a member of Greater Manchester Police, she was short, athletic and dark-haired, but a toughie too, whose pretty freckled face belied her blunt, blue-collar attitude.

'I bloody wouldn't, Heck!' she advised. 'I genuinely wouldn't.'

'Seriously, pal,' DS Eric Fisher added, lumbering up. He was SCU's main intelligence man, and possibly the oldest officer still on the team. He was heavily built and pot-bellied, wore horn-rimmed glasses, and boasted a massive red/grey beard that the average Viking would have been proud of. 'This has hit Gemma too . . . like a bombshell.'

'Yeah, she's been up half the night and she's at her wits' end,' Shawna said.

'So she's in?' Heck replied.

'For the next few minutes, yeah. Then she's off to Norfolk.'

'She taking point on this?'

'Deputy SIO,' Fisher said. 'They're putting a taskforce together as we speak.'

Heck gave a wry smile. 'Let me guess . . . Frank Tasker's running it?'

'He's in there with her now.'

'SOCAR . . .' Heck shook his head. 'I wouldn't pay them in washers. I presume "we have no word about Rochester's location or condition" is a euphemism for the bastard's been sprung, flipping us the finger as he went?'

Fisher shrugged. 'They haven't got a clue where he is.'

'And I suppose SOCAR were in charge of the transfer?'

'Yeah, but that means they've taken the most losses,' Shawna said. 'Look Heck, Tasker seems an okay bloke . . . but he's going to be feeling it today.'

'I knew we weren't done with these murdering, raping bastards . . .'

'*We* are done with them,' Shawna insisted. 'You've heard what Gemma said. *You're* not involved.' But he was already backing to the door. 'Heck, don't do this.'

He left the room.

'Oh shit,' Shawna said.

'You got that right,' Fisher agreed.

Heck walked up the central corridor to Gemma's cramped little office. The door stood ajar and he could hear voices inside. They weren't heated or raised, but there was tension there – he could tell that much already. He knocked.

'This had better be really important!' came Gemma's whip-crack response.

'I'd say it was important, ma'am,' he replied. 'Can I come in?'

There was a brief, telling silence.

'Yeah . . . come in, Heck.'

He entered, finding Ben Kane in there as well as Frank Tasker.

For her part, Gemma was slumped behind her desk, while Tasker was seated on the edge of it – which posture irked Heck no end. Okay, the guy was likely to be under pressure and probably in mourning for the personnel he'd lost, but from what Heck knew of Tasker's reputation, he was one of those ultra high-ranking cops who always made themselves at home whoever's office they were in. His jacket was draped over the only other chair – while Kane stood.

The next thing Heck noticed was that both Gemma and Tasker had drawn pistols from the armoury: Tasker wore his in a shoulder-holster; Gemma's lay on the desk in front of her, alongside a glossy photograph. Guns were never ever a good thing.

It was still relatively early in the day – Heck had made it from Fulham to New Scotland Yard in near record time – but Gemma was already less than her usual pristine self. A strikingly handsome woman anyway, she didn't need much makeup, but she believed in appearances, in making a lasting impression; and yet today she looked tired and worn. Tasker,

72

who if Heck recalled rightly, was also known for being a snazzy dresser, was suited, but in a similarly rumpled state. Even his artificially bronzed looks had paled to an ashen hue. Only Kane seemed relaxed, maintaining his usual air of scholarly attentiveness.

'Heck,' Gemma said. 'You know Commander Tasker? Serious Offender Control and Retrieval. He heads up their Special Investigations unit . . .'

'I know him, yeah,' Heck replied.

'Sergeant Heckenburg,' Tasker said with a curt nod.

'Sir.' Heck turned back to Gemma. 'What a bloody disaster.'

She sighed. 'By any standards. Before you ask, we're working on the basis it's down to a Nice Guys team who've come in from abroad. Somehow or other, they managed to bring an entire arsenal of high-tech weapons with them . . .'

'Unless the weapons were already here,' Heck said. 'I know two or three underworld quartermasters we can lean on straight away . . .'

'For the record!' she interrupted. 'We've lost sixteen officers, two prison personnel and two ambulance crew. There are no wounded . . . no survivors.'

'A courting couple got the chop too,' Tasker added. 'Two civvies.'

'How's that?' Heck asked.

Tasker glanced at Kane, who rummaged through his pocket-book. 'A Jenny Barker and Ronald Withersnap,' Kane said. 'Looks like they were out for a late-night canoodle when the Nice Guys ran over their parked car in a JCB, killing them both in the process. They then used their bodies and the wreck of their car to stage the accident.'

'Jesus Christ . . .' Heck breathed.

'Worst of the worst, this lot,' Tasker said, his eyes meeting Heck's – their gaze was cold, distinctly unfriendly. 'Which

73

of course you won't need us to tell *you* about. Anyway, now you're as clued-in as we are, sergeant.'

It seemed to be a morning for euphemisms. That one clearly meant 'so fuck off back to your own office'.

Instead of taking the hint, Heck continued to ask questions. 'What about Silver?'

'No sign of him,' Gemma said, with another ill-disguised sigh.

'They just whisked him away?'

'Looks like it.'

'Isn't he supposed to be ill?'

'Not "supposed to be",' Tasker said. 'He *is* ill. The prison infirmary confirmed it.'

'Is it serious? I mean, how far do we expect him to get?'

'We don't know, Heck . . . okay?' Gemma replied in a patient tone. 'It's too early to say.'

Heck pondered. 'Well, I suppose the next question is did he actually tell you anything useful before he disappeared? I mean during the prison interviews?' Their expressions remained blank. 'Surely you're allowed to discuss that now he's gone?'

'We're not going to discuss it at this stage,' Gemma said.

'Which means he told you nothing . . .'

'Which means we're not discussing it,' Tasker asserted.

'Heck,' Gemma said. 'You know the kind of intel we were trying to glean from those interviews. We wanted to know about other Nice Guys associates. About Nice Guys operations abroad . . . how many there are, where they are, who they are. Regardless of where Peter Rochester is now, there's still a significant amount of sensitivity surrounding that information.'

Heck shook his head. 'I don't see why.'

'Because if you *must* know, sergeant,' Tasker interjected, 'the various law enforcement agencies we're in contact with overseas are well aware of the damage done to your own enquiry into the Nice Guys by a British police insider. They don't want their investigations to suffer in the same way.'

Which, Heck had to admit, made a kind of sense.

'Subsequently, all info related to the prison interviews with Peter Rochester is still being handled on a need-to-know basis,' Tasker added.

Heck nodded. 'Okay, okay . . . but just out of interest, what's this?'

He indicated the photograph on Gemma's desk, which appeared to depict a dented car door, marked here and there with bullet holes, but in the centre of which a jumble of apparently meaningless letters had been crudely inscribed in the paintwork.

BDEL

'That was carved into the driver's door of the SOCAR command vehicle,' Kane said. 'We're not sure what it means yet . . . if it means anything.'

'*BDEL* . . .?' Heck mused.

'We're not going to town on that yet,' Gemma added. 'For all we know it could have been done before – at the prison, maybe even before then. The car was a fully marked police vehicle. If the driver had parked up somewhere, I dunno . . . to buy chips. Some lowlife with an attitude comes along . . .'

Heck looked sceptical. 'Wouldn't the driver have noticed? It's on his door.'

'We don't know what it is yet,' Tasker replied. 'All options are still on the table.'

'But in the event it turns out to be relevant,' Gemma said, 'and is perhaps some kind of signature, we're keeping it in-house, yeah?'

Heck shrugged. 'Yeah, sure. So . . . I suppose it's down to

practicalities. Do we know how many casualties we inflicted on the ambushers? If we bagged a few of them, we can be checking hospitals and . . .'

'None,' Ben Kane said.

'You mean none that we know about?' When Heck received no answer, he glanced from one to the other. 'What're you saying . . . our people didn't even return fire?'

'A couple of the police weapons found at the scene had been discharged, but it looks as if that was in panic,' Tasker said.

'Seems like they were taken totally by surprise,' Gemma added. 'And by overwhelming forces.'

Heck could scarcely believe what he was hearing. Hadn't SOCAR known they were escorting one of the most dangerous criminals in Britain? Or had they been too busy taking it all in their stride, playing it cool? He wanted to ask that question aloud. Wanted to give full voice to exactly how such arrogant incompetence made him feel, but of course it would be impolitic – it was always impolitic. 'I hear you're forming a taskforce to go after them, ma'am?'

She appraised him carefully. 'It's a SOCAR taskforce, Heck. That means we've more than enough bodies. Every spare officer Frank's got is now on the case.'

'Well . . . *you're* not SOCAR.'

'DSU Piper has maintained a dialogue with Silver for the last few months, as you're no doubt aware,' Tasker said. 'She probably knows the guy better than *anyone else* in the job.' He made a point of stressing *anyone else*. 'It would be impossible to leave her out.'

'Don't worry,' Gemma replied. 'Frank and his team are well-resourced and very experienced.'

But they're not detectives, Heck wanted to say. They're like Special Branch; knuckle-dragging ex-squaddies or pumped-up government agents playing at being CID.

'We'll be getting used to each other in the future, anyway,' she added. 'You know National Crime Group is moving from the Yard next year?'

'Yeah . . .?' Heck said, baffled as to where this might be leading.

'It's early days yet, but we'll likely be sharing a building with SOCAR. We may even be on the same floor.'

Heck gave her a long, blank look. 'That's marvellous, ma'am. Truly. Any more good news today?'

'Look . . . what's your problem, sergeant?' Tasker asked. 'You've had an attitude since you came in here. Call me an idiot, but I can't think there's anything about me or my staff that might have got on your nerves.'

'I don't know, sir,' Heck said. 'If we spent a couple of days together, I'm sure I could produce a catalogue.' He turned and left the office.

For a second, Tasker looked astounded. 'What the actual *FUCK!*'

'Leave this to me, Frank,' Gemma said, jumping to her feet. *'HECK!'*

She caught up with him twenty yards down the corridor.

'You've got five seconds to tell me what that was all about!' she said, pinning him to the wall with her index finger. 'And make it good, because trust me, I'm not in the mood for any chip-on-the-shoulder bullshit today!'

'I don't like seeing fellas I don't know treat your desk like an armchair.'

'I'm not going to dignify that garbage with a response. Try again.'

'Ma'am . . . *I* should be the one going after Mike Silver. Two reasons. First of all, I have unfinished business with him. Very unfinished. Secondly, I'm the one who caught him last time. No one else managed it.'

'Oh yes?' She folded her arms. 'Who made the arrest?'

'Okay, me and you should be going after him then.'

'You know it doesn't work like that.'

'Says who . . . SOCAR? The fucking idiots who let Mike Silver go?'

'Hey! Now just watch how you talk to me, sergeant . . . alright?' She kept it low-key, but as always with Gemma when her back was up, there was intense ferocity in her tone. 'And you might try showing a bit of respect, and remember that most of those "fucking idiots" are dead! *And* that they were fellow police officers! *And* that they died in the line of duty! *And* that they left young families, children . . .'

'Okay . . .' He already regretted that part of his outburst. 'That was out of order . . .'

'We're all upset, Heck . . . but at least stop embarrassing yourself, and more importantly, stop bloody embarrassing me! And get your sodding head screwed on! You know you *can't* be involved in this enquiry. I've explained it to you half a dozen times, so I'm not going to explain it again. Your job, as far as the Nice Guys is concerned, is done.'

'No disrespect, ma'am . . . but that's what you think.'

'Heck . . .' Gemma gave him a searching gaze. 'Be absolutely one hundred per cent sure, I will *not* tolerate any monkey business from you on this. Operation Thunderclap – yes, it's got a name and everything – Operation Thunderclap is way too serious to be jeopardised by an officer as emotionally scarred by past events as you are.' Her tone levelled off, but she continued to nail him with those laser-blue eyes. 'You and me have been close for a long time, but trust me on this, Mark . . . I will take *any* disciplinary measures necessary. Any at all . . . to protect this SOCAR enquiry from interference by outside elements, especially you.'

'Ma'am, Mad Mike Silver will be overseas in a day or so. He'll be gone from these shores, we'll never see him again . . . we'll never get another chance.'

'Commander Tasker's team is already on the move.'

'They don't know what they're doing . . .'

'Are you serious? Tasker is SOCAR Special Investigations . . .'

'And what does that mean exactly?'

'*I'll* be there too. Maybe you don't trust me either?'

Heck shrugged awkwardly. 'I always trust you.'

'Which is more than I feel about you.' She paused. 'When are you back on duty?'

'Tomorrow.'

'Excellent. Until such time as you're needed in the Northeast again, we'll have you here at base, doing everyone's housekeeping. In fact we've got a dozen new case files that need our attention too. So you better get home before I send you in there right now.'

Tasker reappeared outside Gemma's office. He stood with hands on hips as she traipsed back towards him.

'You need to put someone on Jim Laycock, ma'am,' Heck called after her.

She glanced back. 'I'm sorry?'

'If he removed all those files containing the names and addresses of clients the Nice Guys provided totty for . . .'

'Heck, we've been over this as well!' She was clearly trying not to look as exasperated as he was making her feel. 'There's no evidence it was Laycock. You were being paranoid to the nth degree.'

Heck had never been able to shake the suspicion from his mind that former National Crime Group commander Jim Laycock had been a client of the Nice Guys. All through the original investigation, the murdering bastards had benefited from having a police insider; it was the only way they could have continually stayed one step ahead. And then, to top it all, right at the death, the files containing extensive details of all the Nice Guys' clients in the UK – a full list of names and addresses – had simply disappeared, even though their existence was only known about inside the National Crime Group. Which had meant the insider was very close to home.

Heck had come to suspect Laycock, firstly because the bloke had done his level best to reduce the manpower available to the original enquiry, finally closing it down entirely before it managed to gain any real results – and for what Heck considered to be spurious reasons. And secondly, because Laycock, with his background in the military police, was better-placed than most officers in NCG to have known some of the Nice Guys from an earlier career. Of course, Gemma never felt there was any proof of this, and had many times expressed concern that Heck was letting his personal dislike for Laycock cloud his professional judgement. However, after the dust had all settled, she had forwarded a written opinion that Laycock's initial handling of the Nice Guys affair had been ill-judged. In consequence, though the resulting internal enquiry kick-started by Heck finally cleared Laycock of having any connection with the Nice Guys, he was still disciplined for 'displaying a level of ineptitude in office that verged on criminal negligence'. That said, Laycock's demotion from the rank of commander to the rank of inspector hadn't returned the missing dossier of names, nor did it explain who the mole had been.

'Whether I was or wasn't being paranoid, Laycock sank that investigation for no good reason,' Heck reminded her. 'He did everything he could to hamper us . . .'

'For which he got busted down five ranks,' she retorted. 'Good grief Heck, that's not an insignificant punishment.'

'He's a DI at Wembley, ma'am. He's still higher up the food chain than me.'

Tasker snorted. 'So that's it . . . you're jealous?'

Heck ignored the comment. 'The main thing, ma'am, is that Laycock was one of the few people who knew the client list was there. One of the very few who had access to it . . . if it *was* him who removed it, this new crew could be after him next.'

'Why?' Tasker wondered. 'You think they're going to spirit him off to the Bahamas for the rest of his life . . . in reward for sparing their client base?'

Heck shrugged. 'That wasn't quite what I had in mind, sir, but hey . . . you're the one in charge now. Perhaps it's time *you* gave it some thought.'

Tasker bared his teeth, but managed to keep his temper in check as Heck headed back to the DO.

'He can be an irritating sod at times,' Gemma said quietly, 'but he's right about one thing. We never recovered those missing details of the original Nice Guys' clients. I've always wondered about that. Someone moved them, even if it wasn't Laycock.'

'It's not like you didn't look for them,' Tasker replied. 'Anyway, it's history now.'

'Maybe sir, but I've never been totally comfortable with the idea that all those rapists are living free among us.'

He shrugged. 'Now the Nice Guys appear to have returned, maybe we'll get their clients by a different route. I'm more concerned at present about Heckenburg. He's going to give us problems, I can sense it already.'

'He won't,' she said. 'I'll see to it.'

'You used to be his girlfriend, didn't you?'

'That was a long time ago, sir.'

'Maybe there's something you can do on that front.'

She glanced around at him. 'Excuse me?'

'Throw him a little something. Keep him sweet.'

Despite all the chauvinism she'd experienced in her eighteen years as a female police officer, this left Gemma virtually gobsmacked. 'Are you really asking what I think you're asking?'

'It's a suggestion, that's all. Oh Christ . . . don't start going all "inappropriate comments" on me, Gemma. Let's live in the real world for a change, eh? We've got a bloody catastrophe on our hands here. We need to keep the lid on it any way we can.'

She lowered her voice. 'If you think I'd stoop to that, you've got the wrong person.'

'What's the matter, don't you fancy him anymore?'

Gemma was acutely aware they were out in the corridor and that ears could be waggling in half a dozen adjoining offices. That Tasker wasn't was perhaps a bit worrying. 'Maybe we could just get on with what we're supposed to be doing,' she hissed. 'Like you said, Frank, we've got a bloody catastrophe on our hands . . . if we ignore it much longer, it's going to burn *both* our departments to the ground!'

Chapter 8

The landlord of The Maypole Tavern was a pain-in-the-arse wanker.

At least, that was Detective Inspector Jim Laycock's view. To start with, his first name was Hubert – *who the fuck was called 'Hubert' in the twenty-first century?* – and though he possessed the sort of build that might have been designed for innkeepers in North London – broad, sloping shoulders, brawny, apelike arms and a big square head – this was offset by the immensity of his beer belly, which was so grotesque that it wobbled over the front of his waistband as he walked, and meant he had to lean backwards to effect any measure of decorum. He had a receding hairline, but there was still sufficient left of his greasy, greying mane at the back for him to tie it in a pretentious pigtail. Laycock didn't know which he found the more revolting, this, or the round, soft, permanently sweat-shiny 'baby's arse' that Hubert had for a face.

Of course, appearances weren't everything.

If they were, Laycock himself – with his handsome looks and impressive physique (though it might be a little flabbier now than it used to be) – wouldn't be in such a rut as this: disliked by his juniors, mistrusted by his seniors, despised by the villains to a degree where they'd probably kill him if they got half a chance, and more than happy to drown these sorrows each night with as much beer as he could get down himself.

'Kill me, eh?' he muttered, propping up the Maypole bar. 'Yeah . . . let them try!'

They'd get what was coming. And so would that scrote of a landlord, Hubert Mollop – or whatever his full fucking name was. The bastard thought Laycock didn't know he allowed rent-boys on the premises. This wasn't a gay pub, not officially, but Mollop was a shirt-lifter of the first order – Laycock felt certain. He'd had it on good authority there was a private room here, a place unknown to regular patrons, where underage male prostitutes came to entertain their clients, paying the sympathetic landlord a generous cut of their earnings.

As usual, the problem was proving it.

The bastard was too clever to leave anything lying around that might incriminate him, or to trust his dirty little secrets to anyone he didn't know intimately. The local catamites might be able to help – the trouble was that Laycock, though he was now running day-to-day divisional CID operations at Wembley nick, hadn't been there long enough yet to develop contacts with that particular crowd, which meant he had to rely on the two informers who'd first tipped him off about Mollop, neither of whom was totally reliable due to their both having been banned from The Maypole in the recent past. That was one reason the rest of Laycock's CID team didn't feel the info was kosher, and the main reason he hadn't tried to share what he'd learned with the local vice squad.

But there was no rush. Laycock wasn't going anywhere – so he could afford to watch and wait. In any case, this was only one of several pubs on his patch that he increasingly found he had a problem with as he made his nightly rounds of them. There was low-level dealing going on in some of them, not to mention regular underage drinking. In all cases, it stemmed from the uncouth bastards who ran these establishments. They were all either slobs or nonces or druggies themselves. At least, this was the impression Laycock got, and his grasses tended to support this view, even if his team didn't.

Not that he cared what those tossers thought.

It amazed Laycock how the rest of Wembley CID thought he didn't know about the dissent-filled discussions they held behind his back, how they'd tell any senior guv'nor who'd listen how unimpressed they were by his sour demeanour and vindictive attitude – and all because of that one bad call he'd made. They didn't know what a sleek, sharp animal he'd been in the days when he was a high-flyer; how much of an achiever he was; how much of a moderniser. Good Christ, there were five women in the Wembley office. What chance would those dozy bints have had making it into CID if it hadn't been for supervisors like him pulling rank on the old dinosaurs in the job, suppressing the 'canteen culture', paving the way for the advancement of minorities?

Yet it was curious – he finished his tenth pint of the evening in a single swallow and called curtly for another – how right-wing he himself now felt he'd become. It was disturbing how personal disaster, not to mention the ruination of all your dreams and ambitions, could bring out the beast in you.

The slatternly crowd who filled these problem pubs and bars, who even now were milling around him, binge-drinking, puking, falling on their faces – these drunks, these drug addicts – he'd once felt sorry for them, had only been able to imagine the pain of their abusive upbringings, the desolation of their everyday lives . . . and yet now he regarded them as vermin wallowing in sewers of self-inflicted degradation.

Who knew? Maybe he'd always felt that way deep down.

He quaffed another pint. Perhaps all that politically correct stuff – the diversity seminars he'd made his managers attend, the positive discrimination he'd practised – had been so much pointless fluff, so much pretence, so much . . . what had that maniac Heck called it . . . 'spin'? Perhaps at heart Laycock had been just like the rank and file, mainly interested in clearing the trash off the streets. Maybe he'd just been playing at being the good guy. And perhaps now, with the bastards on the top floor having rejected it, he'd decided: *What the fuck? You might as well see the real me, a humourless, judgemental SOB, who'll happily bracket all lowlifes together and pull the trigger on them at the same time if that's the quickest, easiest way to do it.*

He'd show the bastards, he thought, as he left the dregs of his pint on the bar top and tottered to the door connecting with the toilets. He'd make the arrests, get the convictions, clean up this fucking cow-town, and when the pompous shithouses from New Scotland Yard came to give him his medal, he'd tell them to fuck right off.

There was no one else in the toilets, which Laycock supposed he ought to be thankful for. There were far too many scrotes with sleeve tattoos, crappy earrings and Burberry caps loitering in mysterious little groups in pub bogs these days. They really must think the rest of society was stupid. Well, their time was coming. At least in this neighbourhood. He wandered to the nearest urinal, unzipped and let it go – four pints' worth. That was as many as he'd thought he'd had since he'd last taken a leak.

It wasn't something to be proud of, he supposed. It even made him feel a little hypocritical. But then Laycock drank for a reason; for one thing it helped cushion his monumental fall from grace, and at the same time, in a weird contradiction he felt no inclination to try and explain, he fancied it clarified his thinking, focused his aims. And of course he needed to be in these pubs; needed to find out for sure what was going on; needed to know indisputably who the lice were he could earmark for elimination.

So absorbed was Laycock in this line of thought that he only vaguely noticed someone else had come into the toilets. A brief glance over his shoulder detected a man wearing a grey hoodie under a khaki flak-jacket, now with his back turned as he too stood at a urinal. Another fucking hoodie, Laycock thought. Antisocial bastards. Terrorising the world with their pseudo-American gangsta wannabe attitude. No doubt, when the time came, he'd be rounding a few of those losers up as well. But first he needed the evidence to answer those all-important questions. Who actually *was* it? Who was dealing, who was fencing, who was catering to the kiddie-fiddlers . . .

He didn't really feel the bang on the back of his head. Or rather, he felt it and at the same time heard a dull, hollow thump – but he didn't notice any pain.

Not at first.

Not until he'd slumped down amid a deluge of cheap wine and a shower of broken glass, hitting the rim of the urinal with the bridge of his nose, causing an instant fracture. His head flirted backwards, the rear of his slashed-open scalp impacting hard on the dirty, piss-stained floor tiles.

Laycock was so fuddled that he didn't even realise the guy reaching down towards him, the guy in the khaki jacket and hood, was the same guy who'd attacked him. Only when a pair of gloved hands took him by the lapels of his jacket and dragged him across the lavatory floor to the exterior exit, did an alarm bell start sounding in the back of his mind. He struggled, began to feebly kick. But his assailant was strong, hauling his twisting form effortlessly out over the step and down onto the gritty tarmac of the pub car park, from the opposite corner of which the rumbling of an engine, a pair of white reverse lights and the open rear doors of a high-sided van revealed a vehicle backing at speed towards him.

Two indistinguishable figures jumped from the rear of the van as it screeched to a halt in a cloud of murky exhaust. Laycock was in so much pain and confusion that he could barely burble, but this didn't stop him writhing in his captor's grasp, which he did increasingly as his senses seeped back. The guy in the hood responded by punching him, delivering a hard, clean shot to the middle of his solar plexus, driving the wind out of Laycock's lungs. A savage nausea clenched his lower belly. As he doubled up, they clamped him by his knees, his ankles and his elbows, lifted him and slung him into the darkness of the vehicle's interior – where more of them were waiting to receive him.

'What . . . why're you . . .?' Laycock stammered, only for more blows to rain down.

One smashed his gagging mouth; another slammed his already broken nose, sending a jagged lance of pain through his head. Another caught him in the solar plexus, in the same place as before; maybe by accident, maybe by design – either way it induced such pain that Laycock thought it might kill him. For several seconds he couldn't breathe, while one by one, his abductors climbed into the van, and the doors slammed shut, locking him in a stifling void where the stench of his own blood mingled with oil, sweat and the choking stink of carbon monoxide.

'Who the . . . who the fuck . . .?' he blubbered, but another gloved hand, this one spread wide, closed over his mouth, blocking out further words, pressing his lacerated head hard into the corrugated iron floor.

88

The engine growled, drowning out his muffled whimpers, and the vehicle juddered as it pulled out of the car park onto the road network. Laycock struggled harder, but they were literally on top of him, a mass of booted feet and heavy muscle swathed in canvas and waterproofs. Noticeably, no one spoke; there was no reassurance that everything would be okay if he complied; no consolation offered that this would all be over in the morning; no attempt of any sort to reason with or calm him.

Laycock wasn't sure how long they were on the road for; maybe half an hour, maybe less. All he knew in that time was the darkness, the airlessness, and the pain of his injuries, the crushing weight on top of him, and the violent banging and jolting of the vehicle – and then the abrupt crunch of a loose surface beneath tyres, and the prolonged squeal as brakes were applied.

When the rear doors were yanked open, only very little light was shed in – the result of a waning half-moon passing through autumnal clouds – but it was sufficient to show the tall, angled outline of an unlit building, the exposed ribs of its rotted roof suggesting it was derelict. Yet more men were waiting there – in an orderly row, like a bunch of soldiers on parade.

Despite the violence he'd so far been subjected to, the first bolt of genuine horror only passed through Laycock's rapidly sobering mind when he realised they were all wearing black ski-masks. With a wild lurch, he attempted to fight his way out of the van. He was a big guy himself, in his youth a military policeman, and he could pack a punch and a kick. But he didn't get more than two or three inches before he was again restrained. One of the figures outside leaned in. With a metallic click, torchlight speared through the entrance.

'Let's at least make sure it's the right guy,' an American voice said.

The light hit Laycock in the face, penetrating to the backs of his aching eyes, causing him to blink involuntarily. A damp rag was moved vigorously back and forth across his face. He realised they were mopping away the clotted blood.

'Yep,' the American voice confirmed. 'Check.'

The light went out and Laycock was taken by all four of his limbs and flung – literally flung – out onto the ground. He rolled over, thinking to jump to his feet, but when he looked up, the ramrod-straight silhouettes of his captors hemmed him in from all sides. Man by man, each one of them drew something from out of his clothing, and held it up. Laycock's eyes had attuned sufficiently to the dim moonlight to observe that in every case it was the same thing – a claw-hammer.

'What is this?' he gabbled. 'Whoever you are, you've got the wrong fella!'

'No we ain't,' came that casual American voice.

'Are you fucking mad? I'm a cop, for Christ's sake!'

'We'd hardly have gone to this trouble if you flipped burgers.'

'Wait . . . just fucking wait!' Laycock half-screamed, holding up empty palms, trying to press his abductors back with a helpless gesture. 'Whoever you are, whatever I'm supposed to have done, I can fix it . . . there's nothing that can't be undone . . .'

But the first of the claw-hammers was already hurtling at his face, unseen in the gloom. It connected with a smack of meat and cracking bone.

'Ouch!' the American said, and chuckled.

The other hammers arced down from all sides, over and over, thwacking into limbs, torso, skull, shattering those flailing hands like they were porcelain.

Chapter 9

It wouldn't be true to say that Heck didn't dream.

He did dream occasionally, or maybe he dreamt every night and only recalled vague snippets in the morning. But as a rule his sleep was deep and undisturbed. Perhaps this was down to his own body, some internal mechanism looking out for his welfare, preventing him reliving the worst events of each day as he tried to rest. Either way, all he ever knew of his dreams were brief, hazy recollections, though these could be disturbing enough: a prostitute's severed foot still in its pink high-heeled shoe; a female body lying naked in a bathtub, its face covered with clown makeup. But for the most part, given how disjointed and out of context this fleeting, broken imagery tended to be, it was easy enough to shrug off.

Not so on this occasion.

This time he was in his sister's house, which was located in Bradburn, a post-industrial town in a depressed corner of South Lancashire. It was the same house where his late parents had lived, where he had grown up as a child. Normally it was clean and tidy, yet now it was filthy and dilapidated. Heck wandered helpless and teary-eyed from room to room, appalled by the dereliction. What was more, he could hear the giggles of two children playing games with him – darting around, staying constantly out of sight. He never saw them, but somehow knew who they were: Lauren and Genene Wraxford, two pretty little black girls, sisters from Leeds, who as young women would be murdered by the Nice Guys. He shouted at them not to grow up, not to leave this place, which though it was dirty and crumbling – fissures scurried across the walls, branching repeatedly – they would be safer in if they just stayed here. But still he couldn't see them, and now bricks and plaster were falling. He blundered through the dust to the front door, only to find it was no longer there – solid brickwork occupied its former place.

Frantic, Heck scrambled back through the building, which now consisted of empty, cavernous interiors, many made from rusty cast-iron and fitted with grimy portholes for windows. When he reached the back door, he saw that a heavy iron bolt had been thrown. This too was jammed with rust, and only by exerting every inch of strength did he manage to free it. The door opened – but not onto the paved back yard where he'd kicked a football during his childhood, onto another vast interior, this one built from concrete and hung with rotted cables. At its far end, a gang of men were waiting. All wore dark clothes and ski-masks. They approached quickly and silently, and now he saw they were armed with punk weapons – logs with nails in them, bicycle chains, lengths of pipe.

'By the time we get bored with you, son,' a gloating, Birmingham-accented voice whispered into Heck's right ear, 'you'll wish we'd finished you the first time.'

He spun away, stumbling along a passage, at the end of which stood a bathroom, clean and well appointed, filled with warm sunshine. Heck recognised it from a holiday cottage he and Gemma had rented in Pembrokeshire when they'd been dating all those years ago. At its far side, a shapely woman stood naked in the shower. She faced away from him; her long fair hair flowed down her back in the stream of water. He knew it was Gemma – her hair had been much longer then. Before he could speak, the bathroom window exploded, and those hostile forms – more like apes than humans – came vaulting in. Heck shouted, but no sound emerged, and the bathroom door slammed in his face, another bolt ramming home.

His eyes snapped open in the dimness of early morning light.

For several seconds he could barely move, just lay rigid under the duvet, sweat soaking his hair, bathing his body. At last his vision, having roved back and forth across his only vaguely recognisable room, settled on the neon numerals of the digital clock on the sideboard, which read 5.29 a.m.

Gradually, he became aware of a need to urinate. At length, this propelled him from the warmth of his bed and sent him lurching along the chilly central passage of his flat to the bathroom. On the way back, he was still attempting to shrug off the soporific effects of sleep – for which reason he was caught completely off-guard when there came an explosion of breaking metal and rending timber downstairs.

Heck stumbled to a halt, damp hair prickling at the sound of furious male voices and the thunder of hobnailed boots ascending the single stair from the front door.

In a state of confusion, he backed into his bedroom, slamming the door behind him. Whatever was happening here, it struck him vaguely that he had options. He could try to escape, though his sole bedroom window opened over a fifty-foot drop into a litter-strewn canyon, through which an exposed section of the District Line ran between Fulham Broadway and Parsons Green. Alternatively, he had his mobile with him, and could call for back-up if he first shored up the door – but in truth there was nothing in here with which to create such a barricade; no chest of drawers, no dressing table. The other option – and this looked like the only realistic one – was to fight.

Heck kept a hickory baseball bat alongside his bed. He snatched it up just as the bedroom door was smashed inward. When he saw a gloved hand poking through, clutching a pistol, he swung at it with all the strength he had.

The impact was brutal, the *smack* resounding across the room, a squawk of agony following it. The pistol, a Glock, clattered to the floor. Heck made a dash for it, but the injured intruder, who was wearing a motorbike helmet, dived in, catching him around the waist, bearing him to the carpet. Other intruders followed, also armed with pistols, shouting incoherently – and wearing police insignia all over their black Kevlar body-plate.

What Heck had first taken for motorbike helmets were anti-ballistics wear, but he'd already rammed his elbow down three times between the shoulder-blades of the first assailant before realising this. 'Bloody hell . . .!' he said.

'Armed police!' they bellowed as they filled his room, seven of them training pistols on him at the same time. 'Drop the fucking bat! Drop it now!'

'Alright, alright,' he said, letting the bat go, showing empty hands.

'Nick . . .?' one of them shouted, crouching and lifting his frosted visor to reveal that he, in fact, was a she.

'Don't you fucking move!' another shouted.

The point-man, the one called Nick, still lay groggily across Heck's legs. He groaned with pain as he tried to lever himself upright. Heck assisted with his knees and a forearm, shoving the guy over onto his back.

'I said don't fucking move!' another officer roared, aiming a kick at him.

'What's your problem, dipshit?' Heck retorted. 'I'm a bloody cop!'

'Shut up!' the girl replied, hoisting her fallen colleague to his feet.

Whoever 'Nick' was, he was a big fella, Heck realised – at least six-three and broad as an ox. It had been a stroke of luck to get those early shots in. In contrast, the girl was about five-eight, but lithe, and from what he could see of her, handsome in a fierce, feline sort of way.

Gemma Mark Two, he thought to himself.

'You fucking little shit, Heckenburg,' she snarled, ruining the illusion – Gemma rarely used profanity. 'Get on your face now, or I'll put you there permanently.'

Behind her, more of the arrest team were piling into the crowded bedroom, several armed with staves as well as handguns. Heck supposed he ought to be flattered, but he was too busy listening to the crashing and banging elsewhere in the apartment.

'What's the matter with you people?' he asked. 'You obviously know who I am!'

'I said get on your face!' she reiterated. 'Ignore me one more time, and I swear I'll put a bullet straight through that empty braincase of yours.' Her eyes were a piercing cat-green; her gloved finger tightened on the trigger of her Glock, which she pointed straight at Heck's face.

He rolled over, arms outspread.

'Too right we fucking know you!' she said. 'Hands behind your head!'

He complied, and then they were onto him – she and several others landing knees-first, driving the wind out of him.

'Lie still!' she said. 'Keep your hands away from the bat!'

'You idiots have screwed up,' Heck grunted. 'Whatever intel's brought you here, it's either fake or very flawed.'

She holstered her Glock, and twisted his arms behind his back, quickly and efficiently inducing two painful goosenecks, which suggested she knew her martial arts. She slipped his hands into a pair of nylon cuffs, and cinched them tight.

'Save that famous motormouth of yours for the judge,' she said into his right ear – in the same gloating tone he'd heard in his dream, which gave him a mild jolt, though of course the accent was different; this one was Home Counties, strictly Middle England.

They lifted him roughly to his feet.

'I'm DS Fowler from the Serious Offenders Control and Retrieval unit,' the girl said, 'and I'm arresting you on suspicion of murder.' She gave him the full caution. 'Any questions?'

'Yeah,' he replied. 'What do you do for an encore?'

One of her male colleagues punched him in the side. Heck winced but managed to stay upright. Though he was still barefoot, dressed only in shorts and a sweat-damp t-shirt, they frogmarched him into the corridor, where personal items and bits of furniture were already being tossed out from the other rooms. By the continuing roar of destruction, they were leaving no stone unturned. Someone Heck recognised stood in the midst of it, apparently supervising. He was a short, paunchy man, with podgy, hog-like features scrunched under his helmet, though his general proportions – which were globular in shape – seemed equally uncomfortable squashed into his black coveralls. His name was Derek O'Dowd, and he was an officious little twerp formerly of the Met's Accident Investigation department. It was no surprise that he'd wound up in SOCAR. More unexpected, perhaps, were the inspector's pips on his shoulders.

'Just remember, guv,' Heck said to him, '. . . anything you break, you buy.'

O'Dowd swung around, his mouth fixed in its usual O of

outrage when someone had disputed with him. Immediately, he began shouting. 'Have you ever – *ever in your fucking life!* – tried showing respect for rank, Heckenburg!'

'You ever tried ringing a doorbell? What did you think I was going to do, flush myself down the toilet?'

'*Good Christ!*' O'Dowd bellowed. 'Get this fucking sociopath out of my sight! If he opens his trap one more time, one of you stick your fist in it!'

DS Fowler and the guy called Nick, who apparently was another sergeant, a DS Gribbins – hustled Heck to the top of the stairs, and walked him down between them, though Gribbins cringed as he rotated his wrist and flexed his fingers.

'Looks like you've got full movement,' Heck said. 'Not broken, at least.'

'Don't push me, Heckenburg,' Gribbins snarled.

They arrived outside, where the presence of several police vehicles, including a couple of divisional units, and numerous other armoured SOCAR personnel, ensured that, despite the early hour and milky light of dawn, curtains would be twitching up and down Cherrybrook Drive, a typical nosy Fulham street.

'I'm just saying it'll be okay,' Heck added.

Even though they were out in full public view, Gribbins spun around, snatching Heck by the collar of his t-shirt. Briefly they were nose to nose. Gribbins's thick brown moustache made him resemble some TV cop from the 1970s. But he was currently flushed with anger and streaming sweat.

'It may have escaped your notice, *pal*! . . . but we're not taking this as lightly as you seem to be.'

'I kind of got that,' Heck replied. 'But just out of interest . . . maybe as a common courtesy to my fellow-police status, who am I supposed to have murdered?'

'No one important,' Fowler said, stepping between them. 'Just a DI in the Met.'

Heck's mouth dropped open. 'What . . .?'

'Laycock.'

'You mean Jim Laycock?'

'Why . . . how many Laycocks are there on your personal hate list?'

'You . . .' Heck was only fleetingly lost for words. 'You better *had* take me in.'

'Oh . . . had we?'

'Right now.' Shaking free of their grip, he turned and headed to the prisoner transport parked at the kerb, climbing straight into the back of it.

There was no cage inside this one, so when Fowler climbed in as well, looking a little bemused, she sat on the facing bench and pointed a warning finger at him. 'Don't even think about trying something. I'm a karate fifth dan.'

'Suppose that makes me feel a bit safer,' Heck replied.

'And that smart mouth is going to make things even tougher on you.'

The engine started, the vehicle lurching away.

'I'm totally serious.' Heck glanced up at her. 'The only thing is, I'm not sure a *bit* safer is gonna be enough.'

Chapter 10

'I'm guessing interrogation's a skill you guys haven't mastered yet?' Heck said. 'Because in the last five minutes, your questions have revealed to me that Jim Laycock was abducted last night from a pub in Kilburn at roughly eleven p.m. . . . that he died sometime between twelve and one, and that his body was found this morning in an abandoned vehicle in Hornsey. All stuff which, if you'd kept it quiet, you could have used to trip me up.'

'And in return you've told us nothing,' DS Fowler said. 'Which hardly looks good from your point of view, does it?'

'I've told you nothing you want to hear,' Heck replied. 'But it happens to be the truth . . . which is sometimes pretty boring, I'll admit.'

He was clad in a paper custody suit, and slumped in an interview room at Hammersmith police station. On the other side of the table sat SOCAR detectives Gribbins and Fowler, first names Nick and Steph. Though now in civvies, the former of these appeared no less a thug, his brutish looks topped by a curly brown mop. His corduroy jacket and open-necked plaid shirt somehow accentuated his big, powerful frame. Also out of battle-dress, the latter had a rather cool 'Mrs Peel' kind of aura. Her slim-fit pinstripes hugged her athletic form, but she wore her jet-black hair gathered in a severe bun. Detective Inspector O'Dowd was nowhere to be seen, though he was probably watching through the two-way mirror on the wall. Maybe Frank Tasker was through there as well, though Heck hadn't seen the SOCAR boss in the custody suite when he'd first been brought in.

'I got home last night just after eleven,' he explained again. 'Having first bought a Chinese takeaway from the shop on Larkhill Lane, Fulham. You can ask the lady who owns it. She was the one who served me. Now you do the maths . . . Fulham to Kilburn in less than half an hour?'

'It's not impossible so late in the day,' Gribbins said.

'Maybe not, but if I was going to pull that abduction off, I'd have to have known beforehand that Laycock would be in that particular pub at that particular time. Even then I'd be cutting it close.'

'You could have observed him on other nights. Laycock had turned into a pisshead. He pub-crawled all the time.'

'And do pissheads stick to rigorous schedules when they pub-crawl?' Heck wondered.

Gribbins had no answer for this; in any case, he was still cradling his injured right wrist, which had badly discoloured.

'Why don't we talk about this ongoing feud that existed between you and DI Laycock?' Fowler said.

'Hardly ongoing,' Heck replied. 'I hadn't spoken to the guy in a year and a half.'

'And yet yesterday, while talking to Commander Tasker, you said quite specifically that it wasn't a holiday you had in mind for Jim Laycock. True or false?'

'I said something like that, yeah. But take anything out of context and it can look suspicious.'

'You really had it in for Laycock, didn't you?' Fowler argued. 'You blamed him several times for the near-collapse of your first enquiry into the Nice Guys Club.'

'He did his best to scuttle that enquiry – for no obvious reason. As such, I developed a strong suspicion that he was trying to protect a vested interest.'

'That Laycock was himself a Nice Guys' client?'

'Not just that . . . that he was acting as their informant too.'

'Even though there was no evidence to that effect?'

'There was circumstantial evidence. At least by the end.'

'There was *no* evidence, DS Heckenburg,' she said. 'None at all. Thanks to some persistent lobbying by you, Laycock was investigated after the first Nice Guys enquiry and exonerated of having any involvement with them. What he was found to be at fault for was his generally poor decision-making. He was subsequently demoted in rank.'

'And that wasn't enough for you, was it?' Gribbins said.

Heck smiled. 'You make it sound so bloody unreasonable of me. I've just told you, I flat-out suspected Laycock of being the Nice Guys' mole.'

'Yeah, but you couldn't *prove* it, could you?'

'Well . . . obviously not.'

'So why not just admit this drove you round the bend?' Fowler said. 'That you've had a bee in your bonnet about Jim Laycock ever since?'

Heck shrugged. 'If having a bee in your bonnet is the same as suspecting someone of criminality, then yes, I guess that's probably true.'

'And when Mike Silver escaped from Gull Rock, it became a *burning* issue for you, didn't it?' Gribbins said. 'Because that might mean Laycock was about to get spirited away overseas, at which point he'd be out of your reach for good.'

'As I implied to your guv'nor yesterday,' Heck said, 'I'd started having doubts they were planning a safe haven for Laycock.'

'But a minute ago you were trying to tell us Laycock was the Nice Guys' best mate.'

'I don't think the Nice Guys actually have mates,' Heck replied. 'At the end of the day, he was a former customer who was briefly useful to them. But they're a tight crew. Ex-comrades-in-arms. They weren't going to trust an outsider indefinitely – not when he knew as much as Laycock did.'

'So why wait two years to move against him?'

'Clearly something's changed.'

'Such as?' Gribbins said.

'How do I know? I'm sitting here answering your dumb questions rather than going after them. Listen fellas . . .' Heck leaned forward. 'Any investigating officers worth their salt, which I'm sure you two are despite all appearances to the contrary, should already have recognised there's at least a possibility the Nice Guys killed Jim Laycock because they're tying up loose ends before disappearing back into whichever banana republic is currently hosting them. They'd also recognise the possibility Laycock may not be the last.'

'What are you talking about?' Fowler said.

'You've done some homework on this,' Heck answered. 'You must know I suspected that Laycock held details of all Nice Guys' clients in the UK. If this new team have now got hold of those details – which is just possible, don't you think – they'll likely have found there are quite a lot of loose ends.'

Fowler regarded him warily. 'Specify what you mean by "loose ends".'

'Former clients, former contacts, anyone they confided in or did business with . . . anyone in a position to give evidence against them should we move in and make arrests.'

'You're saying the Nice Guys are just going to kill them all?'

Heck smiled at her incredulity. 'DS Fowler . . . murder is their game. It's what they excel at. If they've opted to clean house here in the UK – which seems highly feasible now they've got their boss back – if they've opted to close down the whole British operation, they won't hesitate to wipe out anyone who might endanger that. They won't hesitate for a second. We saw that up at Brancaster.'

Gribbins looked amused. 'Let's get this straight. You're saying that we need to release you quickly . . . because there are going to be lots more murders. Is that really the best you've got?'

'It's bloody better than you've got, Gribbins! I express concern for a suspect's safety, and *that* puts me in the frame? Seriously?'

There was a sudden disturbance in a room nearby – it sounded like muffled shouting. The two-way mirror shuddered as a door was banged open and closed. A split-second later, the door to the interview room flew open and Gemma strode in, raincoat swirling around her.

'I think that seems an appropriate place to end this charade,' she said.

'For the benefit of the tape,' Gribbins said in a casual tone, 'Detective Superintendent Piper has just entered the interview.'

'For the benefit of the tape,' Gemma countered, 'Detective Superintendent Piper is terminating the interview.' She crossed the room and jabbed her finger down like a bayonet, knocking the tape machine off.

'Ma'am!' Fowler jumped to her feet, but not before Gemma had rounded on the two SOCAR officers.

'Are you two actually for real, or did Frank Tasker find a pair of cardboard cut-outs with movable parts!' They regarded her with open mouths. 'Who's the arresting officer?'

'That would be me, ma'am,' Fowler said, pink-cheeked. 'But you need to understand, this was a clean pinch . . .'

'I want Sergeant Heckenburg's underclothes returned to him forthwith! Apparently that's all he was wearing when you brought him in here, which is strictly against the rules, so I could have both your backsides for that if I wanted to. I also want some clean, warm clothing provided for him – right now. And I want every trace of this arrest erased from the databanks.'

'Ma'am . . .' Gribbins stuttered, 'you . . . can't do that!'

Gemma spun to face him. 'What's that phrase we all love and cherish so much in the police service? Oh yes . . . "we're the cops, we can do anything we want". *See to it, Gribbins! Now!*'

Abashed, and still gripping his injured wrist, Gribbins stumbled from the room.

Fowler stood her ground. 'Ma'am, I protest in the strongest possible terms. This is a serious breach of procedure . . . you need to speak to Commander Tasker about this.'

'Oh don't you worry, Sergeant Fowler . . . I will.' Gemma stalked back towards the door. 'And tell Derek O'Dowd . . . when he finally stops hiding in the toilets, because that's apparently the direction he ran in when I parked out back, I want any damage caused to Sergeant Heckenburg's premises and property paid for promptly and without quibble, out of his own pocket. Do you get that, Fowler? Out of O'Dowd's *own* pocket! If I don't see proof of that within the week – proof, as in receipts from contractors, retailers and so forth, I'll be speaking to the tax office about that sideline of his doing up and selling on old Traffic cars, which he thinks no one knows about.'

And she swept out of the room, no doubt to consult again with the Hammersmith custody suite team, a good set of lads who most likely were the ones responsible for tipping her off that Heck had been brought in.

Fowler could only stand there, stunned.

Heck rose to his feet. 'Guess now you know why I didn't ask for my Federation rep. Or a solicitor.'

She scowled. 'You think you're so fucking clever!'

'You know, all that effing and blinding doesn't suit you.'

'I lost a lot of friends at Gull Rock, Heckenburg . . . forgive me if keeping it clean isn't one of my priorities.'

'It's more a pity that using your noggin isn't one of them. Seriously, Fowler . . . if I'd murdered Laycock because of some vendetta from the past . . . why were *you* sent to arrest me when you're investigating the murders of your mates? You think I murdered them too?' Her expression remained taut, but it was clear she was listening. 'Your boss is playing games.' He stepped out into the corridor.

'Why the hell would he do that?' she shouted after him.

'Try asking him,' he called back. 'And when you find out, let me know.'

It took Gemma just under thirty minutes to get from Hammersmith to New Scotland Yard, and when she did, she found Commander Tasker in the old media management suite, which was about four doors down from the Serial Crimes Unit's DO.

It was a scene of semi-organised chaos; SOCAR officers, techies and civvie staff bustling back and forth as they brought in tables, chairs, boxes of files, phones and computer terminals, gradually transforming the once large, dusty space into Operation Thunderclap's main incident room, or MIR. Meanwhile, some of the SOCAR Special Investigations team were already hard at work, bashing keyboards, studying images on display systems.

Gemma zeroed in on Tasker as soon as she came through

the double doors. 'What the devil are you playing at, Frank? You dare put one of my detectives under arrest without consulting me first!' Her voice was loud, harsh. It stopped most of the others in their tracks, especially when they realised it was directed at their boss.

'Now wait a minute,' Tasker said, face reddening. 'Detective Superintendent Piper, I think we need to calm . . .'

'You dare confiscate his clothing! Swab his hands! Stick him in a paper suit!'

Tasker's voice hardened. 'He's suspected of murder, for Christ's sake!'

'He's suspected of nothing . . . except knowing your job better than you do!'

Tasker's snowy eyebrows arched. 'You want to run that by me again?'

'Heck has been saying for months that we ought to keep Jim Laycock under observation. And surprise-surprise, it looks like he was right . . . and how the bloody hell do you respond? *By locking him up, for Christ's sake!*'

Tasker jabbed his finger at a nearby door, which connected with the smaller half-furnished sub-chamber he was planning to use as his private office. 'We'll talk in here . . . *now!*'

Gemma followed him in. He closed the door behind her. Through the glazed partition there was still much interest among the rank and file, so Tasker yanked a chain, closing a blind. 'Heck forecast that Laycock was gonna get the chop,' he said. 'And he did. The very next day. What am I supposed to conclude – except that Heck knew it was going to happen?'

Gemma couldn't keep the scorn from her voice. 'You think he'd broadcast that if he was part of it? You think he'd tip us off?'

'You are too close to this fella, Gemma. You are way too close . . .'

'With all respect, sir, don't piss down my back and tell me it's raining. We're up to our nostrils in a very serious incident here . . . and taking sideswipes at lesser ranks just because you suspect they're more on the ball than you are is not going to help.'

Tasker almost reeled from that comment. He liked to think he was an easy, even-handed boss; never arrogant, never malicious. Sure, he could and would make cruel decisions, but only ever for a reason. He preferred to believe this was why he was rarely challenged by subordinates – because they respected him rather than feared him; because his managers trusted his judgement and were loyal. Of course, it had also been common if unspoken knowledge that an officer in his position could crush anyone who really gave him a hard time. And this was all the more reason why he was so taken aback now by the ferocity with which Gemma came at him.

He'd known Gemma reasonably well before all this. There were few police officers of any rank in the London area who didn't know Gemma Piper, and who weren't aware what a firecracker she could be: tireless and efficient; a smart problem solver; a fearless decision taker – rare traits in the modern police – but uncompromisingly adversarial if there was something she didn't like. Even trying to stare her down now – and he was head and shoulders taller than she was – felt like a fool's errand.

'Let me get this straight, Gemma,' he said, using a calmer tone. 'You won't even consider the possibility that Heck let his animosity towards Laycock boil over? That when Rochester escaped from jail, he lost it – went round to see Laycock and, when he got no change, beat the crap out of him?'

'And what about that word . . . *BDEL*, left at the site where Laycock's body was dumped?' she wondered. 'Did Heck leave that? Did he leave the one on the command car at Gull Rock as well, Frank? Was Heck involved in that too?'

'The appearance of that cryptic word at Laycock's murder scene hardly clears Heck,' Tasker retorted. 'He knew about its use the first time. He could have copied it.'

'That's not the way Heck operates!'

'Really . . .' Tasker almost laughed. 'You ever wondered if Heckenburg's so good at catching psychopaths because he isn't far off being one himself?'

'Oh, for Christ's sake . . .'

'No, listen. I actually pulled his file before all this started. He displays plenty of narcissistic traits. Introverted, self-contained, self-reliant . . . *alarmingly* self-reliant in fact. Doesn't trust others. Doesn't work easily with others. Only transmits intel up the command chain on a need-to-know basis. Resists authority almost on principle . . .'

'He's controllable.'

'You sure about that, Gemma? You know how many kills he has to his name?'

'Like you said, sir . . . we deal with the worst of the worst.'

'He's supposed to be a copper. Not a 00 agent.'

'Each fatality was fully examined by the IPCC, as per the manual. And in every case Heck was cleared.'

'The guy thinks he's at war with the entire British underworld.'

'So?'

'It's hardly rational behaviour.'

'Oh, I agree with that,' she said. 'Heck puts every ounce of strength and energy he's got into this job. There's nothing else in his life, which is more than a little bit sad. But how the bloody hell does that make him a criminal?'

'Look, Gemma . . . you want Heck out of the way of this enquiry as much as I do . . . so stop pretending you're so pissed off!'

'Yes sir, I do want him out of the way. For exactly the same reason as you. But you think that means I'd let you throw his arse in prison?'

Tasker dropped into his swivel chair. 'If he wasn't involved in Laycock's death, the forensics will clear him.' His tone was exasperated but dismissive. 'It was a warning shot across his bows, that's all.'

'A warning shot?'

'It's time he learned that opening his big yap can have consequences.'

'You really don't know Heck, do you?'

'I know him well enough to recognise trouble. I said this from the start, and you assured me you'd take care of it.'

'I will!' She moved to the door. 'But it'll be a whole lot harder after today.'

'Gemma, we *are* going to be able to work together on this, aren't we?' Tasker said sternly. 'We've got no choice . . . but I'm a commander and you're a superintendent. I hope I can trust you to remember that. I also hope I can trust you to understand that I'll find it very inconvenient, not to say completely fucking infuriating, if any more of my orders are countermanded.'

She gave that some thought. 'Sir . . . if the other stuff Heck's been saying turns out to be true, namely that Mike Silver and the Nice Guys, after getting rid of Jim Laycock, are about to start working their way through the client list as well, I don't think we can waste any further time on silly distractions like this. So what you can *really* trust me to do is take any action I deem fit to ensure we stay focused on what might be the most nightmarish murder case in British history.'

And she left, leaving Tasker fuming but helpless in his half-furnished office.

Chapter 11

When Peter Rochester, aka Mad Mike Silver's eyes flickered open, the first thing they registered was the pain of glaring sunlight. But after several seconds of grogginess and stupor, his vision slowly adjusted, and the 'glare' revealed itself to be the milk-pale radiance of a cloudy morning as filtered through a single window, the cracked pane of which was smudged with grime.

For the next few moments, confusion reigned. Silver was numb from the neck down, and felt as though his head had been stuffed with cotton wool. He was also aware he was lying flat on some yielding surface – he even fancied a blanket had been laid over him – but could barely move his limbs, which felt heavy as lead. And then Silver's eyes attuned again, this time sufficiently to focus on the face of a person sitting alongside him.

It was a young, good-looking face, but also angular, strong and very distinctive – not just for its piercing green eyes and the mop of sandy blond hair over the top, but for the tight set-square of scar tissue on its left cheek.

'You seem surprised, Mike,' the face's owner said with

that familiar plastic grin of his. Even after all these years in exile, his accent was recognisably Danish.

'I'm more . . .' Silver tried to speak, but his mouth might as well have been crammed with feathers. The Dane offered him a paper beaker. Ice-cold water spilled over Silver's lips, and then through into his mouth. He managed to swallow a couple of sips before coughing and choking – he was lying flat after all. He tried to move again; only now was sensation returning to his body, but slowly and dully. 'I'm . . . I'm more surprised I'm not in hospital, Kurt,' he stammered.

'We've had you looked over. You'll be okay.'

'Where am I?'

'Apparently you need a couple of days' bed rest. So we fixed this billet up for you.'

Silver glanced around, noticing the cluttered interior of a shed or lock-up. Overhead, its sloped roof was of corrugated metal with occasional wooden lathes laying across it, these latter rotted and hung with ropes of dust-thick cobweb. Its walls were bare, mildewed brick. Aged tools dangled from rusted iron hooks.

'Doesn't look like much,' the Dane said. 'But at least you'll be comfortable. Personally, I'd have liked to keep you on the move, but it seems that's a no-no.'

Silver continued to glance around. Of newer manufacture was the metal pole standing next to him, from which a saline drip was suspended. Alongside that was propped the Malacca cane they'd given him in the prison.

'Hey . . . Mike.' The Dane's mouth curved downward in a fake frown. 'You don't look very happy to see me.'

As his grogginess cleared, Silver felt sick to the pit of his stomach. On top of that, he had a pounding headache. 'Kurt, the way I feel . . . you're lucky I'm even acknowledging you.'

'Now that wouldn't be kind.'

'In case you've forgotten, Kurt . . . I'm *not*.'

The Dane called Kurt chuckled. 'You know some of these guys?'

Silver realised that other men were present. They weren't exactly standing back in the shadows; it was simply that his vision was still adjusting to the half-light. They wore scarves, gloves, dark khaki clothing and waterproof coveralls. They also carried weapons: semi-automatics and submachine guns. But that was no more than he'd expect, and now he looked at them properly, he recognised several of their cold, hard faces.

He nodded at a squat, bullet-headed guy, with black scorpion tattoos visible on the insides of his wrists. 'Alex.'

The man he'd addressed nodded back. 'Mike.'

'Bruno,' Silver said, turning to a handsome, powerfully built black guy.

Bruno didn't reply, merely inclined his head.

'You know Shaun Cullen?' Kurt wondered.

A third guy stepped into view. He was freckle-faced, with a red beard and moustache. Silver suspected that long, greasy, red locks were tucked under his pulled-down woolly cap. 'Sure,' he said. 'Horribly killed anyone recently, Shaun?'

'As a matter of fact, I have, Mike,' the man called Cullen replied in an American accent. His eyes glittered, but no smile creased his lips.

'What happened? He look at you in a way you didn't like?'

'Nah . . . this one was strictly business.'

'So's *this* . . . I'm guessing?' Silver glanced questioningly from face to face.

Kurt chuckled again. 'You think we'd come all the way over here for any other reason?'

'I'm still in the UK then?' Sick though he still was, Silver felt more than a little deflated by that revelation.

112

'We'd like to take you home, Mike,' Kurt said. 'We want to go home ourselves, but we've got a long list of jobs we need to do first.'

Silver knew immediately what he was talking about, and it put a pang of unease through him. 'That's taking a big risk, Kurt.'

'Haven't got much choice, have we?' Cullen replied.

'Shaun's right, Mike,' Kurt said. 'The UK's like a wide-open back door at present. We have to close it somehow.'

'The problem is . . .' Silver tried to sit up in his bed. 'The problem is they're wise to us. They know who we are. They'll be watching, waiting . . .'

Kurt indicated the man called Alex. 'Corporal Mulroony here doesn't rate your modern Brit police services much. Reckons they're one half careerists, the other half barrack-room politicians.'

Corporal Mulroony remained stone-faced and silent, but Silver shook his head. 'It would be an error to apply that judgement across the board. This guy Heckenburg . . . it took him a few months, but he ended up pulling my entire operation apart. And that was on his own, with no back-up.'

'Yes, but Mike . . .' Kurt mused. 'The question is . . . was that about Heckenburg, or about you?'

'Gimme a break, Kurt. You know I always ran a tight ship.'

'Okay, so who is this guy . . . Superman?'

'Not exactly. He has weak spots. He can be hurt and he makes mistakes. But he knows his job and he doesn't give up. He's also a chancer . . .' Silver indicated the beaker in Kurt's hand, and took another thankful sip; his strength was now returning, his head clearing properly. 'He's unpredictable too, and that's something you'll need to watch him for very carefully.'

Kurt pondered this as he fished a fragment of paper from his jacket pocket, and unfolded it. 'To be honest, I'm less concerned about this cop Heckenburg than I am about these two.' He glanced at the paper. 'Commander Frank Tasker and Detective Superintendent Gemma Piper . . .?'

'What about them?'

'Well . . . they've been talking to you recently, Mike. A lot.'

Silver shrugged. 'They were trying to get me to blow the gaff on the rest of you guys.'

'And?'

'I didn't. Obviously.'

'What did they offer you?'

'What could they offer me?' Silver shrugged again. 'I was convicted of kidnapping and murdering thirty-eight women. You think the British public would sit by and let them make some kind of deal with me?'

'So all these interviews in Brancaster Prison . . . they just led nowhere?'

'I strung 'em along . . . but that was to make it look like I was playing ball, maybe crank some petty privileges out of them.'

'You were happy to spend the rest of your life in Gull Rock, Mike?' Cullen asked doubtfully.

'It wasn't like I could do much about it.' Silver had managed to draw his right hand from under the blanket and was slowly, cautiously flexing it. 'But believe it or not, it isn't actually so bad. I was in the Special Supervision Unit. There were only four others in there with me. A crazy old fella who dismembered his two grandkids to see how they worked. A mob enforcer with twenty kills to his name, but who's now virtually blind thanks to getting shot in the back of the head when the screws let him out to attend his brother's funeral. A rape-strangler who specialised in teenage prostitutes. And a fifty-year-old social reject who still relied for everything on his octogenarian mum, and got his kicks setting fire to old folks' homes. Now you tell me . . . who do you think was running *that* wing?'

'Congratulations on being king of a pretty goddamn pathetic castle,' Cullen said.

'Hey, it could've been worse. If I was outside the SSU and in with the general population, it might've turned nasty very quickly.'

'Is that what they threatened you with if you didn't cooperate?' Kurt wondered.

'Once or twice.'

'You had no legal recourse?'

'I may have had. I don't know . . . we never got that far. Like I say, I kept stringing them along.'

Kurt mulled this over. 'The main thing is you never talked to them about us?'

'In truth, there wouldn't have been a lot I could tell them, would there? I mean, I know who you guys are, I know roughly where your respective centres of operation are . . . but I haven't been abroad for quite a few years now. And you'd be damn stupid if you didn't keep moving things around, mixing personnel, switching IDs . . .'

'Like you did, you mean?' Cullen said. 'When one cop on his own pulled your entire crew apart.'

Silver regarded him coolly. 'You might show a little fucking respect, Shaun. I brought you into this line, remember?'

'Yeah, you did,' Cullen said. 'And I'm grateful, Mike, I really am. But let's face it . . . law enforcement bodies all over the world have infiltrated organised crime, international terrorism, dissident political groups. They've even penetrated each other's networks. Everyone out there knows what everyone else is doing. Except us. We've always stayed under the radar.'

'Until now,' Kurt added. 'When we've suddenly got this great big hole in our security wall . . . called Great Britain.'

'I'm aware we fucked up over here, Kurt,' Silver said. 'But we paid the price. It wasn't just me getting slammed inside. Eric Ezekial got blown to kingdom come. You knew Deke, didn't you, Alex?'

'I did, aye,' Corporal Mulroony replied in his Glaswegian brogue. 'Good man.'

'Yeah, well you can thank Heckenburg personally for that one. Sonny Kilmor was shot in the back by some shit-arse London gangster. Tommy Hobbs got his neck broken.'

'Shot in the back?' the black guy called Bruno said, sounding disappointed.

'You knew Trooper Kilmor?' Silver asked.

Bruno nodded. 'He was a legend in 3-Para.'

'There you fucking go. We paid the price, Kurt.'

'You may have done, Mike,' the Dane replied. 'But like I say, you left the back door open.'

'Then close it . . . if you must.'

'We're in the process of that.' Kurt patted the patient's knee and stood up. 'But we've gotta be sure we close it properly. And for good.'

Briefly, they stood looking at him. Their expressions weren't exactly hostile, but they were blank, unreadable – and that was never a good sign. Silver's scalp began to prickle.

'You don't trust me, do you?' he said slowly.

'We've gotta be *absolutely* sure, Mike,' Kurt reiterated.

'And my word's not good enough?'

'There was a time when you were the best liar I knew. That suited us then.'

'But now things have changed,' Cullen added, the left side of his mouth hitching into a lopsided smile. The American was an ultra-reliable operative; a professional through and through. But there were some aspects of his work he enjoyed more than others.

'You bastard, Shaun,' Silver said, a sense of dread knotting his lower belly. 'All the favours I've done you . . .'

'Well . . . you made me number three in this outfit. I owe you for that.'

'I can make you number two. Just say the word.'

'But I'm already number two. And I've got Kurt to thank for that.'

Silver switched his attention to the Dane. 'Come on, Kurt. You know me . . . we're friends.'

Kurt shrugged. 'You just offered my job to Shaun. Is that how you treat friends?'

'You fucking snake-in-the-grass!'

'Despite that, I'm not going to make this personal.' Behind Kurt, a dingy drape was drawn over the single window; dimness flooded in. 'All we want, Mike, is the truth.'

'You wouldn't know the truth if it sank its teeth into your bollocks and twisted them off. You're a fucking caveman, Kurt . . . and you'll lead these guys to disaster.'

Cullen snorted. 'Says the one who's endangered our entire operation.'

Silver glared at him. 'You'd better do what you've got to do, Shaun . . . but don't be surprised if it doesn't lead anywhere.'

'I sure hope it doesn't,' Cullen said with apparent sincerity as he unzipped his combat jacket. 'Whatever today's outcome, I always kind of liked you.'

Chapter 12

'Laycock hadn't taken his demotion well,' Shawna McCluskey said. 'He got the idea he'd washed up in some hellhole, surrounded by society's worst.'

Heck sipped his coffee. 'Wembley, a hellhole? I've seen a lot worse.'

'Exactly. Sounds like he'd lost it.'

Heck contemplated this as they sat together in the National Crime Group canteen. It was lunchtime on the day after his arrest, three days after the attack on the prison cavalcade, and the place was busier than usual, mainly due to the extra bodies brought in from SOCAR.

'Are we absolutely sure some local posse wasn't responsible for this?' Heck wondered. 'Maybe some minor players Laycock had been winding up?'

'Wembley CID reckon he was winding no one up but them. Ever since he arrived there, he was drinking. Occasionally while he was on duty. Came up with loads of ideas, but nothing workable. Spent most of his time signing off other people's paperwork.'

Heck snorted. 'Just like when he was here. Or *not* signing it off, in my case.'

'Whatever else he was, Heck, he didn't deserve to get his brains hammered out.'

'I can introduce you to thirty-eight sets of grieving parents who'd give you an argument on that. It's accurate he was found in a burnt-out van in Hornsey?'

'Yeah. In the grounds of an abandoned house. *BDEL* had been carved on its door.'

'That seems weird,' Heck said. 'Doesn't fit the former pattern. I mean, the Nice Guys never left a signature before. What about Laycock . . . much left of him for the lab-rats?'

'Enough. He was pretty badly burned but they reckon he was dead before the fire was lit. Blunt force trauma all over his body.'

Heck contemplated this. Laycock had been a policeman, but it was a struggle to feel pity for him. The guy had come to a grisly end, but so had a good number of others – and in their case Heck still felt certain Laycock had been partly responsible. Whenever he viewed the gruesome leftovers of criminals who'd been turned on by their own, it filled him with revulsion – the sight of mutilated flesh always did – but no real sadness.

'Any witnesses?'

'Only the CCTV at the side of the pub. It caught the van leaving.'

'The van was a knocker, you say?'

Shawna nodded. 'Stolen from Southall early yesterday morning.'

'More than one assailant, I assume?'

She shrugged. 'One assailant in the pub toilet, they think . . . probably someone else driving the van. Maybe a couple of others to help chuck him into it.'

Heck sat back. 'The more of them the better . . . less chance they'll have got away without leaving something at the scene.'

'Gemma's not expecting the forensics will do us much good . . . if this crew have come in from abroad, the chances are they won't be in the system.'

'It'll do us good if we manage to get our mitts on a couple of them,' Heck said.

'*You* won't be getting your mitts on anyone,' a voice interrupted.

Nick Gribbins had approached them, unseen. His right wrist was in a cast, but not in a sling, and by his formal attire he was still on duty. He no longer regarded Heck with suspicion – Heck's story about visiting a takeaway on the night in question had checked out, while a woman living on the other side of the railway from his flat had confirmed she'd seen the light in his bedroom and had spotted him moving around at about half-past midnight, which made his involvement in Laycock's abduction impossible. But they'd hardly hit things off. The SOCAR sergeant's gaze was still an icy shade of grey.

'You're wanted downstairs, Heckenburg . . . now.'

Heck indicated the dregs of his coffee. 'Gotta finish this first. Might take a while.'

'It isn't a fucking request!'

'Perhaps it *should* have been. That may have been where you went wrong.'

'You really are an obnoxious prat, aren't you?'

'And you couldn't raise a wank in a warm bath . . . and that was before I busted your hand.'

'You want to see how busted it really is?'

Heck jumped to his feet, but now Shawna McCluskey intervened. 'Hey!' She rounded the table. 'What's all this testosterone crap? This is a sodding canteen . . . people are trying to have a quiet cuppa in here!'

The men continued to eyeball each other.

'It's your own DSU who wants you downstairs,' Gribbins

said tightly. 'I don't know why . . . I just said I'd deliver the message. But *she* didn't bloody request either.'

He turned on his heel, and strode to the service counter. Heck glanced at Shawna, who looked vaguely disappointed in him.

'What?' he asked.

'Oh . . . nothing.' She grabbed her jacket. 'I just wondered if it ever occurred to you that laying into bystanders because the real bastards are out of reach might be counter-productive?'

'Come on, Shawna. You heard him . . .'

'Yeah, I heard you too. You're like a kid sometimes.'

'You're like a kid, *sergeant*,' he corrected her, but she only half-smiled. 'Hey, DC McCluskey . . . they turned my flat inside out!'

'Like anyone'd notice,' she replied. 'The point is, we're all on the same side.'

'When you've got a sec, remind SOCAR of that.'

Heck headed out of the door, and walked downstairs in a huff. But in truth, her words had made an impact. His original investigation into the Nice Guys, into the kidnap, rape, torture and murder of thirty-eight women – thirty-eight *at least*, he reminded himself – had been the worst experience of his professional life. On top of that, he himself had been beaten and shot. Lauren Wraxford, a civilian he'd formed a real attachment with, had been stabbed through the heart. The perpetrators, a bunch of mercenary scum, had been plying their filthy trade for years in distant lands – and there'd been nothing insane about them, nothing sick, nothing beyond the scope of human responsibility. The acquisition of wealth was their sole concern, and they didn't care who died in unimaginable terror, agony and despair as a result. Only when they'd brought their business to Britain under Mad Mike Silver had they finally fallen foul of law enforcement, but they hadn't fallen foul of it nearly enough for Heck's taste. Even though several of them had died and Silver had received a full life sentence, Heck had long suspected there were more of them out there – and now he knew it for a fact. He wasn't sure how he'd react if those remaining ever came under his hand; they'd just better hope he didn't have a weapon in it. He'd often been criticised in his career for being too obsessive, too extreme. But it was difficult in the case of the Nice Guys to imagine there could be any other way. And it wasn't as if his worst fears hadn't, at least to some extent, been justified. He ought to have realised there was no prison in Britain secure enough for a bastard like Mad Mike. The notion that he was out again, free to do anything he wanted – and God alone knew what that might be – was more than Heck could stomach. And yet each time he thought along these lines, or even attempted to justify in his own mind the hatred he felt for Silver and that gang of nameless, faceless killers, it reminded him more and more why he shouldn't be involved. And as Shawna had said, taking his frustrations out on those who *were* would hardly help.

He passed the former media suite, the doors to which stood open. Glancing through, he saw that the new MIR was now almost totally functional. Though Operation Thunderclap hadn't officially been launched yet, personnel were already crammed around every desk. Photographs and diagrams covered the walls, and in the centre of the room there was a large VDU display bearing a massive 3D image of the crime scene at Brancaster; evidently it was coming through a live feed, because figures in Tyvek could be seen stepping warily between the ruined hulks of vehicles. Alongside that, on two display boards, were two enlarged photos of the *BDEL* engraving – the first on the police car, the second on the battered wooden door of a derelict house.

Yet what most caught his eye was much lower-tech, and located just inside the main doors, facing into the office.

Heck wandered in and looked it over. It was a large noticeboard covered with purple crepe, on which glossy head-shots of the SOCAR officers who'd died in the ambush had been pinned in four neat rows of four, each with name, rank and collar number placed underneath it on black plastic labels. The other victims of the ambush – the non-police personnel – were displayed elsewhere in the room. This little item was more like a shrine; a reminder to the team perhaps that on this occasion the criminals had struck very close to home. Almost invariably, these shots had been taken in happier times; some of the men were in uniform, some in plain clothes – all ages, colours and creeds were on show, yet all looked like family men. Theirs were the sort of fresh, genial faces you'd find in wedding albums or on holiday snaps. Heck thought about the scrapbook in his own drawer, in which he kept photographs of every murder victim he'd ever got a result for. He knew one or two other coppers who did the same thing, but he'd never put the SOCAR glory boys in the same bracket. Perhaps that had been a bit hasty of him.

Two dozen yards down the corridor, he found the door to Gemma's office open. She was slouched behind her desk, seemingly lost in thought.

'Ma'am?' he said.

'Oh, come in, Heck. Sit down.'

He did so. She said nothing else for a moment or two, still looking distracted. There was something vaguely surreal about the leather strap across the back of her shoulders and the Glock nine-mill hanging at her armpit. She'd drawn a pistol before for use on the job, but by all accounts Operation Thunderclap had been blue-carded for the duration of the enquiry, which was a rarity indeed.

'Surprised you're setting up the MIR here and not at Brancaster, ma'am,' he said.

'Yeah, well . . . the best we could probably get up there is a bird-watchers' hide. Anyway, I doubt the focus of the investigation will lie in East Anglia much longer.' She pushed two bundles of stapled paperwork across the desk. 'These came in today.'

They were two crime reports, with assorted statements and photographs attached. Heck picked them up and leafed through. The first had been forwarded by Hampshire, and it concerned a homicide committed the previous evening just off the A303 near to Andover. Even with Heck's long experience of murder investigations, the photographs almost made him retch. It seemed that just after eight o'clock in the evening, while on his way home from work, a successful sixty-five-year-old haulier, name of Austin Ledburn, had for some reason stopped his Jaguar in an isolated lay-by, and climbed out. There was no trace of a scuffle or fight either inside or outside the vehicle; it had simply been parked, locked and left. Passing police patrols hadn't initially thought it suspicious until two hours later, when it had suddenly occurred to them that whoever left the car had had nowhere else to go, which possibly meant it had been stolen and dumped. A PNC check had produced no reports to that effect, but Ledburn's wife expressed concern that he still hadn't returned home, so a search commenced in the nearby woods. Ledburn's body was found half a mile in. He'd been tied to a tree and doused with petrol – it had even been poured down his throat – and then set on fire.

There could have been any reason why such a death was inflicted on the guy – were it not for the familiar word *BDEL*, which had been notched into the bark of the next tree along.

The second crime report came courtesy of Kent Police, and was just as ghoulish. This one related to a certain Geoffrey Culbrook, a retired banker who'd been found dead in his Maidstone home by his housekeeper at nine-thirty that morning. Again there was no sign of forced entry, though Culbrook had been bound spread-eagled on his own four-poster bed. He'd then been tortured with pliers, razor blades and a cigarette lighter, before being dispatched by a single shotgun blast to the face.

In his case, the *BDEL* had been carved onto his bedpost.

Heck laid the gruesome photographs back on the desk.

'No I-told-you-sos please,' Gemma said gravely.

'You think these are former Nice Guys' clients?'

'Wasn't it you who said they'd start rubbing names off the list?'

'I theorised they might.'

'Well, these may be the first two.'

Heck mused. 'Were they known to us before?'

'Ledburn was. He attempted to rape a girl when he was in his early twenties. Dragged her into bushes while she was going home from a nightclub. He got a year and a half. Twenty years later he was reported for indecently assaulting one of his secretaries. Apparently offered her money to make photocopies of her bare bottom – no comments about SCU Christmas parties! – and pinched said bottom after she told him where to go. He received an adult caution for that one.'

'Okay . . .' Heck mulled this over. 'Kind of puts him in our court. Anything to suggest Culbrook had a sexually chequered past?'

'Kent were initially working on the basis he was gay – fifty-eight and single. They wondered if he might have picked up the wrong bit of rough. But when Culbrook's house was searched, they found a locked cupboard stuffed with hetero porn . . . and it's the nastier end of the market. Whips, chains, thumbscrews.'

'The victimology's a match, then,' Heck said. 'In both cases. But it's this *BDEL* thing that's bothering me.'

'Eric Fisher's come up with something on that,' she said. 'He thinks it may be an abbreviation of the Greek phrase, BDELUGMA . . . which stands for the word "Abomination".'

'Abomination . . .?'

'Eric's wondering if it's a reference to those *abominations* who idolised the Whore of Babylon in the Book of Revelation. It means wretches, wastrels, pleasure-seekers . . . they were ranked alongside harlots as the vilest of the vile.'

'The Book of Revelation . . .' Heck's words tailed off as he considered this. Detective Sergeant Eric Fisher was SCU's secret weapon, a tireless analyst and researcher; behind his big, dishevelled exterior, there was a huge intellect that had contributed enormously to cracking the raison d'être behind many complex murder cases. But on this occasion his thesis sounded like a bit of a stretch.

'In Revelation,' Gemma added, 'that phrase, or something like it, was written on the Whore of Babylon's forehead. It was also, allegedly – though this may be more myth than fact – branded onto the foreheads of prostitutes and adulteresses in the ancient Middle East.'

'Ah . . .' Now Heck thought he saw where Fisher was coming from. Mike Silver and his crew's origins lay in the Middle East and North Africa. That was where they'd run their first sex/murder rackets. 'Branded whores . . .' He pondered. 'The Nice Guys might have witnessed such punishments in hard-line Muslim countries. That may be the inspiration for this. And they certainly regarded the women they abducted as nothing more than that . . . cheap product to be exploited and then chucked away. But it's the whole signature aspect I don't understand, ma'am. The Nice Guys never left calling cards before. Ever.'

'That's what's troubling me, if I'm honest,' Gemma said. 'You're saying you don't think this is the Nice Guys?'

'No, ma'am. Far from it.' Heck perused the paperwork again. 'All these cases have a real aura of Nice Guys efficiency. We know they're professional stalkers. I mean, that's what they do. All their previous victims were tracked over a period of weeks, if not months, and finally, when every condition was right, they were snatched – with scarcely a clue left behind. That's at least partly what's happened here. The offenders zeroed in on Geoff Culbrook and then on his house, and got inside it with relative ease. Austin Ledburn was followed home from work, and somehow induced to stop on the darkest, loneliest stretch of road. And then we've got Jim Laycock . . . who they pursued around the pubs of Kilburn while he got progressively more pissed. He'd have been an easier target, I suppose.'

'But why the calling cards?' Gemma asked. 'Why the casual dumping of the bodies where anyone could find them? Previously, Silver's speciality was making people disappear. I mean, he was cute as a fox. It was years before we even knew there was a series of murders in progress.'

Heck sat back. 'Well, you know Silver better than me, ma'am.'

'Hmm.' Briefly, Gemma looked discomforted by that.

'Did he go through some kind of personality change while he was inside?'

'Not as I noticed.'

'Then maybe we shouldn't assume Silver's in charge.'

She frowned.

'He'd had a heart attack, after all,' Heck said. 'On which subject, I presume we've checked with all relevant medical facilities?'

'Of course. We drew a blank.'

'Well, who knows . . . maybe Silver's dead. Maybe he died shortly after they sprung him.' Heck tapped the new documentation. 'Perhaps these other atrocities are the rest of the Nice Guys lashing out at a world that's deprived them of their beloved leader.'

'Heck . . . are you taking the mickey?'

'Not really, ma'am. Look, Silver doesn't necessarily have to be dead. If he's got heart trouble and he's still alive, but is totally messed-up . . . well, the decision-making could be in someone else's hands.'

'So there's been a change of management?'

'It's possible. And perhaps the new guy isn't quite so cautious. Perhaps he's an out-and-out cowboy, and doesn't mind us knowing it. Hell, maybe he revels in throwing out this kind of challenge. "This is what I do. I'm a reckless maniac. Catch me if you can".'

She heard him out in glum silence.

'There's another possibility too,' Heck said. 'Maybe he's teaching lessons. That's something the Nice Guys have always been big on . . . punishing those who've betrayed them.'

'And in what way have former clients betrayed them?'

'By being a security risk. When they needed to, the Nice Guys never fought shy of making public examples. Remember that poor sod in Manchester . . . the one they hanged upside down and disembowelled? And it worked. Those few snouts who knew about them wouldn't dare say a word. But this . . . this BDEL malarkey . . .' The idea was slowly growing on Heck. 'Abominations. If the Book of Revelation ranks these characters alongside harlots, it may not be a reference to the women as much as to the men who used them. As in, "You slimy bastards mean no more to us than the whores you raped. We can't trust you, we don't like you . . . so you're next". Yeah . . . I can go for that.' He gathered the

128

paperwork, shuffling it. 'I take it you want me to run with these two?'

'I'm afraid not.' Gemma extricated it from his grasp, placing it back on her side of the desktop. 'I'm sorry, but you're still not part of the team, Heck.'

He gave her a long, level stare. 'In which case . . . why tell me all this?'

'As a courtesy.' She met his gaze boldly. 'At the end of the day, you were the officer who originally uncovered the Nice Guys. You did more to expose their activities than all the rest of the police in England and Wales put together.'

'And . . .?'

'I'm keeping you in the loop because you're a friend as well as a colleague. And because I think you've earned the right to know what's happening.'

'And because you wanted my opinion, ma'am . . . evidently.'

'Maybe. But that's as far as it goes. As I say, I'm sorry.'

'Ma'am, Gemma . . .' He tried not to reveal the true depth of his exasperation. 'I could really assist with this enquiry.'

'No can do, Heck.'

'If nothing else, you're going to need a lot of muscle.'

'We've already got it. The taskforce is over two-hundred strong. That lot down the corridor are only the office staff.'

'Okay, you need someone with insight . . . personal experience.'

'Even if I agreed with that, after what happened yesterday it would be impossible to integrate you into a taskforce primarily made up of SOCAR personnel.'

'But they were the ones in the bloody wrong!'

'Heck . . . do *not* raise your voice at me.'

'Gemma, please. Look . . . I've had this monkey on my back for the last two years. You've got to let me have another crack at these bastards.'

'I don't have to do anything of the sort. And I'm not going to.'

'Why?'

'We've been over this a dozen times.' She opened a leather zip-folder, and slid the paperwork in. 'My decision stands.'

'Your decision that I'm too damaged to get involved?'

'That's all, Heck. Even if you're not busy, I am.'

Heck stood stiffly and moved to the door, but then turned back again. 'Funny how I'm not too damaged to be useful on other enquiries.'

'Damn it, Heck, how simply can I put this?' She jabbed a finger at him. 'You'll make it personal! You made it personal last time. Civilians died because you went in without back-up. Your own sister got kidnapped, for heaven's sake! You almost went to jail. I don't need all that now, not this time . . . not when we've got seventeen coffins with Union Jacks draped over them, not to mention six dead civvies, maybe even more.'

Heck was about to reply, when the door banged open and Ben Kane barged in. 'Oh, sorry ma'am,' he said. 'I was looking for . . . erm, Heck.'

'That's alright, Ben, we're just about finished here.' She turned back to Heck and pointed at the door. 'Britain's got lots of other violent offenders. You go get 'em!'

'Here's one to start with,' Kane said, pushing a wad of paperwork into his hands.

Heck wandered disconsolately out into the passage, Kane alongside him, and glanced fleetingly at the new documents. They had been issued by the CID office at Stoke Newington police station, who were in contact about a series of street robberies and face-slashings on their patch.

'Five attacks in total, all the work of the same hand,' Kane explained. 'No deaths yet, but given the paltry amounts pinched and the significant quantities of blood spilled, the local factory are a bit worried it might be more about the knifing than the theft. They've asked us to look it over, which I now have . . . and it's my view we need to nip this thing in the bud pronto, before someone actually *does* die.'

Heck nodded half-heartedly as they walked. It sounded like the sort of case he'd normally cop for, and be interested in – but it was a distraction at present.

'Don't know why you're so keen to mix it with these Nice Guys reprobates,' Kane said. 'Leave that to Tasker and his crew. They're the ones who let Silver escape.'

It was no surprise to Heck that Kane didn't quite empathise with him on this. The guy was a notorious straight bat, primarily because he was big on self-preservation. From Kane's point of view, it was always the same pattern when a crime was reported; investigation of facts, identification of suspect, arrest, interview, charge – after which you filed your paperwork and went home. So long as everything was clean and above board, you could sleep easy in the knowledge you'd done your job. There was never an emotional context to it: no lingering concerns for the victims or bereaved; no prolonged brooding over unexplained elements or incomplete avenues of enquiry. And yet the irony was that this thorough, methodical and utterly humourless approach was exactly the way you were supposed to operate as a police officer. The alternative, they always said, could lead to madness.

'I've told Stoke Newington I'm sending one of my best lads,' Kane added. 'So I'd appreciate it if you didn't fuck anything up.'

'I promise,' Heck muttered.

'I'm serious, Heck. As you may have heard, for my sins I'm now double-hatting. I'm still official liaison with SOCAR as well as running SCU while Gemma's busy. That means I'm getting heat from various directions, which my equilibrium could do without.'

'Sorry . . . your what?'

'It means I like things to be nice and straightforward, and at present they aren't.' Kane nudged the Stoke Newington paperwork. 'So just go and do what you do. Catch this little fish, and let SOCAR chase off over the horizon after the big ones.' They halted at the entrance to the DO. 'That's worth a smile, surely? I'm doing you a favour.'

A favour? Briefly, Heck was puzzled. Ben Kane was about as famous for doing people favours as Gemma was for avoiding confrontations.

'Look, Heck . . . that Nice Guys thing's a nightmare. Seventeen coppers dead, Public Enemy Number One back on the loose. It's a real shit-storm, and it's gonna cover everyone. But thanks to me, you'll now be somewhere else . . . chasing some piddling little street robber who thinks his penknife makes him the big man.'

'Yes, sir,' Heck said. 'Thanks for that.'

Chapter 13

The village of Stanton St John, in South Oxfordshire, was very picturesque in the early autumn. In actual fact, its peaceful, tree lined avenues were scenic any time of year, but never more so than when reds and golds were sparking to life amid its lush cottage-garden greenery. And especially on mellow September evenings like this, when sunlight lay in vivid streaks down grassy verges and across the velvet lawns and mullioned bay-windows of its honey-coloured stone houses. There might be a hint of freshness in the air, it may smell of apples and nuts rather than barbecued steak and chicken, but it still bespoke neighbourliness and content: wives chatted over fences; husbands ambled to the pub together; children played happily and safely, barely concerned by the early advance of evening.

Though it shared a Stanton St John postcode, Woodhatch Gate – the 'Big House', as locals knew it – stood about four miles outside the village and nine miles northeast of Oxford. Formerly a Georgian coach-stop, it was now a resplendent but secluded country residence, located just off the main road to Worminghall, at the end of a lengthy gravel drive, overlooking extensive acres of private wood and parkland.

Beyond that on all sides, the verdant landscape extended away in a rolling quilt of blue, green and dusky purple.

It was a tranquil scene – except for the riot of laughter and good cheer inside Woodhatch Gate itself, at the heart of which, as always, was the lady of the house, Mrs Nina Po, currently in her usual place at the head of the table.

Nina was a pretty, bubbly bottle-blonde in her late forties, but she was also the mother-hen: the chatterbox, the bundle of energy, the arch-organiser. Her husband, Ronald, a consultant heart surgeon at the John Radcliffe Hospital in Oxford, was ten years older than his vivacious wife, and was seated to her right.

This was an official dinner party, and the word 'official' meant something in this company. It wasn't just a gathering of pals for a natter and a chip supper. It was one of Nina's 'special events'; long in preparation, exquisite in execution. However, as Ronald Po wore a jacket and tie all day – when he wasn't wearing scrubs of course – he made a point of never dressing for these occasions. A tall, trim man with silver sideburns and wavy silver hair, he looked neat enough – he would say – in clean jeans and a polo shirt. He'd also add that this put their guests at ease, helped them relax, and would offer the same explanation for his inertia between courses; not for Ronald the back-and-forth bustle from dining room to kitchen, the ferrying of dirty crockery to the sink, or the more careful transportation of the next amazing dish to the table. *His* role was to entertain their visitors, talk to them, amuse them; be a warm and convivial host.

Not that Nina would have accepted assistance from her other half in any case. For that she had her best friend, Mary Entwistle, who, to those who knew her, seemed almost permanently to wear an apron. A legendary cook, Mary aided and abetted Nina in all her culinary creations. Take tonight for instance, with chicken and butternut squash stew, autumn chestnut salad and Moroccan roasted lamb with mint pesto on the menu. Nina had selected the courses, provided the ingredients, the utensils, the work-space and the elbow grease, not to mention the supervisory intellect, and of course was the sole architect of all those delicate last details so typical of a mercurial perfectionist (origami napkins, lilies wrapped in silk as perfumed favours for the ladies, a measure of cognac for each of the men), but it was Mary who provided the gastronomic expertise. She was the same age as Nina but a less lively soul; her barrister husband had abandoned her before she was thirty, leaving her to look after their demanding young daughter, who had now grown up into an obstreperous snob. Despite all this, Mary continued to work full-time at the catering company she'd originally set up with the money inherited from her late father, but the pressure on both these fronts had built so enormously over the years that she was now a semi-anonymous shadow of her former self, and perhaps by her own admission, a little too fond of the G&Ts. But she was still a marvellous cook, and more than happy to be the permanent fixture on Nina's right hand in her zealous quest to wine and dine the socialites of the county.

These were the hosts, but there were several other person-alities gathered at the dinner table that September evening at Woodhatch Gate, on the outskirts of Stanton St. John.

Tim and Trudy Willoughby were the straight couple. Both were in their early forties and keen outdoors folk; if they weren't camping at weekends, they were climbing, or hiking, or kayaking. 'The Lakes is our back-garden,' Tim was fond of saying, usually to the accompaniment of an infectious grin. Despite being only a junior accountant at one of the less important Oxford colleges, he never appeared at any of these functions in anything less than a smartly tailored three-piece suit (though always the same one, Nina had noted).

Apart from the mouse-brown tufts behind his ears, Tim was bald and rangy of build – to an ungainly degree, which was a surprise to many as his wife was a natural beauty with flowing red tresses and a curvaceous figure. But Trudy Willoughby wasn't just a looker; she was incredibly well brought-up. It was impossible to ascertain where she hailed from merely by speaking to her. She never smoked, never swore, never laughed at crude jokes, and always drove because she drank so little ('One dry-white for me, please, and then I'm on Perrier').

Seated at the table opposite the Willoughbys, much to Trudy's quiet discomfort, were the Hardcastles. Ross Hardcastle was a loud, proud Yorkshireman, fifty years old and foursquare of physique – that was the way he described himself, though much of his former rugby union prop forward's frame had now run to plumpness. He was MD of a blue-chip software company based at Kidlington, and owner of a Bentley Continental GT, which he insisted on driving everywhere, even when he'd consumed his usual vast quantities of alcohol – 'There's more chance of our Sal totalling it when she's sober than there is of me doing it when I'm pissed!' For all this, he was an attractive man: bluff, hearty, outrageously amusing, still with a full head of naturally blond hair, a thick blond moustache, and though pudgy in the face, elements of the handsome young devil he'd once been were in plentiful evidence. In professional terms, he was said to be shrewd, calculating and confident; a real shark in the boardroom – though just to meet him, a natural assumption would be that he'd only reached the level of boardroom by pushing and shoving his way there. By contrast, while Ross Hardcastle filled almost every room, both in terms of his body and his personality, Sally Hardcastle was virtually invisible. Pencil-thin, with short grey hair and a dull line in three-quarter-length skirts, flat shoes, grey blouses and strings of beads that were too long, she rarely spoke and certainly never upbraided her husband for any of his more outspoken opinions – he was a Conservative to his back teeth, which was not always to his advantage in a liberal, scholarly town like Oxford. She didn't even comment when, on occasions like this, he would sometimes play footsie with Trudy under the table – though to be fair Trudy didn't comment either, because she never wanted to cause a scene.

But for all the differences between them, it was really the last guest who was the odd one out. He was unmarried and a self-professed bachelor. Nina, Trudy and Mary had always assumed this meant he was gay, but there were no obvious indications of that – he actually lived with his elderly mother. His name was Anton Trevelyan, and he was a fellow of Jesus College, specialising in Classical English Literature. He was in his mid-fifties, white-haired and pale-skinned. A cross-country runner in his youth, it would be a mistake to assume his lean figure meant he was frail, but his athletic days were far in the past, and there was something undeniably wispy and wraithlike about him, even when clad, as now, in bow-tie, frilled shirt and pristine tuxedo. Doctor Trevelyan wasn't always the most attentive guest. When you pinned him on his pet subject, the Age of Sensibility, he spoke interestingly and eloquently, revealing deep knowledge. But when mundane matters were under discussion, he merely nodded when he concurred, or puffed out his lips and blew long breaths if he disagreed. Though he'd chuckle at the occasional quip, he rarely laughed uproariously. Nina said she thought this was because there was some secret tragedy in his past, something tormenting him even to this day – which was odd because, though her husband had known Doctor Trevelyan for many, many years, he'd never thought there'd been anything unconventional in his life. Tonight in particular, Doctor Trevelyan seemed down, only smiling sadly when he smiled at all, and scarcely communicating. Of course, this only increased Nina's fascination with him – because secretly she'd often thought Doctor Trevelyan a rather good-looking chap. Okay, he might be white-haired, it might be said he'd aged before his time, but there was still something there, something noble but also mysterious, something gracious but also . . . could she use the term 'wolfish'? She didn't mean it in a negative way, especially as he was so well mannered, so civilised . . . but she felt certain he had a darker side, and at some point she was determined to discover it.

It was just around nine o'clock when the cups bearing the hostess's famous palate-cleansing lemon sorbet were cleared away. There was more than bonhomie in the air. Most of the diners already knew each other from past events at Ronald and Nina's; though it wasn't always the same combination of guests, there was enough mutual familiarity for the banter to flow along with the wine. Ross Hardcastle was in mid-tirade, mocking the recent Labour Party conference in his usual brash, pseudo-uncouth way, but he kept it light-hearted – to such an extent that even the Willoughbys, who were of a left-wing inclination, had to chuckle. Doctor Trevelyan noticeably didn't, and, as his political affiliations were unknown, it seemed more likely he was preoccupied with other matters. Ronald, who was also a Tory, thought it utterly hilarious and when he started with his hearty, booming laugh, it was difficult for others not to join in.

For all these reasons, it was quite a shock when the dining-room window suddenly exploded inward, flecks of razor-edged glass showering the happy band, and a massive half paving stone crash-landed in the middle of the mahogany table, sending flowers and scented candles spinning, scattering crimson claret across faces and hair-dos and the pastel-shaded walls.

It was even more of a shock two seconds later, when a second missile was lobbed in and landed amid the wreckage with a gentle *plop*.

Because it was a hand grenade.

When it detonated, the hardwood table absorbed some of the downward blast, but mainly ensured that most of it went upward and out. Of course it wasn't just the flash and flame that did the damage, or the concussive, ear-crunching *BANG* – it was also the cutlery, the crystal goblets, the shards of glass and porcelain, and even the PVC place-mats, which went flying like mini guillotine blades.

Nina was in the kitchen at the time, while Mary was halfway along the hall with a covered dish in hand. It wasn't the first explosion that stopped Mary in her tracks; it was the second one – the one that blew the front door in, hinges, chains and all. It hit her head-on at terrific speed, all ninety kilogrammes of it, knocking her flat beside the foot of the grand staircase, and landing on top of her, a mass of heavy, scorched oak. The first of the masked, khaki-clad figures who came charging in through the smoke-filled entrance initially stepped on top of it. Realising there was someone underneath, he lowered his MAC-10 machine-pistol and drilled a dozen shots through its surface. A second intruder spotted Nina at the end of the hall, framed in the kitchen doorway, mouth agape. He opened fire with his Desert Eagle .44 Magnum. Nina, struck four times, tottered backwards amid a deluge of shattered kitchenware.

Other intruders, meanwhile, piled past into the dining room.

The once-ornate chamber had been reduced to a heap of smouldering trash. The encircling shelves and sideboards, and their assorted ornaments had all been demolished. The fine wallpaper hung in blackened shreds, daubed with blood as well as claret. The dining table lay burned and blasted, as did the handsomely carved chairs formerly arranged around it, not to mention those who had been seated in them.

Ronald Po was the first of these to be found. He was still alive. He even managed to rise to his knees as the intruders milled in around him. But he was badly bloodied, a spear of bone protruding from his twisted right arm. He was also agog with shock. He tried to speak to them, as if they were here to help him – but only nonsense spilled from his mouth, along with globs of reddish foam.

'Ronald Po?' a muffled American voice enquired.

Ronald, dazed enough to think they were speaking to him, nodded dully.

'That's him!' came a Euro-accented response.

'Welcome to the wages of sin, Doctor Po,' the American said.

Still unable to comprehend what was happening, Ronald barely flinched as they grabbed him by his besmirched collar and yanked him to his feet. Only now did he seem able to focus on the rest of the smoke- and wreckage-filled room.

Directly alongside him, Tim Willoughby writhed on the floor, his face a blistered pulp, both hands clutched on his jaggedly severed windpipe. By the arcing arterial blood, he was certain to die soon, but a Madsen LAR was emptied into him to speed things along. The same fate befell Ross and Sally Hardcastle, though both looked to be dead already. They sat side-by-side on the floor, against the right-hand wall, which they'd been flung into with back-breaking force. Their shoulders drooped, their heads hung down. A fork had penetrated Ross's left cheek and jutted at a grotesque angle; a shattered segment of PVC was embedded in his capacious belly. Sally bore less obvious fatal wounds, though she streamed blood from both her eyes and her nose. Repeated discharges from a pump-action shotgun ensured there was no doubt in either case.

'We need the other!' the accented voice bellowed. *'Find Trevelyan!'*

But the next survivor they uncovered was Trudy Willoughby, huddled underneath the table. Though incoherent with terror, she was largely unscathed. She'd taken her lead from Doctor Trevelyan, who, on first seeing the grenade, had reacted more quickly than anyone else. Perhaps, maybe – just maybe – he had been expecting something like this? He'd ducked beneath the table, and Trudy had done the same. The table, a tough slab of mahogany, had then taken huge damage, but had still provided enough of a shield for the duo to survive.

'Hah!' laughed the intruder who hauled Trudy out by her long, red hair. He was the size and shape of a Russian bear, with an accent to match. He threw his Borz submachine gun over his shoulder, and ungloved a big, dirty paw, with which he mauled the fulsome breasts beneath her smoke-stained evening gown. 'The last time I see a face so pretty, I drive a steam-roller over it! Happy days in the Balkans, uh!'

'Sergei . . . no fucking around!' the Euro voice commanded.

'Ach . . . sorry babe,' the Russian said, before wrapping his brawny left arm around Trudy's head, then twisting and jerking it sideways, her neck snapping like a branch.

Only now did Ronald Po scream, which merited him a punch in the stomach and a dizzying blow to the back of his skull.

'Find Trevelyan!' the Euro voice roared.

Booted feet stomped all over the handsome house. Cupboard doors were kicked in. Shots were discharged through curtains and pillows, underneath beds, into the backs of closets. But it was the Russian who got lucky. He barged through a door from the dining room into a rear annexe; a beautiful, moonlit conservatory filled with exotic plants and wicker furniture, and immediately sensed movement – only a few feet away, he detected a ragged, white-haired figure cowering behind a wrought-iron stand filled with orchids. Laughing, he hauled Trevelyan out.

The good doctor struck desperately with his fist. His captor retaliated by viciously and repeatedly head-butting him. Other intruders appeared in the conservatory door, the limp, bloodied form of Ronald Po still tight in their grasp. A tall figure in dark khaki and a woollen balaclava shouldered his way through.

'No more playtime,' he instructed curtly, and his was the voice with the Euro accent.

The Russian kicked the figure of Trevelyan – now badly cut around the face – away from him. Ronald Po was pushed across the conservatory as well, so that for several seconds the bedraggled twosome stood together.

'We've been looking for you fellas,' their chief captor said with faux-cheerfulness.

Even in his shell-shocked state, Ronald found himself wondering about the guy's nationality. German maybe? Swiss? Scandinavian?

'Maybe you've been expecting us,' the guy said. 'Maybe you weren't. I bet when you heard the big boss was loose and a load of cops dead, you started shitting your pants . . . wondered how it would work out, yeah? Like, would the case get blown wide open again, would the trail lead back to you this time? Well . . . perhaps it would, perhaps it wouldn't. You understand . . . we can't take that chance.'

'They'll get you,' Trevelyan said, at first querulous but his nerve tautening as the inevitability of his fate grew on him. Angry blood frothed between his shredded lips. 'You think this will save you? Don't be too sure. You can't go around committing crimes like this . . .'

'Could be worse,' the Russian chuckled. 'We could be rapists.'

'You fucking moron!' Trevelyan spat. 'They'll catch you. They'll put you somewhere that'll make your gulags look like kindergarten . . .'

'Sergei,' the chief captor said, tiring of the conversation.

The Russian unslung the Borz from his shoulder and emptied its entire magazine, catapulting the two doctors back across the conservatory with such velocity they exploded out through a twinned pair of double-glazed windows, and landed side-by-side on the rear patio.

Their task complete, the eight intruders filed back out via the front of the house, where a dark, nondescript van was waiting at the bottom of the drive, blocking in all the other cars, which would now never be driven away again by their rightful owners.

They had reloaded their weapons on the off-chance there'd be someone around; a late-arrival at the party perhaps; a villager enjoying an evening stroll. But the surrounding farmland lay still and quiet. The country lane was empty of traffic, basking in the silver radiance of the new-risen moon.

Chapter 14

Heck was headed through Clerkenwell when he heard the news.

He was en route to a rendezvous with Detective Constables Reynolds and Grimshaw at Stoke Newington police station. Both officers had been busy until late evening, but were still keen to speak to him about the series of face-slashings they were investigating, so he gunned his Citroën along Old Street, speeding through the darkened streets. 'There's an appalling news story breaking,' the DJ said, interrupting his late-night music show in an uncharacteristically solemn tone. 'Reports are coming in about a mass shooting in a village just outside Oxford. Details seem sketchy at the moment, but witnesses have apparently reported hundreds of rounds fired and a *considerable* number of casualties. It's not known whether there are any fatalities, but the epicentre of the incident is believed to be a private house on the outskirts of Stanton St John . . .'

The small hairs on the nape of Heck's neck stiffened.

Hundreds of rounds fired.

Twice in the same week? Both incidents unrelated? Not bloody likely.

'That's all we've got at the moment,' the DJ added. 'But obviously we'll keep you updated . . .'

Heck swerved into the first parking zone he came to. He fished his mobile out and went through his contacts. When he found the one he wanted, he placed a call.

'Thames Valley Major Crimes Unit,' came a gruff response. 'DC Forester.'

'Mal . . . it's Heck. SCU.'

'Heck . . . what a surprise.' But Malcolm Forester didn't sound surprised.

'What's going on, mate?'

'What isn't? It's kicking off here tonight.'

'I mean in Stanton St John?'

'Ah . . . thought you'd be interested in that. We've never had anything like it in the past, I'll tell you that. It's thrown us.'

'What's happened?'

'Hard to say for sure. The lads on the scene tell me it's a fucking abattoir.'

'Come on, Mal. Give me any details you can.'

'Well, I mean . . .' Even Malcolm Forester, a twenty-year veteran of specialist CID operations, and before that a soldier who'd served in the Falklands, briefly struggled to produce a coherent description of events. 'It's a place called Woodhatch Gate, halfway along the road to Worminghall. In a nutshell, Heck, we've got a home-invasion that's turned into the night-mare of fucking nightmares. Some bunch of lunatics wiped out an entire dinner party. Just walked in and started shooting with automatic weapons. Sounds like high explosives were used to force entry. First impression is hand grenades . . . can you believe that?' The hairs on Heck's neck no longer stiffened, they bristled. 'They've had the Bomb Squad in first . . . *hang about*! What do you know, Heck? What're *you* working?'

Heck hesitated. 'The prison transit at Brancaster.'

There was a long, low exhalation at the other end, as if only now was this possible link occurring to Forester. 'They used grenades in that job too, didn't they? And there were a lot of shots fired.'

'There's no guarantee it's the same firm.'

'Come on, pal! How many other firms chuck that kind of hardware around?'

'How many died tonight, Mal?' Heck asked.

'Eight that we know of. Multiple shrapnel and gunshot wounds.'

'Presumably Major Crimes are running things?'

'Temporarily. But SECU are on their way.'

Heck cursed. The Southeast Counter-Terrorism Unit would be a royal pain in the butt. They'd take charge of everything, nabbing whoever they fancied, no matter which side of the fence he sat on. And they could sweat you for days with no comeback – they didn't have to follow the complex rules that governed the actions of most British police officers.

'What's going on, Heck?' Forester asked. 'Grenades on village greens. Machine guns in the shrubbery.'

'Can't tell you, Mal.'

'So I give you everything, and you give us squat!'

'I can't tell you anything, mate, because I don't know anything . . . not for sure.' Heck hung up. 'But I've got a damn good idea.'

The trouble was – what did he do next? Everything Gemma had told him made a kind of sense. For all his antipathy to SOCAR, they weren't amateurs, they were well-resourced and, after the deaths at Gull Rock, they'd be as highly moti-vated to go after the Nice Guys as he was. But he resented Gemma's refusal to let him participate more than anything that had happened in his career to date. He didn't even buy her rationale for it, and that was unusual; normally when they fell out over procedure, he at least understood where she was coming from.

Heck put the car in gear and eased it forward. Some might say he was going out on a limb now, though it could also be argued – somewhat imaginatively – that he was simply responding to a serious incident, which was his duty as a police officer. At the end of the day, it didn't matter what anyone said. He had to take at look at this. He just *had* to.

He hit the gas hard almost the entire distance, arriving at Stanton St John just before midnight.

The road to the house had been closed off by incident tape a good three hundred yards from the actual scene. Beyond this barricade, which was manned by several burly uniforms, flickering blue light spilled from the plethora of parked emergency vehicles. These weren't just police cars, but ambulances, fire engines and even khaki trucks bearing military insignia. As Malcolm Forester had said – the Bomb Squad had been sent in first. A yipping and yelping of dogs drew Heck's attention to handler teams making cautious exploration of the surrounding woods and fields, searching for discarded evidence or secondary crime scenes. Choppers whirred high overhead, spotlights trailing in various directions.

Heck parked near the outer cordon, close to a mobile command post, where a growing clutch of journalists armed with mikes and notebooks were clamouring for the attention of a uniformed inspector, and proceeded along the road on foot, passing several checkpoints by use of his Serial Crimes Unit ID. Despite that, he was increasingly aware that he had no authorisation to be here.

The central cordon, which was lit by arc-lamps, entirely encircled the large Georgian house called Woodhatch Gate, as well as its drive and outbuildings and a significant portion of garden and attached woodland, which was being guarded by armed officers who had disembarked from a nearby ARV. But even here, everything Mal Forester had said about the local lads being caught on the hop looked to be true: a photographer prowling the exterior of the inner cordon, flashbulb flaring repeatedly, didn't look as if he was part of Thames Valley Photographic – which might mean crime scene images would appear in the local rag before the deceased's next of kin were even informed. There was also a young woman in a nightie, standing crying at the tape. A female paramedic wearing a hi-viz coat over her green boiler suit was trying to wrap a foil blanket around her.

Inside the central cordon, the interlopers were fewer. Only two uniformed officers were visible, firearms men posted at the end of the drive, on which various high-end vehicles were waiting, now adorned with stickers marking them for forensic examination. As Heck strode up the drive, a detective in the obligatory gloves and protective coveralls emerged from the front doorway to the house, which, owing to its massive smoke and fire damage, had clearly been the main object of attack.

'DI Bennett,' he said. 'Major Crimes. Bloody glad to see you lot.' He was young, short and lean of stature, with smooth features and fluffy blond hair. He was also pale, his lips grey and taut. Beneath his partly unzipped Tyvek, his tie hung in a loose knot, as though he had been constantly and unconsciously yanking at it. He referred to Heck in the plural, but didn't seem to notice the newcomer was here alone.

Heck flashed his ID, and indicated the wailing woman on the perimeter. 'Who's that?'

'Oh . . .' Bennett, who Heck now realised was even more harassed than he'd first looked, barely glanced towards her. 'That's, erm . . . Miss Entwistle.'

'Miss Entwistle?'

'She lives in the village. Her mother's one of the victims here.'

'For Christ's sake, sir . . . you've got to get her away from there! We're going to be working this scene!'

If Bennett was offended by such belligerence from a lower rank, he didn't show it. Only slowly did he turn and signal that the civvie onlooker needed to be moved away.

'Get rid of that scavenger too!' Heck called to one of the armed PCs, nodding at the freelance photographer, who heard and made a bolt for it. 'In fact, he might have tampered with evidence . . . arrest him for obstructing an enquiry!'

The armed officers took off at high speed.

Bennett watched all this in a kind of daze.

'You Crime Scene Manager here, sir?' Heck asked

'Not really. Just providing a situation report for you guys. You're SECU, did you say?'

Heck shook his head. 'Serial Crimes Unit.'

Bennett looked nonplussed. 'I thought SECU were taking this one?'

'They are, but we may have an interest too.'

Bennett shrugged distractedly. 'So long as someone's coming. Don't mind admitting I feel a bit out of my depth on this.'

'I doubt there'll be anyone who isn't,' Heck replied, rummaging in a box at the side of the drive, taking out some fresh Tyvek coveralls and climbing into them. 'Just out of interest, sir . . . we're in the middle of nowhere here. Who reported this?'

'A poacher and his mate, would you believe. They were about half a mile away, back in the spinney, when they heard the shooting and the explosions. By the time they got here it was all over.'

Heck pulled on some shoe-covers and a pair of his own disposable gloves. 'They didn't *see* anything then?'

'They say not. They're at Abingdon nick now, getting debriefed.'

'They'll need checking for firearms residue,' Heck said. 'Just in case they're not as innocent as they say.'

'It's being taken care of.'

'No other witnesses?'

'Not as far as we know.'

When they entered the house, they had to step warily. Smashed, smouldering items lay everywhere. A fog of acrid smoke still hung in the hallway. Myriad bullet-casings were scattered around the first two corpses, both of whom were women. Blood wreathed the walls and radiators.

'No SOCO yet?' Heck asked, moving from one body to the next. 'No Photographic?'

'En route,' Bennett replied.

'FME?'

'Same.'

Heck glanced around. 'This crime was committed over two hours ago. Did they all have somewhere else they needed to be?'

'Yeah. We've had a busy night.'

'Other shootings?'

'No . . . but serious stuff.' Bennett wiped a sheen of sweat from his pasty brow.

Only a couple of light-bulbs remained in the lounge, but these gave sufficient light to penetrate the veil of smoke. Again they had to tread carefully; no safe access-way suggested itself amid the blasted, bullet-riddled wreckage. The dead stiffened where they sat or lay, in most cases hammered to pulp by shrapnel and gunfire.

'Butcher's shop, or what?' Bennett said. He looked queasy.

'Tell me about the other offences tonight,' Heck replied.

Bennett scratched his head. 'The first was two bouncers in Oxford city centre. About eight-thirty this evening. They got dragged down an alley next to a bar, and had the shit kicked out of them. I mean literally . . . the living shit!'

'*Two* bouncers? Must've been a heavy mob?'

'They're lucky to be alive, apparently. We've also had three muggings in the city tonight. No fatalities but all violent – brutal beatings. We're usually looking at one of those a week, tops. There's been a whole raft of burglaries too, an armed robbery at a corner shop, an attempted arson at a homeless shelter, and a young girl got attacked coming home from school. That was around tea-time in Beckley, which is only about three miles from here. The assailant dragged her into some trees, ripped her knickers off and gave her an arse-whipping with a willow twig. It was nastier than it sounds. She's needed stitches.'

'That *is* a busy night,' Heck concurred. 'Is it normally so bad around here?'

'Almost never. Anyway . . . what's all that got to do with this?'

'Maybe nothing . . . but by the same token it could all be an elaborate diversion.'

Bennett remained blank-faced. 'What do you mean?'

'To ensure you lot couldn't respond fast and team-handed to the main event of the evening. And if that's what it was, it worked, didn't it?'

'Christ's sake . . .' Only slowly did the reality of this possibility seem to strike the DI. 'Who . . . who the fuck are we talking about? A terror group, surely?'

'Best if we save the hypothesis for later, eh?'

'Well, this obviously wasn't a robbery.' Bennett indicated the jewellery visible on the women, and the watches on the men's wrists. 'That's a Rolex, unless I'm mistaken.'

Heck bent over a heavy-set male body slumped by the right-hand wall; he was horrifically mutilated, a fork dangling from his mangled cheek. The watch adorning his plump wrist was a blue-faced Rolex Submariner. Five grand's worth, easily. Even the average professional gunman should have been interested in claiming a prize like that. Of course, there was nothing average about these perpetrators. Masses and masses of spent casings strewed the floor – hundreds, maybe even thousands.

'You ever seen anything like this?' Bennett said. 'I mean . . . ever?'

Heck declined to respond. His eyes had now come to rest on another door at the far end of the lounge. The door stood partly ajar, but not so that the large letters crudely carved with a knife or chisel on its smooth matte finish weren't clearly visible.

BDEL

'What's, erm . . . through there?' he asked.

'Two more APs,' Bennett replied. 'What about that graffiti?'

'Yeah . . . that needs looking at.' Heck edged through, entering a conservatory lit only by the moon, though there was sufficient of this to show it had suffered marginally less damage than the previous room. Yet again, there was a wide-ranging scatter of shell-casings on its parquet floor, any one of which could prove a forensic officer's dream. The only people who left this much evidence behind them were either novices – which this lot weren't – or they didn't care, which was probably a lot closer to the mark, and a whole lot scarier.

It was increasingly evident the Nice Guys had either undergone a conscious change of direction, or a change of management – or both. Whereas previously they'd specialised in erasing people without trace, now they left victims where they could openly be found and in a ghastly state of torture;

152

now they indulged in full-on massacres. Yet Heck was certain there was more to this than mere recklessness. He had already mentioned to Gemma that he thought the Nice Guys were teaching people lessons. But maybe they weren't just teaching their former clients, maybe they were teaching the police as well, and the entire British legal establishment.

You fucked up our former operation, he could almost hear them saying. *You killed some of our guys and sent our top man to prison. Well, this is what happens. You mess with us and we leave a trail of blood and chaos like you never imagined. We run you from one end of the country to the next, and all the time we snatch those witnesses you tried so hard to locate right from under your stupid pig noses. And we're gonna leave collateral damage as well. Anyone, anytime, anywhere.* Even Heck found the idea terrifying. But now was not the time for flipping out.

A huge hole had been smashed through the double-glazed wall on his left. When he peeked through it, he saw two more bodies lying face up on the outside patio. Both were grotesquely torn by gunfire; the recipients of multiple gunshots to head and body, which had all but eradicated their personal features, though it could at least be seen that they were male and possibly middle-aged.

'These poor sods look like they were singled out for special attention,' he said. 'Separated from the others, brought in here . . . executed side-by-side.'

'Maybe they just tried to run,' Bennett said.

'Maybe,' Heck replied, not thinking that at all. He glanced back through into the lounge. 'How many IDs?'

'Couple. Some of the villagers have been in, identifying them.'

'You've had some of the villagers in *here*?'

Bennett seemed to wake up at that, and abruptly looked irritated by Heck's disapproval. 'They were already here when

153

we arrived! The poachers ran down into Stanton St John raising the alarm before we even got called!'

'And I suppose you've got their details . . . I mean for elimination purposes?'

'I've started a fucking log, don't worry. Fuck's sake, sergeant! I may look like I need my arse wiping, but I know my job, alright . . .?'

'Alright, sir . . . apologies.' Heck wasn't particularly concerned that he'd offended the guy. But it was important for now that Bennett kept his head.

Still disgruntled, the DI leafed through his pocket-book. 'The occupants of the house are Doctor Ronald Po and his wife, Nina. She's in the kitchen. He's one of those two out there.' He thumbed the shattered window. 'The one on the left. The others were dinner party guests. The one half-lying under the front door's been identified as Mary Entwistle, another woman from the village . . .'

'What about the other guy outside?' Heck glanced back at the corpses on the patio.

'Not much chance of facial recognition with that one, but he had his college parking pass with him. Doctor Anton Trevelyan . . . bit of a name in Oxford. Big noise at the uni. Apparently a good friend of Doctor Po's.'

'Anton Trevelyan,' Heck said, wondering. 'That name rings a bell.'

A voice called through from the front of the house. 'DI Bennett? Deputy Chief Constable Ryerson would like access to the scene.'

'What? No . . . no bloody way!' Bennett retorted.

'Well, can you come and tell him that yourself, please.'

Bennett grunted and headed off through the lounge, leaving Heck alone. He quickly dug his mobile out and tapped in a number.

'Heck?' came Eric Fisher's sleepy reply.

'You at home, Eric?'

'Now . . . at ten to one in the morning, where do you think I am?'

'Listen, mate . . . I need you to look someone up for me.'

'Don't tell me . . . Anton Trevelyan?'

Even Heck was taken aback by that. 'Okay, I'm impressed. How'd you know?'

'I'm psychic, what do you think. So psychic I can also predict that Gemma is gonna kick your arse into orbit when she catches up with you.'

'She's been looking him up too?'

'Yeah. About an hour ago. Just before I came off.'

'She got onto that fast.'

'Give her some credit, Heck. It's not every day we get people chucking hand grenades.'

'Well, she'll be glad to know her instinct was good. We've got the same Greek signature here as at the other scenes. It's been cut into a door inside the house. Course, there are other vics here too, so we need to establish exactly who it was intended for. This guy Trevelyan rings a bell . . . '

'Heck, dare I ask . . . are you in Stanton St John?'

'Didn't have much else on. Thought I'd stick my nose in.'

'She's still going to kick your arse, pal. Probably as a prelude to walking all over you with her four-inchers on.'

'What happy memories that brings,' Heck said.

'Is this really a laughing matter?'

'I wasn't laughing, Eric.' Heck glanced again at the bullet-shredded corpses outside. 'Not at all. What did she learn about Trevelyan?'

'He was arrested in '98 as part of Operation Ripsaw.'

'Yeah, now I remember.' Heck recalled the details. Acting on information received from the US Homeland Security Service, various UK police agencies had identified several thousand British suspects believed to have accessed a network

155

of American-based child pornography websites after paying with credit cards. Houses were searched all over the country, arrests made and masses of computer equipment seized. Multiple charges had followed, and in some cases significant prison sentences resulted for persons formerly regarded as pillars of the community.

'Trevelyan was eventually bailed,' Fisher said. 'His gear was thoroughly checked and no images were found, so about four months later he accepted a caution.'

'Would it be un-PC of me to say that makes him sound a likely candidate for the Nice Guys Club?' Heck said.

'That was Gemma's thinking,' Fisher replied.

'She turn anything up on the other APs, specifically a Doctor Ronald Po?'

'Nah . . . she looked him up too, but he's clean.'

'As far as we're aware. Listen, I know you're in bed, mate . . . but any chance you can give me five minutes? I need everything we've got on Anton Trevelyan.'

Chapter 15

The Trevelyan house was located in a quiet mews in one of the tree-lined precincts surrounding Jesus College. It was a tall, gloomy structure with an ecclesiastical aura: steep roofs and narrow, vaulted windows, behind which heavy curtains were drawn, though lamplight was still visible even at this ungodly hour.

Heck stood for several minutes at the iron front gate.

What he was about to do now was beyond the pale. This wouldn't just be a bit of sniffing around on the edges; he'd actually be injecting himself into the very heart of an enquiry that quite literally had nothing to do with him. But no matter how hard he tried to persuade himself, he couldn't just watch this thing from the sidelines. Gemma would go ballistic; that was a given. But she also knew his value, and if he embedded himself in the enquiry sufficiently she might just find it easier to bring him into it officially. Okay, in a way, he'd be bullying her, trying to force her hand, but it didn't feel as if he had any other choice. He certainly wouldn't be able to work effectively on other cases while all this was going on. And it wasn't like it wouldn't ultimately be a smart move, not when he was the only cop in

Britain with experience of hunting and catching the murdering bastards.

It was now or never, he guessed, the gate creaking audibly as he passed through it. The front door to the house opened at the top of a flight of steps. A youngish woman stood there, wearing a kilt and jumper.

'PC Harding,' she said, looking immovable in the doorway. 'Family Liaison.'

Heck had expected that would be her role, and was pleased to see her even if she didn't seem to reciprocate. PC Harding was short and stocky, with bobbed dark hair. She was pretty-faced but snub-nosed and wore a distinctly truculent expression.

'Quite out of the question,' she said when Heck identified himself and expressed a desire to come in and speak to Mrs Trevelyan.

'She's not in a fit state to be interviewed?' he asked.

'Hardly. She only received the news an hour and a half ago.'

'Of course I'm fit!' came a shrill, screechy voice.

An elderly but tall woman appeared in the doorway. She was skeletally thin but angular-framed under her baggy slacks and buttoned-up cardigan. Straggling hanks of unruly white hair hung to either side of her long, wizened face – apparently Mrs Trevelyan was nearly ninety.

'Of course I'm fit,' the old lady reiterated, glaring down at Heck through delicate, wire-framed spectacles. 'What do you take me for . . . a weakling?'

Somewhat reluctantly, PC Harding stepped aside for her.

'Mrs Trevelyan,' Heck said, advancing up the steps. 'Detective Sergeant Heckenburg. I'm terribly sorry for your loss.' She acknowledged this with a curt nod, seemingly resigned to the terrible situation – which made him wonder if true realisation was yet to dawn. 'Is it alright if I ask you a couple of questions?'

'Of course . . . come in.' Mrs Trevelyan turned and headed indoors.

'Well done for getting here so quick,' Heck said quietly, as he and Harding followed her.

'Things are a bit more disorganised than we'd normally like,' she replied, her tone curt. 'Everyone's a bit thrown by this.'

'Anyone else in with her?'

'She hasn't got anyone else.'

'What about the neighbours?'

'She thinks they're busybodies. Us too.'

'Thanks for the heads-up.'

By the look on Harding's face, she hadn't intended it as a heads-up as much as a piece of well-needed advice. 'Just go easy on her. She acts tough but she's still in shock.'

'She's seen a doctor?'

'Yes. He's prescribed sedatives, but she won't take them.'

'She *will*.'

The interior of the house was richly furnished and yet shabby, the décor dated – all browns and mauves, the furniture dark, heavy and old, the carpets and curtains thick and moth-eaten. In every room, the scents of must and polish competed.

'Be so good as to make the sergeant a cup of tea, would you?' Mrs Trevelyan said to Harding once they'd arrived in the lounge. 'You *do* drink tea, sergeant?'

'Yeah, that'd be great, thanks. One sugar.'

Somewhat grudgingly, Harding left the room.

Mrs Trevelyan sat slowly and wearily on the sofa, which faced onto a large stone fireplace currently without flames. In one corner, a can of Pepsi and an evening paper perched on a small table next to an armchair, indicating this was Harding's station. It had evidently been chosen because the house landline was there; it would enable her to intercept and ward off troublesome press enquiries.

Heck appraised Mrs Trevelyan again, now from closer up. If she'd been in bed on receiving the news about her son, she'd evidently got dressed again; further evidence she was a feisty character. But her cheeks were pale and wrinkled as old tissues. A scrunched handkerchief was clutched tightly in her left hand.

'Mrs Trevelyan . . . how much do you actually know about what happened?'

She scrutinised him carefully. Her eyes were rheumy, moist. 'You mean . . . am I aware my Anton died this evening as the result of a shooting incident?'

That was a fairly blunt statement for someone recently bereaved. Harding's comment jumped into his mind. *She's still in shock.*

'Is it okay if I sit?'

'Not at all.'

Heck settled himself on an armchair to the right. Harding reappeared carrying a cup and saucer, which she placed with a clatter on the mantelpiece alongside him.

'Please tell me, sergeant . . . how did it happen that my son was shot? I mean, was he shot by accident? Did he drive into the midst of some terrible event?'

'I'm afraid we suspect your son may have been one of the objects of the attack,' Heck said.

She nodded – again, strangely, as if this was something she'd expected. But she also swallowed, a tight lump passing down her raddled throat. 'Was . . . was it a robbery then? Did they stop his car?'

'The incident occurred at a house near Stanton St John.'

'Stanton . . .?' Mrs Trevelyan's face creased with puzzlement. 'And . . . did you say there was more than one target of this attack?'

'We have several victims, I'm afraid.'

'Good gracious . . . oh my. He wasn't . . . at the house of Doctor Po by any chance?'

'Why do you ask that, Mrs Trevelyan?'

'Anton often dined there.'

'Were the Po family friends of his?'

'Doctor Po was an old friend of his. They first met when they were undergraduates, and have been very close ever since. Doctor Po's dead too, isn't he?'

'I'm afraid we think he and Mrs Po were also victims,' Heck said.

'Oh . . . oh, my.' Mrs Trevelyan's breathing had shortened, but she was attempting – with some measure of success – to maintain her rock-steady façade.

Harding watched worriedly from the corner of the room.

'Was someone else at the dinner party responsible?' Mrs Trevelyan asked, dabbing her handkerchief at invisible tears.

'We don't think so.'

'A stranger then? And yet you say this wasn't a robbery?'

'The truth is we don't know very much. Mrs Trevelyan – and please understand I have to ask these questions – your son wasn't in any kind of trouble?'

She gave him a freezing stare. 'My son is an Oxford don, sergeant. A fellow of Jesus College.'

'I understand that, ma'am, but even the best of us have things go wrong in our lives.'

Her bottom lip trembled. 'This is a grave impertinence.'

'And a necessary one, I'm afraid.'

She continued to glare at him, but dabbed her eyes again, which were now filming with real tears. Her head slowly drooped as the swift, icy rage thawed. 'There is . . . something. No doubt you're aware of it. Some fifteen years ago, there were accusations made against my son. Foul, disgusting accusations . . . which had no basis in reality. He was completely exonerated.'

Heck didn't dispute this. It would serve no purpose to deny the old lady the solace of a faulty memory.

161

'Is that the kind of trouble you're referring to, sergeant? Did some despicable vigilante decide the law was an ass?'

'Again, we don't know. Has there been anything odd in recent times? Anything curious that might have caught your attention?'

'Anton is a God-fearing man! An upstanding citizen!'

It wasn't reassuring that she was still referring to her son in the present tense.

'What I mean, Mrs Trevelyan is . . . was anything troubling Anton?'

'Anton doesn't get into trouble. He lives a simple life, and divides it entirely between his work at the university and his leisure time . . . of which there is precious little, but which he spends quietly and unassumingly. He's always been a worrier, of course. Doctor Po says he worries about things far more than is good for him.'

'What kind of things does he . . . *did* he worry about?' Heck wondered.

She sniffled. 'Everything. His own academic work – he's given himself ulcers over that in the past. But also the badness in the world. The dreadful problems that afflict his fellow men. For instance . . . several nights ago, he was taken ill during dinner. I feared for his heart.'

'Ill, Mrs Trevelyan?'

'It was a temporary thing . . . it didn't last. But . . .' She swallowed again, fresh tears brimming from her glassy eyes. 'But at the time he staggered away from the dinner table . . . and only just made it out to the rear lawn before he was violently sick. I asked if it might be something he'd eaten, but he told me to stop fussing, called me a silly old woman . . . which is not like him at all. It made me wonder if something was concerning him. I asked more questions, but he refused to speak.'

'And what was the trigger to this episode, Mrs Trevelyan?'

162

'The trigger?' The old lady feigned ignorance of the term, but she now sat stiffly upright, facing him full on. She *wanted* to talk, perhaps because only this way could she face the reality of her son's secret, sordid history.

'What caused this?' Heck asked again. 'There presumably was something.'

'It was an article on the evening news . . .' Her bottom lip trembled again, violently. 'Concerning that dreadful man who escaped from prison. The one they called Mad Mike.'

'That was a disturbing incident, I'll admit,' Heck said.

'Anton was very upset by it. We'd just sat down to eat, but it was the headline story. Almost immediately, I heard him gasping for breath. When I looked at him, he'd gone white. The vomiting followed shortly afterwards.' She hung her head, like a child caught in mischief. 'I'm afraid . . . that's all I can tell you, sergeant. As I say . . . Anton does worry.'

'I'm sure that's as much as we need, Mrs Trevelyan,' Harding said, approaching. 'Why don't you go upstairs and lie down? You don't want to wear yourself out.'

Rather meekly, the lady of the house rose to her feet and allowed herself to be led, still sniffing into her handkerchief, to the door.

Heck remained seated. Trevelyan's reaction to Silver's escape wasn't exactly a smoking gun – it might simply mean that he was an overly concerned citizen – but given what had happened to him, that didn't seem very likely. Just supposing Trevelyan had formerly used the Nice Guys' services. From his perspective, with Mike Silver's escape, the whole ghastly affair had suddenly blown up all over again. For a guy who gave himself ulcers over academic issues, that would be more than enough to convince him that life as he'd known it was back on hold, that something terrible might yet happen.

Heck stood up and followed the two women out into the

163

dim hall, where Harding was gently assisting the old lady upstairs. All strength and feistiness appeared to have drained from Mrs Trevelyan. Tears openly coursed down her cheeks, when she suddenly stopped, turned and stared back at him.

'My son is not a bad man, sergeant . . . not at heart. He has his . . . his demons. His obsessions, you might say. But he always regrets them afterwards. So deeply.'

'We all do things we regret, Mrs Trevelyan,' Heck replied.

'But we don't all expect to suffer for them, sergeant. Not like my Anton. And suffer he does, wouldn't you say? Or rather . . . suffer he *did*.'

She continued to ascend, leaning heavily on Harding's arm, suddenly crooked, looking every inch the eighty-nine-year-old.

Heck exited by the front door, but as he started down the steps outside, he almost collided with two people coming up. It was Gemma Piper and Frank Tasker. They were talking quietly together, but stopped dead at the sight of him.

Gemma, who often professed that nothing Heck did would ever surprise her, could only gape with outraged disbelief.

'What in Christ's name are you doing here?' Tasker stuttered.

'Morning to you too, sir,' Heck replied. 'The Woodhatch Gate murders are a Nice Guys' hit for sure. If you've been to the scene, you'll have spotted the calling card.' He had no option but to go in sure and confident. If he didn't put them on the back foot straight away, they would launch him into the stratosphere. 'You want my opinion, Anton Trevelyan was a former customer. It looks like Ronald Po was too. If the crew were after hitting two birds with one stone tonight, that might explain the excessive nature of the attack . . . but I think that's mainly down to their new *blitzkrieg* policy.'

'Who . . . told you all this?' Gemma said, seemingly because she didn't know what else to say.

'Trevelyan's mother. I don't know how much she actually knows, but she's clearly aware he was no Goodie Two Shoes.'

'I asked you a question, sergeant,' Tasker said flatly. 'What are you doing here?'

'Happened to be in the area, sir. Thought I could help out.'

'You smart-arsed little . . .'

'Frank, why not let me deal with this?' Gemma cut in, acutely aware of curtains twitching upstairs in the house. 'Okay? Please . . .?'

Tasker, who'd looked set to erupt, straightened his crumpled tie and strode red-faced up the steps, shouldering his way roughly past Heck.

'There's something else,' Heck told Gemma, but she put a finger to her lips and beckoned him down to the pavement, from where she headed to her Merc, parked a few yards away.

'There's been an unusually high number of other violent crimes in central Oxford this evening,' Heck said quietly. 'I'd suggest Thunderclap looks at those too . . . they might be diversionary tactics.'

She fished her keys from her raincoat pocket. 'That's all in hand. Thames Valley MIT are assisting.'

'You know SECU are en route?' he asked.

'Not anymore,' she replied. 'Frank's told them *we're* taking this one.'

'Just like that?'

'Just like that.'

Heck was surprised – since when had SOCAR wielded that kind of power?

Meanwhile, Gemma had unlocked her Merc. 'Get in,' she said.

He pointed across the road to his Citroën. 'I'm only parked over there.'

'*Get in!*' she hissed.

'Ma'am,' he protested, 'this is relevant to the enquiry. Now we *know* what the Nice Guys are up to.'

'*We* doesn't exist, Heck!' she said through clenched teeth. '*So get in the damn car!*'

Wearily, he climbed in. Once they were both installed, she hit the central locking – and sat there, staring through the windshield. After what seemed like several minutes, she closed her eyes resignedly and pinched at the bridge of her nose. 'It may have escaped your attention, sergeant . . .' Her tone was curiously calm; if anything she sounded tired. 'But there are actually higher powers in this job than me.'

'Ma'am?'

'I mean . . . you feel free to ignore my orders time and again, which does me no good at all professionally. I used to have a reputation for kicking arse in this job, which seems like ancient history now. But my personal circs are beside the point.' Gemma turned to face him. 'What I'm saying is . . . regardless of how content you are to disrespect me at every turn, there are people higher up the chain who at some stage, probably soon, will get so sick of your lone wolf antics that whatever I say, however I argue your case, whatever clever spin I put on it . . . they'll just lean down and squash you like an annoying gnat!'

'Ma'am, I . . .'

'Shut up, Heck! Just for once, hey? Your role now is to listen, because you've done enough talking for one night! *Way more than enough!*' Again, she took almost a minute to compose herself. 'I'm not going to ask what it is you don't understand when I say you're not involved in this enquiry. Because there's nothing you don't understand . . . about anything! You're the sharpest tool in the bloody box! What's going on here is flagrant, pig-headed disobedience. As usual. The only difference is we've reached the stage where you're

166

leaving me no choice. If this continues, I'll be enacting formal disciplinary procedures with a view to having you suspended from duty. That's not a threat, Heck . . . that's an absolute promise. Can I make myself any clearer?'

Heck looked away; when Gemma's eyes burrowed into you, you really felt it.

'Well?' she demanded.

'Maybe I don't think it's fair, ma'am.'

'This is not about fairness, Heck. It's about one overheated individual jeopardising an entire operation.'

He stared back at her. 'How have I jeopardised it so far?'

'Are you serious? You intruded onto a crime scene where you had no right to be. You interviewed a witness whom you shouldn't have had any access to . . .'

'I'm doing the job!'

'Too many cooks, Heck. Too many chiefs . . . you're not just treading on toes, you're getting in the way, you're likely duplicating the work of others . . .'

'Ma'am, I gave you the heads-up about the Nice Guys working their way through the client list. And lo and behold, that's exactly what they are doing!'

'And we're grateful for your insight . . . but that doesn't excuse your other behaviour. I mean, weren't you supposed to liaise with DCs Reynolds and Grimshaw last night, at Stoke Newington police station, about a series of woundings in Shoreditch?'

'Ah . . .' Heck had known in the back of his mind there was somewhere else he was supposed to have been.

'Those lads had just finished a very busy shift. Apparently, they waited four hours extra, twiddling their thumbs in the DO . . . until you were available. And not only did you not show, you didn't even send an apology or an explanation.' Her voice thickened with disgust. 'And you think of yourself as a bobbies' bobby.'

Heck could hardly argue with any of that.

'Minimal use of time,' she said. 'Disruption of procedure. Wastage of manpower and resources. Do none of these things ring a bell? And you've got the nerve to talk to me about fairness? Is it fair you're still in the job when I'd have launched almost anyone else who did this to me off the front doorstep? Is it fair you keep using my former feelings for you as leverage in your favour?'

That last comment was almost a plea, which shook him a little. For the first time it occurred to him that he might have hurt her emotionally as well as professionally.

'It doesn't surprise me you want to get involved in this,' she said, apparently forcing herself to be calm. 'But surely you can understand my objection? Mark, it's starting to look as if your first scrap with the Nice Guys burned you very badly indeed. Some would say *too* badly. Which brings me back to my former point. I can't wave a magic wand on your behalf indefinitely. So when I say you have to pay attention to me now, you really *have* to. For your own good!' She looked him dead in the eye, with as much concern as anger. 'I need your solemn promise . . . not to Detective Superintendent Piper, but to *me*, to Gemma . . . that you will cease your participation in this investigation forthwith! That you will have nothing further to do with this case unless your assistance is specifically requested. If any promise we've ever made to each other means anything, Mark, this has to be it. Because if you don't do as I say, I'll report everything that's happened to Professional Standards . . . in addition, I will voice *genuine* personal concerns about your mental fitness to continue functioning as a police officer.'

'You don't think that's a bit OTT,' Heck said.

'It doesn't matter. That's how far I'm prepared to go.'

He could tell she was in earnest. And he couldn't blame

her for that; he'd pushed the elastic to breaking-point this time.

'You've got my word, ma'am.'

'Gemma.'

'You've got my word, Gemma. I promise.'

She sighed – it was almost a sigh of relief. 'Now . . . very first thing tomorrow, you get in touch with DCs Reynolds and Grimshaw at Stoke Newington, and you apologise for failing to make the rendezvous last night. I don't care what piece of guff you give them, but make it sound good. And then get up there at the first opportunity, and get after the Shoreditch Slasher, or whatever the press have started calling him.' She paused. 'Do we understand each other, Mark?'

'Yes ma'am. And . . .' he looked away, 'for what it's worth, I'm sorry.'

'You always are. When it's too late.'

'I don't mean for disobeying orders. I can't feel regret for ignoring commands I don't agree with. Especially when they've come down from some flash bastard like Frank Tasker . . .'

'I've worked with Commander Tasker for several weeks now,' she interrupted sharply. 'He's a good departmental boss and a very proficient police officer. And don't treat me like your bloody confidant if all you're going to do is spread dissent!'

'Whatever,' he said. 'The point I'm making is that . . . I'm sorry to you *personally*. I mean, if I've put you in an awkward position.'

'Let's hope you take this on board,' she said huffily. 'So we don't both end up being *really* sorry.'

They sat in silence. There was no sound from the house, where Commander Tasker was presumably going through everything with Mrs Trevelyan that Heck had gone through earlier. There was no doubt, Heck supposed – it had been a tad perverse to inject himself into the enquiry like this. He'd known Gemma was on the trail, yet something inside had provoked him to get there first. It was no surprise she wasn't just furious, but offended as well. The retaliation she'd threatened had been a bit unnerving too, even if she did view it as a necessary last resort.

'You take this job away from me, ma'am,' he said quietly, 'and I'll have nothing.'

'That's something else that worries me,' she replied. 'There's actually a wider world out there than police-work, you know. Are you going to bury yourself in this crap forever?'

He turned to face her again. 'Since when was willingness to work a negative in CID?'

'Since it started endangering your health. You think I don't know what you're doing, Mark? Your career is like the longest suicide note in history.'

'Excuse me?'

'That's why you take on the gunmen when you're not armed yourself. That's why you chase fugitives to the point where it might give you a heart attack.'

'Bollocks.'

'Hit a nerve, have I?'

'That's just bollocks, ma'am.'

'It's not your fault what happened to Tom. You were a school kid at the time.'

'My career has nothing to do with Tom,' Heck asserted.

But deep down, they both knew it did. The death of Heck's brother, Tom, when Heck was still at school, was something he could hardly bear to think about even now. Tom, who was three years older than Heck, had been an out-of-work drug addict. He'd fallen foul of the law several times, but only for minor infringements. But things had turned a hell of a lot more serious when he was framed for a series of burglaries, during the course of which several senior citizens were very badly beaten up. The CID team responsible pinned the crime on Tom because they were under pressure to get a result, and because as far as they were concerned he was a revolting human wreck whom society had no use for. Tom's name was cleared some time later, but only after he'd committed suicide in prison. He'd served one month of a life sentence, but had been raped and tortured repeatedly by fellow inmates. The event had devastated Heck's family, his parents blaming themselves for their failure to cope with their eldest son's problems, but refusing to admit this guilt. Heck himself had then made things a whole lot worse when, a couple of years later, he suddenly – inexplicably and traitorously, where his family were concerned – joined the police.

'That isn't why you enlisted?' Gemma asked. 'To show the rest of us lazy bastard coppers how the job *should* be done? Was that a pack of lies then? Was it just some big sob story you gave me back when we were DCs?'

'No,' he replied. 'But that isn't what you just said. I'm *not* suicidal.'

'Maybe not consciously.'

'Not at all.'

'So why you sitting there like a firecracker's just gone off under your jacksie?'

'I'm not.' He tried to relax his posture.

'Why do you live in the worst flat in London?'

'What's wrong with my flat?'

'It's godawful, that's what. It's got trains under the bedroom window every five minutes, and the best view of litter and rail-side rats anyone's ever seen. Admit it, Heck . . . you picked that place so you wouldn't want to be there. So you'd spend even more time in the office. And that'll kill you as surely as any gun or knife.'

'This is a wind-up, isn't it?' he said slowly.

'Maybe,' she mused. 'But what I said earlier wasn't. You're off this case, Mark . . . for all our sakes. Because the outcome otherwise will hurt me just as much as you.'

He now realised she was keeping it close and personal for a reason, having assumed – correctly – that he'd be more likely to respond on that level than if things remained cold and official. Not that he'd bloody show it.

'I've already said you've got my word, ma'am.'

'You've got my word, *Gemma*.'

'Yeah,' he said. 'Gemma.'

No wonder she'd decided to hold this conversation in the privacy of her car, he thought. Damn, but she was clever.

Chapter 16

'As you're aware, Operation Thunderclap is going to be a cross-department enquiry,' Tasker said, addressing the two hundred or so officers crammed into the MIR. 'Separate incident rooms have now been set up in Oxford and near to the ambush site at Gull Rock, but Gold and Silver Command have been located here.'

The crowd attending him didn't just consist of SOCAR Special Investigations personnel. Members of the SOCAR uniform branch were also present, now in plain clothes, along with senior officers from the Met's SCO19, whose firearms expertise was likely to be necessary, and a sprinkling of detectives from SCU, including Shawna McCluskey, whom Gemma had appointed Chief Statement Reader.

Heck, who wasn't invited to the party, eavesdropped enviously from the open door at the back. Tasker and Gemma were at the far end, making a complex but thorough presentation, aided by flip-charts and videos.

'But there's a real urgency here, people,' Tasker added. 'It's only four days since the prison break, and our targets, the so-called Nice Guys, appear to be shooting people like it's open season . . .'

He'd stripped down to his shirt and tie before he'd started; it was cool, professional, businesslike. There was something reassuring about it. He spoke clearly and articulately, interacting easily with team members when they raised their hands to ask questions. Gemma hadn't been lying when she'd said Tasker was an impressive operator. And she was usually a pretty good judge of character. Increasingly, Heck felt that it was he himself who wasn't.

'As well as the two massacres near Gull Rock and in Stanton St John, which ballistics reports have now connected, we're also focusing on several additional, apparently motiveless homicides, which have occurred in different parts of the country in the last few days,' Tasker confirmed. 'All were apparently the work of pro assassins who were well organised and appeared to know exactly what they were doing, but all were marked clearly . . .' he held up a photograph, 'by this BDEL signature, which we've deduced is an oblique reference to a punishment supposedly doled out to prostitutes in the ancient Middle East. As for Peter Rochester, better known as Mad Mike Silver, there are a lot of unanswered questions. We don't know if he was really taken ill in Gull Rock, or if he somehow managed to fake it. If it's the latter, we don't know how he got word out to the Nice Guys that he was being transferred to hospital. We don't know how they were able to respond to it so quickly. But Rochester's obviously the key to all this. If we get him back, and we've *got* to get him back, ladies and gentlemen, that will enable us to wrap up the rest of these bastards too. But it's not going to be easy, I'll tell you now. These Nice Guys . . . I mean I'm sorry but I hate that term, these *Nice Guys*, are almost entirely composed of combat veterans and spec-ops turned mercenary. That means they're what I'd call "do or die" criminals, who'll show no mercy to anyone who gets in their way. More to the point, they'll have safe boltholes

174

overseas, so it will never be in their interest to surrender. They'll attempt to shoot their way out of every situation when they get cornered . . .'

Heck was still listening intently when someone tapped his shoulder.

He turned, to see Detective Constable Gary Quinnell there. Quinnell grinned and said, 'Someone's been illegally peeing.'

'Come again?'

Quinnell grinned all the more. He was a gigantic Welshman with a dusting of red-gold bristles on his pate, a battered, craggy face and a nose that had been broken more times than he'd had leeks for his tea, mainly while playing rugby union for South Wales Police. 'Up in Shoreditch. You know . . . peeing, slashing? The Shoreditch Slasher, for God's sake!'

'Oh, yeah.' Heck accompanied him along the corridor. 'You on that one as well?'

'Yep, it's me and you. Probably sending me along to puppy-walk you. Make sure you don't lose interest halfway through and bugger off somewhere else.'

Heck wasn't displeased to hear that Quinnell would be accompanying him. The two of them went back some way, having worked together closely on several cases. They weren't natural bedfellows. Quinnell had an affable nature and liked to joke around. He also held staunch Anglican beliefs – which occasionally left Heck nonplussed as they didn't seem to moderate the big guy's effectiveness in a tight spot one iota. But that was a good thing. There was no one Heck would rather go across the pavement with than Gary Quinnell.

Ben Kane was waiting for them in the DO. He regarded Heck with thinly disguised irritation. 'I take it you're not too busy to do some SCU work today?'

'No sir, I'm sorry about that,' Heck replied. They were, of course, Kane's orders that Heck had blatantly flouted the previous day – not intentionally, but it was still disrespectful to a supervisory officer. 'I've had my knackers chewed off about it, I assure you.'

Kane harrumphed. 'I ought to make you drop your kecks and prove it.'

Heck cleared his throat at the sound of suppressed sniggers from the surrounding desks. 'Sorry, sir. It won't happen again.'

'Like I believe that,' Kane said. 'Anyway, enough bullshit. Let's get on with it.' He showed them a couple of photos that had just been emailed through. 'I'm sending Gary to Stoke Newington with you, Heck, because this thing's getting serious at a rate of knots. Apparently there was another one last night. This one also suffered severe damage to her left eye. As usual, the mugger seemed more interested in striping the victim with a knife – probably a Stanley – than in taking her handbag. But he *did* take the handbag.'

'Perk of the job, I suppose,' Quinnell said, hands in pockets.

Kane glanced at him with distaste. 'The Met reckon it's only a matter of time before someone dies.'

Heck nodded, but said nothing.

'I know it's small potatoes compared to the Nice Guys,' Kane added. 'But it's worrying stuff and the local lads could use some help.'

Heck nodded again. 'That's what we're here for, sir.'

'Good. Now's an excellent time to remember that. So get up there. Liaise with DCs Reynolds and Grimshaw.' They slouched to their desks to get their stuff together. 'And get a sodding move on!' Kane bawled after them. 'Take the quickest, shortest route . . . no dawdling or pissing around. That lot have waited long enough!'

'You can bring the worst out of anyone, you can, boyo,' Quinnell said as they sauntered down to the car park. 'Now Schoolmaster Ben's shouting and carrying on!'

'You gonna blabber on all the way up to the East End?' Heck asked.

Quinnell made a zipping motion across his lips.

'Good. Because I've got to think some stuff through.'

'Well, thinking stuff through's one of your strong points, sarge.'

Heck gazed at him suspiciously, but Quinnell only grinned.

They opted to take one car up to Stoke Newington – Quinnell's silver Subaru XV. The Welshman drove, the growling, honking horde of mid-morning traffic testing his good humour to the limit, as did the deluging rain. Heck, meanwhile, slumped in the passenger seat, flipping through the paperwork they'd been sent.

'What do you think?' Quinnell asked after ten minutes.

'I think it should be left to Division,' Heck replied.

'Bit messy, though, isn't it?'

Heck pondered the details of the case. The attacks were confined to the Shoreditch and Hackney districts, and rarely varied. In almost all cases, the assailant, a tall, lean man wearing a black anorak and a hoodie, and described as having 'a pale, skullish face' accosted lone females after dark. His MO was to shove them back against a wall or lamppost with his left hand, pull a small, sharp blade with his right, and demand money. In every case thus far, the terrified victim had handed valuables over. The assailant had then lunged at them with his blade, always going for the face, before running away. A couple of times, the wound had been superficial – no more than a nick, but he was clearly getting better at it. On the last three occasions, he'd created six- or seven-inch incisions, sometimes half a centimetre in depth. Heck could understand the divisional CID office's concern – in the case of the previous night's victim, Angelina Watts, a seventeen-year-old waitress, the blade had sliced clean through her left eyeball – yet he still didn't view this as an SCU case, for various reasons.

'This is five minutes of a job,' he said. 'To start with, he's local. He always leaves the scene on foot, but CCTV footage from bus stops and railway stations has brought no results, which means he's got somewhere close to lie low. He's been chased from the scene three times, but always eludes his pursuers. That means he knows the area. He almost certainly lives or works on the plot. He's white, six-foot-four minimum, lanky build. That narrows the field.'

Heck read on. 'Look at this . . . he left footprints in a flowerbed after vaulting a fence to get away across a nursery school playing-field. They've been identified as belonging to a size-twelve training shoe. That's a big foot, which narrows it down even more. The tread pattern is also identifiable. It gives us the specific brand. So . . . six-four, size twelve feet, specific make of shoe, and all in that same small area. Realistically, how long should it take for the local factory to trace this lad? His signature crime is slashing the faces of female strangers. He robs them too, but the wounding is the object of the exercise. Think about it, Gaz. Face-slashing . . . that suggests he's either got a disfigurement himself, or someone in his family has . . . maybe his mother, his sister.'

'No witness has reported a disfigurement,' Quinnell said.

'No witness had a proper gander at his face. All they did was glimpse it under his hood, calling it pale and skull-like.'

'A disfigurement isn't a given . . . *hey, shit-brain*!' Quinnell hit his horn as the red Alfa Romeo in front took its sweet time moving through a green light. The traffic was still heavy, the dirty grey rain intensifying, drumming the windshield.

'Alright, put that aside,' Heck said. 'He only attacks young women. Non-fatal knife attacks on females tend to indicate a sexual inadequate. Someone who hasn't got the capability to commit rape. The chances are he's committed similar but lesser telltale crimes before. Purse-snatching, skirt-lifting, bottom-pinching, spitting on girls in the street, name-calling . . . especially when he's drunk. You seriously think someone like that won't already be in the system?'

Quinnell shrugged, but snarled. The Alfa Romeo was again dawdling at a traffic light.

'And with all these ID markers,' Heck added, 'how long before you're looking at a shortlist of one? And that's assuming he isn't dumb enough to have used one of the stolen credit cards at a cashpoint and get himself caught on film. It's also assuming the local grasses can't turn something up. Or that a poster campaign or a door-to-door won't drop a name into our lap. Seriously, Gaz, this dickhead should've been topped and tailed in a couple of days.'

Quinnell shrugged. 'This is why they've asked for us. We've got it sorted and we haven't even arrived there yet . . . whoa, what's this now?'

Heck looked ahead. The Alfa Romeo in front had stopped at another red light, but now two passengers, two big young guys – one black, one white – had climbed out, one on either side. They chatted amicably as they sauntered around to the rear of the vehicle; the white one wore a denim jacket and jeans, the other a leather jacket and jeans. Their only precaution in the face of the heavy rain was to wear a knitted cap each. They continued laughing and chatting as they turned to the Romeo's boot.

'What the hell are these bozos doing?' Quinnell wondered.

'Get us out of here now!' Heck said sharply. *'Now, Gaz . . . NOW!'*

'What?' Quinnell's Subaru still advanced, though was slowing to a halt. Twenty yards ahead, the two men had opened the boot and were lifting something out, one item each.

'*Hit the fucking gas!*' Heck bellowed.

A third man, with a red beard, was coming across the road towards them. He wore a khaki flak-jacket and had a rolled-up newspaper in hand. One second earlier he'd been seated in a bus shelter. He too wore a woolly hat – but was now in the act of pulling it down over his face, to reveal that it was actually a ski-mask.

The twosome at the back of the Romeo did the same, and spun around.

Quinnell reacted, throwing his car into reverse, slamming the pedal to the floor. In seconds they were thirty yards away, but had to swerve sideways with a screech of rain-sodden tyres to avoid colliding with vehicles behind, before the two men opened fire with blistering flashes of flame and an ear-numbing *dadadadadada!* A strobe-like burst flared from the end of the rolled newspaper as the man in khaki opened up too.

Heck and Quinnell weren't quite caught in an enfilade; they were moving too quickly for that, but streams of lead raked the Subaru from different angles, safety glass exploding, bodywork buckling and puncturing on all sides, projectiles whining across the interior. Blood and flesh spattered Heck's face as one slug ploughed through the side of Quinnell's neck. A split-second later, the Welshman was hit again, the second slug slamming through the windshield and into the right side of his ribs. Yet somehow he kept the vehicle on track, reversing clean across the A10, a hail of lead still rattling over and through it. He struck the kerb, which collision half-turned the car, spun the wheel and shifted gear.

'Jesus loves me,' Quinnell whimpered through clenched teeth. 'Jesus loves me . . . Holly . . . Sally . . .' Those were the respective names of his wife and daughter.

They blazed through a U-turn, other road-users shrieking out of their way. Heck squirmed around to peek over the top of his seat. The masked man in khaki had discarded his newspaper and was running full pelt in pursuit, in the process of snapping off a spent magazine and banging another into its place. The other two had jumped back into the Romeo, which swung around in a crazy three-point turn, back-ending a waste bin with such force that it cartwheeled through the window of a carpet showroom, and front-ending a Ford Fiesta coming the other way.

'Jesus loves me,' Quinnell gasped, three separate rivulets of blood running from his frothing mouth. He tromped the pedal hard, but his efforts to negotiate the oncoming traffic looked doomed. With a wild wailing of horns, cars and vans swerved aside at the last second, crashing through railings or into shop-fronts.

'Serial Crimes Unit to Stoke Newington CAD, urgent message!' Heck hollered into his radio, despite the rain now blasting his face. 'We're in trouble on lower Stoke Newington Road. Multiple shots fired by unknown number of assailants . . . maybe a Nice Guys hit-team! Repeat . . . maybe a Nice Guys hit-team! One officer injured. Require immediate back-up, plus armed support, over!'

'Holl – eee . . .' Quinnell moaned, the eyelids fluttering in his stone-grey face. Heck realised he couldn't even see the single-decker bus screaming sideways towards them as it attempted to spin out of their way. He grabbed the wheel from Quinnell's bloodstained hands and thrust it left, the Subaru jack-knifing around at speed, shuddering again from bullet impacts to its rear, and now to its offside flank, before shunting its way down a narrow alley.

A collapsible steel market stand blocked the way. Quinnell didn't see this either, because they smashed through it at full speed, its rain-soaked tarpaulin plastering itself across the imploded windscreen. Heck punched at it, but only got it partially clear. 'Jesus!' he swore.

'He's calling me, Heck,' Quinnell stammered.

'No he isn't,' Heck retorted. 'He's telling you to hang tight!' He yanked the wheel left as they approached a redbrick T-junction. They swerved around it, gearbox grinding, jagged cornerstones chewing through the Subaru's nearside flank.

'Gonna die . . .' Quinnell groaned.

'No you're not! Keep that foot to the floor!'

Frantic voices sounded from the radio, but Heck couldn't concentrate sufficiently to reply. Rain still whipped into his face, along with litter. The tarpaulin wouldn't shift either, but even beyond that it was difficult to make things out. They were firmly in back-alley country, more bleak cobbled passages lined with old boxes, rainwater gushing in tumults from the broken gutters and rusty gantries overhead.

Quinnell kept his foot down, but was barely conscious. If his features had been grey before, now they were almost green. Blood clotted his chin and streamed from the gruesome gash in his neck – but it wasn't pulsing out, which suggested no artery had been severed. The wound on his right was more of a worry. Heck couldn't lean across to assess it, but that whole side of Quinnell's jacket, and the shirt underneath, were saturated with gore.

They slid around another corner into a wider thoroughfare, with mountainous heaps of plastic rubbish bags on the left and locked-down steel shutters on the right.

'Holl . . . eee . . .' Quinnell croaked.

'Hang on, Gaz, we'll be out of here . . .'

'Smashed me up, Heck . . . smashed me . . .'

'Fuck!' Heck said, glancing back to the front. '*OH FUCK! Brakes! Gaz, brakes!*'

Quinnell was just adequately compos mentis to pull this off. They skidded wildly on the rain-slick cobbles, Heck jerking forward against his belt, losing his radio through the shattered windscreen. When they came to a halt, another T-junction lay ten yards in front. The left-hand turn was too narrow for any vehicle; little more than a footway. But the right-hand turn would have been wide enough to swing into had it not been blocked by a skip filled with broken pub furniture.

Heck kicked the passenger door open, jumped out and stared back down the passage behind them. Veils of rain swept along it, but there was no sign of immediate pursuit. From somewhere in the near distance, he could hear sirens. It was possible the Nice Guys had called it off. Alternatively, they might have followed and just got lost in this maze of backstreets. He clambered quickly over the bullet-riddled bonnet, and opened the driver's door. 'We've gotta get out of here, Gaz. Now . . . come on!'

'You're bloody . . . kidding.'

'Come on, man! For God's sake, they could be on us in seconds . . .'

'You go . . .' Quinnell inclined his head right, which action seemed to stretch open the glistening wound on his neck – it yawned, fresh blood trickling out. His attempted lazy smile became an agonised grimace. 'You go . . .'

'You think I'm going to leave you?'

'It's you . . . you they want . . . isn't it?'

This had already occurred to Heck, but the Nice Guys didn't have much of a live-and-let-live policy where witnesses were concerned. 'Just get your arse up, you bloody lazy Welshman . . . imagine you've been clouted by some plug-ugly English wing-forward. How'd you feel about that?'

Quinnell grinned again, but his eyes had closed. 'That's . . . fighting talk . . .'

Heck had lost his radio; he had his mobile, but how long would it take to place a call, much less get someone to answer? Instead, he reached down, freed Quinnell's seatbelt, grabbed him under the right arm and around the back, and cantilevered him up and out of the vehicle.

'Owww . . . shit! Sarge . . . that's killing me . . . and it's wet . . .' At six-three and seventeen stone, the bulk of it bone and muscle, the casualty slumped to his knees and then over onto his side, and there was nothing much Heck could do about it.

'Scared of a bit of rain?' Heck scoffed. 'They don't build you men of Harlech like they used to!'

Quinnell lay flat on the cobbles, sinking into unconsciousness again. Even in the downpour, he was drenched head to foot with blood. 'Leave me . . . you go . . .'

'Yeah!' Heck said. Like he was just going to abandon a guy who he'd gone through so many doors with, who he'd burrowed through so much paperwork alongside, who he'd shared more than a few whiskey breakfasts with after coming off a difficult night-turn. The problem was that Heck could hardly carry Quinnell away. He doubted he could *drag* him and expect to stay ahead of their pursuers.

Quinnell's head dropped to one side, mouth agape.

For a second the breath froze in Heck's lungs. He fell to his knees, feeling at the undamaged side of Quinnell's throat. A faint pulse denoted the carotid. Placing a flat palm to the mouth, he felt the breeze of a breath. It was weak and shallow, but at least it was there – yet now there was another problem. Heck heard the approaching growl of an engine, and the howl of tyres as they were rent to shreds taking corners they'd never been designed for. The bastards were still on the hunt. He glanced across the alley at the mountain of rubbish bags.

It wasn't a nice thought, but there wasn't much else for it.

Taking Quinnell by the collar, he lugged him around the front of the vehicle. There was another squeal of tyres. It was difficult to place the direction it had come from. With a grunt, he laid his burden down alongside the rubbish. The meandering, gory trail behind was already washing away.

That was the good news; the bad news was that blood was still flowing. Heck crouched and yanked open Quinnell's sodden shirt. Underneath, the right-hand side of the ribcage had all but collapsed, as though clobbered with a mallet. It was black and blue, and in the middle of it there was a clean, coin-sized hole from which blood was throbbing.

'Shit, Gary,' Heck said, glancing over his shoulder as gears screeched again. By the sounds of it, they were sweeping the entire district.

He fumbled in his pockets, locating a wadded handkerchief. It wasn't fresh, but it was as clean as they could hope for. He twisted it around and poked it into the wound, before stripping off his own and Quinnell's neckties and knotting them together into a single binding, which he swathed around the injured torso. Then he stood up and backed away. The rain was still teeming, hammering the Subaru's mangled hull.

One by one, he lifted down the rubbish bags, and piled them over the prone figure. He'd all but finished burying the Welshman under a makeshift cairn, when an engine yowled again, this time *very* close. More bodywork was ravaged as it turned a sharp corner. A rising rumble drew steadily closer. Heck spun his attention to the right-hand passage, the one half-blocked by the skip. He dashed forward and glanced into it – and saw the red Alfa Romeo proceeding towards him at speed, crashing through boxes, slewing over a discarded mattress.

He turned and checked the left-hand route. It led fifty yards between sheer brick walls, before turning at a right-angle. Possibly it connected with the main road beyond that. He didn't know, but there was no time to try and get the Subaru started. Besides, anything to draw the bastards away from Quinnell.

Heck took the left path, running for all he was worth.

Behind him, the Romeo shrieked to a halt as it approached the skip. Doors thundered open.

The alley was ankle-deep in slimy water. He blundered and slipped as he raced along it and around the corner – only to find another passage, this one filled with rubbish, bricks and collapsed pipe-work from overhead. The massive skeletal remnant of a fallen fire-escape blocked off most of it. As he scrambled around and over these obstacles, shouts rang out behind him. That was when he saw that this second alley didn't lead to a main road, but to a steel mesh fence maybe eighteen feet in height.

He charged on, knowing he wouldn't be able to climb the fence – not in time. But just in front of it there was a door in the left-hand wall. It was featureless and had no handle, but he cast around, spying a broken strut hanging loose from the upper section of fire-escape. It flaked in his hands, but was still stiff, still heavy. If this wouldn't serve as a pry-bar, nothing would. He jammed the strut into the gap on the left side of the door, and used a brick to bang it in several inches. Movement flickered in the corner of his eye. He glanced around. A masked figure in khaki had come into view at the end of the passage.

Heck didn't look to see more, though he sensed other figures appearing – and a communal raising of firearms.

With manic grunts, he slammed the brick against the base of the bar, and from somewhere inside heard the *clunk* of a rusty mechanism fracturing. He threw his weight sideways against the bar, and the door broke open. With a strobe-like glare and cacophony of submachine-gun fire, shells clattered through the fire-escape, but Heck was already in the building, stumbling along a dank, black passage.

Faint exterior light spilled ahead through swirls of ochre dust, but didn't prevent him toppling down the first flight of stairs he came to, tumbling over bare wooden treads, at last slamming into yet another door, which burst open on impact. Heck clambered to his feet, coughing and wafting at the rancid dust. Only the faintest trace of light penetrated down to this point, but it was adequate to show a wide, square room. Its floor was thick with greenish grime, but slippery. He fell again, his leather-soled shoes scraping away sufficient scum to expose yellow floor tiles. High on the wall facing him, a notice swam into view.

Assembly Area 2

Fleetingly, he wondered if he might have blundered into an old air raid shelter, but just as quickly dismissed the notion. More likely it was an old fire-evacuation chamber. These ruminations were shattered when he heard voices echoing down the stairway behind him. There was a tall, arched opening on his right. It was broad enough for two men to pass through, but led into inky blackness.

Again, Heck had no choice. He ventured forward into its depths.

Chapter 17

'Fuck, mate . . . there were two of them,' Brad Perkins said, hefting his TAR-21 and strapping a flashlight to the side of its barrel with duct tape.

He was a burly, broad-chested Queenslander, formerly of the Australian SAS. His rain-soaked denim jacket threatened to burst apart, it was so crammed with muscle. Now that he and the other two were in the privacy of the disused basement, he'd ripped off his ski-mask, to reveal a bull-neck, tanned, granite features, blue eyes and brown hair shaved in a stiff buzz-cut.

'You sure?' asked Shaun Cullen. He wasn't as broadly built as Perkins, but was at least a couple of inches taller. He too had removed his ski-mask. His reddish beard, moustache and sweaty mop of long hair gave him a country boy air, yet his accent was solid Boston Irish, while his combat fatigues and the SIG-Sauer MX slung at his side proclaimed that anything he knew of the wilderness he owed to the US military, specifically the Navy SEALS.

Perkins nodded. 'The other one must be back in the car.'

Cullen turned to the third member of the trio. 'What is this place, Bruno?'

Bruno, real name Leon Fairbrother, was at least as strongly built as either of the others, and though of West Indian descent, he was a Hackney boy born and bred. His reputation as a fighter had extended from _the_ mean streets of his youth into the Grenadier Guards, where he earned his nickname through his physical similarity to the former heavyweight champ. Bruno shrugged as he too taped a torch to his weapon, in his case a Sterling Mk. 5. 'Tube, mate.'

'Which station?'

'Dunno. Feels derelict, but that should help us. One way in, one way out.'

'Okay.' Cullen pondered quickly. 'Work your way through. Perk, take your lead from Bruno. Whatever it takes, find him. You know the RP?'

They nodded.

'Good luck.' Cullen scarpered back up the stairs. 'I'll find the other one.'

All Gary Quinnell knew when he came around was pain – and that he was drowning.

His aching body was ice-cold, but the heavy, waterlogged plastic slumped across his face was the main problem, not to mention the fluid trickling down his nostrils. He coughed and tried shifting to one side, but even small movements agonised him, his ribs in particular. It took several laborious efforts to shove a clutter of sodden, bulky objects off the top of him.

Initially, nothing made sense: the rain, the cobbles, the rubbish bags, pain and sickness akin to shattered bone and punctured inner organs.

And then it all came back – in a migraine-inducing wave of intense horror.

The Nice Guys, Heck . . .

Quinnell craned his neck to look up. There was no one in sight now. His Subaru stood alongside him, though even from this low angle it looked as if it had been through a wrecking machine.

'B . . . bastards,' he stuttered, the interior of his mouth filled with sludge. He spat out wads of clotted, purple blood. 'Bastards . . .'

Slowly and dizzily, he dragged himself up – first into a sitting position, and then to his feet, but only by hooking his fingers into the bullet holes in the flank of his vehicle. The world swayed and tilted as he leaned against the car. He glanced down at his open shirt; much of his blood had congealed, but fresh streams seeped from a crimson rag bound to the side of his deeply bruised ribs.

'Heck,' he breathed again.

From somewhere nearby, he heard a banging and clanging – like someone clambering through rubbish.

'Shit,' he mumbled. 'Oh . . . shit.'

Step after delicate step, he made his way around the front of the Subaru. At any second he thought he'd slip to his knees. But another clatter, another piece of rubbish being kicked over, goaded him to greater efforts. With breaths sounding like the rasping of a saw, and indeed feeling like rusty metal teeth chewing at the innards of his chest, Quinnell reached the other side of the car, bent down and slid himself through the open driver's door.

He usually kept his mobile on a shelf under the dashboard. It puzzled him that it wasn't there, but then he spotted it lying in the passenger side foot-well. He'd just reached feebly down for it when he glimpsed a red-bearded man emerge from the T-junction's left-hand passage. Thanks to the shattered windshield, Red Beard didn't glimpse him back – not immediately. Quinnell kept low, watching through blurred eyes as the menacing figure came forward, hefting a firearm under his unzipped khaki jacket, and halted five yards short of the Subaru, staring at the ground.

It was obvious what he was looking at: the blood-trail Quinnell had left coming back from the rubbish bags. Unlike the evidence of his outward journey, this would not yet have washed away. Even so, it took Red Beard several seconds, his eyes swivelling back and forth, to realise what he was seeing. As he glanced up, pulling a submachine gun from under his khaki, the Welshman turned the key and hit the gas.

He hadn't been sure if the damaged Subaru would respond, but it leapt forward, smashing headlong into the gunman, its front fender impacting his knees with a bone-rending *crunch!* Red Beard slammed bodily onto the bonnet and was hurled backwards, his weapon bouncing across the passage to lie in a puddle some five feet from the driver's door. Though all the pain in the world filled his body, his vision again darkening, Quinnell flopped out onto the cobbles. That impact alone almost killed him, but a sidelong glance at Red Beard, writhing on the floor with hands wrapped around his left knee, gave him new energy.

He got to the SIG-Sauer with time to spare, and swung it towards his target.

Unfortunately, focus was proving elusive as dizziness and nausea threatened to overwhelm him – for a few seconds Quinnell couldn't even see the guy, but tried to bluff this out, gazing hard along the barrel. 'Don't move!' he shouted.

Red Beard swam greasily into view, posed in a half-crouch, reaching slowly under his khaki, presumably for a second weapon.

'Don't fucking do it, boyo!' Quinnell barked.

Red Beard paused, weighing his options.

'I . . . I wouldn't . . .' Quinnell advised, but his voice was wavering, his world spinning, a kaleidoscope of blood, rain and brick.

The yowl of a siren made both of them flinch.

A uniformed patrol vehicle veered into the alley behind the Subaru. Quinnell was just sufficiently distracted by this – he half-glanced around, and Red Beard bolted, limping but still vanishing down the right-hand alley. Quinnell didn't see him escape, simply heard the harshly whispered comment: 'Next time, motherfucker!' followed by the rumble of a car revving quickly away.

A split-second later, two uniforms were running in pursuit. A third, a female, dropped to her knees beside him, and gently attempted to wrest the weapon from his grasp. For no particular reason, Quinnell tried to resist this, but only for a few seconds – before he slid down into total oblivion.

Chapter 18

The corridor was stale and dank, the dust as thick as midnight fog. So thick in fact that, despite the dim blue glow of his phone's fascia, Heck only knew it was a corridor by bouncing from wall to wall and occasionally encountering open doors, beyond which lay tiny spaces heaped with grime-encrusted junk. It wouldn't be true to say there was no sound: rats scuttled away, squeaking and skittering; there were occasional dull booms denoting the reverberations of Tube trains.

He tried to place a call, but of course got nowhere. There was no signal beneath London's streets. He pressed on, turning corner after corner, before seeing what looked like natural light. At first it was a dull smudge, a vaguely visible streak on the wall opposite another open door. When he glanced through the door, he saw the light filtering out of a tiny square aperture where a ventilation fan had once been attached. Its faint radiance revealed what had formerly been an office, again buried under rubbish and masses of mouldy, filth-covered paperwork. It also showed a recognisable insignia on the passage wall: the traditional red roundel and horizontal blue band of the London Underground, complete with a name:

Heck had vague memories of such a station. He thought it had ceased to operate sometime in the 1970s, having once been part of the Victoria Line. How much of it remained beyond this point was another question. It had been a deep-level station, and many of those now disused had been demolished and filled in. That said, it might be possible to work his way through to another station that was still in service. Half a second later it became imperative he at least try – because he spotted the flashing of torches at the end of the corridor. An explosive smashing of wood suggested that his pursuers were kicking in doors as they came steadily nearer.

He extinguished his own phone light and ran on – only for the passage to ramp downward and terminate at a barred gate hung with cobwebs so old and dusty they were more like tatters of rotted fabric. Heavy, corroded chains held the gate closed.

Heck halted in front of it, sweat pinpricking his face.

Only one other avenue presented itself: an open door on the left. Beyond this lay an even smaller room than those he'd previously seen. By the flickering torchlight, he glimpsed shelves crammed with bric-a-brac, a dog-eared girlie calendar hanging above a chair. The bountiful curves of Miss June 1979 were visible through a skin of mildew, but what stood behind her promised more.

A second door.

Heck threw the chair aside and pulled the calendar down, to find the second door had no handle, just a small hole. Frantic seconds passed as the torches outside drew nearer. He scrabbled along the shelves, initially ploughing nothing but foulness and dirt. There were tools here, but they were ancient and useless. And now he heard voices.

'Time-check, mate?'

'Five to eleven.'

The second voice was Cockney; the first voice different – Australian maybe?

'Mate, this is fucked!'

Then Heck's hand alighted on a familiarly angled shape: a lever door handle. There were no screws in it, but its squared-off turning bar remained. He spun around. The passage was now filled with light. Frantic, he slotted the bar into the hole and twisted it. The door clicked open.

Had they heard? It didn't matter.

He withdrew the handle and slipped through into the blackness on the other side, easing the door closed after him. The voices became muffled, but at best he knew the door would only hold them for a couple of minutes. He quickly brought his own phone back to life. Its battery was low on juice, and the glow it emitted so poor that he now saw very little: just maintenance passages leading off; bare brick walls; exposed wiring; fallen plaster.

At least the light enabled him to walk quickly and freely, which was a relief as a furious banging now sounded behind him. Several bursts of gunfire followed.

Heck started running, rounding a corner and proceeding another twenty yards before stumbling into a section of roof-fall. Massed heaps of bricks and dirt prevented further progress. He doubled back, stopping en route to collect a shovel propped against a wall. He had no plans to dig, but it was the closest thing approximating a weapon he'd seen thus far.

The banging abruptly ceased. Heck halted to listen, trying to suppress the sound of his laboured breathing. It occurred to him that his light might be a giveaway, but then a brighter light burst to life at the end of the adjoining passage. It was one of the electric torches; again it was advancing.

Heck edged to the next corner, heart drumming. He shoved

his phone into his pocket, dousing its light. Then he waited – and waited.

Padding footsteps accompanied the advancing torchlight. There was no chatter. Did that mean only one of them was present? It hardly mattered. There was nowhere else for Heck to go. Fresh sweat beaded his brow. His muscles coiled like springs – but it was only as the muzzle of a submachine gun, with a flashlight attachment, protruded around the corner, that he swung the shovel with both hands.

The flat of its blade made ferocious contact with the gunman's face, the deafening CLANG echoing through the passages.

It was the big white guy. He went down onto his back, a crimson font spraying from his nose, and yet managed to retain consciousness. He even kept hold of his weapon, discharging a blind volley across the ceiling, bringing down plumes of dust and plaster.

Heck ducked around this and sprinted back the way he had come. The gunman twisted where he lay and fired after him, but was clearly groggy, drilling slugs harmlessly into the wall. 'Pommie fucker!' he howled in hoarse Australian.

Heck didn't know where the other killer was; nor did he care. He turned a couple more corners and hammered along a much narrower passage, which had steel plates for a floor and wire-mesh on either side. Midway along this there was an aperture on his left. He ventured through it, finding steps dropping into blackness. He descended these for about fifteen feet before he alighted on flat concrete.

The rasp of his breathing reverberated eerily, and he realised he was in some large, vaulted chamber. He fumbled his phone from his pocket. Again, it didn't illuminate much, but was sufficient to show that he was on a long, broad platform with deep black pits lying parallel on either side of it. When he edged left and glanced into the first of these, rat-tails lashed as furry bodies scampered away into holes and crevices. It was the old track-bed, though the rails themselves had long been removed. Overhead, most of the cream and brown tiling had fallen from the arched ceiling and lay scattered. The walls were adorned with aged movie posters. They were mouldy, blistered with damp, but the films were recognisable: *Apocalypse Now . . . Mad Max . . . Moonraker . . . Alien . . .*

With a low, dull rumble, everything shuddered. More dust trickled down.

Another train had passed close by.

Heck hurried along the platform, circling the bare frame of a billboard on which the tattered remnants of a Tube map hung. He couldn't yet see the tunnel mouth at the far end, but it could only be a hundred yards or so. By the sounds of it, living London wasn't too far away. But then he spotted something else a short distance ahead: a low, arched entrance with another stair rising behind it.

More importantly, a light was descending that stair.

For half a second, Heck imagined help had arrived. Had someone posted on the old site been alerted to intruders? Did Shacklewell Street connect with other buildings still in use? And then the truth dawned. No one was posted on this abandoned site, nor had they been for decades. The light he was seeing was the light of the second gunman, who had somehow got ahead of him. Heck recalled the extra bursts of shooting he'd heard. They'd been blowing the chains off the barred gates.

He turned and ran the other way – only to see a second light, this one proceeding along the mesh-covered bridge.

He was hemmed in from either end.

Scalp tingling, Heck pivoted around. Directly across the left-hand track-bed, he spied a recess in the wall with a steel door set in it. Vaulting down from the platform, he hurried over there. Yet even before reaching the door, he saw that this too was closed and fixed with a chain and padlock.

Heck glanced around. The two lights were now on the level, advancing one from either end of the platform. They'd almost certainly seen each other, but had not yet spotted him, which would explain their cautious approach. Even so, it would only be a matter of seconds. He pocketed his phone and swung back to the door. It was solid steel, its chains intact – but there was one other possibility. The door was mounted on a step, beneath which there was a vent: a rusted, circular pipe sticking out several inches from the brickwork, about twenty inches in diameter.

He ripped off his jacket, dropped to his knees and crawled in headfirst, only then realising how small the space was that he was attempting to pass through; its dimensions were coffin-like, its darkness absolute. He could only make ground by worming ahead on his elbows, his groping hands frequently encountering soft, furry bodies, which again scattered at his touch. And there was another problem: it began to slope downhill. Heck had expected this pipe to lead through into whatever space lay on the other side of the door, but apparently not. He passed over a circular rim, and the passage tightened further. Another ten yards, and he entered an even narrower section. He could only progress from here by slithering on his belly, and even then it fitted him like a glove, tearing at his shoulders, weighing on his back, the mere sensation of which set his gut churning.

A Lancashire lad by origin, Heck remembered tales his coalminer grandfather had told about being trapped underground during a cave-in. He'd suffered nightmares for days afterwards, about the pit: all those tons of dirt over the top of you; the blackness; the airlessness; the narrow gaps; the flat crawlspaces under the seams; the creaking and groaning deep in the rock faces. Being held fast in there, being suffocated, being squashed in the depths of the earth.

But now it wasn't a dream.

Heck snaked on, passing another riveted joint beyond which the angle of descent tilted even more steeply. Here, he hesitated. Only the snugness of the pipe's fit preventing him tumbling forward. He wondered what he'd do if he went down and it suddenly tipped upright. That was a hideous thought, and yet it wasn't possible to go back – he could now hear tinny voices at the end of the pipe. He tried to glance over his shoulder, though even if the slender space had allowed this it was too dark to see anything. Not that he needed to. The bastards were no more than thirty feet away; they'd have found his jacket and thus located his escape route.

Pouring sweat, he squirmed over the ridge, slithering down another twelve yards or so – at which point, very suddenly, the pipe seemed to change shape, become oval, turn narrower. Had earth movements outside partly crushed it? With probing fingers, Heck felt lines of jagged teeth where the interior surface had buckled.

He halted again, fighting down panic.

Somewhere behind, the voices sounded louder. He imagined them gazing into the pipe, perhaps preparing to unleash volleys of gunfire after him. Twisting onto his side, he tried to push himself through. The concave metal immediately gouged his chest, crooked steel ripping through his shirt and into the skin underneath. Briefly, he was stuck there. There wasn't room to bring his elbows back to his sides. His arms were fully extended in front, so he couldn't use those to gain leverage. Even the most strenuous efforts to wriggle through had no effect – but those voices were now ringing down the pipe. They knew he was here; they'd hear him gasping, choking. Metallic clicks echoed as fresh magazines were snapped into place.

That was enough.

The pressure on his chest might be adequate to prevent

him filling his lungs with enough air to scream, but it was inadequate to hold him indefinitely, to prevent him driving forward one last time, forcing himself past the obstruction, and then hauling himself bodily on. When the pipe suddenly levelled out, and he found his hands and head emerging into air and space, he almost shouted with relief. He was able to plant his palms against the rim at the end of the pipe, and push hard, sliding his torso out next, then his waist and finally his legs.

Heck lay stunned and filthied on a damp, gritty floor, bleeding from a dozen minor wounds. Another deep rumble somewhere close by roused him.

Sobbing for breath, he dug in his pocket to retrieve the phone. When he hoisted the meagre light, he saw that he was in a secondary tunnel. In this case the tracks were still in place, minus the electrified inner-rail. Some twenty yards to his right stood a set of buffers and behind those, a wall of solid black bricks. To his left, there was a train.

Heck gazed at it in disbelief.

It didn't look like a modern train: it was the same shape, but maroon in colour. One of its rear windows was broken, the other intact, though centimetres-thick with grime. In fact, the whole thing was so covered in dirt and cobwebs that he could barely distinguish the ornate, gold-painted *London Transport* motif.

More worryingly, it blocked the tunnel. There wasn't enough room to get around it on either side, and certainly not underneath it. Another faint rumble suggested a passing train. Meanwhile, a muffled staccato coughing denoted gunfire.

Heck swung around.

Unmistakably gunfire, followed by a metallic grating and crashing, and then the banging of feet on a metal stair. Set above the pipe he'd just clambered through was an identical

200

steel door to that on the higher level. This too was chained and padlocked.

'You've got to be kidding . . .' he said.

A second later, a fusillade of shots ripped through it, lasers of torchlight blasting after them. With a squeal of ancient hinges, this second door was kicked open and two of the Nice Guys stood there. If Heck had been around, he'd have seen that one was tall, powerfully built and black; the other white, his formerly handsome features now flat as an anvil, his pulverised nose thick with clotted gore.

But Heck wasn't around.

He'd re-pocketed his phone and was already at the back of the train, perched on its rear running board and yanking at its handle. To his amazement, it worked first time. The door opened and thick wafts of dust blew out. He burrowed through them, coughing, and then ran down a dim central aisle, breaking veil after veil of cobweb.

When he reached the first sliding door between carriages, it was closed. He tried to draw it back. Initially there was no give; its runners were gummed up. He threw himself against it, bracing his foot on an upright. With agonising slowness, it squealed open a few inches and he was able to slide through.

He sped on, finding further dividing doors open. Torchlight now speared after him, refracting through cracked, grimy glass, bouncing from age-tarnished metal-work – and a storm of gunfire ensued. Dozens of slugs winged through the train's interior, shattering glass, caroming from safety bars, punching into upholstery. Heck dived into a forward roll, glancing over his shoulder. They were no more than two carriages behind. He could see their humped outlines advancing behind the double strobe-like glare. More projectiles whistled over his head, explosive impacts on all sides.

Another sliding door stood five yards ahead. This too was open.

Heck barrelled at it on all fours, inserting himself through before heaving it closed. Panting, he undid his buckle and pulled loose his leather belt, threading one end of it through the door's handgrip and the other around a nearby pole, and then fastening them both together. But even as he did this, a blizzard of lead erupted through, wood and metal fragments flying. Heck was hurled backwards, his face slashed by glass. The belt was instantly shredded, the pole smashed from its mooring.

He clambered onto a row of seats. Deflected slugs had taken out the window behind them. Beyond that stood a brick wall scaled with mould, but to the left of it a narrow slice of blackness was visible; a safety niche for maintenance men. Heck stepped through the empty frame, and slid into the gap, falling full length and landing on a pile of rotted rubber hosing. Behind him, thunder and lightning raged on in the train, casting sufficient luminescence to expose an open door at the back of the recess. He scrambled through it, and was hit across the body by a horizontal bar, which felt like a handrail. He groped left; the handrail sloped downward. Another stair.

He descended, feet clanking metal, and twenty treads down stepped onto a level surface, some kind of slimy grating through which he was assailed by rank odours far fouler than the normal oil and dust of the Underground.

When he yanked out his phone again, its visibly dwindling glow revealed a straight passage running off into dimness. Its floor was a metal grille, a gantry of sorts, though ancient, corroded and slippery with moss. It followed an egg-shaped passage comprised entirely of dripping brickwork. Heck ventured forward, wondering where the hell he was – under his feet he could hear rushing water. Then his weakened battery gave out altogether. Cursing, he continued in pitch blackness, feeling his way along the handrail, though a few yards later the reverberations of the gantry became louder, sounding hollow.

Heck had a sudden sense of vertigo, of open space – as though the aged brick structures overarching him had fallen away. He halted. Had the gantry become a bridge? It suddenly felt rickety. There were metallic creaks from both above and below. His footing wobbled, and the water now sounded as though it was pouring in cataracts on every side. The first glint of electric light from behind set him stumbling forward again, but at the same time allowed him to see more. He'd covered thirty yards or so before stopping to gaze in amazement at the cathedral-like dimensions of the vault he'd blundered into.

It soared to at least sixty feet overhead. There were high vents on all sides, spouts of water pouring down from multiple levels where pipes jutted out. The floor, maybe ninety feet below, boiled and foamed, before the surging torrent roared away down a massive, circular shaft into what seemed like the very depths of the earth.

Dizzied, Heck had to lean on the handrail. Not too far away, engraved in the brickwork, though so crusted with filth that they were initially difficult to read, were three words:

Hackney Brook Interceptory

It was a water-junction. Most likely built by Bazalgette or one of his Victorian engineers, to divert the flow of the Hackney Brook, yet another of London's many underground rivers whose true course had been lost.

Not that this knowledge really helped.

The whole vault was now flooded with torchlight.

The Nice Guys emerged onto the gantry, but they too slowed to a halt, astonished at what they were seeing – so much so that they didn't at first spot Heck.

He lurched on, the gantry groaning and shuddering. It appeared to be suspended by chains, though there weren't a great many of these, and ended at the far side of the junction, maybe forty yards ahead, on a ledge where a single timber door stood. The two Nice Guys only seemed to realise Heck was present when he was two or three yards short of this door. They opened fire as he threw himself headlong at it, exploding through the ancient, worm-eaten woodwork. Slugs travelled through with him, careening in the narrow space on the other side.

For several seconds, he lay dazed on a heap of bricks and broken slabs, amid more choking dust. However, the clatter of feet on the gantry dragged him to his feet and set him scrabbling around. He located a wooden ladder ascending the wall to his left. Glancing up, he saw nothing, yet sensed he was in a shaft of some sort. Even though the ladder was flimsy, he started climbing. The first three rungs snapped, but he drove himself on. Twenty feet up, he passed through an old trapdoor and struggled knee-first onto a narrow platform. Natural light now shimmered down on him. Its source was high up, maybe a hundred feet, at the very top of the shaft. It was a single circular blot, cross-thatched. A grid perhaps? A manhole on a street?

Droplets of rain on Heck's upturned face indicated that it was. From here, the ladder leading up was made of steel and fixed rigidly to the wall. But he knew he couldn't just climb to safety. The voices of the Nice Guys sounded from the gantry – they'd be halfway across at least, and would sight him in seconds. In a narrow space like this, he'd be a sitting target.

Weary, he glanced around for anything he could use.

Only one other item occupied the platform with him. This too was ancient – corroded, dust-covered. Of no use whatever.

It was a wheelbarrow, filled with hardened concrete.

And yet behind it, in the wall of the shaft, there was a timber hoarding – some kind of shutter through which materials had once been lowered.

Lowered.

To Bazalgette's engineering teams.

Working *below*.

Heck grabbed the barrow's handles, wheeled it around and drove it forward, smashing it like a battering ram through the decayed hoarding. Beyond that, it dropped like a stone, and hit the gantry about ten yards in front of the first gunman.

The structure of the bridge collapsed.

It was that simple.

With a massive, explosive impact, the barrow clove through, and then chains were whipping down, broken struts and sections of grille-work spinning into oblivion.

The first of the gunmen – the big black guy – fell too.

Seemingly for seconds, silent but flailing as he plummeted ninety feet into the frothing torrent of the Hackney Brook, just at the point where it plunged downward through that circular maw into London's ultimate bowels.

The second Nice Guy, the Aussie, was more fortunate.

He was a good twenty yards behind, and able to retreat, though he had to do this at speed, for with screams of agonised steel, more chains and girders gave way; more sections of grille went twisting into the abyss. Only when he reached the far side did he feel secure enough to perch there and take pot-shots at the distant aperture – pointlessly of course, as Heck, now unreachable, had ducked back inside the shaft, where he skulked in dimness, shuddering and sweating with relief.

Only after several minutes, as Heck tiredly clawed his way up the ladder, did full awareness of his aches and pains creep back. This in itself would be a difficult journey – he glanced up – and he still had eighty-odd feet to go.

Chapter 19

When Gemma Piper and Frank Tasker arrived at Homerton University Hospital, there were ARVs on the car park, along with several news vehicles. The story had leaked quickly that the lunchtime shooting in Stoke Newington was connected to the mass-shooting in Oxford, which in turn was connected to the mass-shooting near Brancaster Prison; sure proof – one recent TV bulletin had estimated – that a new war had erupted between powerful factions of the British underworld. Local divisional officers and hospital security were doing their best to contain the press pack, who had gathered behind a line of incident tape but were lobbying loudly for updates.

Gemma and Tasker were met at the hospital's front door by a senior nurse, who advised them that Detective Constable Quinnell was undergoing emergency surgery, though the signs were so far good. They were shown through to intensive care, which now, at Tasker's phoned-ahead request, was under the guard of SCO19, all visibly armed and standing in prominent positions. In the first IC waiting area, they found Quinnell's wife, Holly, and ten-year-old daughter, Sally, sitting together tearfully. Ben Kane sat alongside them, talking quietly. He spotted Gemma and indicated with a nod that she'd want the next waiting room along. They moved down to that one, and stopped short at the sight of Mark Heckenburg in an indescribably filthy state, his shirt and trousers reduced to oily, bloodied rags, his hair a mass of dust and cobwebs, the eyes wild in his grimy, sweat-smeared face. For all that, Heck seemed to have it together; he was in the process of briefing three divisional uniforms, an inspector and two sergeants.

'According to a statement DC Quinnell made before they took him into theatre, the redhead's a Yank,' Heck said. 'Course, we don't know that for sure. I didn't hear it myself . . . he told one of the nurses. The physical description's vague too, and probably won't do us much good even if we circulate it – there can't be any shortage of young Americans in the UK with longish hair and goatees. But it's all we've got. Also, check with CAD for a partial index on the nicked Alfa Romeo he escaped in. The other one's defo an Aussie. He may come back out through Shacklewell Street Tube, but knowing these bastards, he'll realise we've got it covered. Most likely he'll have found another way. An all-points is vital, I reckon. Just remember, he's on the run – so he'll be in a state. Plus I caved his face in . . . shouldn't be too difficult spotting him. But he's on his feet, and he's armed with an automatic . . . I think one of those Israeli assault rifles, a Tavor. He may have a sidearm too. Remember, both these guys are as high risk as they come.'

The uniforms nodded and moved away, the inspector talking into his radio. Heck turned and found Gemma and Tasker still staring at him.

'You been checked out?' Gemma eventually said.

'I'm fine.'

'That's not what I asked you.'

'Yes I have, ma'am. A few bumps and scrapes.'

'And how the fuck did that happen?' Tasker wondered. 'Gary Quinnell was shot twice, and you emerge with scrapes?'

'Funnily enough, the plan was for neither of us to get shot, sir,' Heck replied. 'But here's how it went down . . .' He explained as best he could, from the initial ambush all the way through to his eventual emergence from a pavement manhole – courtesy of council workers – several streets away.

They listened, pale-faced.

'And I only got out of there after climbing a hundred feet,' Heck added. He focused on Gemma. 'Not bad for a bloke on a suicide kick, eh?'

'We're just glad you're alright,' she said.

'Yeah, it's written all over your faces.'

'Don't push it, sergeant!' Tasker warned him. 'Just because you've had a tough day, that doesn't give you licence for lip!'

'The main thing is you're obviously on the Nice Guys' hit-list,' Gemma said.

'I don't see why, ma'am. I honestly, genuinely don't.'

'Is that a joke?' Tasker asked.

'Seriously, sir. I met them once before, and kicked their arses. But by the looks of it, that was no more than a local cell. And even then I didn't break their head honcho. I'm hardly their nemesis, am I?'

Gemma shrugged. 'Whether you're a sensible target or not, Mike Silver clearly feels he has a score to settle.'

Heck rubbed his brow. 'For which reason I owe him. I'm guessing this means you're bringing me back in?'

'On the contrary,' Tasker said. 'We're sending you out.'

Heck frowned. 'What's that?'

'There's an SCU officer lying in there at death's door, sergeant . . . purely because he spent the morning saddled up with you.' Tasker shrugged. 'Even if you're prepared to risk your *own* life, you surely don't want to endanger more of your colleagues?'

Heck's gaze flirted between them. 'What're you suggesting?'

'We're not *suggesting* anything,' Tasker said.

'We're putting you in protective custody,' Gemma added.

Heck gazed at her. 'Ma'am? Ma'am . . . *you cannot be serious?*'

'Keep your voice down,' she countered.

'It's already been decided,' Tasker said. 'It's difficult enough hunting these bastards, without them hunting us at the same time.'

Heck could scarcely believe what he'd just heard. Protective custody meant being taken out of action altogether, not just excluded from Operation Thunderclap.

'Look . . .' he stammered, trying his level best to sound reasonable. 'Okay, I see it. The Nice Guys hate me. They want me dead at any cost. But surely that gives us an advantage? You can use me as bait.'

'Even by your standards that's a bloody ludicrous idea,' Tasker said dismissively, spying one of his SOCAR detectives waiting for him in the corridor. 'I'm glad you're okay, Heckenburg . . .' He strode out. 'But this discussion's over.'

Heck gazed at Gemma beseechingly. She returned the gaze blankly.

'Where?' he finally asked.

'Somewhere outside London.'

'That won't make any difference. They've already hit targets in Hampshire, Kent, Norfolk, Oxfordshire. How's leaving London going to help?'

'Only an elite few will know about it.'

'And who's picked this elite few . . . Frank Tasker? That makes me feel safe! Sorry, ma'am . . . you want me in protective custody, you've got to find me first.'

He made to leave, but she caught the collar of his shirt and, rather to his surprise, pushed him back against the waiting-room wall. 'Christ's sake, Heck!' she hissed, pink-cheeked. 'What did we talk about yesterday? I thought I was getting through to you. Did it all go in one ear and out the other?'

'No . . . that would be the bullets they fired at me. When I was on my way to catch the Shoreditch Slasher, *ma'am* . . . or is it "Gemma"? Sorry, I get confused.'

'You little . . .' Her grip tightened on his collar, though she barely seemed aware of it. For several seconds she struggled to give voice to her feelings. 'Do you have any idea how hard you make it for someone to care about you?'

That wasn't something Heck had been expecting. They continued to glare each other out, neither giving ground – but now he noticed how moist her eyes were, and that stumped him further. She was massively stressed by this, of course. A number of policemen had been killed. One of her own detectives had been shot that very morning. A whirlwind of other murders were occurring around the country, all connected to the case, the work of perps so twisted they had no qualms about chucking hand grenades at dinner parties. To call this enquiry 'high pressure' would be somewhat euphemistic. But in all the years Heck had worked with Gemma, and there'd been many, he'd never once seen her cry.

'You're going to a SOCAR safehouse, do you understand?' she said, regaining control, though only with a momentous effort. 'And when you're there you'll have a round-the-clock armed guard . . . at the taxpayers' expense. So you'd better not give us any reason – *any reason at all, Mark!* – to decide this is money badly spent.'

'You've got it,' he said, subdued.

'Yes?' Unsurprisingly, she sounded deeply suspicious.

'Yeah.'

'You need to keep it together, ma'am,' Heck said. 'If you don't mind my saying.'

They were headed along the Chelsea Embankment in Gemma's Merc. Heck had pointed out that his own Citroën was in the car park at the Yard, but she'd replied that he wasn't going to need it in the near future, so it would be perfectly safe there. That hadn't pleased him much, but there'd been no arguing with her.

'Tasker's lot are a glorified PSU,' he added. 'Great at kicking doors down and roughing up suspects – so they're the brawn. But as the experienced murder detective, you're the brain. If *you* lose it, they'll never catch these bastards.'

Gemma stared directly ahead.

'I was thinking when I was under the ground,' he said chattily. 'How crap it would be if I bought it. I mean down there, in a place where no one would ever find me. But more because I'd never get to say goodbye to all you guys. Hell, you know what it's like. Every time we go on duty we wonder if this'll be it. But most of us tend to die in bed, don't we . . . with our loved ones around us. Like Gary.'

'Gary's not dying,' she said tersely.

'No. But if it was going to be me, I didn't fancy my deathbed being a pile of shit at the bottom of a sewer. Wouldn't have been much fun breathing my last without having you sitting there to hold my hand . . .'

'Can it, Heck! It's not gonna work.'

'You know, there was no need to drive me home personally.'

'You reckon?'

'I'm on-side,' he said. 'Grudgingly, I admit. But surely I'm still allowed to have a legitimate concern about the enquiry? I mean, this is real Nice Guys stuff. Okay, they're cowboying it. But apart from that it's the same as the first time. It's like the whole country's their playground. They've got it mapped and planned. They know exactly where their hit-teams need to go to find targets. They know exactly when to be there.

Complex arrangements don't faze them. I mean, they must have waited outside the Yard for me to come out. That takes some balls. And some patience. But that's what you get with ex-special forces. And they're thorough. They do their homework. I don't think they're based in town. I'll tell you why, because they don't need to . . .'

'I thought you said I was the ace murder detective?' she interrupted. 'The one who knows what she's doing?'

'You are . . .'

'Stop lecturing me, then.'

He understood why she was vexed. Gemma valued her reputation for indomitability. She was an exceptionally talented police officer, but she'd earned her high rank through blood and sweat too. She'd always been called 'the Lioness', but her ascent to the higher echelons of CID, a journey during which no form of positive discrimination was possible, had seen her fight battles that had toughened her to an alarming degree. And yet she wore this with pride. It wasn't just her armour; it was her badge of victory, her mark of courage. Though now she'd let it slip, and Heck had glimpsed the raw emotion beneath.

'You underestimate me,' he said.

'What's that supposed to mean?'

'Nothing, look . . . Gemma, you know I have some expertise on this. It could even be deemed negligent of you not to put some protocol in place where you can tap that resource . . .'

'That's why I'm allowing you to keep your mobile phone. If I need to ring you and . . . *tap* your knowledge, I will.'

'Okay. So . . . what's the rest of the plan?'

'It's simple. You're leaving straight away. Soon as you get your stuff, you'll be escorted out of town.'

'May I ask where exactly? I might as well know.'

'You'll know when you get there.'

'At least tell me you've extended the same courtesy to Dana and Sarah.'

'Of course I have.' She threw him an indignant glance. 'What do you take me for?'

Heck nodded, grateful. Even now, a couple of years later, he could hardly bear to think about the brutal hands laid on his sister by the original Nice Guys; it had been nothing short of a miracle that his niece hadn't been present at the time.

'I've put Greater Manchester on it,' she said. 'And I've stressed the importance. You can relax. They know you were one of theirs. They won't drop the ball.'

They arrived at Heck's flat half an hour later. An unmarked car – a black/grey Ford Focus Titanium, an expensive model, which meant it probably belonged to SOCAR – was parked a little way down the road. Heck and Gemma climbed out.

'Don't like it much,' Heck said, indicating his new front door, which was still bare of paint and ornamentation.

Gemma shrugged. She didn't care for it much either, but then, as she'd said, she thought his whole flat was a dump.

Heck produced his shiny new key. 'I trust Frank Tasker's got a spare one of these? If he's planning any more early starts, it'll keep the damage to a minimum.'

Her only reply was an arched eyebrow, so he opened the door and traipsed up the stair. Gemma followed him slowly.

'Thanks for making them tidy up,' he said. 'Mind you, I was hoping for a complete redecorating job and some new carpets.'

'Quit the attempted levity. We haven't got all day.'

'Time for a shower first?'

'Make it quick.'

He turned to face her as he stripped off his muddied shirt. 'If this really is about my welfare . . . you can always pop into the bathroom with me, and wash my back.'

'You're lucky you've been through Hell today . . . speaking to me like that.'

'Yeah, I mean otherwise I might get sent into exile. Imagine, eh?'

He wandered through to his room, where he tore off the rest of his soiled, bloody rags, and dumped them in his laundry basket. He grabbed a towel, wrapped it around his waist and walked back out to the bathroom. He didn't see Gemma on the way, but heard her talking with someone down at the bottom of the stairs. Once in the cubicle, he stood under a hot spray for a good ten minutes – then fifteen – then twenty – then twenty-five – no longer luxuriating in its scalding embrace but determined to punish her. He'd hurt her already in a way, which he regretted, but he'd had a pretty rough morning himself, and now they were doing *this* to him. In that light, he was determined to make her wait as long as possible to show how badly he felt he was being treated. It was a full forty minutes before there was a knock at the bathroom door.

'Come in,' he yelled. 'It isn't locked.' The door creaked open, and he heard her enter. He turned the water off and clawed a towel from the rack alongside the cubicle. 'You're a bit late,' he said, lumbering out, towelling his face. 'I've washed all the interesting bits.'

'So I see,' Steph Fowler commented.

He hastily covered up. 'What the hell are you doing here?'

She couldn't conceal a smirk. 'We've been detailed to take you on holiday.'

'We?' Heck glanced at the open bathroom door.

Nick Gribbins stood there. His right arm was fixed in a fresh cast, but he was smirking too. 'Don't worry, sarge,' he said. 'We've got your back.'

Heck shook his head. 'This just gets better and better.'

Chapter 20

The Ford Titanium belonged to Steph Fowler, and apparently this was the only vehicle they were taking. Once Heck had packed a holdall, they drove out of Hammersmith along the Great West Road, joining the M4 in Chiswick, following this out of London and continuing west.

The arrangement was for Fowler and Gribbins to take it in turns guarding Heck, operating a night shift and a day shift. Gribbins had opted for night, he sneeringly remarked, because the less time he spent having to converse with 'Salman Rushdie Mark II' the better.

'Don't tell me you were protecting *him* as well?' Heck asked from the back seat. 'I'd have thought Alexander Litvinenko would have been more your handiwork. You know, the one who got killed . . .'

'Alright!' Fowler interrupted from behind the steering wheel. 'We're going to be living on top of each other. We might as well keep it civil.'

Gribbins grunted and said he had to get some kip to acclimatise for the new shift pattern. Heck merely gazed through the window as they drove on towards the West Country. It was nearly October, and the vibrant greens of summer were fading. Autumnal shades fringed the edges of woodland. Sparse scatterings of leaves lay on fields and meadows.

Heck saw none of this, his thoughts straying to the almost unreal scenario that Mike Silver was at liberty again, and not only that – that he and his confederates were causing murderous havoc. There'd been occasions before when Heck had pondered the near-unthinkable possibility that Silver might escape, and maybe that it would be the work of other Nice Guys coming in from overseas. He'd considered the vague chance they might try to clean house behind them, disposing of all potential witnesses to their activities: former clients and informers, and even former investigators such as Heck himself. But he didn't think he'd expected it to happen in reality. Most likely, he'd assumed – if Silver ever did get free – that he'd simply go into hiding abroad and never darken British shores again. And who knew, as Heck had suggested to Gemma, perhaps Silver had done exactly that. He was ill, after all. Maybe someone else was cleaning house for him.

It was a pleasing thought – that Heck had thrown such a spanner into the Nice Guys' works that they were having to close down their British arm, seeking to erase any memory of it for fear it would lead to the extinction of their entire operation. But the job clearly wasn't done yet, and being driven away from it all, as Heck was now, was hardly going to help him change this for the better.

'Any offers on where we're going yet?' he asked Fowler.

'You'll find out when . . .'

'. . . when we get there, yeah I know. You don't think this obsessive secrecy's a bit of a joke? We're all adults here.'

She eyed him through the rear-view mirror. 'Do me a favour . . . remember that.'

'It cuts both ways, you know.'

'I don't understand what you're even complaining about. Most coppers would be happy to be in your shoes. A few days off in a beautiful part of the country, full pay.'

'Beautiful, eh?' Heck rubbed his chin. 'The New Forest?' She snorted.

'Cornwall?'

'No such luck.'

'Pity . . . those'd be proper holidays. If I wasn't on call, that is.'

'On call?'

He raised his mobile. 'That's why Superintendent Piper let me keep this. In case someone on your team needs a bit of advice – like how to tie his shoelace, maybe.'

'If you're such hot shit, how come every time you get close to the Nice Guys, innocent bystanders die? Or nearly die.'

'Nice Guys die too,' Heck replied. 'So far, that makes me pretty unique among the world's police.' She didn't respond. Maybe she agreed with him on that score. 'Anyway, you two must have really messed up to get this gig.'

'I think the boss just reckons we know you pretty well.'

'Yeah? Good luck with that.'

'Don't give us any trouble, Heckenburg,' she added. 'You give us trouble, and it'll force us to get heavy . . . and that's not the way we want to play this.'

'Get heavy? I thought you two were supposed to be protecting me?'

'Maybe the person you really need protecting from is yourself.'

Good answer, he thought. *If a tad mendacious.* 'Don't fret. I won't give you any trouble. Denuding Thunderclap of two men just to watch my back is two too many.'

Fowler's eyes again flickered in his direction, as though assessing him, as though attempting to deduce how truthful he was being.

218

He offered her a three-fingered salute. 'Scout's honour.'

She half-smiled, but continued checking her rear-view mirror, this time scanning the motorway. At least she was doing her job, he supposed. Which was more than he was currently capable of. After the events on the Underground, he felt bone-tired – to the point where his eyelids were soon fluttering. He finally fell into a doze, only waking around five-thirty as they pulled into the motorway services at Membury.

Gribbins remained asleep, but Fowler turned in her seat. 'Toilet break?'

Heck shrugged. 'Why not?'

She followed him through the station's main doors, which made him a little self-conscious. He glanced over his shoulder, to find that she was glancing over hers.

'Something wrong?' he asked.

'Nothing specific.'

'Good . . . let's try not to make it too obvious, eh?'

When he'd finished in the lavatories, he went into the shop, bought himself a sandwich, a bottle of water and an evening paper. 'Not sure how much longer we're going to be driving,' he said, sensing her at his shoulder as he queued. 'So I thought I'd get myself some nourishment.'

'That's fine,' she replied, not lulled into revealing their destination.

They drove another thirty miles, finally leaving the motorway at the Chippenham turn-off, but heading north rather than south.

'The Cotswolds, eh?' Heck said. 'Very nice.'

Fowler didn't comment.

For the next quarter-hour, they toured a verdant landscape of rolling hills, thin woods and sumptuous quilt-work farmland – though all was now dwindling in the long, blue dusk. At last they swung onto a single-track country lane winding between deep hedgerows. Ten minutes later, they turned in at a narrow drive set in a hawthorn hedgerow. Fowler hit an electronic fob, and the tall, wrought-iron gate creaked open. Beyond that, they drove uphill through dense birch-woods, in whose shady depths gleamed the crimson eyes of multiple infrared cameras.

'You got trip-wires too?' Heck asked. 'Pits filled with sharpened bamboo?'

'We're well protected,' was all she said.

Three hundred yards up, they halted at another gate, an immense slab of timber, at least ten feet high and surmounted with steel spikes. Towering granite obelisks provided the gateposts, on either side of which twelve-foot brick walls led away through the undergrowth. These also had spiked rail-ings on top, woven with strands of electrified wire.

'The entire place is walled off,' Fowler explained. She hit another button on her fob, and the wooden gate swung aside. 'There are spotlights too, and CCTV checkpoints every thirty yards around the perimeter. No one gets in here, period.'

'All this for me?' Heck was genuinely incredulous.

'It wasn't built for you,' Gribbins said, yawning and stretching. 'But it'll serve.'

They pulled onto a gravel lot alongside a lawn, in front of what had once been an old farmhouse. It comprised various wings and gables, and was built from gold-hued Cotswolds stone, but its mullioned windows were set into tough PVC frames and in all probability had been constructed from reinforced glass. Cables snaked unobtru-sively around the exterior, suggesting alarms at the various entry points.

As Heck took his holdall from the boot, he glimpsed the back of the perimeter wall. It would be even more difficult to cross than he'd previously thought; as well as the spiked and electrical defences on top, it was double-skinned, with a high barbed wire fence on the inside comprising multiple strands and multiple barbs.

'Someone tries to come over that wall from the other side, they'll get nicely tangled,' he observed.

'Uh-huh,' Fowler agreed.

'Not to mention someone trying to go over it from this side.'

'If you want to go out, you just ask us,' Gribbins said.

'You mean I can travel?'

'No.' Gribbins chuckled. 'But you can ask us.'

'You can go anywhere you want in the vicinity,' Fowler said, shooting her partner a look. 'For a walk, a drive, a trip to the pub, or just to the village to get supplies. So long as one of us is with you.'

'Which village would that be?' Heck asked. 'You might as well tell me. I saw signs to Malmesbury. I know I'm in Wiltshire.'

'The nearest habitation is the village of Lea,' she replied.

'Okay . . . I don't know it, but as long as they've got a corner shop, I'll be fine.'

The front door was another slab of timber, this one studded with iron nail-heads. Over the top there was a heavy granite lintel with the words *1705 AD* engraved into it. Somewhat anachronistically, there was no actual key-hole; this door too could only be opened by the electronic fob.

Inside, the porch was floored with stone and walled with hand-painted tiles depicting eighteenth-century hunting scenes. The downstairs rooms beyond were low-beamed and furnished in the style of a bygone age, though there were newish fixtures too: a modern central heating system; a large, flat-screen television in the lounge, with a satellite receiver box and Blu-Ray player; desktop computers in several rooms; full Wi-Fi, and of course security cameras mounted on the ceiling in almost every room. The kitchen, which was enormous, was pristine. There was scarcely a mark on its parquet floor or pine worktops; the large kitchen table, which could have seated twelve, was of polished teak – again there wasn't a mark on it. It was a similar story upstairs, where the oak-panelled bedroom he'd been allocated, aside from its sumptuous four-poster bed and rich, hanging tapestries, boasted a granite hearth without a smear of soot. The bathroom attached to this was particularly elegant: done out in painted ceramic tiles, the bathtub sunken, the electric power-shower combining a steam-room facility.

Heck wandered back downstairs, fascinated but bemused.

He peeked into the security booth, which was located in a triangular cubby-hole that had once been the under-stair closet. It consisted of a central swivel chair, a bank of intercom/radio controls and wall-to-wall VDU screens, on which black and white images flickered back and forth. Gribbins was already installed there, stripped to his shirt-sleeves and checking electrical systems. His holstered Glock hung from a hook on the wall behind him.

'Everything you could want,' Fowler said, approaching. 'You'll find the fridge-freezer in the kitchen fully stocked. Same for the kitchen cabinets. If you want some fresh air, feel free to mosey about the grounds.'

'There are grounds?' Heck asked.

'Extensive at the rear. We've got a croquet lawn, tennis court, an orchard, lots of shady walks. They're walled off from the front and side of the house, just for security. But there's plenty of room back there. Even a swimming pool . . . though I guess you won't want to be using that with autumn coming.'

'I'm not planning to be here that long,' Heck replied.

'Well, if you do want to use it, you'll be the one who has

to scoop the leaves out,' Gribbins said. 'We may be your bodyguards, but we're not your servants.'

Heck mused. 'I notice there's no phone?'

'You've got your mobile,' Fowler said.

'Yeah, but why's there no landline?'

'Landlines are easy to tap or trace. If any of us, for any reason . . .'

'Mobile phones can be traced too,' Heck said.

'The people who'll normally be held here won't have mobile phones,' Gribbins answered. 'The internet link will be cut on those occasions too.'

'Let me guess,' Heck said, 'super-grasses?'

'Something like that,' Fowler said.

'You guys have turned a few players in your time?' Heck asked, thinking that he hadn't heard about a single incident of SOCAR managing this.

'Come on,' she replied. 'You know we're not going to talk about that.'

Heck shrugged. 'It's just that this place looks new to me.'

'Look on the lintel over the front . . .'

'Yeah, I saw that. 1705. Pretty impressive. But I meant the refurbishments. New kitchen, new bathroom. The desktop in the study's still got a shipping tag attached. What are the odds I boot it up and find it's never been used?'

'What difference does it make whether the place is new or not?' Fowler said.

Heck shrugged. 'None, I suppose. I guess I should be grateful I'm one of the first to sample such comforts.'

Gribbins sniggered. 'Don't get too cosy. Soon as we catch Mike Silver, you'll be out of here and back on Shit Street.'

'I hope you do catch him,' Heck said.

'We will.'

'I mean *catch* him . . . as opposed to slotting him.'

'We're not animals, Heckenburg.' Fowler moved off along

the hall. 'Whatever you may think . . . whatever provocation he's thrown at us, we don't do stuff like that.'

Gribbins smirked. 'You really don't want him blown away?'

'I said I don't want *you* to blow him away,' Heck replied. 'That pleasure should be mine.'

Chapter 21

'This brings the murder spree in central and southern England to an astonishing thirty-three in the last week,' the BBC Scotland anchorman said. 'Speculation is rife as to whether this is the result of terrorist activity, or whether a gangland war has erupted in consequence of the escape from prison last week of syndicate organiser, Peter Rochester, better known as Mad Mike Silver, who was serving a life sentence for multiple counts of kidnap and murder. Meanwhile, the British Home Secretary has assured Parliament that all necessary resources and personnel are being placed at the disposal of the police unit charged with halting the carnage. The Prime Minister himself commented while en route to chair a meeting of COBRA, offering his personal assurance that those responsible for the crimes will be brought to justice . . .'

The Most Reverend Desmond Docherty, Bishop Emeritus of the Diocese of Fife, stood up, walked across his small, neat apartment and switched off the portable television. He gazed from his window. The monastery's vegetable garden was directly below. The sounds of the brothers working down there had often been a source of relaxation to him; the soft thump of the hoe, the gentle scrape of trowels as they turned the peaty Highland earth. It was all quiet now at mid-evening. The sky over Sàil Ghorm was streaked in salmon-pink. The sun would soon be down.

Docherty's gaze roved along the whole of the Quinag range with their jagged, granite peaks, their hints of mist. He'd been living here like a hermit for two years, and only now did it strike him how picturesque the world could be. All these simple things – the rocks, the heather, the sweeping purple uplands – they cost nothing; any man could enjoy their innocent splendour. Yet their constant availability was their undoing; only those shortly to be denied such things would appreciate their worth.

He opened the slide door on his walk-in wardrobe. There was a washbasin in its right-hand corner and above that a mirror, in which he assessed himself. For a man in his late fifties, he was well-kept: tall, broad-shouldered, and still with a head of naturally black hair, cut short and parted on the left. With his clear grey eyes and cleft jaw, he'd always been a handsome chap.

Though he'd been dismissed from his post two years ago, he still affected a neatly ironed black shirt and white clerical collar. And why not? Earthly titles might be rescinded, but one never ceased to be a servant of Christ. The rest of his attire comprised neatly pressed black slacks and a pair of black leather shoes. As he glanced down at the toes of those shoes, an amusing thought struck him.

All these decades later, it still made him smile.

While still a young seminarian – a good few years ago now, 1973, perhaps earlier – a question had been raised in class about temptations of the flesh.

'But how do we resist these feelings, Father?' one boy had asked their venerable old tutor. 'It's not as if they're unnatural. They're programmed into us as male animals. The rest of one's life is a long time to remain chaste.'

226

'You are right of course,' the tutor had replied. 'These are natural feelings, but they are feelings bequeathed to us as part of God's great gift . . . so that procreation, which is essential for our species, may be a pleasurable experience. However, we few are special. We have taken a vow to forgo that pleasure . . . to stand aloof from it and serve God in other ways.'

'But Father . . .'

'I understand. These feelings will come to you. They come to all of us. It is an easy thing to say, but we must deny them.'

'How do we do that?'

'There is no easy answer. What works for some fails for others. I can only recommend that when these feelings tempt you, put your mind to something else. Some ordinary thing, which nevertheless will distract you. Perform a mundane task . . . something simple and routine, but which will occupy your thoughts. Polishing one's shoes for example. An easy thing, but it requires care and attention.'

As though some hidden signal had been given, young Docherty and the rest of his colleagues had instinctively glanced down at their tutor's shoes, and found them, without doubt, the most fastidiously polished pair they had ever seen.

Docherty smiled again, but it was easy to mock these things now.

The reality of life as a celibate clergyman was impossibly challenging. Had he known the trials to come he might have left the classroom there and then. He took a waterproof coat from its hanger, folded it over his arm, closed the wardrobe, checked his apartment was smart and tidy, and left. He walked along the passage and down the rear exit stairs to the monastery car park. His rickety orange Volkswagen Beetle was waiting there. The engine coughed and sputtered, but somehow Docherty knew there'd be sufficient life in the old vehicle to take him where he wanted to go.

The scenic vistas of the Stoer peninsula flowed past as he drove west: rolling, boulder-strewn glens, deep tracts of pinewood.

So beautiful, so unspoiled, so virginal.

Virginal.

Not a good choice of phrase really, though in some ways, despite feeling it perverse of himself, Docherty was starting to resent the well of guilt-ridden despondency he'd dwelt in for so long now. The Roman Catholic Church hadn't just been his home; it had been his strength, his courage, his innermost being. He loved her deeply, believed in her absolutely – and yet now felt far removed from her, and even though he had undoubtedly disgraced her and had rightly been punished for that, he blamed the Church herself, at least partly.

How could she ask so much of her children? How could she expect strict adherence to impossible rules and not understand that attempts to observe this law in public would only lead to private defiance, which, owing to its hidden nature, would run without limit? How could the Church be so blind to the errors she herself had made?

But for all this, he *did* love her. It infuriated Docherty to hear her defamed, drove him to the vilest anger the way every unthinking, atheistic pipsqueak in Britain would heap calumnies on her without knowing any of the true facts, without having experienced the love or care she'd extended to millions.

None of that counted, it seemed, thanks to the follies of a few sexually misguided wretches; weak, confused creatures who should never have been ordained in the first place, who had only come to the Church to find sanctuary from the hardships of life. Docherty had to blink back tears, his vision of the narrow road dimming as the last vestige of sunlight retreated west. All because of this handful of undisciplined fools; these hateful, boorish oafs who'd lost control of their primitive urges!

Not that any of this excused his *own* deviations, of course – he couldn't just write himself off as a fool; that would be way too easy. And it certainly didn't forgive them. Only God forgave. And sometimes even that ultimate judge might respond with vengeance rather than sympathy.

There was only one recourse, Docherty had decided that morning – and now he affirmed it again as he drew into the small car park. Direct and determined action.

He climbed from the Volkswagen and pulled on his waterproof coat. The car park was otherwise deserted, which was understandable. The nearest town was Culkein, actually only a fishing village, and that was five miles away; beyond that, the next nearest 'real' town was Ullapool, which was closer to thirty-five miles away. As such, this spot was normally reserved for visitors: climbers, hikers and the like, and there were fewer and fewer of these as the year waned.

A gust of icy sea wind moaned down a gully leading away through piny crags. It set Docherty's waterproof rippling, and he was glad he'd thought to bring it. He crossed the car park to the foot of the gully, where there was a stile. He still had great affection for this place, he thought as he climbed over and ascended the zigzagging path. Though a Kirkcaldy man by origin, in Scotland's east lowlands, he had visited the far northwest numerous times as a boy, and spent many happy holidays here before the bitterness and frustrations of adulthood had pervaded his life.

Docherty's footfalls echoed on the stony footway as he strode uphill. He thought about other pilgrims, in harsher days and harsher climes, ascending towards forgiveness on their hands and knees, their blood smearing the rugged ground. Folly, in his opinion – to damage themselves in that way, when they had a duty to exist and ensure the existence of others. Not that the shoes he'd consciously opted to wear for this occasion were guaranteed to prevent him suffering injury. In his days as a young priest, when he'd brought school parties to the Highlands, he'd been as well-equipped as the next man – in his boots and his hardwearing canvas trousers, and his plaid shirt and his waxed jacket with the big hood that he could draw against the worst of the Atlantic gales. But it was important that none of that was on show now. Today it was the black shirt of office, the clerical collar, the thoroughly polished shoes.

When he reached the top, he threw off the waterproof coat. In front of him stood a waist-high railing, with a coin-operated telescope on a concrete pivot in its centre. Beyond that lay the vast, barren seascape of the northern Minch, rolling and exploding in the fading, reddish light, the sun a dying spark on its distant horizon.

With dull creaks in his knees and hips, Docherty clambered over the railing and walked the five feet to the edge of the cliff top, the wind tugging at his body. He stood there rocking, toes protruding over the brink. Below, by nearly three hundred feet, mountains of spume erupted from heaps of jagged, seaweed-covered rocks. Only vaguely visible far to the north stood the thumb-shaped Old Man of Stoer, the teetering sea-stack around which the ocean literally boiled. To the south, the arrow-thin beam of the Stoer lighthouse crossed and re-crossed the desolate wastes of water, and beyond that, lost in haze, lay the rugged headland of Rubha Mor.

It was a good thing visibility was failing, Docherty decided. No more distractions. No more happy memories with which to hamper himself. Of more importance now was the future – and what might lie in store. Self-destruction with sound mind was a terrible sin, and would incur severe punishment.

But then severe punishment would be the order of the day anyway. And maybe . . . just maybe, he could negate some of it by punishing himself first. He wasn't certain of that, but who knew how the Lord thought?

Anyway, the time for such rumination was over.

As he'd told himself on first arriving here, there was nothing for it now but direct, determined action.

At which point, electric light flooded over him from closer at hand.

For a crazy, near-hallucinogenic moment, Docherty imagined the distant eye of the lighthouse had sought him out, spearing its life-saving glow across acres of foam, as though to reassure him, to advise him he wasn't alone in his pain. But just as quickly, he understood otherwise. He swivelled around.

Three men, indistinguishable behind the light, had emerged onto the cliff top to his rear and had climbed the safety rail, against which they now casually leaned.

'Ready to make peace with God, your grace?' the man in the middle asked. He was the one holding the light. When he spoke it was in fluent English, though his accent was foreign – vaguely Germanic, or Scandinavian. Danish possibly.

'Not . . . not possible, I'm afraid,' Docherty replied confusedly. 'I've never even made peace with myself.'

'And which particular memory prevents this? Your casual abuse of holy women? Your gross misappropriation of diocese funds? Or that most heinous thing of all . . . that filthy service you purchased with those funds?'

'All . . . all these,' Docherty replied, dazed. After brief, absurd notions that in his moment of horror and agony he might be experiencing something transcendental, he now had no doubt who these men actually were.

'Repentance is the first step to forgiveness,' the man added.

231

'But I wonder how repentant you'd be had we not caught up with you?'

'I . . . I already told you . . . I've suffered every day.'

'But not sufficiently to hand yourself in?'

'What good would that have done?' Docherty wasn't sure why he was trying to explain this when he didn't believe it himself, but the words were so rehearsed they fell from his lips. 'It wasn't an offence I would ever commit again. I could atone for it better out here, among my people . . . to whom I had a duty.'

The man chuckled. 'There are certain things one must always rationalise to make them bearable.'

'It's not like that. I knew you would come . . . or someone like you.'

'You did?'

'You *had* to come. First they suspended me from office, then they dismissed me . . . I was mocked, scorned, publicly reviled. But that was never going to be enough. In my heart of hearts, I knew . . . my conscience told me. One can't commit offences so grievous, even secret ones, and expect to walk away unscathed.'

'You're a wise man, your grace, but I think your conscience may have driven you mad.'

Docherty glanced back over the cliff. Nothing down there was visible. It was a void, a maelstrom. 'When I heard about the violence in England, the shooting and killing connected to that fellow from the prison . . . I knew chaos had entered our world through the rent I and others like me opened. It could only be a matter of time . . .'

'Well . . .' The man spoke with an air of finality. 'The fact that you're ready to take your punishment can only be a good thing.' He strode forward.

Docherty wanted to clench his eyes shut, but inner guilt prevented him.

With his clean looks and blond windblown hair, the man did indeed possess the face of an angel. If not for that hideous scar. And that demonic smile. And that glinting blade in his gloved right hand.

Chapter 22

It wasn't long after eight in the morning when Nick Gribbins emerged yawning from the security booth, to find Heck showered and track-suited, turning sausages on a grill and cracking eggs into a pan.

'Fry-up?' Heck asked. 'You may as well . . . you lot are paying for it.'

'Okay,' Gribbins said warily. He wandered into the safe-house lounge, where Steph Fowler, having come downstairs first and polished off a bowl of muesli, was dividing her attention between the TV, on which she was channel-hopping, and her laptop, which sat on the coffee table, a Skype link open to the MIR at Scotland Yard.

In the kitchen, Heck dished up two plates of sausage, bacon, egg and beans, while shoving several slices of bread into the toaster. He'd benefited from a comfortable night in the four-poster. No doubt he'd needed it – he still felt battered and weary, but this was an undeniably restful environment.

He walked through into the lounge, handing Gribbins his food, along with some cutlery and a napkin. Gribbins grunted his thanks, and commenced to eat at the coffee table. Heck stood by the door to eat his own. 'Sorry about the hand,' he said. 'Seriously. I thought you were the Nice Guys.'

Gribbins shrugged. 'You got dragged through the gutters after. Seems like we're square.'

'What's the actual damage?'

'Hairline fracture of the metacarpals. Not too serious, but it hurts.'

'Surprised they're letting you work.'

'We're totally pulled out. Every man and woman we've got is on this job. When I volunteered for light duties, they couldn't very well refuse.'

'Light duties?' Heck said.

'Lighter than they'd be out there . . . on the frontline.'

'Well . . . yeah.' Heck couldn't argue with that, and it irked him. He too was wasting away in here whilst the real battle was being fought elsewhere.

Suddenly, Fowler hit the volume control on the television.

'Police are playing down reports that the body of a man found this morning in the mouth of a sewer connecting with the River Thames, close to Execution Dock in Wapping, is linked with the recent spate of shootings and bombings,' the news anchorwoman said.

The screen displayed a police launch bobbing on a mud-brown tide at the foot of a dockland wall. Police divers were clustered in the mouth of a weed-fringed vent.

'The man, who is reported to have died by drowning, has not yet been formally identified,' the anchorwoman added.

'Your guy?' Gribbins asked Heck.

'Could be.' Heck watched the screen, but there were no further developments on that particular story, and the scene switched to a live broadcast from the ambush site near Gull Rock. He took his crockery back through to the kitchen, slid it into the dishwasher, and returned to the lounge. 'I'm off to check the pool,' he said.

Gribbins shrugged as he mopped his plate.

Fowler glanced through the French windows, beyond which the day looked cool and grey. 'In this weather? You'll catch your death.'

'Just having a look.' Heck walked towards the windows. 'If it needs scooping, I'll scoop. Not hanging around here, catching updates on a case I'm not involved with.'

'Those French windows are deadlocked,' Fowler said. 'Use the back door. It opens from the inside. The key-code to get back in is 78745.'

Heck nodded, leaving the room and heading down the hall. Behind him, Fowler took her place in the security booth, where she could no doubt watch his every move on camera. He left the house via the kitchen, and set off up the extensive garden by a paved central path. As he did, he tapped out a number on his re-energised mobile.

'Incident Room,' Shawna McCluskey answered.

'It's me,' he said.

'Oh great.' She lowered her voice. 'This is all I need.'

'Relax . . . just a quick chat.'

'That's what I was afraid of.'

'No one's said I'm not allowed to talk to people.'

'That's what you think. Gemma reckons the more incommunicado you remain, the safer you'll be.'

'She doesn't even trust *you*?'

'She's just being cautious.'

'Fair enough . . . I'll make this quick. What's the skinny on that corpse found in the sewer at Wapping?'

'Hellfire! I'm definitely not supposed to talk to you about the case.'

'What . . . Gemma doesn't trust *me* either? That's funny, considering I'm the one who's supposed to be in danger.'

'You know what it's like. If these Nice Guy bastards get hold of you . . .'

'You mean if they grab me and torture me, I won't be able to tell them anything? So they'll just keep torturing and torturing . . . until I expire? At which point they'll have learned precisely nothing.'

She hesitated. 'That's the gist of it, I suppose.'

'That doesn't sound remotely like Gemma, and you know it. What's going on, Shawna? At least tell me about the body.'

She lowered her voice even more. 'We're pretty sure it belongs to one of those blokes who bushwhacked you yesterday. The one who fell off the gantry.'

'Black fella? Big bugger, well built?'

'Correct.'

'Wearing a leather jacket and jeans?'

'Yeah.'

'That's him. What've you found out?'

'Nothing so far. We're running his prints and his DNA. Failing that, we'll go for facial recognition.'

'He had no ID?' Heck asked.

'A few bits of sodden paper stuffed in one of his pockets, which don't make any sense. But no wallet, no driving licence . . . if he did have that stuff, he lost it while he was being washed through the sewers.'

'Get back to me as soon as you know something, yeah?'

'Heck . . . I can't.'

'Shawna, this is bullshit. I'm hardly going to blab my mouth off! I just want to know what's going on. I think you guys owe me that much.'

'My job could be on the line here.'

'If anything happens, I'll put my hand up . . . I'll take the fall for it.'

'Oh yeah. If you fell in a barrel of monkey shit, you'd come out clean.'

'I'll sort it, I promise you. Just call me back, yeah?'

'Maybe . . .' She sounded unsure. 'If I get the chance.'

She hung up, leaving him perplexed. He'd always liked to think he and Shawna enjoyed a special relationship. Originally officers in the Greater Manchester Police, they'd known each other from the earliest days of their careers, and after finding their way to London and the Serial Crimes Unit by different routes, had renewed that friendship fiercely. A fellow child of the industrial Northwest, Shawna shared many of Heck's blue-collar traits: she was a roughneck but she looked good; she was streetwise but witty; she also knew her job inside-out and she didn't get fazed or upset. But she was running scared at present, and Heck felt he detected SOCAR behind that rather than Gemma.

This whole thing had a whiff of the extraordinary. How much power had SOCAR been given? They had Gemma, one of the most respected senior managers in the entire National Crime Group, running around at their beck and call, imposing draconian measures she'd never have countenanced were she in control herself.

He'd now drifted almost the entire length of the garden, passing greenhouses and potting sheds, and finally found himself opening a gate and entering a patio area, about fifty yards by forty and set against the rear wall of the property, which, like the others, was comprised of a ten-foot barbed wire fence and then a twelve-foot brick perimeter with spikes and electrical wiring. In the middle of the patio lay a rectangular swimming pool, about twenty yards long.

Heck strolled forward. Unlike everything else here, which was either new or renovated, the pool was a relic of the past – a leftover from whenever this place had been a working farm or a holiday home. It was uncovered, its surface clear and still, but its tiled walls were mottled with algae, its depths greenish and gloomy, filled with several years' worth of autumn leaves. At the south end, there was a wooden storage shed, presumably crammed with tools and the usual poolside junk, at the north end a two-stage diving tower. This was a relic too, a mass of creaky scaffolding, thick with rust. Its lower and upper diving boards, located at about six and twelve feet up respectively, were wooden, but damp with mildew. Still distracted by thoughts of Shawna, Heck leaned against it, and the entire structure lurched to the left – it was mounted on a broad, square base with a wheel in each corner. There was a plastic foot-break over the right rear-wheel, but when he tried to apply this, it snapped.

'Bloody death trap,' he muttered.

He was about to head back to the house when the patio gate creaked open and Steph Fowler came through it. The look on her face was ice-cold.

'Something wrong?' he asked.

'Yeah . . . you.' She held out her hand. 'Give me your phone.'

Heck shoved the mobile into his pocket. 'I was told I could keep my phone.'

'That privilege has been revoked.'

'Privilege?'

'We're not discussing this.' She reached under her pinstriped jacket, and drew her Glock from its holster. 'Just give me the fucking phone.'

'Are you taking the piss?'

'Are you? Do you think we're deaf and dumb, or what?'

'You were listening in to that last call, weren't you? Of all the sneaky little . . .'

'You can spare me the pseudo-morality!' She pointed the pistol at him. 'Give me the phone . . . right now!'

'Or what? You're going to shoot me?'

A look of doubt etched her face, as if drawing her weapon so soon had been a mistake.

'Kind of defeats the object of me being here, doesn't it?' he said. 'Or does it?'

'The phone!'

'Are you seriously telling me you've bugged the phones in the MIR? Frank Tasker's put wire-taps on his own team? How much power has this bloody guy got?'

'It's a reasonable precaution. The last time the Nice Guys were investigated, more women died because a mole on the police force was providing inside information.'

'For Christ's sake,' Heck said, 'that mole is dead! Remember Jim Laycock? Remember him getting battered to a pulp?'

Now Gribbins appeared, looking rumpled and sallow-faced. He tucked his shirt into his belt at the same time as drawing his Glock. 'The phone, Heckenburg.'

Seeing no gain in being relentlessly awkward, Heck handed his phone over.

Gribbins took it – and slung it into the deep end of the swimming pool. 'Let's hope no one needs you urgently,' he chuckled.

Heck gazed at him blankly, and then at the pool.

'Don't do anything stupid,' Fowler warned him.

'Anything *else* stupid,' Gribbins corrected her.

'You mean as stupid as *that*?' Heck wondered. 'Throwing away *my* personal property!'

'Oooh . . .' Gribbins pulled a face. 'I'm really scared.'

'We're under orders to keep you incommunicado from here on,' Fowler said, re-holstering her firearm. 'Back to the house please.'

Gribbins dressed his weapon down, but didn't put it away. When Heck sloped across the patio, Gribbins took him by the scruff of his neck and frogmarched him.

'Even if your gaffer has a genuine concern about security,' Heck said, 'where was the harm in me talking to Shawna McCluskey?' They made no response. 'Look . . . she only confirmed what I already knew. What we all of us already knew.'

'Nice try,' Gribbins said. 'But your mate has already had the bollocking of her life and been sent home pending formal disciplinary procedures.'

Heck stiffened as he walked. 'That's bloody ridiculous!' When they reached the back door, Fowler tapped in the security code. The door clicked open. 'Just answer me one question,' Heck said. 'Is this a safehouse or a sodding prison?'

'It's a safehouse,' Fowler said as Gribbins shoved him inside. 'You've still got full freedom of movement . . . indoors.'

'I can't go out to play in the garden anymore?'

'After that trick with the phone?' Gribbins scoffed.

'Not without supervision,' Fowler said. 'You know why? Because you've just proved that you can't be trusted.'

'If it's a safehouse I can walk out of that front door and go home any time I want!'

She shook her head. 'Not if it's likely to impede the enquiry. For the same reason, you're now being denied access to the internet as well.'

'Hey, how can I live without my daily fix of *Stormtroopers in Stockings*?'

'These are the new rules, Heckenburg,' she said. 'Attempt to break them and we'll arrest you for obstructing an enquiry. And then it'll all get done the hard way.'

'Which we're *that* close to already,' Gribbins added. 'If for no other reason than this latest kerfuffle has disturbed my beauty sleep.'

'It shows,' Heck grunted.

'And here was us, finally starting to think you were alright.'

'Well, they told me you were anyone's for a fry-up.'

'Just keep that smart-mouth going, pal!' Gribbins said. 'And you'll spend the rest of your time here handcuffed to the radiator.'

They might be playing it heavy, Heck realised, but they looked twitchy too. He was giving them a hard time: sending them mixed messages, winding them up – but it was more than that. They were operating well beyond the realms of normality here. DS Fowler had just given him the rules – rules they were making up on the hoof, rules that were unlikely ever to see him brought in front of a disciplinary, let alone a court.

For all that, it was another ten minutes before Heck would decide he'd had enough.

'DS Fowler or DS Gribbins please!' came an impatient voice as they filed into the lounge. Detective Inspector O'Dowd was on the Skype link. His tie was loose, his shirt scruffy, his jowly, hangdog face offset by preposterously short, neat, dark hair, which, though it wasn't actually a toupee, had always resembled one.

'Here sir,' Fowler said, sitting in front of the camera.

'What's been going on?' he asked suspiciously.

'Nothing to worry about.'

'Heckenburg?'

'All under control, sir.'

'You got that message from the boss?'

'We did, yes.'

'He went batshit when he found out Heckenburg has been ringing people.'

'It's okay sir. We won't take our eyes off him from now on.'

'Don't let him pull a fast one.'

'It's okay, sir . . . he's settling down now.'

'Yeah,' Heck said from the doorway. 'With my pacifier and rattle.'

'Good,' O'Dowd said, either not hearing Heck or ignoring him. 'Because the wheels are coming off here. We've had three more suspicious deaths in the last twenty-four hours.

A drowning up in Scotland, a hit-and-run in Portsmouth – bloke got run over seven times by the same vehicle – and now we learn some poor sod in Yorkshire got choked to death on his own Malacca cane.'

'Malacca cane?' Heck blurted, crossing the room.

'Only after he'd been beaten and burned first,' O'Dowd added. 'Poor bastard's totally unrecognisable. Didn't help that he then got dumped ninety feet down a pothole. That info's just come in . . . it was up on the North Yorks moors, near Whernside.'

'Sounds like they didn't want that one found,' Heck said, puzzled. 'Did we get more of these Greek signatures, sir?'

'Apparently we did in Portsmouth. It was painted on the road in blood. We got something similar in Scotland, we think . . . nothing in Yorkshire that I've been informed about . . .' O'Dowd suddenly seemed to realise that Heck was standing behind Fowler. 'What the devil, Heckenburg? Why am I talking to you? Was he earwigging all this time? Get him away from there!'

Gribbins approached, but Heck moved away of his own accord.

'Haven't heard about these other murders on the news, sir,' Fowler said.

'The boss has been talking to the press, and they've agreed an embargo – from ten o'clock this morning. The public were starting to get jittery.'

Heck strode back to the laptop. 'Can you just clarify, sir . . . this bloke who was murdered in Yorkshire, the one who wasn't marked with the BDEL sign. You say he was beaten and burned before they shoved a Malacca cane down his throat?'

'Heckenburg, this has nothing to do with you, okay? You're off duty.'

'So they gave him a going-over first,' Heck murmured.

'What are you driving at?' Fowler asked.

'If I had my way, he wouldn't even be driving a patrol car,' O'Dowd interrupted. 'He'd be on foot again in a tall hat. Don't tell him anything. If he gets shirty, lock him in his fucking bedroom. That's it for now. Just remember, you two have one job to do down there and one job only. Don't screw it up.'

He hit a button, and the laptop screen went blank.

There was a prolonged, tingling silence. At least, that was the way it seemed to Heck as he turned to Gribbins and Fowler, who for some reason were regarding him expectantly. His thoughts were so scattered that it took him several seconds to get them in order, but one thing was suddenly glaringly clear – one thing he now could *not* do was reveal what he had just realised: namely that the Nice Guys hadn't rescued Mike Silver six days ago; they'd ab ucted him. And now they had murdered him.

Piece by piece, it was slowly dawning on Heck.

First of all, the mere fact the Nice Guys had known those prison interviews were underway was worrying. But it was even more worrying they'd learned some kind of progress was being made – so much progress they'd suddenly felt it necessary to intervene. On the face of it, one of three things had happened: Silver himself had let it slip to a fellow inmate that some kind of deal was in the offing – which was impossible to imagine given the danger that would put him in; or Gemma had let it slip in SCU – which was equally difficult to imagine, because if a secret had to be kept for strict professional purposes, Gemma would keep it; or Frank Tasker had let it slip in SOCAR – this was also hard to believe, considering Tasker's obsessive concerns about security. The only other possibility was that they had yet another mole on board.

Laycock had only been the first.

And yet it got worse.

When he'd surmised the Nice Guys had come to the UK

to clean house, Heck hadn't realised just how thoroughly. Evidently, they were here to do it properly, to literally sterilise the place. Any weak links were to be eliminated; not just former clients, and former allies like Jim Laycock, but now their former boss as well – though they'd only got rid of him after beating and burning him, presumably to elicit information concerning his recent discussions with a certain duo of very senior police officers. Whatever the Nice Guys had learned from that torture session, it clearly hadn't alarmed them – because they were still here. Though to be absolutely sure Silver had revealed nothing, they'd next have to pursue the only other people who were party to those prison interviews – namely Gemma and Tasker. Of course, if word reached the Nice Guys about the police finding Mike Silver's body, they might expect a protective cordon to get thrown around Gemma and Tasker, putting them out of reach. In which case, their default position would almost certainly be to run, evacuating all their hidey-holes – both here and overseas – taking all evidence with them. An entire syndicate of gunmen and torturers, with direct contacts to networks of sadists, slavers, rapists, murderers and sex-traffickers all over the world would disappear from under British police noses like the proverbial puff of smoke.

It was a nightmare scenario. Heck either kept his suspicions to himself about the new dead guy being Silver – and in effect allowed the Nice Guys to go after Gemma; or he told SOCAR everything, in which case the new mole would then report to the Nice Guys and provoke them into running.

Only one solution was possible.

'I need to speak to DSU Piper,' he said. 'No one else. Just her.'

Gribbins shrugged. 'You ain't got a phone anymore, pal. And you sure aren't borrowing mine.'

Heck glanced at Fowler. A second passed and then,

reluctantly, she took her phone from her jacket pocket. 'Not in private,' she said.

'For Christ's sake . . .'

She pulled it back. 'Not in private.'

'Listen . . .' Heck tried to keep his voice steady. 'It's very important that you stop being a robot and following orders to the letter, and give me some leeway . . .'

'We gave you plenty of leeway . . . and you chucked it back in our face.'

'DS Fowler, I'm pleading with you . . .'

'I'm sorry, DS Heckenburg. Unless you're prepared to play by our rules . . . we're done here.' She hit the off switch on her laptop, closed it and tucked it under her arm. 'For the time being there are no more private conversations. You've become too much of a security risk.'

She headed out to the hall, Gribbins following her, closing the door behind them.

Neither had been gone more than a minute before there came an explosive shattering of plate glass. Gribbins yanked the door open and charged back through, Fowler following, both with pistols drawn – both staggering to a halt at the sight of the gaping, jagged hole where the French windows had once been, and the twisted wreck of the coffee table lying on the other side.

Heck was already fifty yards up the garden, sprinting.

The duo hurried in pursuit, pistols drawn but neither of them rushing madly. Heck had a small head-start on them, but he couldn't go anywhere. This was what they told themselves – so it was a quite a shock when they burst through the patio gate into the swimming pool area and found the storage shed open, but more important than that, the diving tower wheeled up to the rear boundary wall, its upper diving board protruding over the top into the woods beyond, and no sign at all of Mark Heckenburg.

Chapter 23

Heck charged five hundred yards through tangled thickets, ignoring the motion cameras as they turned on their pivots to watch him, before reaching the rearmost outer boundary, which was composed mainly of thickly woven hawthorn and stood to a height of nine feet.

Hefting the shears he'd brought from the shed, he went at the foliage hard, slashing and hacking his way through its outer carapace, burrowing on and on until he was clean through to the other side, though it cost him, his face and hands scratched, his blue flock tracksuit plucked and torn. Beyond it lay open, rolling farmland, stripped bare of crops and covered with stubble. Heck plunged across, tripping, stumbling. On the far side, he waded a brook that came almost to his knees, then clambered a low rock wall and found himself on another winding country lane. In no particular direction, he ran.

It felt ridiculous to be doing this – an invitation to disaster, but one thing was certain: there was no time for idling around in the company of Tweedledum and Tweedledee. He knew he was disrespecting the chain of command, not to mention breaking personal promises again, for which there might be severe consequences, but some things were more important than that.

He crossed a humpback bridge, and on the other side of that found a payphone on the verge. He entered the booth, grabbed the phone and asked the operator to reverse the charges to Gemma's personal number. It cut straight to voicemail. He spent several costly seconds deliberating about who to call next. The only other number that came to mind was a certain landline in Battersea.

'Shawna McCluskey,' came the response.

Her tone was thick, nasal, as though she'd been crying, but it cracked with disbelief when the operator asked if she'd accept reversed charges from a Mr Heckenburg. There was fierce agreement, and the call went through.

'You bastard!' she said. 'I've been suspended because of you! *For the first time in my sodding career, I've been bloody suspended!*'

'Alright, I'm sorry,' he said, 'I promise I'll make it up to you.'

'Oh, yeah, how? You're not a bloody miracle worker, Heck! You're the top man when it comes to saving your own arse though!'

'Shawna, please . . . listen to me, I haven't got very long.'

'Thanks to you, I've got all the time in the world . . .'

'Come on love, Lancashire loyalties, eh?'

'Oh, is that what you've rung me for? To bag another favour? Not to apologise?'

'Both . . . if you'll let me.'

'Make it quick,' she said sulkily.

Heck glanced over his shoulder to ensure the lane was still deserted. 'First of all . . . I've been trying to get Gemma and there's no response.'

'There won't be. She's in the air by now, on her way to Scotland. She actually rang me from Heathrow to tell me to go home. *She sent me home, Heck!*'

'I know, I understand . . .'

'Yeah, course you do.'

'Look, I'll call Gemma later, but if she speaks to you first, tell her to watch her back.'

'What are you talking about?'

'No details . . . no time for that. Just tell her to keep her eyes open. She and Frank Tasker might be in trouble.'

'As much trouble as I'm in?'

'Shawna, I'll say it again . . . I am sorry about this. I'd no idea Tasker was using such underhand tactics. But it's totally my fault you're in this crap-hole. I'll take full responsibility, I promise. I'll beg and crawl to Gemma when all this is over. I'll stick my own head in the noose voluntarily.'

'She's not going to give you up for me,' Shawna snapped. 'She's mad about you!'

That threw him a little. 'That . . . erm, that's rubbish, okay?'

'It isn't rubbish. But it doesn't surprise me you don't know. Like all fellas, you haven't got a bloody clue. Anyway . . .' Stoically, she attempted to get a grip on her anger. 'Even if it was rubbish, I don't want that either. You're a better detective than me, Heck. You may as well stay on the case and do these Nice Guy bastards some damage.'

'I intend to . . . I promise. But when it's over I'm going to get you out of this.'

'Course, I feel it incumbent on me – as an *ex-friend* of yours – to mention that half the cops in Britain are already after this gang. Every firearms unit going is now attached to the case.'

'The more the merrier. The main thing is you said something earlier. About bits of paper on that body in the sewer. Said they didn't make any sense . . .?'

'Yeah. They'd been soaked in effluent. Most of the ink had been washed off.'

'Was any of it legible?'

'I've hardly got that info to hand now, have I?'

'You can't remember?'

'I suppose I ought to. As official Statement Reader . . . the one supposed to make sense of this whole mess.' She sighed as she threw her thoughts back. 'I seem to remember letters were missing, but what was there said something like "whips n stot".'

'What?'

She repeated it, spelling it letter by letter. 'Told you it didn't make sense. There were three dockets in total, and that was printed along the top of each one.'

'Dockets?'

'Yeah . . . or till receipts. Square bits of paper.'

'And you say it was printed?'

'Like a stamp or letterhead.'

Heck pondered this. 'It didn't mean anything to anyone?'

'No one in the MIR.'

'And these three dockets were in the dead guy's pocket?'

'Yeah . . . just crammed in there and forgotten.'

'Well, the fact there was three of them means he had more than a passing interest in wherever it was they came from.'

'So?' she said.

Heck didn't immediately respond. 'You know . . . that term, "whips n stot", it sounds vaguely familiar to me.'

'You're a mine of useless information. If *you* can't suss it, no one can.'

'I'm serious.'

'So am I . . .'

A crunch of gravel drew Heck's attention outside, where a silver-grey Ford Focus Titanium was pulling up in the lay-by.

'You're a gem, Shawna,' he said.

'Somewhat tarnished . . . thanks to you.'

'How's Gary?'

'It was touch and go, but he'll make it. So if you don't do it for anyone else . . . get the bastards for him.'

'Wilco.' He hung up and stepped outside.

Gribbins, his gun concealed beneath his cord jacket, clambered from the passenger seat. Fowler came around the front. They regarded him warily, but with some relief.

Heck almost laughed. 'You two think this is over?'

'Don't be stupid!' Fowler warned him.

But he'd already taken off, dashing around the other side of the booth, vaulting a low wall and sprinting into the undergrowth.

'*Bloody shit!*' he heard Gribbins bellow.

Fowler's whipcrack voice followed. 'Nick . . . *NICK!*'

'*Get in the car . . . head him off at the Canoe Club! This time he's fucking had it!*'

Heck ploughed on, dodging around trees and through patches of briar, crashing into and out of dense masses of undergrowth. The woodland was muddy, and he slid constantly, landing hard on his back at least once. Not far behind, foliage threshed as another heavy body forced its way through. From Gribbins's London accent, he wasn't a local, so he couldn't know this area very well – but he'd said something about a Canoe Club. He must have a vague knowledge.

The ground dipped steeply. Heck plunged down it on his knees, tobogganing through heaps of soggy leaves, rolling when he hit the bottom. He'd blundered into a woodland trough, which he scrambled up the other side of, using roots to assist him, skidding in mud again as he stumbled onto a path. It bisected the line he'd been running in, heading roughly southwest to northeast. There was a further crashing in the leafage behind – he couldn't loiter.

He took the path, heading northeast. A timber footbridge led over a deep, fast stream; probably the same brook he'd waded earlier. Forty yards after that, the path began to curve north rather than northeast, and then northwest. Heck glanced left, seeing lower ground covered with impenetrable underbrush. There was a rankness in there, insects whining. It was some kind of woodland basin, wherein the stream may have burst its banks, turning everything boggy. Was that why the path arched around it? He kept running, wondering why he could no longer hear sounds of pursuit. The path's curve sharpened; it veered west, turning at such an angle it would soon be heading southwest. Was he running around in a circle purely to avoid getting his feet wet? It only occurred to him belatedly that Gribbins might take no such precaution – and right on cue, the big guy broke out of the underbrush in front of him, his corduroy trousers muddied to their knees. He was red-faced and sweating, his curly hair hanging in tendrils, but his lips twisted into an angry smile.

Heck slid to a halt. 'Don't be daft,' he said. 'Your arm's in a cast.'

Gribbins pulled the Glock from his shoulder-holster, cocked it and pointed it. 'Won't stop me using this.'

'Gribbins! Try ditching your "I'm a twat" badge just for a minute. You're gonna shoot an unarmed fugitive? A fellow cop! Even Frank Tasker would have trouble explaining that.'

'Don't make me do it,' Gribbins advised him.

'I'm not making you do anything.' Heck walked towards him. 'You'll be doing it, yourself.' The moist flesh twitched between Gribbins's brows. 'Your call, pal.'

Gribbins threw the Glock aside and aimed a haymaker with his left hand. Heck blocked it and caught him on the collar bone with a downward counter-punch.

'*Fuck me . . .*' the big guy gasped, sinking to his knees.

'You alright?' Heck backed off. 'Look . . . you've got an excuse. You've got a broken hand . . . so let me by. Say you couldn't find me.'

'Like you would . . .?' Gribbins rose gingerly to his feet.

They grappled like wrestlers, but Gribbins, though he was bigger, was immensely disadvantaged. Heck twisted him around and threw him – Gribbins hit the ground heavily, the wind whooshing from his chest. But instead of lying there, he got straight back to his knees, and then to his feet.

Heck shook his head. 'I don't bloody believe this.'

'You know the rules . . .' Gribbins lurched at him again. 'The only ones you can let go are the ones who've beaten the absolute crap out of you.'

Heck swung a left, but Gribbins ducked it, and barrelled into his midriff, wrapping bearlike arms around him, sending him tottering backwards. Heck clamped his fists and slammed them down like a mallet between Gribbins's shoulders; once, twice, the third time knocking him down to the ground. Heck overbalanced too – he tottered from the path, falling full length into mulch and brambles. By the time he was back on his feet, Gribbins was up as well, but stooped and grimacing, drunk with pain.

'Think you've done your bit,' Heck said, circling around him.

Gribbins lunged for Heck's collar with his good hand. Heck drove in a right, but smacked the plaster cast, raised as a shield. He yelled, yanked his hand back. Gribbins struck with the head, butting him – it only glanced the right cheekbone, but still stung, and made the retaliatory knee Heck rammed into his groin all the sweeter.

Gribbins gagged and staggered away. Heck followed with a crisp right, which caught him cleanly on the side of the jaw, snapping his head around. The big guy slumped to the ground, mouth running blood, eyelids fluttering closed.

Panting, Heck dropped to one knee, feeling the carotid in Gribbins's throat. It pulsed normally. Gribbins groaned but remained unconscious. Heck rummaged inside his jacket pockets, finding what he was looking for: handcuffs. He took the inert form by its left leg and hauled it across the path, where he rolled it over into the recovery position, and then clapped the first bracelet around its left ankle and the other around a root arching up from the ground. A further search of Gribbins's jacket located the handcuff key. Heck tossed it away into the trees, before searching again – only to come up with an empty holster.

Gribbins had thrown the Glock somewhere, but it was anyone's guess where. Neither had really been watching, and there was no time to go foraging now.

Heck checked Gribbins one final time – his vital signs were in order, and patted him on the head. 'Had you down as all mouth and no kecks, pal. But you've impressed me. And that doesn't come cheap.'

He traipsed on along the path, still unsure which direction he was headed in, or what he was actually going to do. The woodland opened, and he found himself on the broad bank of an expansive river, almost certainly the Avon. It flowed deep and glassy, emerald fronds streaming like tresses of hair under its surface. On the far side, which was maybe a hundred yards away, there were a couple of houses with a car parked outside.

Heck glanced along the river in either direction. Some eighty yards to his left, a steel footbridge with latticework sides extended to the other shore. On the right, closer, he saw a row of boatsheds, several kayaks beached on a pebbly slope and a tall steel rack with paddles arranged on it and a hi-viz coat hanging at one end. Evidently, this was the Canoe Club, but there didn't seem to be anyone around. The sheds were closed and padlocked. About thirty yards beyond the sheds, the path veered inland between trees, connecting to an open stretch of tarmac. This looked like a car park, but at present it was deserted. Heck gazed across the river to the houses again, eyeing the parked car, not liking what he was thinking. He glanced left at the bridge. The riverside path led straight up to it. Slowly, he began walking that way, brushing off fragments of thorn and leaf. He was about fifty yards short of the bridge, at a point where the path ramped up, the riverside turning from a slope into a brick embankment, when DS Fowler stepped from the bushes.

'For a so-called top detective, you're very predictable,' she said. Then she noted the swelling under his left eye. 'What's happened to Nick?'

Heck shrugged. 'Gone to that great karate lesson in the sky.'

'*You piece of shit!*' She yanked the pistol from under her jacket.

'Joke!' he said, showing empty hands. 'He's chained to a root back in those woods. You'll need to go and help him.'

Slowly, suspiciously, she lowered the gun. 'Turn around.'

He did as instructed, and she came up behind. He heard a slither of leather as she slotted her weapon into its holster. 'Don't try anything. Just remember . . .'

'I know . . . you're a fifth dan.'

She grabbed the nape of his neck and pushed him. 'Show me . . . now!'

He proceeded. 'Don't you think you should actually arrest me? Make this official.'

'That depends what state Nick's in. If he's in a bad way, I'll be arresting you . . . you can guarantee that. Fuck Frank Tasker and fuck Gemma Piper!'

'You really are a potty-mouth, you know that?'

'Shut up!' She shoved the back of his left shoulder.

He toppled forward. She attempted to grab him to keep him upright and he snatched her left arm, twisting it into a goose-neck. But as DS Fowler had threatened, she was better at this sort of thing than he was. Before he'd managed either to turn her or drive her to the ground, she'd wriggled free and caught him with three rapid blows, the first to his instep, the second to the median nerve in his forearm and the third to his solar plexus. Agog with pain, he staggered to the edge of the footway.

'No you don't!' She locked an arm around his neck to prevent him falling.

But Heck wasn't falling, plus he enjoyed a height and weight advantage – so when he dropped to his right knee and ducked his right shoulder, gravity did the rest. Fowler slid forward and over him, and though she kept hold of his tracksuit top, he merely had to unzip it. It tore loose, and she plummeted ten feet, body-slamming the river, before vanishing beneath its surface.

Heck rose shakily to his feet, prodding at his numbed arm. Sensation was only slowly returning to it. In reality, this was all he needed. Now he'd definitely attract attention, naked from the waist up. He remembered the waterproof coat he'd seen back at the Canoe Club, and was about to head back when a spluttering shout caught his attention.

Fowler had re-emerged, but the river's current had already taken her out of reach of the wall. Superficially, the Avon was a calm body of water, flowing smoothly and slowly, but it was seventy-five miles in length, and an awful lot of water travelled down it, which might explain why the policewoman was being pulled inexorably out into the middle and pushed downstream with increasing speed. She briefly ducked under the surface again, and reappeared splashing and choking.

'For Christ's sake!' he called. 'Just swim to the side.'

'Can't,' she gasped, a broth of brackish water bursting from her lips.

'You're not telling me you can't swim . . . I don't sodding believe it!'

Heck kicked his trainers off and hit the water straddle-legged.

It wasn't merely the cold that took his breath away: he went deep and had to kick his way up through the greenish gloom, breaking the surface to discover that the current, which wasn't just strong but swirling, had already lugged him thirty yards from the embankment. Fowler was a significant distance ahead, splashing frantically, drifting ever further into midstream.

Heck set off after her in a front crawl, the force of the river adding invisible flippers to his feet. By the time she passed beneath the bridge, he was only about twenty yards behind, but the overarching steel amplified her chokes and screams. He saw her sink underneath again, a single hand flailing. He swam harder, the iciness of the current dwindling as he worked his muscles, generating extra heat.

When she briefly re-surfaced, she was ten yards beyond the bridge. Open meadows lay to either side, dotted with cattle. The banks were flatter, but swampy, thick with bulrushes, which would make it difficult getting Fowler ashore if she was in a bad way. He glanced up, again spotting only her hands as they churned the water to foam. Then they too vanished, at which point Heck plunged under, changing to breaststroke, driving himself forward with a big frog-kick – and catching sight of her in the murk, turning upside down as she struggled and convulsed.

He dived deeper as he approached, and then kicked himself upward, catching her torso in the cradle of his arm. She clamped to him, wrapping arms and legs around him like an octopus, impeding his progress. But he'd been expecting this. He levered her off his body with his elbow, but fixed a talon-like grip on her left armpit as he struck for the surface.

They broke out side by side, Heck gasping, Fowler gagging.

'Oh God . . . Jesus,' she coughed, threshing against him.

He manoeuvred himself behind her and clapped a hand under her chin. 'Lie back!'

'Oh Jesus . . .'

'Lie back! Do it now or I'll let you drown!'

She did as instructed and he was able to backstroke towards shore, towing her behind him. She continued to cough and twitch, but had the presence of mind to cease struggling and lie level on the water. He glanced behind. They were about twenty yards from land, but still moving due southwest. They'd bypassed the swampy area, and a lengthy stone quay had appeared. There was a recess in the middle of it, through which timber steps led down into the water. Heck adjusted position, steering them towards this. River weed brushed his legs and feet, and they hit the stair side-on. It was slimy and rickety, but Heck raised his haunches and slid himself up onto it, ascending backwards, hauling Fowler by the collar of her jacket. She was limp as a doll, wheezing heavily. Her black hair had come loose, and hung over her shoulders in sodden, glossy tangles.

'Here,' he said, pulling her onto the riverside path, pulling off her jacket, which had already rucked downward, twisting her arms at her back. At the same time, he covertly slid the Glock from her shoulder-holster and stuck it into the back of his tracksuit trousers.

She fell onto her face, shoulders heaving.

'And you're supposed to be a fifth dan,' he said, searching the jacket. 'Unbelievable.'

'They weren't training me to fight . . . to fight fishes, were they?' she stammered.

'You're lucky you didn't fall into the river where I grew up. The toxicology report on your corpse would be off the scale.'

'Fall in?' She coughed again and tried to get up. 'You call that falling in . . . you bastard!'

'Let me help.' He leaned down, and in a quick movement snapped one handcuff to her left ankle, and the other to a steel mooring-ring in the quayside.

'What . . .?' She glanced uncomprehendingly down her leg. Slow realisation dawned. 'What . . . *what the fuck do you think you're doing?*'

Heck stepped back as he continued to search her jacket. *'Is this some kind of sick joke?'* She went for her holster, only to find it empty. Her expression changed from angered outrage to utter disbelief. 'You're mad . . . that's the only explanation. You're fucking mad, Heckenburg!'

'It's been said,' he agreed, pulling out four seventeen-round magazines.

Regulations stated that an armed officer was not supposed to draw more ammunition than two magazines per operation – not without special authorisation. Further evidence that SOCAR were playing well beyond the bounds of normality.

'You'll not get away with this,' Fowler said, as he shoved the magazines into his tracksuit trouser pockets. 'You'll just not. It's gone too far.'

'Not nearly far enough.' He dug her mobile phone out next, which he tossed into the river, and then a keyring. As well as the keys to the car and her handcuffs, it had two electronic fobs attached to it. He turned and set off along the path.

'Hey . . . wait!' Fowler shouted. She lobbed handfuls of grit after him. Her voice rose to a screech. *'Heckenburg! Don't leave me like this . . . what if some pervert comes along?'*

'God help him,' Heck said over his shoulder.

'Christ's sake, it's only lunchtime! No one'll check on us until this evening!'

Heck halted in mid-stride.

Lunchtime.

Such an innocent word, and yet it kick-started a deluge of ideas. That phrase on the printed papers in the sewer guy's pocket – *whips n stot*. Okay, Heck didn't know what it meant, but he now recalled exactly where he'd heard the phrase, or something like it, before, because that had also been one lunchtime.

A couple of weeks ago now, but a memorable lunchtime all the same.

The lunchtime he'd spent in the company of PC Jerry Farthing at Gillbridge Avenue police station, Sunderland. Farthing himself had used the phrase: 'Mind my whips and fucking stottie.'

And yet still it made no sense. Some colloquialism of the Northeast maybe? But if he wanted to find out more, he knew where he had to go. He carried on down the path.

'Heckenburg . . . you're not leaving me like this!' Fowler shouted.

'No choice,' he called back.

'I'll catch my bloody death!'

'I'll send someone to find you.'

He followed the path back to the bridge. On the other side, he found his trainers. He brushed the grit and pebbles from the soles of his feet, and pulled them on.

When he reached the Canoe Club, it was still deserted, so he helped himself to the hi-viz coat. The car park wasn't as empty as he'd first thought – Fowler's Ford Titanium sat in a distant corner. The first of the two fobs opened it; the key brought it purring to life. He eased the classy ride up a twisting, gravelly track, back to a country lane he recognised. When he reached the outer gates to the safehouse, he opened them with the second fob and headed up the drive. Time wasn't on his side, and the temptation was simply to put as much distance between himself and here as he could – but now it was a case of less haste, more speed.

The same fob opened the second pair of gates, and then the front door. He hurried upstairs, peeled off his sopping clothes and jumped into the shower. After that, he pulled on a pair of clean jeans and trainers, a black roll-neck sweater and his black leather coat. The Glock and its magazines, he distributed between his two inside pockets. He also grabbed his wallet; he wasn't going to risk using his credit cards, but his warrant card might come in useful, plus it contained a hundred and fifty pounds in cash.

Initially, he headed south, making for Chippenham, which he reached in just under twenty minutes. Here, he parked outside a newsagent, and placed a quick nine-nine-nine call via the payphone next door.

'Two officers from the Serious Offenders Control and Retrieval special investigations unit need assistance,' he said curtly. 'You'll find both in the vicinity of the Canoe Club on the south bank of the River Avon, just east of Malmesbury. One officer is halfway along the woodland path connecting the club to the Malmesbury road. The other is also on the south bank, close to the Canoe Club. Take hacksaws.'

He climbed back into the car and this time headed north. The car provided a smooth ride as he took first the M4, then the A34, then the M40.

When he fiddled with the radio, it came on a station pre-tuned to low, easy jazz, which kind of suited his mood. Of course, he knew he couldn't keep the Titanium for long. An all-points would go out on it at the first opportunity. On top of that, they'd already have traced the call he'd made, and none of this meandering back and forth across the South Midlands would hold them at bay for long. As such, an hour and a half later, he swung into the car park attached to Northampton Railway Station. He parked at its farthest end, and bought himself a permit for five hours. He affixed this inside the windscreen, and checked around carefully before locking up.

He strongly doubted SOCAR would have caught up with him already, but the Nice Guys were another matter.

There were plenty of cars and vans parked up, but the only visible person was a bag-lady in a ragged dress, long scarf and colourful, woolly hat. She had a supermarket trolley filled with tin cans, and was adding more to it from one of the bins near the car park exit. Heck strolled past, not attracting her attention, and wasn't followed by anyone as he entered the station lobby, where he went straight to the desk and paid a sizeable chunk of cash for a one-way ticket to Sunderland.

Chapter 24

Frank Tasker waited alone in the canteen attached to the Police Scotland office at Inverness Airport. Beyond the windows, an EasyJet airliner taxied towards the runway, its jet-engines shrieking as the air-crew tested their RPMs at full power.

The SOCAR chief barely heard. He sipped at a beaker of coffee, so wrapped in his concerns that he completely failed to notice whether or not his usual stipulations that the beverage be hot and sweet had been satisfied.

Only after several minutes, did he sigh and glance at his watch.

It was mid-afternoon already. The Eurocopter scheduled to fly them the sixty-odd miles up the northwest coast was currently on its way from Glasgow City Heliport, and ought to be here soon. It was only an hour and a half's flight from Glasgow, but he felt useless, redundant – as if time was slipping away while the case spiralled out of control. The door banged open as Gemma entered, her raincoat over one arm, her own coffee balanced on a pile of plastic-covered documents.

She sat down at the table, opposite him.

'Anything?' he asked.

She'd spent the last half-hour engaged in a quick video conference with various bods back at the Yard, and now flipped open her pocket-book. 'The guy in the sewer is one Leon Fairbrother, aka "Bruno". Thirty-two years old. Well known to us as a juvenile, but later joined the Grenadier Guards, 16th Air Assault Brigade. He served with distinction during the invasion of Iraq, but in 2005 was investigated for the abuse of prisoners at Abu Naji, court-martialled and sentenced to two years in Colchester. He broke out after one, and went on to commit three armed robberies, during the course of which a security guard was shot and wounded. This was presumably to acquire sufficient funds with which to leave the country . . . which he duly did. He hasn't been heard of again until now.'

Tasker grunted. 'First time round it's Scorpion Company rejects. Now it's guardsmen turned blaggers. This Nice Guys Club's a regular Legion of the Damned, isn't it?'

She closed her book. 'It's the old story. We train these guys to fight. Afterwards, we don't know what to do with them. They don't know what to do with themselves.'

'My heart bleeds for them.' Tasker finished his coffee. 'Speaking of damned rankers, I take it Heckenburg hasn't been accounted for yet?'

Gemma shrugged, as worn out by the Heck business as Tasker was. They'd been hit by this particular bit of bad news via text the very second they'd disembarked from the aeroplane outside.

'They're trying to trace his route as we speak,' Gemma said. 'He borrowed a set of SOCAR wheels to make his initial getaway.'

'Borrowed?' Tasker snorted. 'That's one way of putting it. And how long is he likely to hang on to those?'

'No longer than he needs to.'

'Which knowing him, won't be long.' Tasker gave another sigh. 'The only reason I'm not bawling you out again, Gemma, is because it was my two monkeys who let him go. Are they badly hurt?'

'Gribbins is hurt . . . not *too* badly. Fowler was incapacitated.'

'She's supposed to be a sodding black belt! This bloody guy, I'm telling you . . .'

'You know, Frank . . . Heck's on our side.'

'For the present, yeah.' His brow knotted. 'But what about when the shit hits the fan? Who'll he be batting for then? I told you, Gemma . . . you should've pulled him back into bed at the first opportunity. Give him something else to think about, break his little heart . . . anything, so long as it took his mind off this.'

'The Nice Guys tried to frame him for a crime he didn't commit,' she said. 'They beat him and chained him up. They murdered his friend, and drugged and kidnapped his sister. And that's before we even consider the thirty-eight women whose rape and strangulation he was investigating. I think even I would have trouble providing a big enough distraction from all that. And now there's something else . . . while we were off the air, another body's shown up in North Yorkshire.'

'One of ours?'

'There's no signature on this one, plus it was ninety feet down a pothole. But it's got some of the hallmarks. Middle-aged white guy. Tortured to death for no known reason. That's all I've really got.'

'Have you assigned someone to check it out?'

'Of course.'

'Let's see what they say. If it's one of ours, we open another incident room.'

A Scottish officer appeared in the doorway and gave them a nod.

Outside, the streamlined shape of the Eurocopter EC135 T2 waited on the police helipad, resplendent in its bright red and yellow markings. Gemma had flown in choppers many times before, but mainly over southern England. By contrast, this would be a truly spectacular ride. Not that it wouldn't be in keeping with an investigation that was assuming unreal dimensions. At no stage in their careers had either she or Tasker ever envisaged they'd someday be investigating the murder of a one-time bishop.

Apparently this death had initially been thought a suicide, but the first medical officer to assess the body had noted some kind of inscription carved into the victim's chest. It hadn't been entirely legible – apparently the fierce northern seas could do that to a body pretty quickly, but it had read something like: 'BDE'.

That had been good enough for Tasker, and for Gemma.

But even so – a bishop!

Gemma was numbed by the mere thought of the scandals that could be exposed when this case was finally blown open. Presuming it ever would be.

Chapter 25

The train journey from Northampton to Sunderland was scheduled to take five hours and thirty minutes. Not an inordinately long time, but it included two changes of train – one at Birmingham and one near the end, at Newcastle – which Heck always found exasperating.

Things were further complicated half an hour into the first leg of the journey. The London Midland train was clean and comfortable enough, and it was only half full, so Heck was able to stretch out and relax. Now he was really feeling the pummelling his body had taken in the last few days. Muscles were aching, joints stiff, none of which was helped by the jarring and jolting of the train – but he was only seriously discomforted when another passenger entered the compartment, and for no apparent reason, sat in the seat directly facing him.

There were three things about this that seemed odd.

Firstly, there were several empty seating bays along the aisle, and most passengers would opt for a bit of privacy, choosing not to cram themselves in alongside or facing someone else if the alternative was available. Secondly, what had this passenger been doing for the last half-hour? He certainly hadn't been wandering up and down the train looking for a seat, because Heck would have spotted him before now. And in any case, he would have found one. This meant he must have sat somewhere else, and then for some reason changed his mind about it. Thirdly, this passenger didn't look like an ordinary Joe. He wore a suit, a shirt and a tie, and he immediately took a laptop from a briefcase, opened it and began to work; but before he did any of this, he removed his jacket, revealing a bullish physique – broad shoulders, a tree-trunk for a neck. He was also shaven-headed, and had a face both brutal and sly: a small slit for a mouth; pitted cheeks; apelike brows overarching tiny eyes.

Heck watched furtively as the guy rolled his shirt sleeves back, exposing thick, powerful wrists. His hands were heavy-knuckled and bore old scars. A mauler's hands, if Heck had ever seen them.

Stations came and went as they proceeded north: Rugby, Coventry. The passenger continued tapping at his keyboard. At one point, Heck got up and walked past him, ostensibly to use the lavatory but in reality to glance at his screen. He had a better look on his way back. The guy was writing some kind of report. It was difficult to see what it was about but Heck caught the words 'mortgage' and 'insurance'.

Did this mean he was legit? Heck wasn't sure, but they'd know soon enough.

The next station, Birmingham New Street, was where he changed. It was three o'clock when they reached it. Rush hour hadn't yet commenced, but New Street was a major crossroads on the rail network, and the platforms were bustling with commuters. Heck sidled through them, refusing to look back, either at the train he'd just vacated or those who'd disembarked with him – at least not until he had a bona fide reason to do so. That came on the main concourse, where he turned and glanced up at the departures board, and at the same time checked the passengers streaming down the corridor from the platform. There was no sign of a shaven head among them, or a brutish ape-face.

Heck relaxed, but only a little.

His connection to Newcastle was on time. He pivoted before climbing aboard, just to ensure the coast was still clear. But now his mind strayed back to that bag-lady in the Northampton Railway Station car park. Why hadn't he noticed her standing there when he'd first driven in? It seemed increasingly strange. Where had she suddenly appeared from? Was it possible the Nice Guys could have tracked him all the way from Scotland Yard to the Cotswolds, and from there to here?

The next train was more crowded than the previous one. Initially, Heck had to stand, but made sure to position himself at the end of the rearmost compartment so that he could see everyone in front of him. There was still no sign of that shaven head. Again it was a minor relief – but were a team like the Nice Guys going to put a *single* tail on one of their targets?

Owing to the extra bodies, this was a hotter, stuffier ride than the previous one. The train rocked and tilted as it wound across the East Midlands and into South Yorkshire. The stations rolled by, more passengers coming aboard, more disembarking. Now there were short-haul travellers among them: gangs of kids in school uniform, office workers. However, by late afternoon considerable numbers were leaving the train, especially at Sheffield and Doncaster. Soon there was room to sit, and Heck chose a seat close to where he'd been standing. Outside, the sun slipped down in the west, and another of those long, blue dusks drew its mantle over the woods and hills. Even so, it took another hour, during which they passed York, Thirsk, Northallerton and Darlington, before Heck begin to properly unwind.

He even felt torpor creeping up on him, and tried to fight

it off, lurching to his feet and swaying down the aisle. The mere act of walking woke him a little, but just to be sure, he made his way to the buffet and bought a large coffee. He removed its lid on his way back, and sipped – only to halt in the middle of the next compartment.

The shaven-headed man was there.

He was no longer working on his laptop, but slouched down, buried in an evening paper. It was neither a disguise nor an attempt to hide, but it had been sufficient to conceal him from Heck on the outward journey to the buffet. The question was how had the guy got on the train without Heck noticing? He had to have done it covertly. Heck eyed him sidelong as he walked past. If the guy was aware of Heck, he didn't show it.

Heck took his seat in the next compartment, thinking furiously. When a flickering red light caught his eye, he glanced up: neon text scrolled across a glass panel.

The next stop is Durham, 12 mins.

How far was Durham from Sunderland? Heck had been up in the Northeast for several weeks, working the neo-Nazi murders, but he hadn't used that time to memorise the geography. He guessed ten or fifteen miles, but it might be more. Ordinarily, that wouldn't be a problem – except that he didn't have much money left.

'Christ's sake!' he said under his breath, but loud enough for the elderly lady two seats ahead to glance around disapprovingly.

He had his credit cards of course, but he couldn't use those to pay for a taxi. All it would take was SOCAR to put a trace on his financial transactions and it would lead them straight to the door of his destination.

But one thing was absolutely clear. He couldn't stay on this train.

The shaven-headed guy was clearly tailing him. But the

bastard might not be as clever as he thought. In his efforts to avoid being spotted, he'd positioned himself far up the train. From way up there, he wouldn't necessarily see if Heck climbed off near the back – not until it was too late.

Heck glanced at his watch. They were now ten minutes out of Durham. He gazed back along the compartment. The few people remaining were facing away from him. Even if there was more than one of them on his case – the second one in here – they weren't observing him at present.

He glanced at his watch again. Nine minutes.

He stood up, stepped into the aisle and backtracked the two or three yards to the slide door connecting with the rearmost boarding area. No head turned to look at him.

He retreated into the boarding area itself, and stepped out of sight, jamming himself against the exit door. Six minutes remained.

Funnily enough, of all the people he'd tangled with during this investigation, including those madmen in the Underground, none had looked as tasty as this shaven-headed character. That didn't necessarily mean anything, though in Heck's long experience it sometimes paid to judge a book by its cover. He adjusted the Glock in his inside pocket, pushing one of its magazines further down, so the weapon was raised, its grip more easily reached.

With laborious slowness, they pulled into Durham station.

Still no one else entered this particular boarding area. The train came to a shuddering standstill. There was a tannoy announcement from the train manager, and the exit door slid open. Heck stepped out, immediately glancing left. Significant numbers of passengers were disembarking, while at least an equal number were waiting to climb aboard. The station's canopy lights counteracted the dimness of the evening, but all he could see for several hundred yards was a chaotic scrum of figures.

Heck backed away along the platform until he was level with the rear of the train. The end of the platform lay thirty yards behind that; it terminated at a horizontal chain with a *No Passengers Beyond This Point* sign in the middle. Beyond the chain, the concrete ramped down to trackside gravel, where a deck of sleepers had been laid to form a footway across the lines, no doubt for station staff.

Glancing up, he saw a red light suspended between the two railways, indicating that no train was about to come hurtling through. It was a risk, but hell, this whole thing was a risk. He stepped quickly over the chain, descended the ramp, and crossed the lines via the footway. No one shouted, no emergency lights were activated. On the other side, he ascended to the next platform and stepped over another chain – still no one seemed to notice, let alone object.

This next platform was also busy, and Heck purposely lost himself in the crowd as they awaited their connection. The Newcastle train drew slowly out again. Heck watched warily. By the time its last carriage had passed, only a few of the passengers who'd disembarked from it remained on the opposite platform. The shaven-headed man was among them.

He stood rigid, his briefcase clutched under one brawny arm as he looked left and right. Heck backed away, almost knocking a woman over. He apologised profusely before stepping behind a stanchion. When he risked another peek, the shaven-headed guy's back was turned. He'd spun on his heel, as though to shield whatever he was doing – but it was quite clear that he was talking into a mobile phone.

Heck made a beeline for an exit stair, his eyes riveted on his opponent, who was so engrossed in his call that he only glanced once over his shoulder, and by then Heck was out of his eye-line, already descending.

He reached the bottom of the stair quickly, finding himself in a white-tiled corridor, which led only to the right, crossing underneath the two railway lines and passing the bottom of the stair from the other platform. Heck ventured towards this, but before he got there he heard trudging footfalls coming down.

He froze. Two options remained: the stair leading back to the platform he'd just left – though in truth there probably wasn't enough time to reach it; or, much closer, the door to the Gents. He took the second, as there might be a staff door connecting from that to another section of the station.

But there wasn't.

He entered the room through two back-to-back doors, to find it spacious but horseshoe-shaped, an island of washbasins and mirrors down the middle, a condom machine fastened to the stanchion at one end, a chewing-gum machine at the other. The urinals stood on the left, the cubicles on the right. There was nobody in there, and nowhere else to go.

With a *thud*, someone pushed against the outer door. Heck darted around the island and ducked into the middle cubicle, closing it behind him and locking it. As an afterthought – and just as a second *thud* signalled that someone had barged the inner door open – he clambered onto the toilet. There he waited, helpless, barely seeing the obscene graffiti scrawled on the walls around him, hardly noticing the stench rising from the unflushed mess in the bowl between his feet.

Feet clipped loudly across the lavatories, halting somewhere else in the room. Heck wasn't sure where, but he heard no water trickling, either from a running tap or a voiding bladder. Sweat seething on his brow, he eased out the Glock.

The flat wooden door in front of him was mesmerising in its blankness. As he tried to picture what was happening on the other side of it, he slowly extended his arm, staring down the pistol barrel. His thoughts whirled with nightmarish imagery: Austin Ledburn forced to swallow a gallon of petrol before he was set alight; Jim Laycock, his skull and bones shattered by the frenzied blows of a dozen claw-hammers; Mike Silver – choked and squealing as his own walking-stick was thrust down his gargling oesophagus. There were no further footsteps, but Heck was convinced his opponent had now focused on the only toilet cubicle that happened to be closed.

That wretched door – less than an inch of hardboard, and it was all that protected him. Some chance against a hail of bullets. His hair prickled as he heard a low, dragging sound – seemingly drawing closer. He imagined the shaven-headed man, gun in hand – a Tavor? a Chang Feng? a SIG-Sauer? – crawling forward on his knees to check under the panel.

Did Heck fire first? Drill the cubicle door from the inside, in the vague hope he'd catch his enemy off-guard? But what if it was some innocent person?

Sweat dripped from the end of his nose. He knew it was impossible that his hoarse breathing would go unheard. And then he heard humming. It was nothing he recognised – some distorted version of a modern ditty.

But *humming*?

The Nice Guy was *humming*?

That didn't compute.

Heck let out a slow exhalation of breath.

The dragging sound seemed further away. The humming ceased as someone hawked phlegm and spat. It was impossible to imagine the person Heck thought it was being so . . . casual. Stealthily, he slipped the pistol under his coat, stepped down from the toilet and planted his ear against the door.

The humming resumed briefly, transforming into a low, tuneless singing.

Whoever that was, they thought they were here alone.

Suddenly, Heck had to get out of this upright coffin. He disengaged the lock. The door opened silently as he peeked around it.

It was something of a surprise, perhaps a worry, that he couldn't see anyone at all – and he didn't notice the singing/humming had stopped until he'd come out into the middle of the room.

He froze. What the devil . . . had he been tricked?

He made for the door, lurching around the pillar with the condom machine – only to find a man waiting on the other side. Heck whipped out his Glock, aiming it squarely at the man's face.

The man, who was wearing dirty green overalls and aged somewhere in his late sixties, gazed back through big bottle-lensed glasses. He was leaning on a broad-bottomed broom and in the process of unwrapping the foil from a stick of gum. His mouth dropped open.

'Sorry . . . mate,' Heck stuttered. 'Erm . . .' He thrust the gun away and fished out his warrant card. 'Police officer. Don't worry . . . nothing to be alarmed about.'

He brushed past the gaping functionary, and shouldered his way out into the corridor. Cheeks burning, he hurried up the stairs to the ticket hall, straight to the outer doors and then down onto the station approach.

Full darkness had fallen, but the place was well-lit. Behind the wall directly facing the station, there were deep thickets of trees. Cars and taxis were coming and going, collecting or dropping off, and he could hear the distant sounds of the city. Thirty yards to his right, tucked half out of sight behind a corner, there was a bus stop. No one was waiting there, but a notice board was fixed to its post. He walked towards it, knowing he'd be met by a wall of information; place-names and bus route numbers which meant absolutely nothing to him.

The shaven-headed man stepped into his path.

Heck was midway between pavements when the burly figure appeared alongside the bus stop. His mouth was fixed in a feral smile, his eyes almost luminous as they locked with Heck's.

Heck half-stumbled; his mouth dried. His hand itched to pull the Glock, but the shaven-headed guy already had his right hand in his jacket pocket. What if his sidearm was already primed and pointed? A vehicle screeched up at Heck's back, its doors bursting open.

The shaven-headed man advanced, his smile a broad grin.

Heck still reached for his gun. He didn't care that this was a public place. He wasn't drinking a gallon of petrol, or being hung upside down and sliced . . .

'*Dadd-eee!*' the two children shrieked, as they charged past him – into the arms of the shaven-headed man, who crouched to hug them.

Heck was a hapless spectator as the man handed one of the children his briefcase – the little tot insisted on carrying it for him – and continued to hug them both as they all strolled forward together. Heck turned stiffly, watching as they passed and climbed into a chugging Mini Cooper, behind whose steering wheel an attractive, dark-haired woman was sitting, smiling. The Mini's doors slammed closed and it circled around Heck, rumbling down the approach road in a swirl of exhaust.

Chapter 26

PC Jerry Farthing had long been aware that his small two-up-two-down in Southwick had never been much to look at: another anonymous unit in a decrepit redbrick terrace, with a tiny yard at the rear.

A low-rent district from way back, it wasn't perhaps an ideal place for a policeman to be living. You might have expected him to be pestered to death by his neighbours, either looking for help or looking to cause trouble. But Farthing had managed to keep it quiet that he was a copper, primarily by having no interaction with those around him, and by never leaving or returning to the house in uniform. Maybe it wasn't the best way to live, but at least the place hadn't cost him much. His parents had owned this house originally, and by the time Farthing had come to inherit it, the mortgage was paid in full, so if nothing else it was cheap. But as he sat up late that night watching the footy in his darkened lounge, he was finally wondering if he should get out of here, maybe head for the suburbs. There were all sorts of romantic myths about the old working-class north. About how the houses might be ancient and rotten, but how their occupants were good-natured, generous and always looking out for each other. Well that might be true, though with the best will in the world, what use were good-natured neighbours against a man with a gun?

It was an easier thing to say than to fully comprehend, but Farthing's day-to-day existence had been ruined by the incident with Ernest Cooper. Okay, it was unlikely he'd ever come up against a maniac like that again. But those pale blue eyes, that bland, emotionless exterior . . . they were burned indelibly into his thoughts. In his younger days, Farthing would have hated himself for the lack of innate courage this exposed, but he was long enough in the tooth now to know that bravery was for suckers. Over the last few years, he'd seen far too many fellow bobbies get severely hurt by going up against impossible odds.

That said, there was no pleasure to be found in *this* – sitting up at midnight, rigid as a fire-poker, just waiting for that suspicious sound outside: a cat hissing, a milk bottle rolling. Just thinking about it brought sweat to his brow, but no more so than the thought of returning to work – and that was equally a source of shame to Farthing, because there was a distant time when he'd been a damn good bobby.

At present, he didn't know how long he could stay on the sick, 'bad with his nerves' as they'd say at the office, though the whispers would doubtless adopt a more ominous tone in due course, wondering if he wasn't shaken as much as shattered. Perhaps they'd add that they'd seen this brewing for some time: wasn't he always the last to respond to an emergency call these days? Wasn't he the one who always wanted to swap his shifts to avoid working Friday and Saturday nights?

Farthing filched a tissue from his cardigan pocket and dabbed his brow, but it only seemed to make him sweat more profusely. The price of refusing to share, he supposed. He hadn't even revealed the full extent to which he feared he'd lost his nerve to his Fed rep or his official stress counsellor. They'd only agree he was finished as well.

It wasn't as if he could just resign. That would cost him his pension, and what else could he find at forty-five when he'd only ever been a copper? It would be another six or seven years before they'd consider granting him early retirement, while medical departures weren't thrown around like confetti anymore – certainly not for stress. They wouldn't even be able to slide him into an inside job, not when most of those roles were performed by civvies these days. Not, if he was honest, that he felt much like sitting at home all day. He'd just done a couple of weeks of that, and it was amazing how mind-numbing daytime TV could actually be.

Farthing glanced at the clock on the mantel. It was ten past midnight, but fleetingly the hour didn't matter. The mere sight of the thing, an ornate wooden pillar-design timepiece, brought a fog of tears to his eyes. It had formerly belonged to his father, donated as a farewell present after forty years on the docks: Jack Farthing; an iron-hard roughneck with forearms like ham-shanks and a plethora of tattoos in an age when inked skin actually meant something, but with a loving heart too.

'Dad,' Farthing said under his breath.

Jack Farthing: a roaring giant reduced to a wheezing skeleton within five years of retirement.

Bastard cigarette companies.

How he'd fought, even then, to his last ounce of faltering strength.

And in the light of all that, how would he feel about his son's current fight – or lack of it? Farthing regarded the clock as though mesmerised by the bitter-sweet memories it invoked. Even so, the sudden rapping at his back door brought him sharply to his feet. Perplexed, his focus tightened on the clock face.

Ten minutes past midnight.

And someone was at his door?

Not only that, they were at his *back door*?

Which meant they'd entered his back yard, meaning they must have climbed over the rear wall or gate.

Farthing turned. There was no light on in the kitchen, but the connecting door was open, which meant the shimmering glow of the TV would be visible. Whoever it was out back, they'd know someone was home.

The temptation was just to ignore it, to make them think he was out.

Unless that was what the caller wanted. Why else would someone knock at this hour? Had they been watching the house maybe, and owing to his hideaway existence of the last few days, was it their assumption he was off on holiday?

But even then, why knock on the *back door*?

Farthing uprooted himself from the patch of carpet next to his armchair. But he didn't venture to the rear of the house; he went to the front, into the tiny hall at the foot of the stairs. Did he run from here? Just open the front door and bolt into the street, screaming for help? Good God, that really would be the end of his career as a copper. The reality was that he had to check this out himself. There was no point pretending an alternative was possible.

Hanging from the post at the bottom of the stair was his utility belt. Breathing hard, he took the CS spray out of its pouch, and his baton, snapping the latter open to its full two feet of flexible polycarbonate resin.

Slowly, Farthing ventured back into the lounge and edged to the kitchen door. Despite the glow from the TV, it was very dark in there; there was no light on the other side of the kitchen window – so if someone were looking in, they'd see him before he saw them. But wouldn't that be a good thing, if it meant they ran? Just showing there was a householder present was usually enough to dissuade opportunist burglars.

With slow steps, he crossed the kitchen, which was strongly redolent of baked beans, macaroni cheese, tomato soup – anything from the stock of cans in the under-stair closet, which he'd warmed up whenever he'd got hungry during his recent hibernation here.

Eight years since Mum died, and you can't even cook, you waste of space!

He knocked the bolt off, turned the key, and opened the back door.

There was nobody there.

The narrow yard was dank, black, empty.

Had they fled after all? Had they seen him coming?

Farthing stepped outside, both weapons clearly displayed. His eyes slowly adjusted, the faint yellow of sodium streetlights diffusing over the encircling rooftops, exposing his surroundings with incremental slowness: the wheelie bin on his left; the tall, brick outline of what had once been the outside loo.

'You alone?' a husky voice asked.

Farthing almost jumped out of his slippers, before spinning left, baton at his shoulder, CS canister extended as per the textbook.

'Whoa, it's me!' Heck said, palms raised.

'What . . . what the . . .?' Farthing's eyes bugged in utter disbelief.

It wasn't just the shock of finding Heck in his yard in the middle of the night – though that was shock enough – it was how tired and bedraggled Heck looked. The normally relaxed SCU cop looked exhausted: his hair was a damp straggle, his face drawn, his shoulders drooped. He approached with a footsore limp.

'Can I come inside?' Heck asked. 'I'm knackered . . .'

Bewildered, Farthing indicated the open back door. Heck

lumbered through it. He halted briefly in the kitchen, nostrils twitching, before moving through to the lounge, where the *Match of the Day* summarisers were giving their round-up. Without invitation, he collapsed into the armchair.

Farthing followed him in, switching on a sideboard lamp. The arrival of Mark Heckenburg at his home address would have been remarkable under almost any circumstances. They'd got to know each other reasonably well in the days following Ernest Cooper's arrest, but it had been cool and professional. They'd hardly become what he'd call friends. They hadn't even gone for drinks together after work.

'So . . .' Farthing finally stuttered, 'exactly what the fuck is going on?'

'I've come a long way to speak to you, Jerry.'

'You've . . . eh?'

'I'll explain everything in a minute . . . look, sorry about this, mate.' Heck sat up. 'I've got to have something to eat. I'm famished.'

Farthing eyeballed him, still with disbelief, before pivoting round on his heel and heading into the kitchen. He reappeared a minute later with a plate of cheese and crackers, and a cup of tea – only to find Heck by the sideboard, gulping from a bottle of Black Grouse.

'Hey . . . come on, that was a birthday present!'

'Sorry.' Heck put the bottle down. 'Been flying on empty for hours.'

Farthing pushed the plate into his hands. 'Best get these down.'

'Cheers.' Heck sat again. The cheese and biscuits weren't up to much – stale and vaguely tasteless, thrown together at speed – but Heck wolfed them anyway, and then swilled down the mug of tea. When he'd finished, he glanced up at his host, who stood there with hands on hips, like a disapproving housewife.

'How'd you get my address?' Farthing asked.

'There're only three J. Farthings in the Sunderland phone book. The first two were wrong numbers. I didn't bother calling the third. Anyway, never mind that. I take it no one's said anything? At your nick, I mean. You haven't heard anything on the grapevine?'

'About what?'

'Me.'

Farthing shrugged. 'I've been out of circulation for a few days.'

'Oh . . . how come?'

'My nerves are shot . . . I'm on the sick.'

'Cooper?'

'What else?'

'Put the shits up anyone, that.' Heck's tone was conversational, but his thoughts seemed to be elsewhere. 'And there's not been anything on the telly?'

'Telly?' Farthing looked alarmed. 'Have you got yourself into some kind of trouble?'

'No . . . well, not really.'

'Not *really*?'

'SOCAR'll be looking for me.'

'Yeah, and what's SOCAR?'

'They're sort of halfway between us and MI5.'

'Great.' Farthing paled. 'So they kick arse and don't even have to answer for it.'

'Hear me out,' Heck said. 'SOCAR are cops. The Serious Offenders Control and Retrieval unit. They're not officially part of NCG, but they have a multi police force remit. They're like the judiciary's strong right arm. They protect the courts, juries, witnesses, investigate jail breaks, chase fugitives . . . transport high-risk prisoners.' He winced as he peeled off his leather coat. '*Sometimes* they transport high-riskers. Sometimes they even get them to their intended destinations.

Must admit I've never known them have this much clout before. They even overruled SECU, the most empowered firm in British law-enforcement since Henry VIII's mob went crown green bowling with a bunch of severed heads . . .'

'*What the fuck?*' Farthing shouted.

Heck glanced down. He'd assumed the object that had just thudded to the floor was his wallet – but it wasn't, it was the Glock.

'Don't panic,' he said. 'The safety's on.'

Farthing's gaze jumped from the weapon to his visitor. 'So . . . hang on. Let me get this straight. You're currently an armed fugitive. Is that what you're trying to tell us?'

Heck placed the gun on the sideboard. 'It's not that simple.'

'This SOCAR mob . . . are they bent?'

'One of them is. I think. The point is . . . you've heard about the Nice Guys Club?'

'That mob who whacked those lads escorting the prison caravan five days ago?'

'Correct. And they've whacked a few more since then.'

'It was all over the news till this morning.'

'The latest is they've green-lit my boss. And if that doesn't work out for them, they're gonna leg it . . . either one of which will leave us with a mountain of scrambled egg on our faces, but knowing how efficient these bastards are, they may actually manage both.'

'Okay.' Farthing shrugged. 'But I guess I've missed the bit where this involves me.'

'If I'm going to take the fight to them, Jerry . . . you're all I've got.'

'You want to run that by us again?'

'I'm onto them,' Heck said. 'And I'm gonna get them before they do any more damage. But I can't do that on the run. I need somewhere to lie low.'

Farthing's expression of disbelief slowly lengthened. '*Here?*'

'You owe me, remember?'

'Are you kidding?' Farthing shook his head energetically. 'I owe you a pint. Or a lift when you decide to go and turn yourself in. I'm not getting involved in this . . .'

'Hey . . .' Heck's tired mask hardened; he glowered at his host. 'I put my life on the line for you!'

'For Christ's sake, Heck, think what you're asking! You want to use my house – my home address – as a base of operations from which to attack this bunch of professional psychos!'

Farthing's outrage was perhaps justified. It had long been police tradition that home didn't enter the equation; that you fought the enemy on their own patch. Bizarrely, it was often the case that even criminals respected this. But Heck was weary and irate, and for a moment all he could see was the same lump of sweating, wobbling jelly he'd been lumbered with in the abandoned factory at Hendon. He levered himself to his feet with such force that Farthing backed away.

'All I need is a roof,' Heck said harshly. 'You can provide that much, can't you? Look what I provided for your non-existent family. You! Still fucking alive!'

'Alright, alright . . .' Farthing wheeled away from him.

'And I need something else,' Heck said. 'Your local knowledge.'

'Eh?'

'When me and you first met in the canteen at Gillbridge Avenue . . .' Heck knuckled at his brow. 'There was a phrase you used. "Mind me whips and stottie". Something like that.'

'What's that got to do with anything?'

'"Whips n stot",' Heck said. 'Does it mean something? I hope it does, because it's the only lead I've got.'

Farthing looked baffled. 'You're from Lancashire, aren't you?'

'By origin, yeah.'

'You'd call it "a chip barm". Whips means Jockey's whips
. . . chips. Stottie is a kind of loaf made in the Northeast.
So . . . chips and buttered bread.'

Heck regarded him dully. At first he didn't know whether
to laugh or cry. Something that simple, and yet . . . it had
appeared in print, like a letterhead. 'Is there a local business
with that name . . . a fish and chip shop maybe?'

'There's a café.' Farthing spoke matter-of-factly, as if this
could surely be of no importance. 'It's fairly well-known up
here. Whips n Stottie.'

Heck felt that old tremor of excitement. 'Where is it?'

'Just off the A1, on the stretch between Newcastle and
Berwick.'

'How far from here?'

'Forty miles.'

Heck groaned. 'Might as well be a thousand for a bloke
on foot.'

Farthing looked startled. 'You're on foot?'

'Want to see the blisters?'

'How did you get here?'

'Walked.'

'Where from?'

'Durham.'

Farthing's mouth dropped open. 'All the way from
Durham?'

'Managed to get a taxi part of the way . . . about a third
of the distance.'

'No wonder you're . . . *hang on*!' Farthing moved to the
kitchen door, staring into the darkness beyond the rear
windows. 'You sure no one followed you here?'

'I'm sure.'

'I'm not talking SOCAR. I'm talking these Nice Guys
fuckers.'

'Jerry, I've just dragged my arse along every kind of road

286

you can think of. High streets, suburban avenues, country lanes covered in horseshit, and most of that time I was alone. If they wanted to jump me, they've had half a dozen chances.'

Farthing still opened his back door a crack and peeked out. It was several seconds before he closed it, locked it and returned to the lounge.

'Can I make a call?' Heck said, indicating the telephone.

'Who to?'

'My boss.'

'The one they're after?'

'They *may* be after her. They may also decide she's too hard a target. Truth is, I don't know.'

'Won't she trace it back here?'

'I'm trusting that she won't.'

'Come on, Heck, this is my home address . . .'

'Yeah, and why is that a problem?' Heck tried to keep the exasperation from his voice. 'Christ's sake, Jerry . . . there's nothing weird about me showing up here. We're in court together soon, giving evidence against Ernie Cooper. We have to talk, compare notes. How the hell were *you* to know I was on the run?'

Despite this logical argument, Farthing looked increasingly alarmed. For a second Heck almost felt sorry for him, but he truly was in the last-chance saloon here.

Eventually, Farthing shrugged and gestured at the phone.

Heck picked it up and made the call. As before, it went straight to voicemail. He was tempted to leave a message, but that would be a risk. He hung up.

'No reply?' Farthing asked, unashamedly relieved.

'Didn't think I'd get one. At present, she's in the Highlands of Scotland, probably in a chopper.'

'No signal then.'

Heck stood silent, not seeing the TV weatherman running

his hands across a meteorological map of England's Northeast coast.

Farthing loafed around the room. 'Look . . . you're clearly shagged. I'm not going to turf you out now. Why don't you get your head down, and we'll talk about this in the morning?'

Heck nodded. This was probably the best he could have hoped for.

'You'll have to use the armchair,' Farthing said. 'There's only one bed here. Don't worry about me. I'm not going to dob you in or anything.'

Heck eyed him curiously. It had never occurred to him that Farthing might 'dob him in'. But then – here was a guy who seemed to have broken off from the police family in more ways than one. Farthing's expression was suddenly inscrutable; it betrayed no obvious emotion, which Heck thought strange given that two minutes ago he'd had the weight of the world on his shoulders. In fact, Farthing was now the considerate host. He made Heck another mug of tea, and brought a pillow and some blankets down from upstairs, along with a hot-water bottle.

'I know you're tired and all, so it might be tough getting a proper handle on things,' Farthing said, after checking the downstairs doors and windows were locked. 'But you need to think about this. Can you really go after these killers on your own?'

'Hopefully I won't have to,' Heck yawned. 'If I can get through to my gaffer, we should be sorted.'

'When's she due back from Scotland?'

'Dunno.' Heck adjusted the pillow behind his head. 'All we can do is wait.'

Farthing nodded, said goodnight and traipsed up the stairs. Heck remained where he was, slumped in the armchair. He picked up the remote control for the TV, turned the volume down and channel-hopped, scanning various late-night news programmes. Nowhere could he find references to the shootings and bombings, which suggested the press embargo was holding. At least that meant the Nice Guys couldn't learn their handiwork in Yorkshire had been discovered by simply watching television.

He turned the television off and pushed his head back into the pillow. The lamp was still on, but he was too tired to get up and switch it off. And yet, despite this deep bone-weariness, sleep proved elusive. It had been an incredibly long, arduous day.

Tomorrow had to be easier. It had to.

Chapter 27

The northwest coast of Scotland didn't always equate to wild winds and raging sea, but on this occasion Gemma had a definite feeling she'd arrived on the extreme fringes of Britain.

The last hour of the flight had been dramatic to say the least, a tableau of barren, rocky summits unfolding below them, the deep glens in between filled with pine trees or the mirror-flat surfaces of lochs burnished red by a sun setting in embers on the western horizon. Like all seas when viewed from height and distance, the North Atlantic, on their left, seemed almost benign: a vast expanse of misted blue, shot salmon-pink by the sunset, its myriad waves little more than ripples. Needless to say, once they got down to it things were different. It was dusk when they left the Eurocopter on the car park at Clashnessie police office, a squat, pebble-dashed building located just inland from Clashnessie village, and then had to travel another couple of hours to the coast in a Police Scotland Range Rover.

It was nearly midnight when they arrived there, and dark in a way that only Britain's most remote hinterlands can be dark. In single file, they descended a teetering flight of steps cut through the granite of the shoreline cliffs, lit every dozen yards by fluorescent lights scaled in waterproof cases. Below them, breakers boomed with increasing volume. To avoid going dizzy, Gemma focused intently on the broad back of their chaperone, PC Kevin McKenzie, who, aside from his flat hat, was shrouded in a luminous, ankle-length slicker. When an ice-cold spray began spattering them, she wasn't sure if this was rain or the ocean itself.

At the foot of the stair, they crossed a narrow steel bridge, still in single file. There was much turmoil beneath their feet, massive waves exploding on blade-edged rocks. The sea wind felt strong enough to hurl them into the abyss were they not clinging to tubular handrails fixed on either side. Ahead, on an island composed almost entirely of offshore crags, stood Clachtoll coastguard station. Though it was brightly lit, it wasn't possible to gain an impression of the entire structure. Gemma glimpsed high mesh fencing surrounding a square, whitewashed building. A cluster of radio antennae and receptor dishes were visible on its roof; there was also apparently a helipad up there, but the weather conditions being what they were, their pilot had opted to put down in a sheltered location inland.

Once inside, they were shown to the crew room, and offered a hot cuppa, which Tasker declined on behalf of both of them because, as he said, they were in a rush. Gemma was irritated by that, but said nothing. They'd booked into a bed and breakfast at Clashnessie for the night, which was hardly ideal; she too felt an urge to rush back south and get on with stuff rather than 'dawdle about up here at the top of the world' (Tasker's words, not hers), but Police Scotland had only one Eurocopter available and it had now been called to other duties. It would return for them first thing in the morning, which was eminently reasonable of their hosts. Until then, there was nothing else they could really do.

They were provided with the necessary paperwork, before the watch officer led them through to a small mortuary at the rear of the station. This was a temporary facility, normally reserved for the victims of maritime accidents, though at present it only contained the one corpse. A stark halogen light filled the small room, which was completely bare except for a central porcelain slab with runnels down either side connecting to a drainpipe underneath. A wall of freezer cabinets stood on the right.

The watch officer was a young Highlander; stocky, red-haired and freckled. 'Hope you two haven't got a dinner date due,' he said.

'It's okay,' Gemma replied, snapping on a pair of disposable gloves.

He opened the drawer, and lifted the opaque plastic sheet covering the figure on the tray, before discreetly withdrawing.

Both Tasker and Gemma had seen worse – though not often.

It was quickly evident that most of the damage they were viewing had been caused naturally: mainly by the rocks the unfortunate victim had been battered against as he'd rolled in the surf; probably also by the crabs that had scuttled all over him when he'd finally lodged in the crevice where he was later found.

Nothing remained of his face. It was scrunched inward like a decayed football. One pulverised eye-socket was just about visible, though strands of shredded nerve tissue hung where the eyeball should be. Only flesh held the rest of the skull together, though this too was crushed, gaps in the matted, blood-gluey hair revealing jagged bone and deep fissures. The remainder of the body was equally mutilated; throat hollowed out, ribcage flattened, limbs rent, torn and twisted.

'Do we have a death certificate yet?' Tasker asked.

'Yes sir,' replied PC McKenzie, who, having removed his slicker and taken advantage of the tea offered on their arrival, now entered the mortuary behind them. He was an older man with a white beard and a thatch of bristly white hair. 'It was signed by Doctor Baltillie. He's our local practitioner. It's in with the paperwork, I believe.'

Tasker flipped through the documents. They included photographs of the body as it was found on the rocks, which were even more revolting than the sight before them.

'Do you get suicides here often?' Gemma asked. 'I mean . . . there are high cliffs all along this coast. Are they bad for jumpers?'

'Not so many as you might think, ma'am,' McKenzie said. 'This is a lightly populated region. We do get bodies washed up. Usually after boating accidents. The Minch can be a real bugger.'

'How was Bishop Docherty identified?' Tasker asked.

'His height, sir – six foot, two and a half inches. His cleft chin – what there is left of it. His proximity to his abandoned vehicle, and his clothing. That's awaiting inspection in the drawer on the right.'

Despite all, it was relatively easy to spot the lacerations in the wrinkled flaps of salt-eroded flesh still covering the body's mangled ribcage, though the writing itself was only partially visible:

BDE

But it was evident what it was; the entirety of the inscription would have been clearly visible before the victim went over the cliff top.

'Anything else to suggest this guy is one of ours?' Tasker wondered idly.

'Accusations of sexually inappropriate behaviour dating back to the 1990s,' Gemma said. 'Most of them from nuns. Plus some stories three or four years ago that he'd misused Church funds. There was a significant hole in the bishop's accounts, which he never explained. Something like eighty thousand pounds. The Vatican probed that one, but got nowhere.'

'They might have got nowhere, ma'am,' PC McKenzie spoke up, 'but Bishop Docherty was suspended from office and resigned shortly afterwards.'

Tasker remained po-faced. 'Before he was sacked, you mean?'

'That's correct, sir. He went off to live in obscurity, which perhaps was better than he deserved. But there wasn't much publicity and no one's been harassing him to my knowledge. So if you're still thinking suicide . . .'

'I'm afraid not,' Gemma said. 'As of now, this is officially a murder enquiry.'

'Yes, ma'am.'

Tasker eyed the local bobby. 'You didn't much care for the bishop?'

'The *ex-bishop*, sir. No, I can't say I did. I was born and raised a Roman Catholic . . . like many here in the North Highlands. But men like him have their way, and all Catholics must answer for it.'

'But if he was never convicted of anything . . .?'

McKenzie merely replied with that thin smile typical of time-served coppers the world over when asked to judge a man purely on his *official* record.

'There were sus circs leading up to his death, I understand?' Gemma said.

'That's correct, ma'am.' McKenzie opened his notebook. 'Apparently the bishop was seen driving his car along a coastal track yesterday evening at around seven-thirty.'

'Who saw him?'

'Pair of American students here on a hiking holiday. I took full statements from both.'

Tasker leafed into the paperwork again.

'They reported the bishop driving slowly and carefully,' McKenzie added. 'A bit too carefully, they thought . . . seeing as the road was empty.'

'They mention a second vehicle?' Tasker said, speed-reading the statements.

'Apparently it was following the bishop's Volkswagen Beetle at a distance of about four hundred yards, sir.'

Tasker grunted irritably. 'They noted the Beetle, but can't remember what the second vehicle was . . . or spotted its VRM.'

'They didn't think anything of it at the time,' McKenzie explained. 'The witnesses only came forward this morning, when the news broke that the bishop was missing and his Beetle abandoned on the cliff top.'

'And this nondescript second vehicle contained a group of men?' Tasker said. 'An uncertain number . . . but no less than three?'

'That's my understanding, sir.'

'And again . . . no descriptions?'

'I did press the students on that, sir, but as I say, they didn't realise they were witnessing a criminal event.'

'Where are the two hikers now?' Gemma asked.

'A hostel at Inverkirkaig, ma'am. They've agreed to stay in the area an extra week.'

'Okay, good.'

'Thank you, constable,' Tasker said.

McKenzie nodded and backed out of the mortuary.

Tasker gave a deep sigh. 'This is getting out of hand.'

'Heck said they were enjoying themselves,' Gemma replied. 'Running us all over the country, revelling in it.'

'*Heck!*' Tasker snorted. 'Jesus, all we need now is for him to show up and the party's complete.'

'I think we're even out of Heck's range up here, sir.' Gemma tried not to sound as irked as Tasker was making her feel. He was tired and disgruntled – she understood that. But he'd supposedly absolved her of all responsibility for Heck's break-out of custody – *illegal* custody, she reminded herself – and yet whenever the subject arose, his tone seemed to imply annoyance with all those around him, especially her.

'The main thing now is that we speak to those two hikers,' she said. 'See if we can get a bit more out of them. They might actually have *seen* the Nice Guys.'

'Yeah . . . great. Unfortunately, they can't remember what they looked like.'

'We'll take new statements, have some e-fits made. If we get someone in custody later, we can put them on an ID parade.'

'That'll be next to no use in court, Gemma. These aren't private roads. Anyone can use them for any kind of legitimate reason.'

'It's still a new lead.'

'Not to mention a new layer of bureaucracy.' He grimaced. 'I know we were half-expecting it, but now we're going to *have* to liaise with Police Scotland.'

'They've been pretty helpful so far.'

'We'll need them to be a lot more helpful from here on.'

'I'm sure the local MIT will assist,' she said, referring to the Police Service of Scotland's ultra-efficient Major Investigation Team, at least one division of which was permanently allocated to its North Command. 'If we ask them nicely, that is.'

'We'll visit their HQ in person. A phone call won't cut it.'

Gemma nodded, glancing again at the corpse. 'Talk about

your sins will find you out. Wherever you try to hide . . . Scotland, Yorkshire, Oxford, East London.'

'Yeah.' Tasker chuckled without humour. 'Turning into a bit of a travelogue, this, isn't it? I wonder who's paying the Nice Guys' expenses?'

'Who do you think?' she said. 'The poor sods they're doing this to. Gotta be the last word in irony.'

Chapter 28

It was after three in the morning when Jerry Farthing prepared to descend the stairs. He hadn't set the alarm clock because he hadn't been asleep. Instead, he'd sat upright for the last three hours, fully clothed, gazing at the yellow-lit square of curtain over his bedroom window.

For some time he'd sweated, icy globules clustering on his brow.

As so often in his life, it briefly seemed that he hadn't thought this through properly. He'd reached the decision to turn Heck in at an early stage. It would be a tad disloyal, given the guy's selfless antics at the derelict factory in Hendon, but getting involved in this mindless fight with the Nice Guys was totally out of the question. The problem was, Farthing now lacked the means to this end.

In an effort to cut himself off these last few days, he'd allowed his mobile phone's battery to run dry – so he couldn't make a call from the privacy of his bedroom. The only alternative was to sneak back down and take the landline through into the kitchen. Its cable would extend that far; but he'd then have to hold the entire conversation within a few yards of his snoozing target. The mere thought of that had set his few remaining hairs on end, but he'd continued to think it through, and it had gradually seemed less risky. Heck was beat and would surely be out for the count. And in truth, all Farthing really had to do was get in touch with the duty officer at Gillbridge Avenue, and tell him he had an armed fugitive at his home. Once the cavalry had arrived and Heck was in custody, he could give them the rest of the story.

He took his slippers off before descending. The stairs were old and creaky, but he knew the treads that were particularly bad and stepped over them. When he reached the bottom, he glanced into the lounge. The sideboard lamp was still on, but his guest had flopped in the armchair; head slumped, arms draped to either side – like a life-size ragdoll. His breathing was slow, shallow and regular.

Reassured, Farthing trod stealthily to the sideboard. He picked the phone up and turned towards the open kitchen door.

'You've got to ask yourself one question, Jerry . . . if you grass me up now, who will you actually be helping?'

Farthing froze, heart pounding. He risked a sideways glance, and spotted the Glock still lying on the sideboard. Relieved by that at least, he turned the rest of the way around. 'And how about you?' he said boldly. 'Because from what I've heard about these Nice Guys, you go after them on your own, and you won't last five minutes.'

Heck looked grizzled and sallow-faced, but his eyes were wide open. 'I've lasted this long, haven't I?'

'God's sake, man, this is madness. Not only that, it's illegal, and I'm . . .' Farthing shook his head, '. . . I'm not being part of it.'

'You don't have to be.'

'It's a bit late for that . . .'

'No it isn't.' Heck shrugged. 'I've got a gun. So you're

299

only doing this because you're under duress. What more do you want . . . you're covered.'

Farthing shook his head. 'What's the matter with you?'

'This isn't something I *want* to do, Jerry. It's been forced on me. But don't worry. I'm not totally bonkers. I'm not going to try and tackle this crew alone . . . I just want to know where they are. Pinpoint their position, and then make the call.'

'Then why not do it through the correct channels?'

'For some reason I can't yet fathom, those channels are closed to me.' Heck sat up. 'The investigating team have gone out of their way to shove me aside . . . but this was my original case, and it's gonna be my collar.'

'Oh . . . so you've actually got no good reason for this? It's like a totally selfish motive?'

'And why, pray, would *you* be grassing me up? Let's see . . . you're bad with your nerves, so dobbing me in might improve your situation. Might secure you an inside job for the rest of your service . . . maybe grease the wheels towards an early finish?'

Farthing regarded Heck balefully, but saw no point in denying the obvious.

Heck smirked. 'Yeah, Jerry . . . we're neither of us white knights.'

'Okay . . . I'm lazy and scared. But I wouldn't trade that for what you're doing.'

'I only need a couple of days,' Heck said. 'You don't even have to come with me. Just point me in the right direction and turn a blind eye.'

'But why are you doing this . . . why not just let them go?'

At first Heck thought he'd misheard. 'Excuse me?'

'What was it you said . . . if they don't have a pop at your boss, which won't be easy if she's flying all over the country, they're going to go home, yeah?'

'Probably.'

'So let them. Then they're out of our hair.'

'Let them go? Seriously? Do you know how many they've killed?' Heck got to his feet, straightening out the crick in his back. 'Anyway, like I say . . . this has been my case for ages, so it's damn well going to be my collar.'

'Heck, you think saying that over and over makes you sound any less a maniac? Especially when both you and I know there isn't going to be any collar! I may not be the smartest bobby, but even I can tell this isn't going to end in a neat little line of arrests.'

'You haven't got a bloody clue, have you?'

'Neither have you, and you'd realise that if you stopped and thought about this.'

'I'll tell you what I'm thinking, Jerry.' Heck was now pacing the room. 'All the pain and misery I could have prevented in my career . . . if I'd put a bullet through the head of every criminal I've ever met, instead of locking him up so he could eventually get released and inflict his misery all over again. Arrest is too good for scrotes like these.'

'You're not a fucking soldier, Heck! You're a copper . . . you have to do things according to the law.'

'I have to do this any way I can. Look Jerry, mate . . . this thing's haunted me for years. The sodding Nice Guys! I was *that* close to knuckling them last time, but I blew it. And now suddenly they're in my back yard again. I cannot turn a blind eye . . .'

'So go to CID at Gillbridge Avenue. You know most of them. Barry Grant's a good lad. Talk to him. Try and enlist Major Crimes. They'll pay this café a visit.'

'Yeah, and tramp all over it with their size sixteens.'

'Don't be a bell-end . . . they know what they're doing.'

'They don't know the Nice Guys! Look . . . this isn't going to be as bad as you think. There'll be no unnecessary shooting.

If there's any, it'll be because the Nice Guys started it.'

'That doesn't make me feel a whole lot better.'

'Maybe this will.' Heck grabbed the Glock from the sideboard and tossed it onto the sofa. '*You* take possession of the gun if it helps.'

Farthing gazed down at the weapon. 'It doesn't.'

'If you don't know how to use it, I'll show you . . .'

'I know how to use it. I was a shot myself, once.'

Heck was startled by that. 'You were?'

'Only a few months. Didn't finish the training course.'

'Who binned you?'

'What does it matter? I learned one thing from that valuable experience, Heck. Stay out of the line of fire . . . *always*.'

'Well, I prefer to work unarmed too, if I can.'

Farthing slumped onto the sofa. 'You know, you say things like that . . . and for a minute you sound completely sane. And then I remember how you got here and how you're going to leave, which most likely will be in a coffin.'

'At the end of the day, Jerry, we're coppers.' Heck shrugged tiredly. 'We don't get a choice what kind of bad guys we have to pursue. We just do it.'

'Oh fucking hell, the philosophy of the street-cop. Spare me that at least.'

'If you feel you've got to turn me in, get on with it . . . don't bore me with some professional cynic routine. I've given you a way out. You can say I oppressed you into helping me. Who knows, the experience may traumatise you so much they'll have no option but to let you leave early. But if all that isn't good enough, there's nothing more I can do.'

Farthing pondered this for several seconds, and then sighed. 'You realise there'll be no way back for us after this?'

'Well, that'll suit you . . . won't it?'

'Christ, Heck . . . you're deranged. You must be.' He stood

up and stomped across the room to the hall door. 'I don't believe I'm not just chucking you onto the street.'

'It'd be easier doing that if you had the gun.'

'I'm not leaving my prints on some murder weapon, thanks very much.'

'And you said you weren't a smart bobby,' Heck called after him as he banged his way upstairs. 'If it's any consolation, Jerry, you're doing the right thing.'

'Right and wrong don't come into it,' Farthing's voice echoed down. 'Thinking about these next few days, it was a straight choice between you and Jeremy Kyle. And even *you* win on that score.'

Chapter 29

'Just so long as you know I'm not getting out of this sodding car,' Farthing said.

'That's okay,' Heck replied, distracted by the map book on his knee.

It was late morning and Farthing's scruffy blue Chevrolet was thirty miles up the A1, having passed Gateshead, Newcastle, Cramlington and Morpeth. Heck's original plan had been to set out first thing, but the breakfast rush-hour traffic would have provided a major headache, plus, after the late night they'd had, it had been nine-thirty before either he or his reluctant host had come around fully. On top of that, Heck had then had to persuade Farthing to act as his driver for the day, which hadn't been easy. At least the A1, a broad dual-carriageway, was largely clear. The rugged northern moors and their occasional belts of wild, wind-stunted trees undulated away on all sides, dotted with blue-faced Swaledale sheep.

'So you reckon this Whips n Stottie place is famous?' Heck said.

'Only round here, like,' Farthing replied. 'It's a caff . . . a truck stop.'

'And how close are we to the sea?'

'Not far. It's about three or four miles. You thinking they came here by boat?'

'Dunno.'

'Assuming it's them, why are they up here in the first place?'

Heck shoved the map onto the dashboard. 'The Northeast's as good a place as any. They're hitting targets in Yorkshire and Scotland as well as down south. That makes it pretty central to their plan.'

Farthing looked puzzled. 'But how did they get into the country?'

'How do criminals normally get into foreign countries? Through Customs, using fake passports, fake visas. The Nice Guys are nothing if not connected.'

'And they just carried all these weapons in with them? From what I've heard, it's high-grade stuff . . . and there's enough of it to start a civil war.'

'The weapons may have been acquired over here. That kind of kit isn't found easily in the UK, so they must have paid top-dollar. But I can't see that being a problem. Christ knows how many millions they've earned from their rape-to-order racket. Alternatively, they might have smuggled them in through some diplomatic channel.'

'Get away!'

'No one checks the diplomatic bag, Jerry.'

'So when you say these guys are connected, you mean they're *really* connected?'

'All their customers I've encountered so far have been high rollers. Big men in big jobs. No one else can afford the Nice Guys' services.'

Farthing checked his rear-view mirror, seemingly in knee-jerk response to that. Heck understood why. One of the biggest problems during his battles with the Nice Guys was the extent to which they were protected, and how many men in positions of influence they could call to their assistance. The last time it had been Laycock, and this time it was probably someone in SOCAR. With that kind of support, they could head off an investigative pursuit with relative ease, assuming they hadn't killed those allies beforehand. In one way, the Nice Guys' very reason for being here might weaken their position. Even so, Heck couldn't help glancing into the wing mirror too.

'Worrying thought though, isn't it?' he said. 'That when we're running in the pervs and peepers and kiddie-fiddlers, we're only scratching the surface. That the real predators are so well insulated we don't even know they're out there.'

They arrived at their target destination just before noon.

As Farthing had said, it was little more than a roadside diner, a small flat-roofed building. The legend *Whips n Stottie* was emblazoned on a rectangular hoarding over the main entrance in mock-medieval typeface, alongside an image of an enormous bun crammed with chips. The same motif flew from a banner atop a tall pole at the car park entrance. A considerable number of vans and trucks were already packed into its extensive parking area.

They reversed into a parking bay some forty yards from the main building, and there waited, watching the comings and goings through the restaurant's main front door, which was located at the top of a short flight of steps. The majority of the customers had the look of ordinary working men: some in overalls, some in jeans and t-shirts. The occasional sales rep appeared, jacket draped over shoulder. Most tended to re-emerge after a few minutes, carrying bundles wrapped in newspaper.

'I suppose it would help if we knew who we were actually looking for,' Farthing said. He'd slumped behind the steering wheel in the hope he and Heck wouldn't get spotted, though in his tatty jumper and hooded cagoule, there wasn't much chance of someone taking him for a copper.

'Military men,' Heck replied.

'That doesn't really narrow it down.'

'Military men who look like they could serve now.'

'So . . . what are we saying? Young, fit, short haircuts?'

'Forget the haircuts. These are mercs. They're also stone-killers, so if we do meet them, you don't get in their faces . . . okay?'

'You must've missed the bit where I said I'm not leaving the bloody car.'

The wait went on. Twelve o'clock became twelve-thirty, and then one o'clock. More customers came and went. The place was busy as hell, but Heck was increasingly aware that someone would notice the stationary Chevrolet at some point, even if it was only a member of staff, and if they came out and asked questions, that would be the kind of attention he didn't need. He opened the passenger door.

'I'm going in.'

Farthing reached into his pocket. 'I was getting a bit peckish.'

'I don't mean for lunch.'

'Oh . . .'

'You're right. We don't know enough about these guys, and I haven't come all this way to sit in a car park hoping to get lucky.'

'What're you gonna do?'

'What I always do . . . wing it.'

Heck entered the diner with the breezy air of a hungry customer. The atmosphere was steamy, greasy, throbbing with voices. Most of the tables were occupied, while a number of men were seated along the counter, all tucking into plates piled high with fish and chips, pie and chips, egg and chips, or just about anything with chips. He wove through to a hatch at the end of the counter. The girls working there wore pinafores, transparent gloves and paper hats. One, a young lass with short sandy hair and freckles, turned to face him. 'Eat in or take out, sir?'

Heck showed his warrant card, though with more trepidation than usual. As he didn't know what most of the Nice Guys looked like, one of them could be sitting right next to him. He glanced sideways, but no one was paying attention.

'It's nothing serious,' he told the girl, 'but I'd like a chat with the manager.'

A middle-aged woman emerged from a room on the right, which, owing to the clashing of pots and cutlery inside it, was probably the main kitchen. She was short and foursquare, with a head of tight, bronze-rinsed curls. She too wore a pinafore and gloves. 'Can I help?' she asked.

'Detective Sergeant Heckenburg. You are . . .?'

'Mrs Broadhurst. I'm the owner.'

'Nothing for you to worry about, Mrs Broadhurst. But I'm looking for a bunch of guys who may have been in here as customers in the last few weeks.'

Mrs Broadhurst didn't look particularly worried, but was keen to take the conversation out of earshot of her customers, which Heck also thought a good plan. She beckoned him through the kitchen area – another hive of activity, staff dashing back and forth – and into a cluttered office, on which she closed the door.

'We get groups of men all the time,' she said. 'Can you be more specific?'

'They'll have been in more than once. Bunch of young fellas . . . twenties, thirties. A mix of foreign accents most likely.'

'Dear me, pet. We get all sorts of accents here too. A lot of East Europeans . . . you know, seasonal workers, labourers, drivers. Plus we're on the tourist route. This is the Heritage

Coast, you see. It runs all the way up. Alnwick, Dunstanburgh Castle, Bamburgh Castle, Holy Island. We get all sorts.'

'Americans?'

'Yes . . . there was one in yesterday teatime.' She relapsed into thought. 'Now you mention it, *he's* been in here before.'

'What does he look like?'

'Longish red hair, red beard.'

Heck recalled the gunman partially described by Gary Quinnell.

'*He* was a youngish man too,' Mrs Broadhurst added. '*And* he sometimes has a few others with him.'

'Other Americans?'

'No . . . different accents, like you say. Some British, others foreign. I assumed they were working locally, because there's usually two or three of them, but they buy pies, chips and stuff, and always in bulk . . . like they're providing for a site or something?'

'Is this every lunchtime and every teatime?'

'No. Sometimes I don't see them at all, but then I'm not always on the counter.'

'Is it usually the same men?'

'No, there are different ones on different days, but you get the feeling they're together. I'm sure they're working local. They must be.'

'You said you saw this American chap yesterday?'

'I'm not sure . . . hang on. My husband might know.' She opened the office door and shouted into the kitchen. 'Ken . . . can you come in here a sec?'

A big, angular man in his late sixties appeared. He had a craggy, weather-beaten face, a pendulous strawberry nose and silver hair slicked into a quiff.

'You spoke to that young American customer who was in yesterday teatime, didn't you?' Mrs Broadhurst asked.

Ken frowned. 'I did . . . why?'

'What did you speak to him about?'

'Well . . . he'd had a shave and a haircut, hadn't he?'

'You've definitely seen him in here before?' Heck said.

Ken looked at Heck, puzzled.

'This is a police officer,' Mrs Broadhurst explained.

Ken pursed his lips. 'I've seen him before. He's usually with those other foreign lads who come in. But he had longish hair and a beard before. All that's come off now. I asked if it was a new look for him.'

'Anything else strike you about him?' Heck asked.

'He's got a limp from somewhere,' Ken said. 'That's new as well. Didn't ask about that though.'

'Any of the others showing injuries? A broken nose maybe?'

'Didn't notice.'

'What about the others' accents?'

'Various. Some British, others European . . .'

'Australian?'

Ken nodded. 'There *was* an Aussie. Big fella too. He was last in quite a few days ago. Haven't seen him since.'

Heck knew why that was. If it was the same Aussie who'd tried to kill him in London, his flattened nose would now be one distinguishing feature that every police force in the UK could look out for. The risk of being spotted also probably lay behind the Yank's change of appearance. He knew Gary Quinnell had survived, which meant there'd at least be a rudimentary description out on him.

'So what does our American friend look like now?' Heck asked.

'Hair's very short,' Ken said. 'Flattened off. Pale-faced too. Light freckles.'

'How old exactly?'

'Mid-to-late thirties.'

'Build?'

'Well . . . athletic.' Ken turned to his wife, who was furtively glancing at her watch. 'We'll have him on film, won't we, love?'

She nodded, but reluctantly, as if there were other things she needed to be doing. 'We have a CCTV over the counter.'

'Can I look at the footage now?' Heck asked.

'Does it need to be now?' she said. 'Only it's lunchtime, you see, and . . .'

'This is a murder enquiry.'

She paused, mouth open. Then glanced at her husband, who looked equally discomforted by the revelation. 'Are these fellas dangerous then?' he asked.

'They'll pose no danger to the public unless someone confronts them,' Heck said. 'So if you do see them again, it's business as usual. It might not even be the same people, but I need to check the footage to know that for sure.'

Ken glanced again at his wife. 'Yes, well I think we'd better take care of that now.'

A couple of minutes later, he was seated in front of a computer, tapping on its keyboard. Mrs Broadhurst stood nervously by. If she had things she needed to be doing elsewhere, she was in no rush to attend to them now.

'If you could find some with the Aussie lad too,' Heck said, 'that would help.'

Ken continued tapping. 'Ah ha . . .'

The relevant footage appeared. It was in black and white, but surprisingly clear in quality. It had been shot from overhead, so all it initially portrayed was the usual jumble of customers at the counter, primarily the tops of their heads. In the midst of this chaos, one man stood out for the sheer breadth of his denim-clad shoulders. Heck leaned forward, squinting. It was possibly the brawny Aussie he'd tangled with on the Underground. The figure sported a distinctive buzz-cut, but it was difficult to be sure.

'That's the American we were talking about.' Ken pointed to the person alongside the big shape. 'Before he had his crop.'

This was a slighter, leaner man. As they'd said, he had collar-length locks and thick facial hair. He was wearing a khaki flak-jacket. With a cold thrill, Heck now remembered the ambush at Shacklewell Street, and the beard he'd glimpsed on the khaki-clad figure advancing from the bus stop. They watched the footage for several minutes, while the two suspects bought what looked like a dozen packages of food, but at no stage were their faces clearly visible. When it finished, Heck dug an ID card from his wallet, took a biro from the desktop, underlined his personal email address and handed it over. 'Can you email this particular file to this address?'

'I suppose so,' Ken said.

'Just out of interest. How do they arrive here? I don't suppose you've noticed what kind of vehicle they come in?'

'I saw the one they came in yesterday. It was a maroon Ford transit van, a flatbed.'

'Registration number?'

'Sorry.'

'Don't suppose you've got exterior CCTV?'

'On the car park, but yesterday they didn't park there. They pulled up out front.'

'Presumably they've parked in the car park on other occasions?'

'Well, yeah,' Ken said, 'but we'd have to go back through the files and that would take time.'

'We can do that.' Heck indicated the card. 'Can you email all the files to that address – say for the last four weeks?'

Ken glanced at his wife. 'It would still take time. I mean, they're big files.'

'Look . . .' Heck chose his next few words carefully. 'I don't want to alarm you unduly, but the men we're looking

312

for may be involved in more than one murder. Several more. As I say, there's no threat to the everyday public, but more lives may be forfeited if we don't start making ground on them. Seriously folks, we need those files as soon as possible.'

'Okay . . . erm, right.' Ken exchanged another discomforted look with his wife. 'Erm . . . well I'll get onto that straight away.'

'Thanks. That would be helpful.'

Sensing that he'd outstayed his welcome, Heck thanked his hosts again and made his way outside, having to suppress his excitement. Not only had the bastards been in this area, they were *still* here. There was a payphone at the foot of the steps. He popped into it to call Gemma. As before, it cut to her messaging system. Frustrated, he hung up and lurched outside.

And that was when he saw the van.

The maroon Ford transit.

It was parked directly in front of him, about twenty yards away.

Heck went rigid. How long had they been here? Had they been inside the café while he was there? Would they recognise him if they'd spotted him? Highly likely, given that he'd been made a priority target.

With a judder, the van's engine was shut off.

That was a break – it looked as if they'd only just arrived. Even so, Heck could barely move. He watched, half-paralysed, as the van's driver and passenger doors opened. Only at the last second was he able to spin around and re-enter the booth, where he slammed the phone to his ear and began wittering in mock-Geordie. His neck hairs stiffened as two pairs of feet clumped across the car park.

He had the Glock under his coat. But he could hardly use it out here, with truck-stop customers everywhere. Sweat greased his forehead as the feet approached him.

And then passed by. Ascending the steps to the diner's front door.

He shot a glance in their direction. It was only a fleeting glimpse, but the one on the left was nondescript – no one Heck had seen before. The one on the right, however, wore a khaki jacket, walked with a pronounced limp, and though his red hair was all but shaved to bristles, Heck knew him straight away.

The door closed behind them, and he darted from the booth. By a no-risks estimate, he had four minutes tops during which time the Nice Guys would queue at the counter, place their order, get served and return to their vehicle. That didn't mean they wouldn't casually turn around while waiting and glance out through the window. If they did that, he'd be in clear view, but this was too good an opportunity to miss.

He walked quickly over to the flatbed van, throwing a brief signal in the direction of Farthing's Chevrolet, which was parked diagonally opposite some forty yards to the right. Whether his nervous chaperone had noticed what he was up to, Heck was unsure, but there was no time to find out. He circled to the rear of the van – which was clearly a hire-truck of some sort, probably for use in the farming trade. A blue tarpaulin lay over its rear deck. When he glanced under this, he saw tools, old empty feed-sacks and the like. There was plenty of room.

Heck hovered there, ripped by an indecision that was almost painful. The obvious thing to do was to return to the Chevrolet and either cajole Farthing into following the bastards, or push the guy out of the way and take charge of the wheel himself. But the chance of not being noticed on these empty moorland roads was poor.

It really was a no-brainer.

Heck threw a quick glance in the direction of the diner, then clambered over the van's tailgate and squirmed beneath the tarpaulin. It was dank and musty under there, redolent of compost and swelteringly hot. He also had to insinuate himself between rough-edged spades and forks. After that, all he had to do was lie and wait. Within a couple of minutes, he smelled the two men approaching before he heard them: the aroma of fresh fish and chips, the tang of vinegar. They chatted together as they reached the car. It sounded as if the American had brought a Brit with him today, but no actual dialogue was discernible.

A second later, the engine started and the vehicle shuddered to life. It was still possible they'd noticed him and were now taking him away to some private place of execution. His muscles tensed at the thought, and he felt at the Glock. If nothing else, he'd take both the sons of bitches with him.

They drove for quite a few miles, apparently headed north. When they swung off the dual carriageway, it was in a westerly direction, the van jolting along what felt like an unmade track. Heck lifted the tarpaulin and risked a glance over the tailgate. The A1 bisected his vision horizontally, rapidly receding as they followed a dirt road away from it. There was loud juddering as they passed over a cattle-grid. After that trees and thickets closed in, and they swerved around bends and curves. Heck was thrown back and forth, the tools rattling and clashing. So noisy was it that he couldn't hear any conversation in the driver's cab. All of a sudden, this felt like a bad idea. His breath came hard and ragged as he drew the Glock and cocked it. They wouldn't expect him to be armed. The moment that tarpaulin was ripped away, they'd each get a nine-millimetre slug in the face.

The brakes screeched as the vehicle suddenly slowed to a halt. Heck twisted around so that he lay sideways across the deck, but in a good position to aim the Glock with both hands.

A voice sounded, and this one wasn't muffled by the driver's cab. Heck recognised those dulcet Aussie tones, but he still couldn't distinguish what was being said, even though he listened intently, drenched head to toe in freezing sweat.

A metallic rattle suggested a chain being removed. He realised they'd stopped at a gate, probably with a guard on it.

It had to be now. Or it was never.

Heck fumbled for the bolts at either side of the tailgate, sliding them loose. Gripping the top of the tailgate with his left hand, he lowered it gently, and clambered out, pushing it back into place and managing to slide one of its bolts home before dropping to a crouch on a dirt road. There were only woods to his rear, but he felt horrendously exposed – especially as the vehicle edged forward again.

Heck's thoughts raced. Whoever had opened the gate ought to be standing on the left – so he went right, still at a crouch, plunging headlong into a mass of brambles and nettles. They plucked at his face and hands, but then he was through into a leafy dell, where he halted again, listening hard. There were no immediate sounds of pursuit. In fact, a clang signified the gate had closed. It was followed by a metallic rattle as the chain was replaced.

It was still two or three minutes before Heck dared to breathe normally, let alone move. He slotted the Glock back under his coat, and pushed forward on hands and knees through more tangled foliage. It was five or six yards before he reached the footing of a dry-stone wall. Warily, he rose to three-quarter height.

On the other side of the wall, there was open ground. In the midst of it, only partly obscured by a belt of birch trees, stood a large, rambling farmhouse. From what Heck could see, it didn't look like a working farm. There were no animals; there was no sign of traditional farmyard activity. But a number of vehicles were parked in front of it, including the maroon van, and various figures moving around – all of them youngish men. About thirty yards to Heck's left, another youngish man – a burly, big-shouldered guy with a distinctive buzz-cut and an almost comically broad sticking-plaster across what could surely be no more than a stub of nose – leaned on a gatepost, picking at an open bag of chips. He wore a thigh-length waxed coat, beneath the lower hem of which protruded the stubby steel barrel of an automatic rifle.

It was an unnerving sight, but also a reassuring one. Because now there was no doubt in Heck's mind – he'd found the Nice Guys' hideout.

Chapter 30

It was a difficult journey back to the A1.

Not so much because of the distance – it was probably no more than a mile and a half – but because Heck didn't want to stay on the road. Another Nice Guy vehicle could easily happen along. In addition, there had to be sentries, though he was making a guess there wouldn't be too many. The Nice Guys were team-handed, but they had a lot of targets to hit, so how many men could they realistically spare to put on guard in the woods – especially when no one else knew they were here? Most likely, there'd be one or two, and they'd probably be watching the main approach.

This meant he should veer far from the actual road, and stick religiously to the undergrowth, which he did, moving cautiously and at a crouch, constantly scanning the high branches for vantage platforms and the surrounding ground cover for anything resembling a woodland hide – and thankfully seeing nothing of the sort.

When he came unexpectedly to another road, he sank to his haunches and waited. Only after several minutes did it occur to him that this one was different. For one thing, it was laid with tarmacadam. Plus, as far as he could tell, it ran north to south rather than west to east. He still hung back, but moved parallel with it in a northerly direction. About four hundred yards further, he reached a crossroads with signposts and a payphone.

The place-names on the signs meant nothing to Heck: Christon Bank, Stamford and Dunstan. But the phone was a godsend. Again, he attempted to call Gemma. As before, there was no reply, but this time he had a contingency plan. Under normal circumstances, Ben Kane would be the last person Heck would confide in. He was the archetypal by-the-book man. But if nothing else, he would put the machine in motion. Okay, once Kane knew, the rest of the office would also know – word would hit the mole in record time, but as long as it also meant there were armed units from Northumbria en route ASAP, it wouldn't really matter.

'Serial Crimes Unit, DCI Kane,' came the clipped voice.

'Boss . . . it's Heck.'

'Heck . . .?' Kane stuttered. *'HECK . . . WHAT THE DEVIL ARE YOU PLAYING AT?'*

'Listen, please . . . I've found the Nice Guys.'

There was a short, breathless silence. By the background noise, it sounded as though Kane was in his car. 'What're you . . . Heck, what're you jabbering about?'

'They've rented a farmhouse in the countryside.'

'Are you pissed or something?'

'I'm sitting on them right now. The whole shebang. All their ops are probably carried out from here. I bet all their kit's here, the vehicles they've been using . . . everything.'

'Are you serious?'

'No, I always make up really amusing lies like this. Of course I'm bloody serious! I've followed them all the way to Northumberland.'

'Whereabouts specifically?'

'Not far off the A1, somewhere south of Berwick. You'll

have to put a trace on this call to get the exact location. I'm in a payphone at a crossroads between three villages I've never heard of . . . Christon Bank, Stamford and Dunstan.'

'It shouldn't be hard pinning that down. Heck . . . how've you managed this?'

'With no little difficulty.'

'You're absolutely sure it's them?'

'Bloody right, I am. The Aussie bastard who tried to nail me at Shacklewell Street's here. So's the Yank who half-did Gary. I'm telling you, sir, this is them . . . one hundred per cent.'

'Okay . . . how secure is your position?'

'They haven't spotted me yet, I don't think. The farm's about a mile and a half away, through rough woodland. I'm going back in a sec, to keep an eye on it.'

'Negative, Heck . . . do not do that!'

'They don't know I'm here . . .'

'And what if they've posted sentries?'

'That's occurred to me, sir. I'll be careful.'

'Heck, no! And that's an order.'

'Copy that,' Heck said after some hesitation. 'There's something else . . . I've been trying to get hold of Silver Command, with no joy.'

'They're on their way back from Scotland, as I understand,' Kane said. 'But Gemma diverted to the North Yorks moors to have a look at another body. They should be back in range soon.'

'Soon's no use. We have to take these bastards down now!'

'Heck, the soonest I can get the team up to Northumberland is four hours.'

'We need to move well before then . . . look, I think SOCAR have a mole in their ranks.'

'What makes you say that?'

'It's a long story.'

'Even if they do, I can hardly keep this thing under my hat.'

'I know . . . so speed is of the essence.'

Kane pondered. 'Listen . . . stay put while I make some phone calls. I'll try and mobilise armed response units from Northumbria. They can hook up with you pretty quick. If nothing else we can throw a ring around them till everyone else arrives.'

'Sounds good to me.'

'In the meantime, we'll be on our way up. But you stay exactly where you are, okay . . . so the shots aren't running round the woods like blue-arsed flies. What time have you got?'

Heck checked his watch. 'One-forty.'

'Same here. I'll try and get them with you for three-thirty at the latest.'

'Sir . . . that's two hours.'

'Heck, be realistic . . . you're in the fucking boondocks. First I've got to persuade them I know what I'm talking about, and in case you'd forgotten, I'm a DCI, not God. Then they've got to gear up and mobilise. Then they've got to find you.'

'Okay . . . look sir, just remind them it's a silent approach priority. That farm doesn't look particularly defensible, but if it's old it'll be solidly built . . . thick-walled, small-windowed. And we already know what a bad attitude the Nice Guys have got.'

'You just stay put. You hear me, Heck . . . stay put!'

'I hear you, sir.' Heck hung up, stowed his leather coat to the rear of the booth, shoved the Glock into the waistband of his jeans, covering it with his sweater, and set off back to the farmhouse.

He understood the DCI's concerns, but Kane wasn't just Mr By-The-Book, he was also Mr Over-Cautious. Anyway, it didn't matter. Heck would ensure he'd be back at the crossroads for three-thirty, when the RV was due. But there was no way in hell he intended to kick his heels alongside an empty phone box for the next two hours. Besides, he needed to scope the farmhouse out properly so they knew what they'd be facing. He'd go carefully and quietly, and would take the same route back that he'd taken coming out. Again, it was slow progress, and took him almost forty minutes to reach the farmhouse perimeter, where he crouched below the dry-stone wall's parapet, listening to a faint gabble of voices from the other side.

By Heck's own reckoning, he was about fifty or sixty yards west of the main gate, which ought to be distance enough from the Aussie sentry. Slowly, holding his breath, he raised his eyes above the top of the lichen-covered stonework.

Initially, he thought the Nice Guys were leaving.

He was sufficiently west of the tree belt to see that various cars were being readied at the front of the building, though there was so little urgency on view that it soon became apparent this was not an evacuation.

A sizeable group of the Nice Guys, maybe eleven or twelve, was standing outside the farmhouse's front door, conversing. All were clad for the hunt in khaki, canvas and waterproofs, and all of them were gloved. It was cool for late September, but it wasn't really autumn yet – such packaging looked like overkill, even for men used to the balmy climes of North Africa and the Middle East. Of course, its main purpose was to prevent them leaving traces of themselves in the cottage.

Some loaded kit bags into car boots, but others loaded weapons as well. Even from this distance, Heck could identify assault rifles, submachine guns, and pistols tucked into the waistbands of trousers.

It was an ugly thought that he was kneeling here, safely concealed, while the Nice Guys were systematically dispatched on hit-missions. How many more people were going to die while he lurked behind this wall? And there was another worry. It increasingly nagged at him that whatever evidence this farmhouse contained relating to the murders and to the wider activities of Nice Guys networks overseas, it could all be destroyed very quickly during the course of a protracted siege. It was a particular concern that the list of Nice Guys' clients in the UK might get flushed. That was the piece of vital evidence they'd lost last time, thanks to Jim Laycock. Okay, it might be a contradiction. The Nice Guys were in the UK to kill off their former clients, but Heck didn't want them killed – he wanted them put in front of a court, convicted, exposed to the whole world as the rape-murderers they were, and then subjected to some exemplary sentencing.

One by one, the cars reversed from the front of the building, swinging around and rumbling towards the main gate, which the Aussie sentry held open for them. Each one held a complement of three or four Nice Guys.

Heck switched his attention back to the crowd at the farmhouse front door. There were only a handful left now, along with a couple of cars. A tall, fair-haired man seemed to occupy centre stage. It was difficult to make out his distinguishing features from this distance, but he seemed to be issuing orders. He was about six-two, wearing green army surplus trousers and a zip-up brown bomber jacket.

The last of the others climbed into the first of two remaining vehicles, a Renault Mégane, leaving the blond leader and one other – the American. The Mégane reversed away, pivoted around and swerved along the farm track after the others. The Aussie stood aside as it growled past, sipping a soft drink through a straw.

The two remaining Nice Guys reached some agreement. The tall blond man closed the farmhouse door, before they climbed into the last vehicle, a tan Ford Mondeo estate. As that too pulled a three-point turn and headed to the main gate, Heck sank behind the wall, toying with various options. He glanced at his watch. It was still an hour before his RV with the Northumbria shooters. So what did he do – leg it back to the payphone, call Ben Kane again, and tell him the birds had temporarily flown? Maybe put an all-points on the vehicles? Not that he'd had a chance to memorise any of their registration numbers. He perhaps ought to warn Northumbria that at least a few of the Nice Guys were currently not here. That meant they'd have to make a very covert approach, and find a lying-up point somewhere close by. Of course, he was due to meet them himself in an hour's time. He could give them that message personally.

He surveyed the house again, wondering how many targets were still on the premises. Their skipper had closed the front door firmly, ensuring it was locked.

Crazy thoughts played through Heck's mind. The house itself was pretty standard for these parts: gabled and built from plain grey stone. It consisted of a central block, but like so many old farmhouses that had been added to over countless ages, various wings and annexes jutted out, each with a different levelled roof. As a sop to the holidaymakers who'd normally rent this place, there was a lawn on the right side, while the drive and the forecourt were covered with fine gravel. Now the present occupants had left, there wasn't a hint of life there; not a flicker of movement beyond its small windows. But Heck's concerns still carried weight. There'd likely be a treasure trove of evidence behind that closed door, which he could expect to go up in smoke if Northumbria Firearms – how had Ben Kane phrased it? – threw a ring around the place. Warnings would go out to other Nice Guys units not on site.

Quite simply, the investigators stood to lose too much if Heck just remained on the perimeter, watching. He glanced at the Aussie sentry. The guy's back was turned. He'd closed the gate and was taking a long leak against its left-hand post.

Though every molecule in Heck's body told him this was a bad idea, he stood upright and swung his legs over the wall. Scalp tingling, he walked quickly towards the house. It was tempting to break into a run, but he maintained a leisurely pace. When you ran you made ridiculous mistakes – like kicking over unseen bottles, or tripping and falling. The front door was directly ahead by about twenty yards. It was made of solid oak, with a narrow frosted glass panel in the centre – and of course it was locked. He risked another glance towards the sentry, whose back was still turned. Thanking God for cans of takeaway Cola, Heck veered left towards the northwest corner, sliding thankfully around it so that he was out of sight of the main gate.

He pressed on down the side of the house, a clutch of stone and timber outbuildings coming up on his left. Most looked closed and locked, but it meant there were plenty of places for Nice Guys to be lurking. He also had to pass several ground-floor windows, through any one of which he'd be visible from the inside, though in all cases he saw only empty, wood-panelled rooms, one containing a table heaped with rubbish. Away from the front of the house, the windows were more functional than ornate – sheets of glass in basic PVC frames. He tried each one, but found them locked. He was fully prepared to break and enter if necessary – whatever the legal consequences might be, they were far outweighed by the larger gain of taking the Nice Guys off the street. He'd find some way around the irregularity – he always did; though it would help if he didn't have to smash something.

Heck rounded another corner. A potting shed stood to the left, alongside a disused garage. Beyond those, the encircling trees encroached closely – he'd be able to nip to cover quickly in the event he heard someone coming. But this didn't resolve his problem of how to gain entry.

He rounded another corner, entering the farmyard proper. This was a paved open space, rectangular in shape and partially covered with straw. It extended about sixty yards by forty to a wire fence, beyond which lay empty paddocks. More farm outbuildings stood down either side of it. Several hung open, exposing rank darkness inside. Heck halted and listened. Only after several seconds did he venture forward, proceeding along the back of the house – where he halted again.

The rear door stood ajar.

This gave him real pause for thought.

An open door likely meant someone was on the premises. In fact, as Heck's ears strained, he fancied he could hear something beyond the farm buildings. Music, very faint and tinny. Someone was working over there but wearing earphones. He stood rigid by the wall as he processed this information. A guard at the front, and someone out here at the back. It felt like madness to continue. But an open door was a big invitation. It also offered the advantage of a silent entry.

He'd come this far, he decided, proceeding. He peeked through another window before passing it, scanning a traditional farmhouse kitchen: stone worktops, a cast-iron range, a brick floor, crockery and ironmongery on walls and shelves. It looked improbably neat. They clearly hadn't been preparing their own food; another measure against the risk of leaving DNA. No doubt their heap of takeaway refuse would be incinerated before they departed. In fact, giant-size plastic bottles of bleach and white spirit were visible in one corner, suggesting the entire place would be cleansed after use. An enclave of professional killers, he reminded himself – who had come here unnoticed, wreaking indescribable carnage, and then would simply vanish again. An amazing notion. Even more so, given that he was about to walk into their centre of operations and sign their communal death warrant.

Steeling himself with that thought, he slipped past the window and pushed at the kitchen door, which eased open. The Glock was still tucked into his waistband, but he kept his right hand on its grip. He wasn't even authorised to be carrying it at present; he didn't want to use it if he didn't have to – but he wasn't going to become the centrepiece of the Nice Guys' next bonfire.

Again, he listened long and hard. The only sound from the interior was the steady tick of a grandfather clock. Heck glanced again over his shoulder – no one was in sight – then wiped his feet on the mat and stepped across the threshold.

The interior of the farmhouse was rougher and readier than the safehouse in the Cotswolds. It hadn't been modernised, but it was handsomely finished in the Jacobean style, with plenty of beams and panelling, original stone features, and numerous rural ornaments on show, from horse brasses to hunting bugles. Aside from the kitchen and hall, there were four spacious reception rooms, though none seemed to have any specific or individual purpose. The grandfather clock stood by the front door, at the foot of an awkwardly twisting staircase. Thanks to the small windows, the place was dim, almost gloomy, and as Heck prowled from one chamber to the next, this heightened his awareness that he was on dangerous ground. But still he heard nothing: no creak from overhead; no sounds of movement aside from his own.

There was evidence everywhere that the house was in use by a number of occupants. The dining table was heaped with the rubbish he had spied from outside, mostly cartons and wrappers adorned with the *Whips n Stottie* logo. Much clothing was on view, mainly cagoules and anoraks, but also flak-jackets and windbreakers. Some of it hung in the hallway, either from pegs, or over the stair banister, but plenty was littered around the reception rooms as well, strewed across the furniture, on the various camp beds that had been set up, or over the haversacks and Bergen kit bags dumped alongside them. This was no more than a crash pad, Heck decided; a camp they could break at a second's notice.

But the find of the day came in the room adjoining the lounge.

All four of its wainscoted walls were hung with documentation: maps, both local and national, covered in scrawled biro; printed lists and itineraries; sketched diagrams; masses of surveillance photographs – so many that they hung in untidy wads – with every kind of location on view, from town to country.

This was so reminiscent of the original Nice Guys operation that Heck was almost physically sick as he assessed it, but now his thoughts were racing. He wanted to seize it all, every scrap, but that wasn't practical. He could fill twelve bin-liners and there'd still be materials left over. Instead, he should go for quality rather than quantity – remove something vital, something undeniable, something that would totally incriminate these bastards. Because there was no question in his mind that as soon as the Northumbria lads closed in, whichever Nice Guys were present, they'd put a match to this pile of kindling.

And then he saw it.

Pinned to the doorframe connecting with the hall.

It was a list – another list. The Nice Guys so liked their lists; they were meticulous, methodical. They'd almost certainly created this one on the basis they were already loaded down enough without having to carry a half-ton of 'client files' around. The list was very neat, carefully typed, arranged in alphabetical order. It consisted entirely of names and addresses. Four pages of them in total, stapled together.

Heck snatched it down, sweat stippling his brow, but it was only when he flipped a couple of pages that he noticed how some of the names – well over twenty, in fact – had been scribbled out with red marker. A few of those rang a bell straight away. Ronald Po and Anton Trevelyan – the two university pals shot to death in Oxford. Austin Ledburn; wasn't he the haulier doused with petrol and burned in the woods near Andover? It shouldn't have surprised him the Nice Guys were working to a fast timetable – they wanted to get the job done and get home again. But it was a shock that they'd already clocked up so many victims, many of whom were presumably still waiting to be found. Even given the murderers' high level of improvisational skill, it was amazing they'd been able to put together so many missions so quickly when they'd only got hold of the client info from Laycock five days ago.

Despite that mystery, Heck wanted to shout in triumph – but his excitement was tempered by the overall number of names on the list. At least eighty.

Eighty.

SCU had established that the Nice Guys' tally of victims in the UK was thirty-eight at least. They'd estimated that another ten or so might still be unknown. But another forty-two! Raped and murdered, still lying in undiscovered graves!

And that was assuming each of these men had been content with one victim each.

Heck folded the list and crammed it into his back pocket. It would be tricky presenting this as evidence, but he didn't care. They had the all-important names.

He backed into the centre of the room, pivoting around. An inner sense advised him that time was running out. But there had to be something else here he could use.

He went back into the hall and began searching coats and jackets, rifling their pockets, finding a train ticket stub, a pen or two – and a phone.

A rather smart one. An expensive-looking iPhone.

The coat he'd taken it from was a khaki overcoat; no different to many of the others there. He pocketed the phone and was about to search some more when a shadow flickered past. He whipped around, staring along the hall towards the front door. No one was visible on the other side of its glass panel, but he knew someone had just walked past. He back-tracked a few yards, flattening himself against a wainscoted wall to peer into the dining room. Half a second later, someone trudged past its window, headed towards the rear of the property.

It was the Australian sentry.

Heck ran hell-for-leather back along the hall, but when he reached the front door, it was locked. He jerked around as booted feet clumped on the kitchen's brick floor. From this position, he could see clear through to the cast-iron range, a shadow swelling across it as the feet clumped louder. He had no choice but to dart up the stairs, hoping the dull, repeating thud of the grandfather clock would mask the sound of his own footfalls. When he arrived on the landing, he crouched to listen. The heavy feet plodded around downstairs, in and out of various rooms. At the same time, there came the gravelly growl of an engine from outside. Heck stood up and ventured to an arched window, beyond which he saw a Mondeo estate and a Peugeot 207 re-entering through the main gate. The Mondeo came straight on, but the Peugeot halted, and one of the Nice Guys climbed out, taking up the sentry post.

Downstairs meanwhile, those feet were crossing the hall towards the foot of the stairs. Heck snatched again at his Glock. Did he just go for it? Try and arrest them all now?

That was a crazy idea. This Aussie shithead alone was armed with an assault rifle, and would easily outgun him.

Heck entered the first bedroom he came to, where there surely had to be a hiding place. The room was neatly if sparsely furnished – a real holiday let if ever he'd seen one, but the sheets and coverlet on the bed were unruffled. None of the Nice Guys were sleeping up here; another defence against leaving DNA, and yet a door led into an en-suite bathroom, in which a Bergen kit bag was dumped against the radiator. There was something else in there too – a tall, arched window. At the sound of boots on the stair, Heck skedaddled into the en-suite. If the window was locked he'd have no option but to kick it through, jump out and run for it.

Jump . . . yeah. And how was he going to run with two broken ankles?

But the window wasn't locked. It was merely on the latch. As quietly as possible, he opened it. The boots had now reached the landing, and came thudding in this direction. In addition, now the window was open, he could hear the slamming of car doors. But the cars were parked at the front of the house, and this window looked down on the north side, on the footpath running past the potting shed and the old garage. The window was also part of a gable-fronted dormer, set into the slope of the roof. It would be risky underfoot, but at least he'd have a parapet to balance on. Heck sidled out, more grateful than he could say for the rubber grips of his trainers. Clinging with fingertips to the rugged slates composing the dormer roof, he pushed the window closed with his left foot, before clambering around the side of the structure, out of sight from within and hopefully from below.

Then he could do nothing except wait, pressing himself into the join between the dormer and the roof, arms and feet outspread, sweat beading his face. He heard movement inside the bathroom. There was a dull thumping. He pictured the Australian rooting through his kit bag. A second later, those sounds fell silent.

Had the Aussie withdrawn, or had he spotted the window open a crack?

With a clunk, a slate under Heck's backside broke and he felt himself sliding downward. He struggled desperately to brace himself and at the same time catch hold of the errant slate – both of which he achieved, though with no little scuffling. He held his breath again, listening. The silence inside persisted. Very cautiously, he adjusted his position – at which point something else detached from his person.

Heck watched in disbelief as the list of Nice Guys' clients slipped down the roof, unfolding as it did and fluttering out of sight.

He hung on there for several more heart-stopping moments, listening intently but hearing no commotion, either from inside the bathroom or down on the footpath. Then, slowly and clumsily, he straightened himself up, took a grip on the dormer corner, and leaned forward, peering first into the bathroom, which was indeed empty, and then down into the passage below – just as one of the Nice Guys came trudging along it. The stapled list lay in plain view, just left of the path.

But face-down, presenting nothing more than a blank sheet of paper.

Heck sucked air through tight-locked teeth as he watched. The Nice Guy strode past, never giving it a glance, vanishing around the back of the house.

Heck swallowed bitter saliva. They were all over the premises now. He could hear their voices. Even if he didn't get spotted up here, the list would be found, and sooner rather than later. In addition – he glanced at his watch – he had only twenty minutes before his RV with the Northumbria firearms team.

It was two or three metres down to the edge of the roof, and Heck had to cover that distance on his heels and backside, constantly aware that slates were cracking and slithering. When he reached the guttering, it was made of aged, scabrous iron, clogged with old nests. About six yards along that, a drainpipe descended. Whether it would hold his weight, he didn't know, but he balanced his way towards it on all fours, and lowered himself over the edge.

The pipe shifted and creaked, and he clambered down it quickly. When he hit the bottom, he dropped to a crouch, snatching up the list and glancing in both directions. Voices were encroaching from all sides. He heard the Aussie twang again, the broken-nosed maniac conversing with someone who replied in a Scandinavian accent. That exchange was at the rear of the house, but drawing closer. Heck bolted down the narrow gap between the potting shed and garage. He scrambled over the perimeter wall, and sprinted away into the trees, ears pinned back for any sounds of pursuit – and hearing nothing of the sort.

Only as the property fell behind him, did he shove the client list back into his pocket, and fish out the iPhone. He prodded at its keyboard, managing to open its directory. There was no time to search it properly, but he immediately saw reams of telephone numbers, many of which looked as if they were located overseas. When he scrolled down the directory of contacts, it went on and on. He ran faster, perhaps no longer exercising the necessary caution, but eager to put as much distance between himself and the farmhouse as he could. He glanced at his watch. It was twenty-five past three. He was due at the RV point in five minutes, so he had no option but to sprint. It wouldn't matter; the vanguard of the Northumbrian firearms response should already be in position. Help was close at hand.

However, when he burst out of the bushes onto the road

leading to the junction, it was suspiciously quiet. It was possible they'd had the common sense to find a covert lying-up point, but Heck was suddenly uneasy. He stepped back into the undergrowth before heading on towards the cross-roads. When he reached it, there was a single vehicle parked there: a purple Land Rover Discovery. It was parked by the phone booth, at the end of the road approaching from the southeast. No one was inside it.

Bewildered, Heck walked across the road. It was possible this vehicle had nothing to do with him. Maybe Northumbria had yet to turn up. But why had this car been left here unattended? And why did it seem vaguely familiar? When a foot scuffed the road surface behind him, he attempted to turn – only for a sharp, stinging blow to impact on the back of his neck.

Chapter 31

Gemma Piper felt as if she was midway through a whistle-stop tour of the entire British Isles. She'd spent the previous night in the Highlands, while most of today had seen her on the move – over yet another empty, desolate landscape.

The Police Scotland Eurocopter had brought both she and Frank Tasker back from Clashnessie to Glasgow City Heliport, at which point they'd parted ways. The original plan would have seen both of them continuing by chopper to Edinburgh, if a message hadn't been waiting for them at the police office at Glasgow City. This was from Detective Constable Charlie Finnegan, the officer she'd assigned to check the body found in Yorkshire. Far from giving it the once-over and dismissing it from the enquiry straight away – which is what they'd expected given there was no writing on or anywhere near it – Finnegan had felt some immediate concerns and now wanted supervisory back-up. As there was no one from Bronze Command even close to North Yorkshire, Tasker had opted to continue to Edinburgh alone, leaving Gemma under orders to head back to the MIR in London, visiting North Yorks en route to see what the problem was.

Gemma had thus waited by the Glasgow helipad for another hour after Tasker had lofted away in the Scottish chopper, before transferring to the North East Air Support unit's own Eurocopter. Now she was back in the air, traversing more barren summits, thick forests and rolling moors. Like those north of the border, they stretched on interminably. It didn't help that she hadn't been able to speak directly to any of her team all day – she was still very much out of range – but at least this break was giving her a chance to sift through the facts and try to gain a little perspective on an investigation which, like so many others SCU had become embroiled in, appeared to be expanding in every direction at an exponential rate. Her attention flirted between a personal notebook crammed with handwritten observations, and her iPad, which was equally crammed with page after page of information: statements, reports, data of every type, though none of it made for encouraging reading.

The rate at which the Nice Guys were hitting their victims was the most unique and unsettling aspect of all this. Their efficiency was a big worry too. Despite adopting the cowboy approach this time around, they still weren't leaving much physical evidence. Usable prints and DNA samples were non-existent at every crime scene. Incredible though it seemed, they were almost invisible and yet at the same time happy to leave their crazy calling card, not to mention the bodies of their victims on show like grim totems of their power. Of course, this had been the Nice Guys' business from the outset, as former commandos and mercenaries – professional practitioners of homicidal violence. The skills of the hunt and the ability to melt unnoticed into whichever community they'd infiltrated were ingrained into them. It was no wonder they could come and go like ghosts.

The chopper put down on a moorland car park seemingly in the middle of nowhere. Sweeps of rough, tussocky pasture undulated away in all directions, rising in the west to sheer limestone scarps. According to the pilot, this was a popular tourist spot; hikers, walkers, bird-spotters and the like tended to park here, though there was no other vehicle present now, save a Vauxhall Astra with North Yorkshire Police markings.

The driver, a stocky, dark-haired uniform, Sergeant Lisa Manfredi, introduced herself and said she was at Gemma's disposal for the rest of her shift.

'When does your shift end, Sergeant Manfredi?' Gemma asked as she stowed her bag in the rear foot-well and climbed into the front passenger seat.

'Ten o'clock tonight, ma'am.'

'Well . . . hopefully I won't need to keep you that long. Once I've made an assessment of the body at Ripon, I could do with visiting your HQ at Northallerton.'

'No problem on that, ma'am. DSU Benford, from the Northeast Regional Organised Crime Unit's expecting you. Your man on the spot seems to think this might be one of yours.'

'We mustn't jump to any conclusions, Sergeant Manfredi.'

'Course not, ma'am.'

'If this body was found ninety feet down a sink-hole, that suggests the perpetrators, or perpetrator, was trying to conceal it,' Gemma explained. 'That would be quite a divergence from the pattern that's emerged so far. Makes it more likely, at least to my mind, that it belongs to another case entirely. What do we actually know about the victim?'

'We've no name as yet, ma'am. I mean, he was severely beaten and then burned with an accelerant – probably petrol. It cost him all his fingerprints apparently. But he was a white male, somewhere in his late thirties or early forties.'

'Who found him?'

'Bunch of cavers. Bad luck on the killers' part.'

337

'Or ignorance,' Gemma said. 'If, for some reason, they didn't know this is potholing country.' And given that the majority of the Nice Guys – as far as the police knew – were foreigners, that was not a pleasing thought.

They arrived at Ripon Community Hospital half an hour later, pulling into an empty bay in the personnel car park, close to the mortuary entrance. Charlie Finnegan was already waiting there, pacing up and down. He was a lean, peevish-looking man with slick black hair.

'Ma'am,' he said with the semi-exasperated air of someone who'd been kept waiting an unnecessary length of time.

'What've we got, Charlie?'

He checked his notes as they headed across the car park. 'Male IC1, around forty years old. Suffered multiple injuries consistent with severe and protracted torture, but according to the local examiner, the eventual cause of death was asphyxia.'

'Asphyxia?'

'He was choked on a stick. They shoved it down his throat.'

'Good God . . .'

'After that he was doused in petrol and set alight.'

'That was definitely post mortem?'

'Apparently so.' They entered the hospital together, Finnegan leading the way along a white-tiled corridor smelling strongly of disinfectant. 'The aim seems to have been to destroy any distinguishing features, which it more or less did.'

'Doesn't *sound* like a Nice Guys' hit.'

'That's what I thought before I got here, ma'am . . . but I've spoken to the examiner, and to be honest . . . this guy wasn't just beaten up. They gave him a real going-over. Over a period of hours. We're talking pliers, razor blades . . .'

Gemma glanced sidelong at him.

338

'I know,' he said. 'That guy Culbrook down in Kent. That was a Nice Guys' hit, wasn't it? And they used pliers and razor blades in that case.'

'There was definitely no calling card?'

'None on the body or clothing. I've even been looking down the cave, which wasn't easy, I can tell you, and there was nothing there either. Ma'am . . . there's another matter. I've had SOCAR bending my ear all day about Heck.'

'Who at SOCAR?'

'An Inspector O'Dowd.'

'Oh yeah . . . why was he bending *your* ear?'

Finnegan shrugged. 'I'm guessing because he knew I'd be seeing you.'

'Why didn't he ring me personally? He's got my number.'

'Reckons he'd been trying, but you were out of range. So was Commander Tasker.'

'And?' she said.

'Well he wants to know what we're going to do about Heck. Apparently one of their lads got a real kicking.'

'So will Heck, don't worry . . . metaphorically speaking, of course.'

'Can you call O'Dowd back?'

'All in good time, Charlie.' They turned into the mortuary. 'We're investigating a murder here. It's about priorities.'

The mortuary examination room was not busy. The majority of the porcelain slabs had been mopped down recently; the tiled floor was sparkling clean under the big fluorescent lights. It was the kind of place Gemma and her crew visited often, yet when she set eyes on the single body lying there, it stunned her into silence. She walked slowly forward, and said nothing for several seconds – before turning and walking stiffly out again, even vacating the outer corridor, only stopping when she was back in the car park.

Finnegan glanced down the passage after her, puzzled,

before re-entering the examination room. He gazed blankly at the corpse, which was gruesomely burned, its entire epidermis missing, the organs and musculature crisply flambéed. It was no pretty sight, especially the way its head had jack-knifed backwards on a neck rendered stiff by the charred Malacca cane jammed so deeply down its gullet that only its handle protruded from the melted orifice that had once been a mouth. But even then her reaction had been a surprise.

'Funny,' he said to the attendant. 'She's seen hundreds of these. Thought she had a stronger stomach than that.'

Outside, Gemma hastily produced her phone and was about to stab in Tasker's number, but managed to stop herself in time. Only now were the possible repercussions of what she'd just seen dawning on her.

There was no mistaking who that was in there. They'd need forensic confirmation of course – for anyone who didn't know him well, he'd be unrecognisable. But she'd sat face to face across prison interview-room tables too many times with Peter Rochester, aka Mad Mike Silver, to make such a basic error. In fact it was all too easy – horribly easy – for her to superimpose those sneering, arrogant features over the burned mask of the atrocity in the mortuary. If that hadn't been enough, she would never have failed to recognise the distinctive Malacca cane that Silver had been given by the prison medical wing. She'd likely have made that link earlier if she'd known the actual cause of death, but thanks to her flitting about all over the North Highlands she'd been too far off the grid for the full details – including any specific reference to a Malacca cane – to be passed on in advance.

All that aside, it was the import of this that frightened her most.

Silver had not been rescued after all. He'd been abducted, tortured and murdered. More importantly, they'd tried to commit this crime quietly rather than publicly, leaving no signature – because if this body was ever found it would have revealed that they knew she'd been wearing him down in the interviews, that there was a danger he'd soon talk.

Suddenly it all made a terrible kind of sense. Why else would the Nice Guys make their move to nab Silver now, two years into his sentence, only to kill him? Why go to all that trouble, expense and risk – if not for their somehow knowing that he was very close to spilling the beans on their overseas operation? And of course there was only one way they could have known that, just as there was only one way they could have known in advance that Silver was being moved to hospital . . . It was clear they had another informer in the higher echelons of the investigation team, someone who'd been watching every move the police made and reporting it back. Or maybe it wasn't another informer; maybe it was the same one who'd hamstrung Heck's original enquiry into the Nice Guys two years ago, which narrowed the list of suspects down dramatically . . . a list which, for rather obvious reasons, no longer contained Jim Laycock.

It took a minute or so before Gemma could compose herself enough to make a phone call that would sound sufficiently normal. She knew she couldn't make a song and dance about this. If she let it out that she was now aware the Nice Guys' former boss had not been sprung from custody by his old mates, but in fact had been kidnapped and murdered because they knew he was close to turning evidence on them, the Nice Guys would also expect her to have realised she had a mole in her ranks – a mole she'd probably find quickly – and in response they'd simply bolt for cover. She'd lose any chance of arresting them.

She had to be careful how she played this – she had to be *so* careful. Which wouldn't be easy, as she was still fizzing like a bottle of pop.

There was no answer on the number she initially rang, so

she then tried Eric Fisher at SCU. He answered in his usual gruff manner. But when she told Fisher which officer she wanted to speak to, he replied in a perplexed tone that he hadn't seen that person for most of the day. No one had, in fact. And Fisher was at a loss to explain this.

'Thanks very much, Eric,' she replied, cutting the call.

Somewhat sheepishly, Charlie Finnegan reappeared in the hospital doorway. Hands in pockets, he ventured across the car park.

'You alright, ma'am?'

'I'm alright, thank you, Charlie,' she said. Despite her best efforts, she knew she still looked shaken. But could she trust Finnegan with the information she'd just uncovered? It was probably best not to, though it would only, in truth, be a matter of time before they all found out.

'Sorry if that caught you by surprise,' he said. 'I should have warned you it was bad.'

'It's okay . . . I'm fine.'

'Erm . . . don't want to harp on about this, ma'am. But what about Heck?'

'Heck?'

'What I said earlier.'

'Oh yeah . . . Heck.'

'SOCAR have been trying to trace his movements. They actually reckon he was heading up this way, to the Northeast.'

'How convenient,' she said, still distracted. 'Or how inconvenient, depending on your perspective.'

'Ma'am . . .?'

'Just humour me a minute, Charlie.'

'Yeah sure, but . . . well, they reckon it's a real problem. According to the SOCAR detail who lost him, Heck's . . . well, quote, "behaving like a fucking maniac".'

'Is he?' Gemma almost laughed. 'You'd better get onto SOCAR . . . tell them they ain't seen nothing yet.'

Chapter 32

'I'm going to kill you slowly,' Heck said through gritted teeth. 'And I'm going to kill you last . . . so you know exactly what's coming to you.'

He was seated on the floor, propped up against the Discovery's wheel-arch. But even though his eyes had only just fluttered open and his head still thumped, he was struggling to get to grips with the sight of his captor. 'You know why I'm going to do that, Ben?' he said. 'Quite simply, because you deserve nothing less.'

DCI Ben Kane chuckled, but noticeably kept the Glock trained squarely on his prisoner, while at the same time stuffing the Nice Guys' client list and their iPhone into his jacket pocket. 'Codswallop, Heck. You're the one who's operating outside the law . . . again. You're the one who's here when you should be in custody; you're the one who stole a police vehicle and a police firearm. On which subject, thanks for *this*. It would have been difficult me leaving the office and for no good reason drawing a pistol on the way. You've solved that problem for me.'

Heck could still hardly believe it. There had never been a second mole. There'd only ever been one – and they'd even got *his* identity wrong. 'Just for clarity's sake, Ben, does this seriously mean *you* were the Nice Guys' insider all along?'

Kane chuckled again. 'You mean you hadn't worked that out? Perhaps I blew my cover too soon.'

'I thought their original snout was Jim Laycock.'

'Laycock was certainly guilty . . . but in his case of arrogance and incompetence. I'm a cannier operator.'

'No . . . no, just let me get this straight,' Heck said. 'You're telling me Jim Laycock had nothing to do with the Nice Guys?'

'Nothing whatsoever. He was never their client, never their snitch.' Kane's grin widened, the eyes strained and glassy behind his spectacle lenses. 'Talk about getting things arse-about-tit, Heck. You genuinely never thought it might be me? An unmarried bloke of my age . . . who never spoke to anyone about the women in his life, never brought a girlfriend to a Christmas do?'

Heck shook his head, at first too appalled to reply, not just by the critical error he'd made, but also embarrassed at how easily Ben Kane – studious, scholarly 'Mr Prissy' Ben Kane – had pulled the wool over all their eyes.

'How the world changes, eh?' Kane said. 'Twenty years ago it would have been "Shirt-lifter Ben", not "Schoolmaster Ben". But of course they'd have been wrong then too. I prefer women, but I prefer them subservient. *Very* subservient. Hey, don't look so stunned, Heck . . . you're the arch psycho-hunter. You ought to know deep in your gut by now that it's – what's that phrase? – *always the quiet ones.*'

'I'm more surprised they even took you on,' Heck replied. 'One look at you, Ben, and most crims piss themselves laughing.'

Kane's grin tightened. 'I think you'll find the Nice Guys knew my capabilities from an early stage. I first fell in with them as a paying customer. Made contact with them through

344

connections I had in Vice. Word had got out, you see – to a select bunch of pimps and traffickers, that I could be greased. I mean, I wasn't the only one, was I, Heck? I'm not the only one now. Though my price-tag was a bit different from the norm – and ultimately, only Mad Mike Silver and the Nice Guys could meet it. Of course, their price was a bit different too. You see, I was very well placed to keep them advised about various missing persons enquiries – about the progress being made, or lack of it – and later on, about the somewhat more insightful investigation being run by a certain bolshy young DS in the Serial Crimes Unit.'

Even Heck found trouble providing a snappy response to this. It almost defied logic that Ben Kane was the reason the Nice Guys had been one step ahead these last few weeks; that he was the reason they'd been one step ahead the first time; that he was the one who'd spirited away their original list of clients. Though at least it explained how the killers had been so proficient in tracking and assassinating their recent targets. They'd had the list longer than Heck had thought – months, maybe years.

'I knew my name was on that client list when it first showed up in London,' Kane explained cheerily. 'So, seriously . . . what would you have done other than make it disappear?'

'In which case why was Laycock murdered and not you?' Heck asked.

'Well . . . *duh*!' Again Kane looked amused, but also surprised at how little Heck knew. 'Why would they kill their own super-grass? They need me now for the same reason they've always needed me. I'm their all-hearing ear. I especially won brownie points with them when I let them know Silver was getting close to spilling the beans during those prison interviews with Gemma. That was what finally brought them back to Blighty.'

345

'And let me guess . . . killing Laycock was a diversion? It would make us think the SCU mole had been disposed of once and for all.'

Kane grinned again and nodded. 'Got it in one.'

'Tasker thought we still had a mole. Otherwise, why bug the office?'

Kane rolled his eyes. 'Tasker's one of those blue-eyed boys who always seem to rise in this job without actually ever being right. You know . . . one of these slimy characters who always get invited to the Commissioner's table while the rest of us have to work that little bit extra just to get noticed. His main aim in bugging the phones was to keep you in the dark about the enquiry. It could also have netted him a mole, had I, as a senior supervisor, not been party to his plans. But if it had done, it would have been a fortunate accident – not an unusual occurrence in his career, I suspect.'

'Jesus . . . Jesus H. Christ.' Perhaps now wasn't the time for Heck to feel guilty. But it was slowly striking home how horrendous his misjudgement of Jim Laycock had truly been.

Kane seemed to sense this line of thought, and had no hesitation rubbing it in. 'And who made it possible for big Jim to take the fall, if not you, Heck? All those nasty, unfounded allegations. I mean, come on . . . condemning another copper to certain death! Even by your standards, that was something of a faux-pas.'

Heck briefly felt sick. Laycock had never been much of a copper. For him it had all been about appearances – meeting targets, massaging the figures. As long as things *looked* good he was happy, because that would only reflect well on him. But he'd never deserved the fate Heck had indirectly sent him to.

Not that it was Heck who'd wielded the claw-hammer, of course.

'And it wasn't just Laycock, was it?' Heck said. 'You tried

to dispose of me too. You set me and Gary Quinnell up in Stoke Newington.'

Kane gave an expansive shrug. 'I even set up the crimes you were due to investigate there.'

'What . . .?'

Kane chuckled again. 'The reason Stoke Newington CID got nowhere near the Shoreditch Slasher, couldn't track him for love nor money, is quite simple . . . he didn't exist. Well, technically he *did* exist, but not as some malfunctioning lowlife who got his jollies ripping women's faces . . . as one of the Nice Guys doing a specific job, with a bit of "sex offender" coaching from yours truly.' Kane mused. 'I think he quite enjoyed rearranging a few Plain Janes' fizzogs.'

'Ben . . . are you fucking insane! One of those girls lost her eye!'

'Had to make it real, Heck. I needed some reason to get you up there, firstly to keep you occupied, but failing that, to set up some kind of ambush. And then look what happened. I gave them your exact route, your exact timings . . . but you proved your usual tricky self. Of course, I couldn't send them after you once you were installed in that safehouse in the Cotswolds. If you'd been hit there, Gemma would have realised we still had a leak. It crossed my mind briefly that she might have been setting a trap – using you as bait to see if the SCU mole was still functioning despite Laycock's death. But now I think she just wanted you out of the way. It's not like she didn't have good reason, is it?'

Despite his desperate urge to jump to his feet, try to dodge the inevitable bullet and beat the living shit out of his gloating captor, Heck couldn't help but sit there and listen. Because it sounded as if he was yet to hear the biggest revelation of the day.

'So you hadn't worked this bit out either?' Kane laughed. 'You're not going to like it, Heck, you really aren't. But the

347

irony is . . . it's all your fault. Ever since the first Nice Guys enquiry, and your incessant blabbing, Interpol and Europol have been leaning on the Home Office. They've got lists of their own missing women the size of phone directories, and yet in Mad Mike Silver we had the world's only known Nice Guy prisoner. The pressure was on to get him to talk, and so as you know, Gemma and Tasker were trying to cut a deal with him. What you don't know is that he would only play ball in exchange for his freedom. Obviously that wasn't possible, but it was eventually proposed that, in return for chapter and verse on Nice Guys operations abroad, more comfortable accommodation – *significantly* more comfortable – might be found for him. He said he'd think about this – he wanted to try it out before he made up his mind. Of course, simply moving him to this new home was out of the question. The public would never have forgiven us. So it had to be done secretly. An escape was staged. Silver was given drugs . . .'

Heck's face slackened in disbelief.

Kane laughed again, loudly. 'Yeah, that's right, pal . . . *we* smuggled in those drugs to induce that fake heart attack. We – or rather SOCAR – were the ones set to ambush the cavalcade. Unfortunately, thanks to yours truly, the real Nice Guys learned all about this – and I mean, what a break for them! The cavalcade got bushwhacked a good ten miles before it reached the point where our ambushers were waiting. And how easy was it? Thanks to the intelligence blackout, no local forces knew anything out of the ordinary was happening. Even if word had got out at the time, they'd have been hard-pressed to respond effectively.'

'How . . . how did you know all this?' Heck stammered. 'You weren't party to those prison interviews.'

'Gimme a break, Heck . . . I was Gemma's deputy. I was always there, always hanging around. She may not have consciously trusted me with the top secret stuff, but it wasn't difficult sniffing it out. I've got keys to her drawers, passwords to her encrypted files. But who'd have thought it, eh? DSU Piper! Britain's top lady detective! Once the love of your life . . . aiding and abetting a prison break by the most reviled criminal in history. And so many lives lost in the process.' There was a loud bleeping from his pocket. He fished out his phone. 'Good . . . they're on their way back.'

Heck was still attempting to digest what he'd been told. It was almost inconceivable, and yet it made a grotesque kind of sense. No wonder SOCAR had tried to imprison him rather than let him join the investigation . . . no wonder Gemma had gone along with it. Though understanding why didn't necessarily forgive. He doubted he'd ever be able to forgive her anything after what he'd just heard.

'I told the NGs not to wander off too far,' Kane added by way of explanation. 'Just enough to flush you out.'

'Why didn't you just tell them where I was when I first rang you, so they could grab me there and then?'

'Because I know you, Heck. How you don't bother following orders. How you wouldn't be waiting by this phone, even though I specifically instructed you to. How you'd find some covert position from where you could do your own thing. At the very least, you'd have seen them coming. In addition, I wanted to be here personally. As you may have guessed, I was already halfway up the A1 when I got your call. How else could I have made it so quickly?'

'Getting jumpy, were you?' Heck wondered. 'All these bodies stacking up. And your name on the Nice Guys' paperwork.'

Kane shrugged. 'I will admit to deciding it was time I had a face to face with Mr Klausen. See if I could persuade him to depart these shores again. It wouldn't have been easy, even then. He always lacked Mike Silver's wider vision . . . not to mention his professional control. Plus . . . well, I think he enjoyed it all a bit too much. I mean, all that calling card stuff. I advised against it, but he really wanted to inflict pain and fear. Wanted to leave you guys in no doubt there was a new bad boy in town. I said all along that once Silver had been removed from the picture, there was no point them staying. That their former clients were weak, frightened nobodies who couldn't grass on anyone because they knew nothing. But Klausen's always been one to try and kill two birds with one stone . . . or two dozen, come to that.'

'Klausen's the tall guy with the blond hair, I'm guessing?'

Kane nodded. 'Kurt Klausen. He was Mad Mike's second-in-command in the Foreign Legion. Good soldiers by all accounts. Paratroopers, Counter-Terrorist Brigade. But as a Brit and Dane, their opportunities for promotion were limited. When Mad Mike broke away to form a mercenary company, Klausen went with him. When he formed the Nice Guys, Klausen went with him again.'

'And does Klausen run things in Europe?'

'I'm not party to all these details, Heck. At the end of the day I'm just their grass. But you'd be an idiot to imagine there aren't others like him. This octopus has many tentacles.'

The Ford Mondeo Heck had seen earlier now approached from the northwest, cruising to a halt about fifty yards from the junction. At the same time, another vehicle, a Toyota Corolla, approached from the southwest. That too parked about fifty yards down the road.

'You know what I hate most about these pals of yours?' Heck said, noting that quite a few men had arrived in the two vehicles.

'Do tell.'

'Our country's always at war. Every generation sees its young guys come home shattered. They do the best they can, but they're never the same again. And yet these scrotes you've fallen in with . . . they don't suffer, they don't regret. They seem to thrive on it . . .'

'So do you, Heck.' Kane signalled to the figures climbing from the newly arrived vehicles. 'Least, that's the impression I get. Do you consider yourself a scrote? Or what is it . . . that old cliché? It takes a wolf to catch a wolf. Is that how you excuse yourself?'

'And how do you excuse *your*self, Ben?'

'I'm a survivor, that's all. I'm not fond of my indiscretions. But I dare say we all have sexual tastes we'd be ashamed to admit in public.'

'Except that in most cases they don't amount to rape and murder.'

'Then you're very fortunate you have no uncontrollable chemical imbalance that's likely to ruin your life should word about it get out.'

'What are you saying . . . it's not your fault?' Heck tried to scoff, but was uncomfortably aware of the Nice Guys – nine of them in total, five from one car, four from the other – encroaching on foot along the adjoining roads.

'I'm saying I'm not going to prison for a sexual preference I have no control over,' Kane said. 'Not at all. I'll continue to do whatever it takes to keep me alive and functioning in this world. I don't believe there's an afterlife . . .'

'Good thing, given what you'll be facing if there is!'

'This is the only time I've got, Heck. And I don't intend to waste it.'

'You're still gonna pay for this, Kane.'

'But you first. Stand up.'

Heck clambered to his feet, nausea gripping his guts as the two groups of figures came together at the crossroads, and then, with the man called Klausen at their centre, spread out like a clutch of Wild West outlaws, drawing various firearms from under their coats and jackets. Kane kept the

351

Glock trained on Heck, but took several steps backwards until he was alongside his Discovery.

The only Nice Guy who didn't draw a weapon was Klausen himself. He stood with arms folded, an odd fixed grin on his handsome yet scarred face. 'Well . . . Sergeant Heckenburg,' he said in his distinctive accent. 'You really are quite a guy. In London, I sent three of our best men after you. Only two came back, one with a smashed nose, the other with a fractured kneecap.'

'The pleasure was all mine,' Heck replied.

'Wiseass fucker, ain't he?' came an American voice, and Heck focused on the figure to Klausen's right; he had a shaved-down flat-top and a limp. Up close, there was something particularly disturbing about this character. He was ashen-cheeked with freckles, almost boyish – he didn't look old enough or mean enough to be involved with this crew. And yet his glittery grey eyes were the closest organic things to broken glass Heck had ever seen.

'Give my regards to your Aussie pal,' Heck said. 'Pity he's not the handsome devil he once was, eh?'

'He'll sure be sorry he missed you.'

As though at some unspoken command, the Nice Guys raised their weapons. Heck's spine went rigid, but it was half a second before he realised the roaring in his ears was not the blood rushing into his head, but the fast approach of an engine.

Despite the narrowness of the northwest road, the blue Chevrolet came hurtling around its bend, swerving past the parked Mondeo with a speed beyond reckless. An attempted handbrake turn saw it skid sideways into the junction, all four tyres smoking, the Nice Guys scattering. Heck dived out of the way too, and rolled as it slewed past him and hit Kane's Discovery with jarring force – *WHAM!* – spinning around in the middle of the crossroads. Kane's car was buffeted onto the verge, shattering the telephone booth, and slamming into its owner side-on. Kane half-somersaulted, the tarmac smacking him in the back like a sledgehammer, the Glock skittering away.

That was the first thing Heck went for, at the same time taking cover behind the Chevrolet. With a crunch of crumpled metal, its driver's door burst open.

'*Heck . . . get in!*' Farthing shrieked.

But Heck was still scrabbling after the gun, and that half-second was all the Nice Guys needed. Their training initially had them going to ground, but they still opened up on the intruding vehicle. Heck hit the road surface, Farthing falling out alongside him as an Amazon of lead ripped through his pride and joy, its windows and bodywork exploding.

One of the bastards, thinking them cowed, ran around the front end of the Chevrolet, boots slamming the tarmac. 'Hold your fire, boys!' he shouted in loud, brash Cockney. 'I got 'em!' He was tall and lean, with an oval, eerily skullish face split crosswise by a deranged grin. He hefted a Steyr TMP, taking careful aim.

But Heck was already shooting.

The Cockney's visage exploded as five rounds hammered through the middle of it, the sixth smacking him on the left temple, his blood and brains ejecting every which way as he tottered backwards.

'How's that for a rearranged fizzog?' Heck said under his breath, continuing firing, hitting the bastard four times more before he crash-landed – though in retrospect that had been a mistake. He only had seventeen shots in this clip, while the others were still in his coat, which was out of reach.

The fallen Nice Guy had his Steyr of course, but that had clattered a few yards across the road towards Ben Kane, who had recovered sufficiently to go lumbering after it. Heck pegged a shot at him, punching it through his left shoulder, spinning him like a toy. Twirling back, he spotted another Nice Guy peeking around the rear end of the Land Rover. Heck pegged two shots at him as well, forcing him to retreat.

By luck rather than design, he and Farthing had finished up in a defensible position. The two half-wrecked vehicles had created a chevron across the junction, blocking off the southeast exit, thus providing them with a retreat but at the same time creating a barricade – though the Nice Guys were now giving it all they'd got, systematically shooting the two vehicles to pieces. Fleetingly, Farthing's face came into Heck's eye-line: white, sweat-drenched, but not haggard the way it had been in Sunderland, not sickly with fear. The dumpy copper was kneeling, cringing, but his jaw was set, his mouth clamped with determination.

Another flicker of movement caught Heck's eye. He spun, seeing Nice Guys attempting to flank them through undergrowth on the west side. He blasted wild shots in their general direction, again forcing them to cover. In the same motion, he hunkered down, scuttled after the Steyr and tossed it at Farthing, who caught it smartly.

More Nice Guys sidled to the rear of the Range Rover, only to fall back as Farthing, still kneeling, sprayed lead at them. Heck meanwhile, crawled over to Ben Kane, who lay on his back, his glasses skewwhiff; blood seeped copiously from the back of his shoulder, and he writhed slowly – as though only semi-conscious. When Heck began rifling his pockets, he tried to speak, but a swift head-butt to the mouth put him out for the count. Heck continued searching, finding first the list and then mobile phone, both of which he shoved into his own pockets.

He turned back. The crossroads was now a battlefield, thick with the stink of gun-smoke, wreckage and shell-casings littered everywhere. Farthing had moved closer to the narrow gap between the two car-wrecks, still returning fire as the

Nice Guys scampered across the road, but now in short, sharp bursts. Heck fired a couple more shots in support of him, emptying his clip.

'Get out of here!' Farthing shouted over his shoulder.

'What?'

'If you've got what you need, whatever you came for . . . just go!'

Heck hovered there, helpless. To leave Farthing behind was the last thing he wanted, but it was all true. He had everything he needed to take the Nice Guys down for good. But he wouldn't have it long if he stayed here. And they wouldn't be able to fight it out much longer, either. Heck was out of ammo. Farthing couldn't be far off the end.

'Go!' Farthing shouted again. 'While the coast's clear.'

Heck went, running low along the southeast road, diverting into the southern line of underbrush about forty yards along, discarding his empty pistol en route.

PC Jerry Farthing wasn't quite sure what it was that had possessed him.

Something about being a coward, being a failure, being a loser. Something about being forty-five years old, with nothing but a lifetime of daytime telly to look forward to – if he was lucky. More important than that, it was something about his dad: the genial giant, the working-class hero, the iron man with the heart of gold, who'd been so proud that day of his son's passing-out parade at Durham, when Jerry had emerged into the world as a young policeman, that he'd taken the lad and his mum for dinner, a meal they couldn't really afford, in honour of 'the first among us to really make something of himself'.

For all that, it was still a bit of a dream; Farthing's body deadened, his hair standing on end, the Steyr jerking in his hands, its heat embracing him.

355

'*Bastards!*' he howled, horrified and delighted at the ease with which these notorious killers were driven to cover. Allegedly, there were more than a few combat soldiers among them, experienced guys. But they'd been professional bully boys for the last few years. Maybe they'd forgotten what it was like to take fire in return. He was so absorbed that he never really saw Ben Kane come lurching up at his rear, stooping to pick up a broken strut of steel from the flattened telephone booth. Farthing glanced around at the last second, just as his weapon ran dry – but it was too late. The impact on his skull was a bomb going off.

He managed to get to his feet and swing the Steyr at the tottering, bloodied figure. But fleetingly, Farthing's world had turned searing white. He tried to focus on the Nice Guys advancing beyond the smashed cars, gazing at him along their barrels.

When five rapid shots followed, each striking Farthing's midriff, he barely felt them. But they still knocked him down in a twisted, tangled heap.

'*After Heckenburg!*' Klausen barked, vaulting over the Discovery's bonnet. Three of his men set off at a gallop, vanishing through the bushes. Kane lumbered forward, grey-faced and bloody. 'You didn't tell us Heckenburg had a partner,' the Dane snarled, kicking at Farthing's crumpled body.

'I don't know who that moron is,' Kane stammered, spitting crimson phlegm.

'Are you alright?'

'The wound's superficial, but I've also had half my sodding teeth knocked out . . .'

'It's less than you deserve. This is a fuck-up!'

'Listen . . . Heckenburg's got one of your phones . . .'

The Dane's eyes narrowed. 'What's that you say?'

'It had a lot of foreign contacts in it. I got it off him, but he snatched it back . . .'

Klausen turned to Cullen. 'Was he in the house?'

Cullen's face fell. 'If he was . . . Goddamn, that's the company phone!'

'*Lort!* All of you . . . *QUICKLY!*'

Chapter 33

The woods ended abruptly. Which wasn't really ideal.

Heck had woven maybe half a mile through dense trees and undergrowth, to suddenly see open space ahead. He increased his pace, breaking from cover – only to pitch forward over a low dry-stone wall. He found himself sitting half-winded on open grassland, which slanted several hundred yards down to the thundering coastline of the North Sea. The only living things in his immediate vicinity were sheep, all of whom glanced at him with mild curiosity.

The sound of voices in the woods behind jerked him to his feet.

Red-faced and sweaty, he stumbled on downhill, the flock bleating as it cantered away. It was late afternoon, but the sun poked through lacy cloud, and cast a mellow light over the sloping pasture, bringing out its verdant green, turning the sea a livid royal-blue. Of course, in that typical deceiving way of coastal scenery, the crashing waves weren't quite as close as Heck had initially thought. He tottered down over a grassy ridge, only to see that it was another several hundred yards to the next ridge, and another several hundred to the one after that.

'Gemma, Gemma,' he chunnered as he scrambled on. 'We're gonna have a chat, me and you. We really are.'

As well as the shouts behind him, he could now hear voices in front.

Beyond the final ridge, it was only fifty yards to the water's edge, the heavy surf blasting spray along a shoreline mainly comprised of jumbled rocks and natural granite pavement. Just inland from this was a straggling procession of people, maybe two hundred strong. Heck halted, panting. They combined numerous ages, and wore variously coloured cagoules and walking boots, and in many cases were equipped with backpacks and staffs. They moved single file, or in twos and threes, and stretched out southward along the beach for a very considerable distance. None initially noticed him, because they were mostly wearing headphones and appeared to be engrossed in whatever it was they were listening to.

Heck's initial response was fright for these innocent passersby.

Whatever happened, the Nice Guys couldn't afford to let him escape. What was more, they were in a kill-frenzy, trigger-happy beyond belief. But there had to be a point where common sense kicked in. If he went and joined these walkers now, would his pursuers really come after him, still shooting, mowing down anyone who got in their way? Heck's heart hammered at the horror of such a thought. But surely they wouldn't be so rash as to create as big an incident as that? They were unmasked, with fully exposed faces – and most of these people would have mobile phones with them; they could raise the alarm instantly.

He glanced again at the people roving past, trying to work out exactly who they were. At their head, he sighted a kind of point-man, a diminutive, bespectacled scarecrow, also in a cagoule, his bare brown legs like pipe-stems between over-large boots and baggy, khaki shorts. If that wasn't ludicrous enough, he had a mop of white, wind-tossed hair and a bushy white beard. He didn't notice Heck as he strode on, talking energetically into a microphone.

Angry voices again drew Heck's attention to his rear. A significant number of humped ridges now lay between himself and the wood, so he couldn't see its edge, only the tops of its trees. But he knew the Nice Guys' frontrunners had emerged, and were now probably baffled as to his whereabouts.

It was a terrible risk, but in truth there was no other option.

He hurried down the final slope, still unnoticed by the coastal walkers as he tagged on halfway along, hands in his pockets, assuming an air of innocence.

Surreal moments followed. A strong salt tang blew from the rocks to Heck's right, which he saw were covered in weed and bladder wrack. With each explosive impact, foam surged through their nooks and crannies, droplets of spray hitting him. Meanwhile, on the left were the Nice Guys – three or four of them, the blond-haired figure of Klausen among them. They moved parallel to the walkers along the last ridge, watching in silence. They'd opted for caution – at least for the time being. Not that this really improved Heck's position.

Casually, he increased his speed, one by one overtaking the others, most of whom were still too fascinated with their tour guide's discourse to notice. Directly ahead, maybe a quarter of a mile away, there was an immense headland crowned by the ruins of a medieval castle, its sandstone walls glowing gold in the late afternoon sun.

'Dunstanburgh Castle is one of the highlights of the Heritage Coastal Walk,' came the cultured voice of the guide. He was still forty yards ahead, his wiry legs setting an impressive pace, but his voice carried on the sea wind. 'It was built in 1313 by Earl Thomas of Lancaster, not so much as a bastion against Scottish raiders . . . which was the cover story, but in defiance of King Edward II.'

Heck glanced left again. More Nice Guys had appeared, and were keeping pace with him – but Klausen had trailed down the slope. He was going to join the tour, and was already close enough for Heck to see the repressed rage in his face.

Heck increased his pace, again overtaking people. He was now past halfway up the straggling line. On the ridge, the American was on a phone. Despite the vast openness around him, Heck couldn't help but feel boxed in. More breakers erupted to his right; there was no escape that way. In front, the castle was now a hugely impressive chunk of ancient architecture, its eroded outer wall and soaring, broken towers filling his vision.

'Most of the destruction you see today resulted not from the border wars with Scotland,' the guide's voice added, 'but from the Wars of the Roses a century later. Yorkist forces all but annihilated it during two separate sieges.'

Heck hurried forward. As he did, he glanced over his shoulder. Klausen had fallen in line with the rest of them, but he too was walking at pace, passing one preoccupied tourist after another.

'What happened to Earl Thomas?' Heck asked, now almost at the front.

'Oh, he met a singular fate,' the guide replied, glancing airily back. 'He finally rebelled in 1321, but was defeated in battle.'

'Here?' Heck wondered.

'At Boroughbridge near York. If he'd made it back here, he may have evaded capture and his subsequent execution, which was decapitation by axe . . . it apparently took the headsman nine blows.'

Heck looked around again. Klausen was about five yards behind, walking alongside a thirty-something couple. The tubby, bearded father had a baby suspended on his chest in a papoose.

'There are some things you don't do, eh?' Heck said, ostensibly addressing all three of them. 'Challenging the king. Imagine thinking you can get away with that?'

'They breed 'em tough up north,' the father said laconically. By his accent, he was a Londoner.

'He considered he had a legitimate grievance,' the tour guide explained. 'Edward II was weak and famously ill-advised. His court was filled with self-interested schemers. They too were torn down eventually.'

'What do *you* reckon?' Heck asked Klausen. 'Worthwhile sacrifice . . . a hero who brought down a bunch of nasty little sods?'

'I think some people bite off more than they can chew,' Klausen said quietly.

'We're almost there,' the tour guide said aloud, his tone implying he was less interested in discussion than he was in making announcements. Ahead of them, the ground ramped slowly up towards the castle. 'We'll take a break once we get inside. You can wander around and look at the ruins, and then get out your flasks and your sandwiches and what-not.' He treated Heck to a chirpy grin. 'Bet you'll be glad to take the weight off, eh?'

'I've had busier days,' Heck replied, 'but not many.'

Back at the crossroads, Ben Kane knew he was in trouble.

It had always seemed likely the Nice Guys would prove to be fair-weather friends, if any kind of friends at all. He perhaps should have expected them to abandon him in his hour of need. But he found it odd they would do so when it was potentially so much to their disadvantage. If he got picked up now, the only living presence at the scene of a mass shooting, with two dead bodies on the road, two bullet-riddled cars, a bullet hole in his own shoulder, bullet casings strewn like grass cuttings, an orgy of evidence to connect the many rounds discharged here with those discharged in the various other shooting and bombing murders to have occurred in the last few weeks, and all that only ten minutes from a house they had rented, how did they think he could explain it away?

It all served to underline Kane's increasing concerns, the ones that had brought him up here to the Northeast in the first place – namely that Kurt Klausen was out of control. Kane didn't know him that well, but by all accounts Klausen had always been muscle rather than a thinker; an arrow compared to Mad Mike's bow. In getting rid of Silver, he'd thought he was taking charge of the entire operation. Clearly the rest of the men had at least partly bought into that. Thanks to Kane's regular reports, they'd quickly become concerned that Mad Mike was about to cut a deal with Gemma and Tasker, and had taken to this second mission in Britain with determination and no little relish. But Klausen's insistence on cowboying his targets, making an example of each and every one, instead of doing it covertly and subtly, as Kane had suggested, had backfired. On top of that, Heck had been his usual infuriating self, refusing to relinquish the case, doggedly chasing every lead until it had finally, miraculously, got him somewhere. And wherever Heck was, Gemma wouldn't be far behind. It was like they were telepathically linked, those two. Whatever was going on here, it was highly likely the police powers in Northeast England would be mustering by now. In which case, it was time for Kane to cut out, though this wouldn't be easy either. The initial gut-thumping agony of his wound had subsided a little, but there was no question he'd broken at least one bone in his shoulder. The bullet had passed clean through, and now the bleeding had staunched itself, which meant no major blood vessel had been damaged, but though he was on his feet, he could only stumble around in an agonised daze, his left arm hanging like a piece of lead. If he was having trouble walking, he didn't have the first idea how he was going to drive, but he had to find out.

Groggily, he folded his body into the driving seat of his Land Rover Discovery. The car was Swiss cheese. He'd already seen that. Its interior was slashed and torn, filled with broken glass and splintered metal. God knew what state the engine was in. He was under no illusion that, even if he managed to get it started, it wouldn't take him far – not without being noticed. But he needed to try. The trouble was, when he scrabbled at the ignition port, the key was missing.

Sweat dripped from Kane's face as he gazed at it uncomprehendingly. He fumbled in his pocket, but there was nothing there. He felt sure he'd left the key in the ignition in the event he'd need a quick getaway.

That was when someone dangled it outside his shattered window.

It hurt Kane just to turn and look. But he was still stupefied to see Jerry Farthing on his feet. The Northumbrian copper was pale as ice, with congealed blood speckled up his right cheek, as though it had spurted from under his collar.

'I actually learned two things when I was a shot,' Farthing said, breathing hard. 'Always keep out of the line of fire . . .' He yanked open the remnants of his jumper, exposing a cluster of flattened-out slugs embedded in body armour. 'And always wear your vest.'

Then he reached into the car – but not with the key, with his CS canister, which he emptied into Kane's face. Kane jerked away, but it was too late. His eyes and nose immediately began sizzling, feeling as if they were clogged with pepper. He glugged and choked, and as such he didn't see Farthing snap his left wrist to the steering wheel with a pair of handcuffs.

'For . . . for Christ's sake,' Kane gagged. 'I can't breathe . . . get me to hospital . . .'

Farthing turned and tottered away. Slowly, gingerly, he filched his mobile phone from his jeans pocket. The problem was, reality was ebbing around him. Though his vest had saved his life, he knew that at least one of the slugs had penetrated. It had taken a momentous effort to reach the car, had taken so much out of him that he now struggled to make sense of his own phone. He coughed up a mouthful of blood, spattering its keypad. He so wanted to make a call, so wanted to help Heck – but his head was seething, his vision fogged, his legs giving way at the knees. He toppled a couple more yards across the tarmac, and when he finally collapsed, it was into the roadside undergrowth.

Chapter 34

Heck glanced back along the line of walkers several times as the path now veered hundreds of yards inland, rising towards the castle entrance on its west side. It was difficult to tell how many of the Nice Guys had joined the group, but behind the tall Dane, every six yards or so there was a face that didn't quite fit: cold, sneering, feral.

To his left, there was only moor and rising meadow, though a farm track led straight west from the castle, presumably connecting with a main road of some sort. The tour guide diverted along a narrower sub-path, which curved sharply north, ascending ever more steeply but finally bringing them around to the front of the ancient structure.

Dunstanburgh towered over them, but now they were close to it, it was clear there wasn't a great deal of it left. Its encircling outer wall rose in some sections to about twenty feet, but there were big gaps and fissures, and beyond that very little else. The gatehouse itself, through which they were to enter, was more impressive. Much of that remained, and its arched access tunnel passed between two immense towers, the lower halves of which were intact, though their upper portions had long ago collapsed, leaving jagged monoliths of weed-grown stone. As they approached the tunnel entrance, they passed a floor plan of the structure. According to this, there were almost no other buildings after the gatehouse. The bulk of the castle's interior, though it projected right back to the shoreline, mainly comprised open grassy space. This was a bit of a gut-punch, as it meant the maze of rooms and corridors Heck had been banking on to lose himself in didn't exist.

Before entry, there was a prefabricated kiosk on the right with an English Heritage logo on it and a smiling elderly lady waiting inside. The tour guide, shorts flapping in the breeze, skipped ahead to speak with her. Heck glanced behind again. The majority of the group were removing their headphones and digging into haversacks, bringing out flasks of tea and packages of sandwiches. The Nice Guys walked stiffly and in silence, most of them making their way to the front. Fleetingly, Heck locked eyes with Klausen. The Dane's disfigured face creased into a mocking smile.

'This way, ladies and gentlemen!' the tour guide called, standing to the left of the arch, ushering them through.

The stony footpath gave way to ancient cobbles worn by time. Heck led the way, his footfalls echoing in the arched passage. Some ten yards ahead, the vast emptiness of the interior beckoned, all paved walks, green grass and blue sky. Before reaching it, they passed an entrance on the right, but a barred gate was drawn across this, blackness skulking beyond. The next entrance was on the left, but this had been adapted for modern use. Its wooden door stood open; Heck glimpsed electric lighting and shelves cluttered with mugs, pens and cuddly toys in knitted chainmail.

He turned abruptly, stepping through, hoping no one would follow but sensing immediately that someone had.

It was similar to many 'ancient monument' shops – not a large room, but well stocked; more mugs and toys arrayed along the walls, along with guidebooks and local crafts, while in the middle several rotatable racks carried postcards. Another English Heritage lady stood behind a small counter. She smiled politely on seeing Heck. Then she glanced at those behind him – and her face fell.

He recalled that age-old tenet so beloved of homicide investigators: 'Monsters rarely look like monsters.' Though occasionally it was possible to *sense* what they were, and then again – he thought about that disfiguring scar on Klausen's cheek – sometimes they looked the part too.

Ahead, just left of a fire-extinguisher suspended in a basket, there was an internal door marked 'Staff Only'. Heck turned towards it. Behind him meanwhile, numerous feet now scuffed the linoleum. Some might be innocent – but another quick backwards glance told otherwise. Klausen was closest, his jack o' lantern grin plastered in place.

Heck darted at the internal door without warning, but stopped to grab the extinguisher and twirl around, knocking out its safety pin. The exploding fountain of foam caught Klausen full in the face. The Dane coughed and choked, clawing at it with both hands, but gallons of the stuff had been compressed into the sealed vessel, and jetted out in a frenzy, filling his eyes, nose, mouth, coating him from hairline to crotch. As the counter lady squawked in outrage, Heck launched the extinguisher over Klausen's shoulder, the white spray arcing, the cylinder catching the Nice Guy behind him on the left temple. The Nice Guy went down, the one behind him falling over as well.

Blinded and coughing, Klausen dug through foam to reach under his coat, but Heck now swung a foot, making a crunching impact in the Dane's groin. As Klausen dropped to his knees, Heck spun to the door, pulling down a postcard rack. Two more of them fell over it, while he dashed out into a bare corridor.

On his immediate left stood a room with nothing in it except coats hanging on hooks. The other way, a stone stair spiralled up into dimness.

Heck took the stair, and within seconds was in the ruined section of the gatehouse. There was no modernisation here: no lighting, no heating. The first window he came to was a recessed arrow embrasure, too narrow to fit through. Guttural shouts echoed after him as he hurried up to the next level. In several places here there was no roof – just crumpled polythene supported by scaffolding, but passages still led off in various directions. The immediate one on his right terminated at an open aperture with a knee-high chain looped across it. Heck estimated there'd be at least a thirty-foot drop from there, so he went left, and then left again, now hearing many pairs of feet on the spiral stair. He came abruptly to a door-shaped gap with pitch-darkness beyond it. Some vague instinct prevented him blundering straight through it – and with good reason. Venturing forward, he found himself teetering on the brink of an abyss, which stank of mould and damp.

Hair prickling, he gazed up a hollow stone cylinder, some twenty-five feet in diameter and ascending maybe seventy-five feet to a diminutive patch of sky. In the faint bluish light this cast down, some thirty feet below – his estimation had been correct – lay nothing but stones, thistles and a few bits of broken scaffolding.

More shouts bounced along the passage behind. Heck contemplated the gutted tower. There was no obvious way he could climb down – but as his vision adjusted, he saw there might be a way he could climb up. The eroded stubs of a stairway wound up the interior wall, but at no point protruding out more than a foot or so. It was so narrow he'd only be able to ascend with his back braced on the stonework, much of which was rugged and thick with vegetation. And how greasy would those stair treads be?

'*Find him and kill him!*' came Klausen's semi-hysterical voice.

Ben Kane had been right about that at least. The Nice Guys should be fleeing this place by now; they were acting beyond reason, or at least their leader was.

Just to reach the internal stair, which began on his left, Heck had to cross a crevice of nearly four feet. He made it with a single leap, but the tread he landed on was loose, grating out of place under his weight. Only by hooking his fingers into the moss-damp wall did he avoid toppling into the chasm.

'No fucking arguments!' an American voice snapped. 'It's the company phone, Goddammit!'

Heck started up, his body flattened backwards against the bricks, the horrific drop only inches in front. To avoid looking down, his eyes remained riveted on the doorway. Shadows flickered inside it. It was a miracle they hadn't already reached this point. There were various places to search in the gate-house – but not many.

Another tread shifted under his foot. This one jutted out no more than seven inches as it was. He could barely perch both heels on it. He held his breath as it shifted again in its rotted socket. Only a rash, desperate lurch took him onto the next step, but there were further perils after that. In some cases, treads were not just short and slippery, they actually sloped downward. In others, entire treads were missing; he had to step sideways over those, constantly sure that he was about to overbalance; the blackness below yawning in expectation.

But he *was* ascending. The entry door was soon directly opposite, and lower down by a good ten feet. Such signs of progress emboldened him. He increased his pace, the entry door sliding round to his left; in a minute or so, it would be under him again. That would be the opportune moment for one of the bastards to stick his head through – Heck would be completely out of sight.

But he'd never had much luck.

A dark form appeared in the narrow slice of light when Heck was perhaps at eleven o'clock to it. He froze, flattening himself again, arms outspread, not daring to breathe. Whichever Nice Guy it was, he scanned the interior of the tower from top to bottom; for several moments he peered straight at Heck – and then withdrew.

Heck's breath burst from his chest with such force that he almost toppled forward. He was briefly baffled, but then it occurred to him that he was wearing dark clothing. And whoever that was, they couldn't possibly have taken sufficient time scanning the tower for their eyes to attune to the gloom.

He continued up, sidling ever higher, though his calves and hamstrings ached from the stress he placed on them. It must now be fifty feet down to the rock-strewn floor, but he tried not to think about that. He heard the Nice Guys' voices again: angry, squabbling. Some of them must want to leave. They had too much to lose by not leaving. But then again, he had the company phone. It occurred to him to fish it from his pocket and conceal it, perhaps insert it into a chink between the stones, on the off-chance they caught up with him. But that would mean he'd have to let someone know it was there, and if he wasn't able to do that it would never, ever be found. He couldn't even text the information to Gemma – the mere act of fiddling around with the phone in this gloom would take up valuable time and threaten to overbalance him; being an adult, it had never come natural to Heck to text with one hand. The good thing was that such extreme action might no longer be necessary. They'd lost him – they'd checked this part of the castle and seemed to have missed him.

Heck had now circled clockwise around the inside of the

tower two and a half times. The aperture overhead looked larger, but it was still a significant distance away. He didn't know if the stair led all the way to the top. If it didn't, he resolved that he'd climb as high as he could and then perch there, hanging by his fingernails if necessary. They'd be mad to hang around much longer.

And then he noticed two things at once.

Firstly, way before the top of the tower, the stair passed a large hole in the wall through which light shone. The second thing was a sudden silence; the shouting and arguing had abruptly ceased.

The vibration in his pocket came next.

It was the company phone.

A second later its trumpeting ringtone sang raucously down the tower.

Heck clawed at his pocket, but with a thunder of feet, several figures had already crammed into the doorway below, heads swivelling. The phone continued to jangle before cutting to voicemail. Heck sidled up what remained of the stair with desperate, reckless speed, slipping on another mossy tread. He scrabbled desperately, catching the wall behind with spiderlike hands. Fragments of ancient mortar fell, clinking on the rusty scaffolding at the bottom. The result was a burst of gunfire trained downward. Stroboscopic flashes filled the barrel-like interior. Sweating, Heck continued up. The doorway was only a couple of yards above and to his left. He almost slipped again; the tread wobbled, but he kept his balance and now was slapping around the door jamb with his left hand.

'*There!*' came a harsh shout.

He swung himself out of range just as the fusillade erupted, a storm of lead ricocheting around the doorway, caroming past with spatters of fire.

Gasping, he found himself in a turret room, a squat,

boxlike chamber, with another square aperture facing him, presumably the point where decayed masonry had fallen out around an arrow port. Beyond that he saw only the sea, though from much higher vantage than before. He limped forward and gazed down – to find that it had not been an arrow port, but the entrance to another stair. The overarching masonry might have collapsed, but the stair itself remained. It was horrendously narrow, with no safety rails and strong wind gusting across it, but the treads were intact, and they descended twenty feet to a battlemented walk along the gatehouse's north side.

With a speed bordering on the suicidal, Heck scampered down. It seemed he was going to have even more to tell Gemma about than he'd first thought. Assuming he didn't murder her for her deception first.

A few yards along the wall walk, a scaffolding frame was clamped to the outside of the curtain wall. Heck stepped onto it, and descended through its bars, monkey-like, half-falling at the bottom, but so relieved to land on solid, grassy ground that he barely felt the impact through the soles of his trainers. He ran along the side of the gatehouse, slowing as he approached the front. Some of the Nice Guys might have been posted there. From the sounds of it, there was much consternation inside, but that was perhaps understandable after the commotion in the castle shop.

He glanced warily around the north gatehouse tower, and spied an unexpected opportunity. At the foot of the slope, a blue Bedford van bearing an English Heritage logo had pulled up at the end of the track. The driver, unaware of the problems inside the castle, was at the vehicle's rear, unloading boxes.

Jamming his hands into his pockets, Heck walked down there. From the corner of his eye, he could see people milling at the front entrance. The tour guide was among them, gesticulating wildly as he shouted at a mobile phone that some maniac was discharging firearms. Heck increased his pace, making a beeline for the van. One glance through its windshield showed the keys still in the ignition. Heck didn't like doing this, but saw no other way.

He opened the driver's door and slid inside. The driver only noticed when the engine rumbled to life. He charged around to the front, but the vehicle was already in motion, swerving away from him and pulling a smart U-turn at the head of the track, turf spurting from its tyres.

Through the wing mirror, Heck watched the driver, red-faced with outrage and falling steadily behind. He didn't feel good about this, but reminding himself there were more important things, and patting the iPhone in his pocket, he gunned the vehicle on – only to note the needle on the petrol gauge resting just above empty. It was several seconds before the reality of that struck, and then he swore volubly. If that wasn't bad enough, he was now passing the entrance to the castle car park, the track broadening out into a proper road – and he saw a caravan of vehicles approaching from the opposite direction. At the front was a tan Ford Mondeo estate.

Heck snatched a cap from the passenger seat, pulled it on and tried to tug it down. But it was too small. At the same time, he veered past the Mondeo, which carried several men, but unavoidably exchanged glances with its driver – there was no mistaking the smashed, plaster-covered nose of the Australian.

Heck hit the gas, but he had almost certainly been spotted – even if they didn't recognise his face, they only needed to glance at his behind, and the van's swinging rear door would be a massive giveaway. As if proof of this were needed, the Mondeo jack-knifed around in his wake, the other cars shunting together in their efforts to brake.

Heck glanced into his mirror as he drove hell for leather, seeing frantic figures emerging along the track from the castle. In no time at all, it seemed, the whole posse was on his tail again. He slammed his pedal to the floor, passing various turn-offs. Embleton, Craster and Stamford didn't sound like the kinds of villages he wanted to lead a bunch of killers to. However, another idea – a real wildcard – was now unfolding. He didn't know exactly how much fuel remained in the tank, but it was a reasoned guess there wouldn't be enough to get him back to a major centre of conurbation like Berwick or Alnwick, where the Nice Guys might be loath to follow. Fortunately there was somewhere a little nearer than that. Again, innocent bystanders would be endangered, but the innocent were in danger anywhere and anytime while this gang were loose.

He reached the end of the access road, barely breaking speed as he swung right onto the A1, horns blaring from other vehicles as they screeched out of the way. He threw a glance at his petrol gauge. It was right at the bottom of the red. Behind him, one by one, the Mondeo, the Toyota, the Peugeot and the others, swerved out into the traffic, more road users skating across the carriageway to avoid them. He floored the pedal again, but the van was old and struggling to bypass seventy. Heck swore. If those bastards got alongside him, they'd shoot his tyres out – and they were gaining fast.

It was pure good fortune that cardboard boxes, apparently loaded with books and toys, now began to fall from the back of the van. At this speed, they broke apart spectacularly, bouncing and spinning across the blacktop, scattering their contents. The Mondeo was the first to come unstuck, a particularly large box still loaded with goods jamming under its front fender. It skidded and slewed, tyres squealing, before sidewiping the Toyota, which struck sparks from the central barrier. Behind that, the Renault Mégane spun off onto the hard shoulder.

Heck whooped as he drove, his clutch of foes falling further and further to his rear – only for the van to start juddering and shaking.

He glanced nervously at the gauge. It hadn't dropped since he'd last checked, but there could scarcely be a speck left in the tank. Just then a signpost flickered by – literally in the blink of an eye, but he'd seen it, and it gave him new heart. It read:

Holy Island 4

Chapter 35

Holy Island's warning notices slipped by as Heck raced along the approach road.

This Could Be You
(framed above an image of a car door handle deep in rippling waves)
Please Consult The Tide Tables

Danger
Do Not Proceed When Water Reaches Causeway

Picturesque scenery lay ahead; immense tidal flats extending in every direction, broken by the occasional upturned hull or hummocked by dunes crowned with marram grass. Beyond those was the sea, deceptively flat as a millpond.

Heck didn't bother to check the tide tables, which were arrayed at the side of the road on a tall pole; partly because he already had a vague idea the tide turned on this coastline at around six in the evening, which was about twenty-five minutes ago (memories of childhood holidays had to be good for something, if only as a basis for educated guesswork), and also because he couldn't afford to stop. His pursuers had been delayed by his shedding cargo, but not halted.

He drove straight onto the raised roadway that passed over the causeway, though as wavelets were already swimming over it, it was only clearly discernible by the reflector posts arrayed along its parallel verges. It seemed crazy – he had two miles to go, by the end of which the tide would be up to his wheel-trims, but the alternative was worse. He was perhaps a quarter of a mile out when he glanced into his wing mirror and saw the procession of battered cars also risking the causeway, froth billowing around their tyres. His own vehicle was cutting a V-wash as he pressed boldly on. But he'd already passed the refuge tower, and the landmass of Holy Island itself drew steadily nearer. Though the causeway would bring him ashore at the island's bleak, largely uninhabited western tip, the point they called 'The Snook', he could already see the roofs of the shops and cottages southeast of there.

He also felt his first real twinge of guilt.

Heck was making this up as he went along. It had only become his intent to bring the Nice Guys here in the last fifteen minutes. It wouldn't be a pleasant experience for the two hundred or so islanders, though it wasn't as if this ancient, sacred place – better known these days as Lindisfarne – hadn't suffered a brutal assault once before. In truth, despite his one-week childhood holiday here, Heck only had a rudimentary knowledge of the place, mainly that it was made famous because Vikings had once sacked and burned its monastery, murdering all the monks. It was about two and a half miles square, he thought, and it only had the one village on it. The ruins of the Norman monastery, built after the Vikings had gone, were still present, and it boasted the impressive remnant of a sixteenth-century castle on its southeast corner. It also possessed the usual smattering of coach

378

parks, visitor centres, shops and pubs, though in his youth much of it had been given over to agriculture – and as he rolled up onto the Snook, that didn't appear to have changed. He saw meadows and flat fields, many broken by low fences or dry-stone walls, extending away to the north and east, while to the south there was lower, soggier ground – salt marsh riddled with minor tidal inlets.

The road now ran due east along the island's southern coast. Heck slammed his foot down and tore along it, glancing again into his wing mirror. One by one, the Nice Guys' vehicles were also reaching dry land, though not without difficulty, having first to negotiate a tide surging to their wheel-arches. Was the company phone really so important that they'd risk this? Was it the key to their entire operation?

Increasingly, Heck felt certain it was. There were so many reasons now why he had to make this thing work.

Thanks to the turning of the tide, it looked as if most day-trippers had already departed the island. The streets of Holy Island village were largely clear. He hurtled into its centre along Crossgate Lane, screeching to a halt beside the green. It was an almost impossibly well-kept place: the cottages and shops whitewashed or built of local pale-grey sandstone. There were treed areas, gardens and flowerboxes. And despite initial appearances, it wasn't empty. A woman walking a dog along the other side of the green had stopped to look at him. A few curious faces appeared at windows. Again, Heck felt guilty about having brought the Nice Guys here; the trick now was to draw them away from this centre of population.

There was a 'No Parking' sign opposite, which he ignored as he abandoned the van – the more people who called the police now, the better. Heck bolted away on foot, heading northeast along a passage between the houses. Again, if residents saw him and thought something amiss, that could only be good. He threaded across several allotments, and vaulted a low, slatted fence onto rough pasture. Open, flat countryside now lay ahead. As he vaulted a second fence, he heard a skidding of tyres from the village, and the sound of car doors slamming open.

He ploughed on, pulling out the iPhone and tapping in a quick number. It gave him a mild jolt to think this might be the last time he'd ever call Gemma. He was tired and stiffening, and the Nice Guys were a lot fitter than him. Plus there were more of them and they were heavily armed. If there was ever a time he needed his former lover to answer the phone, it was now – but yet again it cut straight to voicemail.

'Gemma . . . it's me,' Heck said, panting as he tripped and struggled through corn husks. 'Whatever level of Hell you've got me consigned to . . . please hear me out! First of all, don't believe a word Ben Kane tells you. You may already have worked this out, but in case you haven't, he's the Nice Guys' mole and I can prove it . . . but of course, first you've got to find me. And that won't be easy, because I'm on Holy Island. That's right, Lindisfarne . . . Northumbrian coast. Gemma, the Nice Guys are here too. Not all of them, but most of the ones currently in the UK. I don't know their total strength . . . maybe as many as nineteen. Put it this way, they're team-handed and they're packing massive firepower. So you'd better bring your mates with you. On the upside, they're going nowhere for the time being. The tide's come in and the causeway's flooded for the next five hours. But all that time I'm stuck here with them. So get a scoot on, eh? Or they're going to turn me into a colander.'

He was tempted to add a few additional choice thoughts, but barking male voices now drew his attention behind. A small group of Nice Guys were already on his tail. Klausen and five others openly sported firearms as they athletically vaulted the first fence.

'Gemma . . . however you feel about me,' Heck said as he hammered on, 'and I imagine you're pretty pissed off at present . . . and hey, maybe those feelings are mutual! . . . I've never needed you more in my life than I do at this moment. So please get this message soon. Over and out.'

Though Gemma was airborne again, back in the NEAS Eurocopter, she was no longer out of range of the mobile networks, but initially, thanks to being engaged with a series of urgent phone calls to senior officers in various northern forces, she was too busy to pay attention to the unrecognisable number from which some previous caller had just left her a message.

And it wasn't as if she didn't have other things to occupy her thoughts.

She only knew PC Jerry Farthing as a uniform from Northumbria. She'd no idea how it was that Farthing now lay in a wood dying from gunshot wounds, unable to tell his office specifically which wood, except that it was off the A1 somewhere north of Alnwick. But the search wasn't just on for Farthing. It seemed that several firearms-related incidents had recently been reported in the Alnwick district. It hadn't needed a genius to make a link between Farthing's garbled message and those other offences, but it had taken a certain DS Barry Grant, based down in Sunderland, to connect Farthing to Operation Thunderclap due to the wounded PC's former association with Heck. In response to this, Gemma was already headed for the Northeast coast, with several other choppers close behind her, drawn from various forces but mainly containing armed SOCAR personnel who had flown up from the south. Meanwhile, specialist firearms teams from Northumbria and Durham were en route on the ground.

With all this going on, it was nearly ten minutes after she'd first noticed the unidentified number before it struck her that no one of inconsequence knew they could reach her on this line. She hit playback – and listened, at first trying not to flinch from the desperate, breathless voice at the other end, then trying not to show any emotion in front of the pilot.

As soon as the call terminated, she stabbed in another number.

'Talk to me, Gemma!' came Tasker's voice. He was currently headed south from Edinburgh by hire car, by the sounds of it at high speed.

'It's Holy Island, Frank!' she shouted. 'The Nice Guys are on Holy Island!'

Chapter 36

The eastern shore of Holy Island wasn't an especially long way from the pubs and cottages of Holy Island village; a third of a mile at most. But long before Heck reached it, the atmosphere of quaint rural community had gone, and he was crossing rough, uncultivated ground. Gulls wheeled raucously overhead, riding the cold wind blasting in from the sea. It was torturous on his leaden limbs and tired joints. He only reached the waterline after stumbling through ranks of age-old dunes thinly capped with tussocky, wiry grass – yet the beach itself was mainly shingle, the dark green waves rumbling up it and retreating again with much sucking and grinding.

He halted, sweat-soaked. Some distance away to his right reared the mound on which sat Lindisfarne Castle, noticeable for its solid outer wall and the flag streaming from its central spire.

'No more bloody castles,' he said, turning left.

In that direction, the desolate shoreline stretched on northward, but about fifty yards along there was a row of buildings. Heck slogged towards them, feet crunching in the debris. The bungalow-like outlines gave away their purpose. They were built entirely from wood, and painted in various bright colours. Chalets, holiday lets; five in total. Each had a small, carefully laid garden at the front, and a narrow paved path leading through to the rear, presumably to a larger garden. Of course, on the North Sea coast the off-season came early, and as it was now late September, there was nobody here. The chalets' front doors were closed, shutters covering their windows. The grass on their lawns and the bushes in their flowerbeds already looked straggly and overgrown.

There might be a hiding place among one of these, except that the Nice Guys could easily put a match to the whole lot. Heck glanced back along the beach. There was no one else there yet, but they couldn't be far. Tracking a fugitive over open ground ought to be a forte of theirs. They might even be encroaching through the gardens to the rear of these properties right now, fingers on triggers.

Exhausted, he stumbled on.

Just beyond the chalets, he saw what looked like a fisherman's hut, a ramshackle timber thing perched on props on the waterline. Most of its windows had been broken, presumably by gales and heavy seas, and were plastered from the inside with old newspaper, but a jetty jutted out some sixty yards, at the far end of which there was a mooring with a small motorboat tilting on the tide. As Heck hurried towards it, voices clawed his attention back. Two of his pursuers had appeared at the far end of the chalets, one tall with blond hair.

Heck scrambled forward to the hut, diving to the ground and rolling underneath its propped-up porch, scrabbling through driftwood and weed, and emerging on the other side where he was screened from them. He climbed breathlessly onto the hut's leeward step, on top of which there was a door. Thrusting his hand through the urine-yellow newsprint covering its central panel, he reached down, yanked the bolt back and stepped inside.

It was musty and damp, and smelled strongly of fish. There appeared to be all kinds of junk in there, but the first thing he really noticed was a set of four large plastic containers arranged in a row along the back of the hut, in a section sheathed with corrugated tin. Each one was filled with liquid. He unscrewed a top and sniffed. It was petrol, presumably for the motorboat. He looked farther. Other gear was heaped higgledy-piggledy: ravels of netting, lobster pots, hooks, lines, barrels and crates, shelves groaning beneath various ocean-faring knickknacks, a heavy oilskin coat and cap hanging from a hook next to the door – but nothing that was obviously a weapon. Then he heard the voices again, much closer – along with a shattering of wood. Heck lifted a sheet of newspaper and peeked out.

Klausen and his men, all five of them now, were prowling the front of the chalets with hunched, angry postures. With a bellow, Klausen launched himself at the second chalet's front door, splintering it inward. He and another of his men went in; there was much clamour as they tore and smashed everything they found.

The Aussie with the plastered nose did the same with the next building along, while a fourth invaded the one after that, but the remaining two, which included Klausen's American deputy, bypassed the chalets altogether and came on towards the fisherman's hut. They walked slowly but with purpose, their weapons by their sides. Even from this distance, Heck recognised an Armalite rifle in the American's hand, an L22 carbine wielded by the other. These two alone were packing enough firepower to stop a herd of elephants.

Shaun Cullen didn't open fire on the dilapidated hut simply for fun. Nor did Alex Mulroony, the bullet-headed Glaswegian by his side. They knew Heckenburg was around here somewhere. The guy wasn't Rambo; he had to be out on his feet by now. Concealment was his only option, and there were few opportunities for that here.

The L22 and the Armalite spat fire on the ancient building, blowing out planking, glass, sections of window frame. When they'd emptied their clips, the structure remained upright, but only just – hanging together loosely, creaking, the wind whistling through its multiple jagged wounds.

Cullen went up first, kicking at the windward door, the very little of which remained falling from its hinges. Inside, it was knee-deep in wreckage: broken barrels, shattered crates. Shelves had fallen on all sides, spilling seas of bric-a-brac. Dust and splinters swirled. Cullen advanced in, Mulroony following – both surprised to find themselves sloshing to their ankles.

'The fuck . . .?' Mulroony said. 'That fuel?'

'Gas,' Cullen replied.

'Smells like petrol!'

'I mean that, fuckhead! Look . . .' Cullen twisted to the rear of the interior, where four large plastic drums had ruptured, spilling their contents.

'Place is swimming,' Mulroony said.

Cullen peered more closely at the four drums. Slugs had gone through them, but by the looks of it each one had also been sliced down the middle, as though with a knife. 'What the . . .?'

The sudden 'rattlesnake' *hissss* might have warned them, had they known where it was coming from. They spun around, guns levelled, but when the brilliant red flare arched in through the leeward window, there was nothing they could do.

The blinding flash would have been seen for miles. An ear-pummelling *BOOM* followed as the fisherman's hut was engulfed in a searing holocaust of flame.

Kurt Klausen and the other three Nice Guys watched agog

from alongside the row of chalets, barely flinching as burning shrapnel cascaded around them. Only the sight of Heck leaping up into view on the far side of the jetty, and sprinting along it towards the motorboat jerked them into action. They charged forward, checking their weapons, but struggling as Heck had done on the heaped shingle.

The jetty was actually longer than sixty yards; more like eighty. It was also greasy, and Heck was going full belt – yet somehow he kept his balance, his shadow spearing ahead of him, reflected by the inferno at his back. Of the two sodium flares he'd found on the fisherman's shelves, he still had one left; it was crammed into his pocket next to the company phone. He didn't know how it would help him, but he was hanging on to it. More useful was the key he'd found in the old oilskin coat. It would be ridiculous if it was the wrong one, but something told him it wouldn't be.

His rubber soles skated the last five yards as he attempted to stop, and he rocketed down, landing on his back in the boat, which bounced and swayed on the oil-dark waters. He jammed the key into the ignition and turned it. The vessel revved to life, pivoting around as its propeller began chopping. Heck glanced at the mooring rope knotted around a hook at the back end of the boat. He also threw a single glance down the jetty.

And saw something incredible.

A figure in tatters was jerking towards him along the timber footway; blackened and melted all over, smoke hissing off it in gouts. Still limping on its injured left knee.

Heck yanked at the rope to loosen it.

The figure was coming at pace, already halfway along the jetty.

Heck crammed his fingers in to try and widen the knots, but sodden with freezing sea water, the rope was proving difficult.

The terrible shape, now only thirty yards away, audibly slobbered for breath. 'Motherfucker,' it gasped. 'I'll kill you . . . motherfucker . . .'

Heck's fingernails tore and split as he rent at the rope. With painful slowness, it began to unravel.

The figure was less than a quarter of the jetty away, the woodwork shuddering to its heavy footfalls – so close he could smell its burned flesh.

'Gotcha!' Heck shouted as the last knot sprang apart. He unwound the rope from the hook, turned and dived for the wheel, hitting the accelerator, the boat surging away – but the roasted husk that had once been Shaun Cullen had now reached the end of the jetty. With a choked howl, it launched itself into space – landing squarely in the back of the boat.

Chapter 37

Even chargrilled, Shaun Cullen was a frightful opponent.

He was in a hideous state: little of his clothing remained – just scraps of smouldering fabric fused to his crisped, semi-liquid flesh. His hair had gone, as had much of the skin from his face, leaving only a purulent, melted mask stretched on visible bone structure: peg teeth, lidless eyes rolling like golf balls in their orbits. His stench alone could knock most men unconscious, and yet he got back to his feet with incredible ferocity.

Heck attempted to steer the boat away from the jetty, heading south yet far enough from shore to be out of range of the gunmen on the beach, but now he had to leave the wheel to defend himself, because Cullen came at him, howling, arms windmilling.

Heck grabbed the fisherman's knife with which he'd gutted the petrol drums in the hut, and slashed out, incising a deep wound across Cullen's left forearm. But the American, with so many nerve-endings destroyed, barely flinched. He struck at Heck with the bloody knot of bone and pus that was his left fist. It caught Heck full on, smearing body fluids across his cheek and mouth. Heck tottered backwards, knocking against the wheel, which turned them sharply to port – so they were now headed away from land into the roaring, rolling surf of the North Sea.

Heck tried to duck out of the way, but Cullen kicked at him. He was still wearing a pair of boots, the scorched hobnailed sole of the left one clamping Heck's hand to the gunwale with crushing force; the hand jerked open and the knife was lost into the bilge. Charred teeth gnashing, Cullen followed through with a right hand jab; Heck wove away, and though it missed his Adam's apple, it jolted the left side of his neck.

Heck sagged against the wheel a second time, his consciousness reeling as pain engulfed his head and his shoulder. A backhand chop came down at the other side of his neck, but he had sufficient strength to block this, and then stamp out and down with his left foot, driving his heel onto Cullen's injured knee.

Some nerves were clearly still functioning: the American gave a choked squeal, and toppled across the boat, which was now buffeting and bouncing on an ever-heavier swell. Heck managed to steady himself, his head still ringing. Cullen lurched towards him, shrieking, leaving himself wide open for the right hook that hammered into his mouth, busting in those many exposed lengths of tooth, jarring him sideways.

Even then, with fresh blood spouting from the blistered hole in his face, Cullen tried to bounce back. Heck caught him with another hook, this time a left, and the American went down heavily, more corpse than man.

Heck staggered back, reaching for the wheel and gazing shoreward.

Holy Island was already little more than a narrow green/brown line on the western horizon. A tiny spark denoted the fire at the head of the jetty. He lugged the wheel around. He was acutely conscious of Klausen and his men's assault rifles, but he didn't know how much fuel this boat contained, and the last thing he wanted was to run out a mile from land. But no sooner had they changed direction, waves hitting the vessel side-on, rocking them like a cradle, than Cullen swayed back to his feet, now with a secondary weapon drawn from his left boot.

It was a Desert Eagle, an ultra-powerful pistol. It would have changed the game there and then, had the American's fleshless fingers not found trouble trying to cock it.

Heck relinquished the wheel again. On the inside of the starboard gunwale, a paddle hung in stirrups. He snatched it and spun around, smacking the pistol, flipping it overboard. Cullen still threw himself forward, and they grappled chest to chest, the paddle crosswise between them. The boat continued rocking, throwing them this way and that, one falling on top of the other, first to starboard and then to port. Heck head-butted Cullen. The bastard head-butted him back. Though Cullen only had fragments of teeth left, he tried to clamp them on Heck's nose, but Heck drove him back by shoving the point of his elbow into his throat. Cullen gurgled, his exposed eyes finally registering pain. Heck caught him again, this time under the chin, breaking the madman's hold, and stumbling away.

They were now headed inshore, the landmass approaching at speed. The blazing wreckage at the foot of the jetty was more clearly defined, as was the row of chalets – where Klausen and his men would be waiting.

Heck grabbed at the wheel with one hand, and with the other clung to the paddle. Cullen hung on to the other end – in fact he wrenched at it feverishly, finally tearing it from Heck's grasp, so that it went spinning over the side. But now, for the first time, Cullen's strength seemed to be flagging. He hunched there, bloodied, putrid, the air rasping through his lungs. Doggedly, he threw himself at his opponent. Heck broke from the wheel to smash his right fist into the mangled face, and drive his foot as hard as he could into the side of the damaged knee.

When Cullen landed in the bilge this time, it was with a hollow thud – and an air of distinct finality.

Gasping, Heck turned back to the wheel. They were still headed inshore, and were perhaps no more than a hundred and fifty yards from the beach. The swell here was lighter, and he was able to bring the vessel about due south, the line of chalets falling to his rear. His own lungs were wheezing, his heart throbbing; every part of his body ached. He'd known all along that to mix it hand-to-hand with these guys, even one as badly injured as the American, was ill-advised.

But even from a distance, they could be deadly.

Klausen and the other three were running along the beach in pursuit, but its pebbles were slowing them down and the boat was drawing further ahead.

The Dane skidded to a halt. 'Elwood!'

Keith Elwood, who while serving with the Blues and Royals was consistently the best long-range marksman in his unit, dropped to one knee, unslung his Parker-Hale M82 sniper rifle and put it straight to his shoulder. Through its telescopic cross-hairs, the small motorboat flying across the whitecaps and the weary figure slouched over its wheel looked a lot closer.

'Got him,' he said.

'Do it,' Klausen replied.

Elwood adjusted position slightly, his bead fixed directly between Heck's shoulder-blades. His gloved finger tightened on the trigger – just as a second figure leapt up to block his view.

Heck would never have believed Cullen had enough malevolence left in him, let alone energy, to jump up yet again

– this time with the fisherman's knife in hand. But Heck barely had time to turn before a distant boom rolled across the waves, and a 7.62mm slug hit Cullen with such force that it chopped his spine, punched through his cardiovascular system, and erupted from his chest at a deflected angle, leaving an exit cavity the size of a dinner plate.

Heck dropped into the bilge and stayed there, panting and sweating, gazing point-blank and for long minutes at a travesty of flesh, bone and shredded inner organs that no longer resembled anything human.

There were three more booms as the boat roared on, each one diminishing further into the distance. It might have been Heck's imagination that the craft juddered at least once in response, but there was no damage caused that he could see. When he finally risked peeking over the gunwales, the entire shore was different: the beach had given way to broad, flat, weed-slathered boulders. To the southeast, the castle on the mound, while still a quarter of a mile away at least, was so much closer that he could see its windows and turrets. He peered back northward. He couldn't see them, but they'd be coming; they couldn't afford not to – but now at least he had a head start. It struck him that if he had enough fuel to get around the island's southeast corner, he might be able to reach the mainland. Then it would be game, set and match.

He straightened up, one hand on the wheel as he dug the company phone from his pocket – and spotted three missed calls. He hit the log, and saw that each one had come from Gemma. Giddy with relief, he made to call her back – only for the boat to judder again, and shake as it suddenly decelerated.

Heck overbalanced and grabbed at the gunwale. Glancing around, he saw a plume of brackish smoke unfurling at the rear, and an erratic, purplish trail zigzagging across the sea behind. The sniper had got lucky after all, and had punctured the fuel tank. Heck turned the craft towards shore, which was still over a hundred yards distant. If it conked out on him now, with the paddle gone, he'd be in big trouble. He could easily swim, but not with the iPhone.

'Shit,' he said through clenched teeth. The bloody thing was already chugging.

When it finally did die on him, he was perhaps thirty yards from the beach. A dull, ear-pummelling silence followed as he rode the green swell. When he peered over the side, he could see the bottom, but that didn't mean anything. With no choice, he clamped the phone and the folded list of Nice Guy contacts between his teeth, and carefully lowered himself over. It was freezing, as he'd expected, but that wasn't his main concern – it could be three feet or thirty.

But in actual fact, it was just over five.

The waves slopped under his chin as his feet found purchase on greasy, shifting stones, and then, his treasures held overhead, he commenced the slow march to shore. That whole distance he kept his eyes skinned northward along the beach. He'd almost fully emerged, the surf crashing around his waist, trying its level best to upend him, when he spied them coming.

They were a good distance away, but were approaching paratrooper-style: moving in single file at a fast jog, guns across their chests. Klausen was at the point.

Heck scrambled up the beach, determined to cut back inland. In the right of his vision, he saw them halt – they'd spotted him – and then come on even faster.

He struggled to breathe as he followed a muddy path running between arable fields. The castle loomed large on his left, but was no real option. Sure, he could bar its door. But the only route to that was steeply uphill, at which point the special forces-trained Nice Guys would easily overhaul him. Besides, directly ahead now lay buildings – the eastern outskirts of Holy Island village. Surely there was somewhere he could find sanctuary here?

With this thought in mind, Heck clambered over a wall and found himself crossing an open space, and the next thing weaving among the ruins of the monastery; through broken gateways and along roofless cloisters, but seeing no one around. Perhaps this wasn't a surprise. It was early evening now, the daylight leaching slowly away. On top of that, the Nice Guys most likely had imprisoned the populace at some central point, where they could guard them all together. He jumped over an iron gate onto a village road with terraced cottages down the other side – only to round a corner and spot one of the bastards.

The Nice Guy was standing at the next corner, partially turned away. He was lean and tall, about six-three, with a shaven head and dark ebony features. The weapon in his hands looked like a high-tech pump-action shotgun.

Heck edged back onto the previous road until he was out of sight. Again, the remnants of the monastery lay before him. Lindisfarne Priory – a holy place for sure. With the sun slowly setting in the west, multiple shadows lengthened through its crabbed, lichen-covered monuments. But there was nothing encouraging about this pretty scene. At any moment, Klausen and his team would emerge through the ruins.

Heck glanced at the modern structure alongside it: a single-storey, pebble-dashed affair, attached as an annexe to a larger, less functional building done in decorative salt-and-pepper stone. He currently faced it from its rear, in the middle of which an exit door stood open. Over the top, a notice read:

Museum Staff Entrance

Heck slid along the pebble-dashed wall, and stepped inside. He attempted to close the door behind him, but found that it wouldn't catch – the exit-bar was bent and stained by a bloody handprint. Someone had attempted to escape this way, but had been caught in the act.

Stepping around an overturned wire-mesh wastebasket, he pressed on along a narrow passage with unlagged pipes across the ceiling. It took him past various rooms filled with boxes, paperwork and other curios, finally joining a broader corridor laid with carpet tiles. The several offices adjoining this were deserted but wrecked, a desktop computer lying smashed in the first one. As Heck checked the second, he heard voices. He crept in and peeped around the side of a Venetian blind – to find that he was on a level with the shaven-headed black guy, who had now been hailed by someone walking towards him along the street. Heck shifted position, and saw Klausen and two others approaching, all three of them drenched with sweat. The black guy exchanged a few words with them, and shook his head. Klausen shouted: *'Fuck!'*

Which was when Heck heard movement elsewhere in the building. He darted back to the corridor and glanced down it. It was empty, but somewhere beyond his vision there was a metallic clatter – a stray foot had struck the overturned wastebasket.

Klausen had chased Heck along the coast with three men – but only *two* had come up the street with him outside.

Heck hurried on, passing through another staff door, entering the first of the exhibition areas. Maps adorned the walls in here, not just covering the Northeast coast, but the whole of Britain and Ireland, and much of western Scandinavia. Sea lanes were marked with the sorts of pins and different-coloured ribbons that crime scene analysts used in incident rooms. On his right, a long glass cabinet was filled with tarnished Dark Age trinkets: brooches, buckles, knife-hilts blackened by rust, each one carefully labelled. But what most caught his eye was on the other side of the chamber, against the wall. It was a raised, roped-off dais, on which a life-size wax mannequin of a Viking in a chainmail coat and an elaborately carved full-face helmet stood over the kneeling form of a black-habited monk. In the Viking's two hands, which were high above his head, he clasped an imitation battle-axe.

Beyond this, an arched passage connected with another area. Heck ventured that way, only to stop after ten yards. He could now see a glazed outer door, but on the other side of this Klausen and his two minions were standing in debate. Again there was movement in the building. Somewhere behind Heck, a door was kicked open.

Native Queenslander Brad Perkins had a bigger beef with that pommie bastard cop than he'd ever known in his life. Though he'd fought often and savagely as a juvenile gang member in Mount Isa, not to mention being bombed and shot at during his countless actions in the military, he'd never felt antipathy like it as he wended through the empty rooms and passages of the Lindisfarne Museum.

Despite his many scrapes, Perkins had always somehow maintained his 'surfer guy' looks, which in turn had helped him keep a lot of ladies busy in a lot of ports. But now his conk was so squashed that he couldn't breathe through it; he was constantly gargling blood and snot. He also thought he might have fractured his left cheekbone and maybe the eye-socket too.

To say he had unfinished business with Heckenburg would be the understatement of all time. They'd said the bastard was a hard-case, and he'd sort of proved it – but he wouldn't be hard enough.

Perkins kicked another door open, Tavor levelled – but the room beyond contained nothing more than a shattered desktop. He prowled on. Heckenburg had actually done incredibly well making it this far. But according to Elwood, he'd looked half-dead in that boat. He couldn't keep going much longer.

He opened another door, and slid into what looked like a display area. There were charts on the walls, and a glass case filled with archaeological treasures. Directly in front, a wax monk cowered in terror from a wax Viking holding an axe. It seemed deserted, but when Perkins walked forward, he did so slowly, warily, surprised to feel sweat on his brow. There was something about this that bothered him. It was tempting to open fire, to blow the room to pieces and hopefully smoke the shit-arse out. But unfortunately he was low on lead. He'd left the farm that day with only two magazines, and now had only half of one remaining.

He stood in front of the dais, scanning every corner, and finally spotted something curious: on the wall opposite, alongside the fire alarm, there was a hook from which the fire axe was suspended – except that this fire axe, inexplicably, resembled a plastic medieval battle-axe.

Perkins spun back to face the Viking facsimile – just as its eyes rolled towards him and the real fire axe descended. Instinctively, he blocked the blow with his left forearm, the blade cleaving flesh and bone. It didn't pass all the way through, but lodged deeply – only jerking loose as the Aussie threw himself backwards, gore spurting from the wound. He tried to swing his Tavor around, but it was difficult with one hand, especially as the Viking now tore off its fake helmet and leapt over the rope, kicking at the gun, sending it flying. Perkins landed on the floor hard, gasping, hot blood raining all over him. His legs were spread, and Heck drove his foot between them with battering ram force.

The Aussie yelped, but still managed to roll away, heading for the fire axe. Heck dived, body-slamming on top of him, grabbing for the axe as well, reaching it at the same time. Neither was able to use it as they rolled together, blood streaking the pair of them, one of Heck's feet smashing through a low cupboard, the dismembered wax parts of the real facsimile spilling out. But his opponent's gasps had now become snarls. Though gruesomely injured, the Aussie's superior strength and training were telling. He threw Heck over onto his back, the axe and the hand grasping it trapped underneath, exerting downward pressure on Heck's throat with his good forearm.

Heck gasped, choking. Dizziness set in as, with his one free hand, he raked at the Aussie's nose. Perkins jerked his head sideways, the plaster coming away in Heck's hand, revealing a jagged piece of cartilage. With a roar, the Aussie drove his forehead down. White fire exploded between Heck's eyes: his own nose had clearly just broken. But that was nothing compared to the compression of his larynx. A last, desperate thought occurred to Heck before his awareness expired.

He stuck his sweat-soaked hand into his pocket, fumbling out the second sodium flare. He banged it on the floor to strike it – a searing crimson flame blazed out – and drove it upward, grinding it into the right side of the Aussie's head. Flesh sparked and sizzled, and with falsetto shrieks, Perkins rolled away, one hand clamped to his right ear. Heck scrambled upright, hurled the flare across the room and lunged for the fire axe again – only just grabbing it in time, because almost immediately the Aussie was also back on his feet, froth and bile venting from his snarling mouth.

Heck swung the axe two-handed, aiming it downward. The blade bit deep into his opponent's left knee, hacking both that and the right knee clean out from under him.

Perkins landed on his back with pile-driving force. Heck dropped down on top of him, pressing the axe handle across his throat. Horribly wounded though he was, his entire right ear a blackened, seething mass, Perkins still fought like a wildcat. So Heck dragged his knees forward, planting one at either end of the handle; his entire weight was now compressed downward.

The blows the Aussie struck with his good right hand were initially savage, but gradually weakened until they were no more than slaps. Even then it was another minute and a half before that hand locked into a rigid, shuddering claw, and slipped lifeless to the floor. With a low gurgle, his breathing abruptly ceased.

Heck fell onto his side, lungs heaving . . . it was several seconds before the blood-red glow and noisy hissing of the flare faded away. But almost immediately after that there came a series of clattering impacts on the main doors at the front of the museum.

Heck grabbed up the Tavor, cracking off its magazine. The thing was half-empty.

The impacts on the door stopped. As abruptly as they'd begun.

He moved to a curtained casement and peeked out.

Two Nice Guys had been attempting to force entry: the shaven-headed black guy, who, from the slanted horizontal scars on either cheek, was clearly an African, and an equally tall but thicker-set white guy with a black beard, whom Heck recognised from the pursuit along the coast. They'd now moved away from the museum into the middle of the road, heads cocked as though listening. A few yards away, Klausen reappeared with two more henchmen. They too halted, listening. And now Heck could hear it as well: the distinct whirring of a helicopter.

Rapidly, Klausen began issuing orders. His men split up,

vanishing over fences or down side alleys. Heck dashed from the window, tearing off his fake chainmail. He ran down to the museum's glazed double doors. Their glass had been partially shattered, but was holding. A few blows from the butt of the Tavor put it through. He stepped outside. The racket of rotor blades was much closer now. In fact Heck sighted them – six copters, sailing in neat formation over the island from the west, three bearing official police insignia, while the other three were larger-bellied and coloured dark blue.

As Heck watched, their formation broke apart and they commenced circling, two of the heavier craft descending first. He hurried across the road, rounded a corner and peered over a garden fence. They looked to be putting down on the open farmland northeast of the village. Even as the first two landed, large numbers of men in black coveralls, body armour and ballistics helms, armed with shields and MP5s, began piling out and deploying to cover behind clumps of scrub. Almost immediately, there were bursts of shooting from concealed positions among the houses. At least one police assaulter dropped, though other officers now under cover returned fire.

From somewhere nearby, Heck heard Klausen barking hoarse commands.

'Check the villagers are locked in the Town Hall! Doesn't matter if we've missed a few – don't waste time looking for them. They'll only go to ground! No guards! Put extra men on the harbour. And find that fucking phone. Never mind the list . . . just the phone. We can't exfil without it!'

Heck bolted back down the road. He was minded to secrete himself inside the museum, where, if the worst came to the worst, he could hide the iPhone and send Gemma a text explaining its whereabouts. But he was only halfway back, running along the wall bordering the monastery ruins, when two figures rounded the corner in front of him. It was

401

the same two as before: the African, now carrying his pump shotgun across his belly – at this proximity Heck recognised it as the much-feared Remington 870 combat shotgun – and the bearded guy, who by the make of his own weapon, a Borz, was possibly Russian.

They skidded to a halt. Neither had expected to see Heck out in the open. Nor had they been expecting he'd be armed with an Israeli TAR-21, which he now levelled at them, unleashing a hail of fire as he scrambled left to the wall. But frantic flight was not conducive to good marksmanship. Slugs ricocheted everywhere, from the road surface to the walls of the nearby cottages. The two Nice Guys ducked and dived, and though neither of them were hit, at least they weren't able to return fire straight away, allowing him to vault the wall and fly back into the ruins.

They reached the wall seconds after him, taking aim and discharging, the rapid-fire *dudududu* of the Borz alternating with the louder *clack-clunk-BOOM* of the Remington 870. Heck dashed among the ancient pillars and arches, bullets careening around him, kicking off chunks of weathered stone. He slipped on the grass and threw himself flat behind a step, from where he tried to return fire, only to find that his clip was empty. Scenting blood, the Nice Guys clambered onto the wall, shooting and reloading as they did – consummate battlefield professionals – until another big-bellied helicopter swept without warning about sixty feet overhead, abruptly turning and wallowing back towards them. Gunfire erupted from its starboard port, sending the duo back over the wall and scampering for cover among the cottages.

Heck watched and waited, determined to keep his head down – there was no guarantee the glory boys in the chopper would ID him as a cop – until that vehicle too had lofted away. He got warily to his feet, discarding the Tavor.

He could now hear shouting and bursts of gunfire from what sounded like every quarter of the village. Palls of smoke rose above rooftops. He could also hear a loudspeaker; the Nice Guys were being ordered to surrender, to lay their weapons down. He scaled several feet up a nearby flying buttress, from where he could scrutinise the surrounding landscape.

Some of those choppers that had landed had lifted off again. Others had taken their place, and were depositing further sticks of armed, black-clad assaulters. By the echoing cacophony, fire-fights were underway everywhere, but the armed units had already worked their way into the conurbation. Another loudspeaker began hailing. This one sounded as if it was coming from the direction of the anchorage and pier. Highly likely the Northumbrian Police would have offshore launches they could bring across. Heck gazed in that general direction, and was able to see along several streets and passages beyond the museum. Motion was visible, but it was mainly armoured cops advancing behind ballistics shields, pistols and rifles levelled over the top.

'No time to be hiding in church,' Heck said to himself, jumping down and alighting on the grass.

He placed another call to Gemma, but now the phone appeared to be lacking a signal – which he perhaps should have expected. Most likely the Nice Guys had activated some kind of scrambler device, to try and cut themselves and the islanders off. He crouched, wondering how he could help. The best thing seemed to be to hook up with the police assault teams. He could then hand over the company phone personally, and tell them everything he knew. He poked his head above the boundary wall, and saw the coast was clear. He clambered over and scampered across, taking a side alley, which brought him into a narrow road next to a bakery, the front door to which stood wide open.

He glanced left and right. Again, the coast seemed clear. But some instinct nailed him to the spot.

The white stucco cladding on the wall above his head was then cross-stitched by gunfire, showering him with dust and debris. Heck dodged inside the bakery, slamming the door behind him and throwing a bolt. Through the window, he glimpsed two figures advancing up the adjoining road – Klausen and the bearded Russian. Both opened fire again, the bakery's door and plate-glass windows flying inward.

Heck raced back through the building, crashing amid pots in the kitchen, then opening a door at the rear and running into a small yard with a slatted gate.

'*Get him now!*' he heard Klausen shrieking.

The gate was closed, but Heck barged through it shoulder-first, the flimsy wood breaking apart, and finding himself in a cobbled alley.

Where the African was waiting.

He was no more than a yard away, and treating Heck to a manic, pearly grin. He'd laid his 870 to one side, and now hefted a gleaming, foot-long machete.

Heck swayed to evade a vicious backhand swipe, and then threw himself forward, landing a heavy right hand, which seemed to take his opponent by surprise. The African tottered, spitting blood – but now goaded to greater fury. He lurched forward, grappling with Heck, twisting and flinging him across the alley. Heck bounced over the cobbles, slamming into the brick wall. The African lunged after him, the machete flashing in an arc. Heck rolled aside, as its blade drew a streak of sparks along the bricks. Heck tried to crawl away, but a second figure now appeared at the bakery's rear gate. It was the Russian. He saw what was happening, and bawled with harsh laughter, lowering his Borz.

'You the man who give us so much trouble?' the African said. 'You give me a broken lip too, man.' Heck winced as

404

he was caught by the ankle. The African raised the machete in his right hand. 'You can have this quick or slow . . . you give us the phone, or tell us where . . . or you lose first one foot, then the other. After that, we show more imagination, yeah?'

'Fuck you,' Heck murmured.

Laughing, the African took him by the waistband and flung him back across the alley, slamming him into the other wall. Every inch of Heck's wind was driven out.

'Okay, White Lightning . . .' The African stood over him, briefly spinning the machete between his two hands, one finger at the point, one at the pommel, and then raising it again. 'Say goodbye to your foot!'

He never even saw the flying roundhouse kick that caught him in the middle of the back and basically pole-axed him. Heck barely saw what happened either.

Someone clad in tight black coveralls, as well as a glinting ballistics helm, and yet moving with extreme athleticism, cavorted past, going into a balletic martial arts routine. The African blundered to his feet, still wafting his machete, but it was kicked from his hand, and three quick-fire karate blows knocked his head left, right and backwards, dropping him to the cobbles in a senseless heap.

The bearded Russian was up next. He came from the gate with Borz levelled – only for another flying kick to send it spinning, its overheated barrel striking the gatepost and bending double. A second kick caught his crotch, and as he lurched over, a chop to the nape knocked him cold.

'Bravo,' Heck said, as his rescuer turned and lifted his visor – to reveal, yet again, that 'he' was in fact 'she'. 'Oh great . . . you again.'

'Like it warms the cockles of my heart to find out *you're* here,' Steph Fowler said, dabbing sweat from her brow, drawing her Glock and moving to the wall alongside the smashed gate. She peered through it towards the bakery. 'You injured?'

Heck realised she was referring to the blood clotting his clothes. 'Not significantly.'

'Good . . . get up. Any more in there?'

'One . . . Klausen.' Heck hobbled across the alley and picked up the 870. He turned it in his hands. It bore a 'US Army Rangers' stamp on its stock, suggesting it had probably been pillaged from a dead US serviceman at Mogadishu back in 1993.

'Who's Klausen?'

'Their gaffer.' Heck tried to pump a new shell into the shotgun's breech, but found it was empty. He glanced at the body of the African. The guy still lay unconscious, but now Heck knew that he wasn't just a merc, he'd probably been a Somali guerrilla too. On top of that, he was a big unit – even unarmed he could probably break most opponents to pieces. Deciding he didn't want to get any closer than necessary, Heck discarded the 870 and fell into place bare-handed at the other side of the entrance. 'He ought to have shown himself by now.'

Fowler shook her head. 'If he's in charge, he'll have more to worry about than you. We're closing them down fast. A few have surrendered already, but others seem pretty hardcore.'

'You got that right.' Heck prodded at his broken nose.

She darted past him along the alley. 'That's only a taste of what you actually deserve.'

'How's Nick?' he said, following.

She turned, lip curled. 'How do you think? He's got a fractured collar bone and a fractured right wrist. *And* he lost three teeth.'

'He said I had to batter him.'

'It was hardly a fair fight.'

'He was the one who volunteered for light duties.'

'I'm not laughing, okay?' She jabbed a finger. 'The only reason I'm not kicking your arse right now is because you saved my life in the river. Sort of.'

'*Sort of?*'

'And because there are others here who deserve it more.'

They moved on, turning a corner and following a passage between gardens.

'Don't let that stop you,' Heck hissed. 'I'll meet you on some car park after.'

'Deal!' She halted as they reached another road.

They waited, listening. Sporadic shots were still being fired elsewhere. But more choppers lofted by overhead, and they could hear further loudspeaker messages. On the opposite side of the road, there was a small row of shops.

'How's the fight actually going?' Heck asked.

'We'd taken the harbour when I last looked,' she said. 'We've got at least forty guns on the plot from SOCAR. Another twenty from Northumbria, ten from Durham. These idiots can stick it out all they want, but it's only a matter of time. Okay . . . keep low and move fast.'

'I *have* done this before, you know.'

'Yeah. And you've been shot before too. Follow my lead.'

She took off across the road in a crouch, pistol dressed down. Heck followed, and almost immediately a shot was fired. Fowler fell with a scream, one hand clamped to her right hip. Heck didn't halt to commiserate, just grabbed her by her harness and continued across, lugging her after him – which induced more screams. He dragged her into the recessed doorway of an estate agency, the door to which opened under the impact of his shoulder. He thrust Fowler inside, where she curled in an agonised ball on its parquet ball.

'H . . . Heck!' she stammered. 'Here . . .' Her gloved hand

shook as she offered him her Glock. 'Eight . . . eight rounds left. Go easy . . .'

He took it and glanced around the corner. Klausen was advancing up the other side of the road, assault rifle in hand – it looked like an L85. He ducked repeatedly behind parked cars, never visible for more than half a second, though he still managed to unload three more rounds, banging holes the size of hubcaps through the estate agency window, forcing Heck to withdraw inside.

Fowler still lay in a foetal posture, face white, blood pooling around her.

'Guess our car park date's off,' Heck said, pulling down a display stand covered with property photographs, and jamming it across the open door.

'Could . . . do you on one leg,' she stuttered. 'Oh God, oh Christ . . .'

'Shhh!' he hissed.

Voices sounded outside. One of them was Klausen's. The other sounded like the African's. There was a sharp *clack-clunk*.

'Shit!' Heck said, diving for cover.

The entire middle of the display board, an area approximately five feet by four, was blown through with a single blast of the 870. Dust and splinters fogged the shop, as Heck knelt up and fired three rapid shots back through the aperture.

'*Sergei!*' Klausen shouted. '*Round the back!*'

'Our Ruski friend's come round too,' Heck said, hearing heavy boots recede down a side-passage. He heaved Fowler up into a fireman's lift. 'What did you hit them with, sugar plums?'

'I didn't see . . . see you knocking 'em round like skittles. Oh, Christ . . .'

Lifting the hatch on the counter, he sidled through it, still carrying her. On his immediate left was an arch with a curtain. He stumbled towards it, and as he did something clinked across the parquet tiling behind. From the corner of his eye, he glimpsed a grenade.

'*Hang tight!*' he yelled as he fought his way past the curtain.

The ear-numbing explosion almost certainly demolished what remained of the agency's front office. In the adjoining passage, Heck was showered with plaster and other debris, and blown from his feet, dropping Fowler heavily. The pain of her collision with the floor knocked her unconscious. Behind them, the curtain had caught fire. There was a smashing of wood and glass as the assailants forced their way in. Heck levelled the Glock at the arch and pegged off three shots, only for movement at the rear of the shop to distract him. He spun around. At the far end of the rear corridor was another room, a dimly lit utility area. A shadowy shape was stealing forward from this – straight into a patch of light. Heck recognised the Russian, just as the bastard opened up with a Serdyukov pistol. Heck flattened himself on top of Fowler, shells like cannonballs whipping over their heads. On the other side of the curtain, there was a familiar *clack-clunk*.

Heck had two shots left. He pegged one through the smouldering curtain, the other down to the rear of the shop, where the Russian dived for cover, then wrapped his arms around the casualty, hoisting her up again, heaving her to his shoulder.

The only avenue of escape was a narrow wooden stair. He tromped exhaustedly up it. The stair switched back on itself once, the upper flight ascending steeply to a small landing with a single door. Grunting and sweating, Heck made it up there, barging the door open – to find a store-room. It contained a table and chair, and filing cabinets down either side. The single window was tall but narrow – too narrow for an adult human to climb out through.

Feet hammered up the lower stair. Heck dropped his burden, turned to the nearest filing cabinet and lugged it out of place – which he only managed with difficulty, as its drawers slid open, revealing masses of paperwork. With every muscle screaming, he manoeuvred it around and shoved it at the open doorway. The Russian was halfway up the final flight, when the cabinet appeared overhead – and toppled down towards him with a sound like a train derailing, the entire building shuddering.

Half a second later, Heck risked a glance.

The stairwell was filled with dust, splinters and fluttering sheets of paper.

When it cleared, Sergei lay motionless at the switchback corner, his face a mask of blood, the entire cabinet, its back broken, lying skewwhiff on top of him.

But Sergei hadn't been alone, and even now a grinning ebony face peeked around the switchback corner. The enormous muzzle of a Remington shotgun followed. Heck ducked back as the blast tore up the stairwell, a cascade of shot ripping the walls, peppering the ceiling. As the African bounded up the last flight, Heck slammed the door in his face. There was only one bolt, which he rammed home before backing across the room. He had no time to make use of another cabinet. The only thing he could do was overturn the table, turn it into a barricade, and drag Fowler behind it – all of which he duly did.

The African's feet halted at the top of the stair.

Fleetingly there was silence. No *clack-clunk* of the 870.

For some reason, Heck's skin crawled.

Then he heard a furtive fumbling at the foot of the door – and a thunder of boots descending. He threw himself behind the table, again covering Fowler with his body.

When the grenade blew, it blasted the door inward, cata-pulting it across the upper room in blistered, smoking frag-ments, which, if it hadn't been for the bulwark of the table, would have smashed the cowering police officers to pulp. The usual gale of smoke, plaster and masonry followed as the walls to either side of the door also shattered. The concus-sion alone was so much that it almost did for Heck, who afterwards lay only vaguely conscious amid broken, charred wreckage.

It seemingly took an age for him to wriggle his way back to wakefulness, and all that time he heard the slow, steady tread of boots re-ascending the stair. Through watery eyes, he focused on the lopsided entrance – and the tall figure with the sickle-shaped grin who appeared there and looked down at him.

This time the African didn't bother speaking; he simply raised his shotgun to his shoulder. He was only nine feet away. With a weapon like that, one shot would tear them both to bloody chunks.

But in fact, two shots were fired.

And not from a shotgun.

Heck's eyes narrowed, his dazed vision clearing – as the African staggered in the doorway, fresh gore bursting from his nose and mouth. Without a word, the eyes rolled into his head and he fell backwards down the stair.

Heck lurched weakly to his feet and crossed the room.

Gemma, in helmet and partial body armour, was standing midway up the stair, peering along the barrel of her Glock, its muzzle smoking.

They gazed at each other blankly for several moments.

Gradually, Heck became aware of multiple voices outside, dogs yipping, the crackle of radio static. He descended towards her. She lowered her weapon.

'Where's Klausen?' he asked.

411

'Klausen?'

'Tall, blond, scar-faced.'

She shrugged, looking too shaken to string two thoughts together. She *had* just shot someone of course. 'I . . . haven't seen anyone like that.'

'Oh . . . brilliant!' He shouldered past her. *'Bloody brilliant!'*

'Excuse me!' she snapped at his back. 'Some gratitude would be nice!'

Heck glanced around and pointed up the stair. 'Sergeant Fowler's up there, ma'am. Gunshot wound to the hip. Losing blood fast. Needs an ambulance.' He continued down, passing the point where Sergei lay groaning beneath the cabinet, ensuring to step on the Russian's face as he did.

Outside, the air was rank with acrid smoke. There were armed cops everywhere, both SOCAR and Northumbria. Many had their weapons holstered, their relaxed state suggesting the battle was over. From their gruff conversations, it became apparent that quite a few of the Nice Guys had surrendered early on, giving full info on their former comrades' strength and disposition. In consequence, the rest had soon been overwhelmed by sheer police numbers – teams were still searching properties on the outskirts of the village, but most hostiles were believed accounted for. Heck still waylaid a few cops, asking if there was a tall, scar-faced Dane among the prisoners. The majority shrugged, or stared at him as if he was some kind of buffoon. A couple looked as shaken as Gemma; ashen-faced, cheeks stained by smoke. It eventually took a Northumbrian firearms inspector to confirm that he hadn't spotted anyone matching that description among the captured.

'Sent those last two bastards in while you hightailed it, did you?' Heck said to himself, as he turned up a nearby alley, scanning every adjoining passage and doorway. 'Sent 'em in as rearguard, eh . . . while you got your fucking arse out!'

He stopped alongside a half-open garage door, from beneath which protruded two upturned feet clad only in socks. Warily, he lifted the door.

Aside from its socks, the blubbery white body inside wore only Y-fronts and a bloodstained vest. Its throat had been cut with such savage but professional precision that the blade, no doubt one of those big bastard commando knives, had almost severed the spinal cord. It wasn't the sort of fate Heck would have wished on anyone – not even Inspector Derek O'Dowd.

'Looks like you were finally of use to someone, Dezzer,' Heck said glumly, before running from the garage.

The fat cop had been an easier picking than Klausen had anticipated.

Heckenburg had surprised them all with his fighting spirit and his stubborn refusal to be beaten, but by contrast the fat cop was everything they'd originally hoped for.

Klausen had first spotted him two streets away from the estate agency, moving nervously from doorway to doorway, fully armoured and with an MP5 and a Glock at his hip. At first he'd looked a threat, even if he had been overweight, his sagging guts squashed inside his flameproof coveralls and ceramic plate. But his sluggish gait had suggested a man out of condition, while neither weapon had even been drawn; his Glock buttoned into its holster, his MP5 locked to his harness, implying extreme inexperience.

It was no trouble to sneak down an entry after him, accost him from behind, slice his fat neck and strip him of his outfit and weapons. As an added bonus, there'd been two pips on his shoulders – this would now prevent the rank and file querying Klausen as he strode casually through Holy Island

413

village. And that was the way it panned out. The Dane strolled easily and unhindered among bustling law officers. Even though his visor was raised, no one batted an eyelid. One or two of the numerous dazed civilians who had now been released from their confinement might have recognised him – perhaps they spotted him through a window earlier. But they were too busy weeping and embracing each other. Of course, the police kit helped, not to mention the spreading dusk, which only now was being illuminated by streetlights springing to life.

It was a pity about Ali and Sergei, he thought as he wandered along the pier, but everyone's usefulness had its limit. He'd already given up on the company phone when he'd sent them into the estate agency to retrieve it. He knew when a battle was lost. With half of the remaining team by then in custody, he'd had no option but to beat a tactical retreat. If the police managed to get hold of the damn phone, they'd be able to roll up much of the existing network, but not all of it. They would never get all of it. And if Klausen could successfully spirit himself away from here, he'd be able to start anew somewhere else. He had boltholes all over the world, and any number of aliases with false paperwork to match.

He reached the end of the pier, where two boats from the Northumbria Police Marine Unit waited: impressive thirty-foot offshore cruisers, their hulls patterned with distinctive turquoise and yellow Battenberg. They weren't exactly designed for comfort, having open front decks where the salt spray could engulf you, and small, enclosed wheel-houses at the rear – but neither of them were presently occupied, and that was all that mattered. Klausen opted for the one on the left, casually stepping aboard and sidling into the wheel-house, and almost laughing when he saw the keys dangling from the ignition. He pulled off his gloves, removed his helmet, and leaned over to assess the panel of controls – and a door clicked open behind him.

An immediate second click denoted the cocking of a firearm.

'Mr Klausen, I presume?' said a low voice. 'Hands up please. And no quick or furtive movements.' Warily, Klausen complied. 'Turn. Verrrry slowly.'

Again, Klausen complied, his back to the exterior door.

Though it was clear from the insignia on the tall, white-haired cop's armour-plated shoulders that he was someone of senior rank, the Dane didn't recognise Commander Frank Tasker.

'Seriously,' Tasker said, Glock aimed with both hands, 'you thought you were just going to sail away from here? You think we haven't got radios, don't talk to each other?'

Klausen said nothing, merely fixed his captor with an ice-green gaze in which his status as merciless murderer was subtly implicit. His mouth curved into an upward smirk. He'd already clocked the nervous sweat glinting under Tasker's raised visor.

'Okay . . .' The cop approached, halting about four feet away. 'The first thing you do is unhitch the submachine gun. Use one hand. Let it drop.'

Klausen lowered his right hand to the side of his harness.

'Watch it!' Tasker said sharply. 'I won't hesitate to pull this trigger.'

There was a *snap*, and the MP5 fell to the floor.

'Kick it to me.'

Klausen did so, the weapon clattering across the wheel-house.

'Now the Glock. Same thing . . . one false move, dead Nice Guy.'

Klausen reached with his left hand to the weapon at his hip.

'Don't take it out of the holster . . . let the whole thing go.'

Klausen's smirk twisted into a smile, his hand sliding away from the holster to the buckle on his tactical belt. 'I assure you,' he said, 'I've no intention of trying anything.' He released the buckle, and the belt slid to the floor. Almost casually, he kicked that across the cabin as well.

Tasker's face still shone with sweat, but now he too smiled. 'Why's that? Never part of the script you'd meet someone who can shoot back?'

'I know when I'm beaten.'

'Hands back up! Keep 'em up!'

Klausen raised his hands again. 'You've got me. It's that simple.'

'Simple? I think not . . . not when you murdered so many of my officers!'

'Pull that trigger if you wish, but I know a lot of things that will be useful to you.'

'I don't doubt you do, but . . .' Tasker shook his head, 'I'll need to think about that, you see. Because when I get you into some official interview room somewhere, we won't be able to do it *this* way, will we? You'll just clam up.'

Klausen's beaming smile never faltered, and all the while, surreptitiously, his raised hands edged closer to the sides of his head, behind which, a couple of inches down, tucked out of sight beneath the high collar of his flameproof armour, was his back-up weapon, a Ruger SR9.

'Course, it's always possible you might try to escape . . . like Silver did,' Tasker said, his confidence growing, so much that he lowered his guard slightly. 'Only this time it'll be *you* who gets shot.'

'What is that . . . some kind of threat?' Klausen's hands were now behind his head.

'More a possibility,' Tasker said. 'Anything can happen, my friend.'

416

'*It can indeed!*' Klausen snatched the Ruger from his nape – only for a sharp karate blow to break his grip on it. He cursed as he tottered forward.

Tasker raised his Glock again, fleetingly bewildered.

'Weren't trying to get this, were you?' Heck said, stepping into the cabin properly, jamming the Ruger into the side of the Dane's neck.

Klausen was twisted at a painful angle, but froze on hearing Heck's voice.

'Is this a day for surprises, or what?' Heck added, grabbing him by a hank of hair and slamming his face into the bulkhead wall. 'You know . . . when I got up this morning, having spent last night in someone's armchair, I never had the first clue I'd be nailing you bastards into coffins by teatime.'

'Easy, Heck,' Tasker said.

'They've had their chance, sir!' Heck slammed Klausen's face into the bulkhead again, then grabbed him by the collar and spun him roughly around.

The Dane was cut deeply across the bridge of his nose, red droplets trickling down to the end and dripping off. He tried again with that confident smile, but this time he wasn't fooling anyone. Heck shoved him back against the bulkhead, and trained the Ruger right between his eyes.

'Heck . . .' Tasker said. 'We need him.'

'We don't actually, sir. We've got a few of the others. We've got their company phone – and there's a telephone directory of contacts in that; everyone who's ever done any business with these creeps. We don't need this one at all.'

Klausen's breathing was slow but steady. His eyes almost crossed as they fixed on the steel glint of the Ruger.

'This is what it's like, pal,' Heck said in low monotone. 'The last few seconds before you die. Not very pleasant, eh? Well . . . tough shit. It's high time he who dealt it, felt it.'

'Heck . . .' Tasker warned. 'You think Gemma will ever look at you again?'

'Gemma!' Heck snorted. 'There's a name from the past.'

'I can give you other names . . .' Klausen said.

'Shut the fuck up!' Heck snarled. 'You think you can rape and murder like you're some kind of latter-day Viking! Lock people up! Throw hand grenades? You think Gull Rock plus satellite telly and an internet link is adequate payback for that . . . just because you've turned evidence?' He retreated a couple more steps, the Ruger still locked on Klausen's forehead.

Klausen attempted a shrug. 'This will be murder. Your boss is a witness.'

'Uh-uh,' Tasker disagreed. 'You went for his gun . . . he had no choice.'

Heck threw the commander a fleeting glance.

Tasker gazed back, po-faced. 'Your call, Heck. This bastard deserves it for sure, but what was that case you recently had in Sunderland? Some citizen taking the law into his own hands because a bunch of in-breds were beyond the pale? Go on, do it . . . shoot him like the dog he undoubtedly is. Isn't that what your crazy Nazi-hunter did? What his dad did before him?'

Heck shook his head. In truth, these thoughts hadn't been a hundred miles away even before Tasker brought them up. But there were some things you just couldn't tolerate. Some offences were so heinous they simply had to be punished.

All the pain and misery I could have prevented in my career . . . if I'd put a bullet through the head of every criminal I've ever met, instead of locking him up . . .

'You've got me covered, sir, is that correct?'

'That's what I said, Heck.'

Heck looked back at the prisoner, who despite his empty smirk was now bathed in sweat, his palms fixed at shoulder height.

'Trouble is, sir,' Heck finally said. 'I wouldn't trust you as far as I could kick your bloody arse.' He fixed his attention on Klausen. 'And *you* shouldn't trust him either. Just remember that . . . whatever he tells you, whatever he offers you. Not that it'll ultimately be his call, because I can assure you now, Kurt, whichever holiday camp you think you're going to . . . there are men in prisons all over Britain who owe me favours. Big ones.' Even then, Heck shook his head at his own weakness. 'In the meantime, Kurt Klausen, you don't have to say anything unless you wish to do so . . .'

Chapter 38

The aftermath of the Holy Island gunfight was massive and chaotic.

High-ranking officials from almost every department, including senior politicians, and news crews from all over the country, had converged on the Northumbrian coast long before ten-thirty that night, when the causeway was due to re-open. By various means, some of them had even got across the narrow waterway before then, and were soon busying themselves up and down the milling streets of the normally quiet settlement, exploring the scene of what – according to one anchor-man – was 'a terrorist-related incident on a par with the Siege of Sydney Street or the battle with the Balcombe Street Gang'.

Significant areas of the island, of course, had already been taped off for crime scene examination. Numerous medical staff had been ferried over from the mainland, and were treating casualties. Military units were on hand with dog teams to search for and take possession of unexploded ordinance. Also, mysteriously, a number of street-vendors had appeared and were providing the various police officers present with tea and rolls.

In the midst of all this, a mobile command HQ had been set up on the village green. This was basically a caravan crammed with telephones, computers and a raft of tea-making equipment. Gemma Piper hadn't enclosed herself in there to take refuge from the bedlam outside as much as to try and get her thoughts in order – though it wasn't easy doing this while attempting to field several phone calls at the same time, check half a dozen reports and also write one of her own. On top of all that, she was tired and stressed, having shot and killed a suspect that day (only the second of her entire service).

But her overall feeling was one of cautious relief.

This thing had never been likely to end peacefully, if it ended at all, but the incident's toll of fatalities was markedly less than she'd expected: ten Nice Guys and one police officer. None of the civilian occupants of the island had suffered more than superficial injuries. It still didn't feel like a victory, but the sight of the Nice Guys' so-called 'company phone', sealed in a sterile evidence sack and carefully labelled, lying on the desk alongside her, was some kind of achievement.

There was a rapping on the caravan door.

She hooked the phone under her chin – Joe Wullerton, Director of the National Crime Group, was keeping her on hold – but only because he himself was being kept on hold by the Home Secretary. 'Make it quick!' she called.

Heck came in looking as battered and bruised as he had earlier, though at least he'd now removed his blood-caked clothing, which would all need to go to Forensics. He was currently wearing a blue and white Northumbria Police tracksuit.

It was a miracle he was alive, of course. Thanks to her. Not that she felt like hearing any fawning gratitude. They'd studiedly avoided each other during the two hours elapsing since the estate agency rescue, but she would have words to say to him in due course. She'd have plenty.

'Two bits of paper for you here, ma'am,' he said. 'Both very important.'

'Leave them on the desk. I'll look at them later.'

'I think you'll want to look at them now.'

She glanced irritably up again.

'This first one is the list of all the Nice Guys' former clients in the UK,' he said, placing a scruffy hunk of pages on the desk beside her. 'Forgot to mention it earlier. Looks like you've got a lot more locking-up to do here before you go overseas.'

She cut the call and unfolded the document. 'Good God . . . this is excellent.' Fleetingly she forgot her annoyance with him. 'You've heard that lad, PC Farthing, is going to be okay?'

Heck nodded. 'Yeah. It's good news . . . if a trifle amazing. He deserves a commendation. At the very least.'

'And that Ben Kane got locked up by Northumbria?'

'He's a lucky bunny too,' Heck said.

She flipped a couple more pages. 'We've also received word the Navy intercepted three speedboats out in the North Sea, not far from Tynemouth. Seems they'd disembarked from the Netherlands earlier this evening. The armed crews manning them have also been taken into custody.'

Heck nodded. 'These goons have always been able to organise on the hoof. Probably realised the game was up once I compromised their hideout.'

'It might have worked,' she mused. 'If they'd managed to hold out a bit longer . . .'

'Or if you hadn't been tipped off so early,' Heck said.

'You were certainly in the right place at the right time,' she conceded, taking another evidence sack from a drawer and inserting the list. 'Once the causeway was flooded, they started cutting phone lines, disrupting electronic communications. We'd have been blind to everything happening here.'

'And instead you've got nine prisoners.'

'More than a few of whom have indicated a willingness to sing like canaries.'

He nodded again. 'So it's job done.'

'Maybe.' She spun her chair around to look up at him. 'What's the other one?'

'What's that, ma'am?'

'The other bit of paper. You said there were two.'

'Oh, that . . .' Rather casually, he dug a small square of frayed cardboard from the front pocket of his tracksuit trousers and dropped it on the desk. 'That's my request for a transfer out of the Serial Crimes Unit.'

She stared at it, initially too puzzled for his words to sink in.

'Sorry it's on the back of a pub beer mat,' he said, turning it over to reveal a near-illegible biro scrawl. 'But I didn't have the correct forms.'

'Hang on . . .?' She gazed at him, assuming they were at cross-purposes.

He returned the gaze blankly, unconcernedly.

'Heck . . . what . . . sorry, what are you talking about?'

'Obviously I'll help you clear this lot up. My collar, my case, and all that. But the first opportunity that comes along afterwards, I'm out of here . . . ma'am.'

'Wait a minute . . . sit down.'

'I'd rather stand, if you don't mind. Got kicked in the butt.'

She regarded him as coolly as she was able to under the circumstances. 'Is this pathetic nonsense because I put you into protective custody?'

'You didn't put me into protective custody, ma'am. You put me into custody. The intention was to keep me out of

423

the way because you knew I'd find out you and Frank Tasker had made a deal to let Mike Silver escape.'

She placed her pen on the desk. 'That isn't entirely true.'

'Oh, it's not *entirely* true?'

'Silver would never have been allowed to escape. The idea was to put him under secret house arrest somewhere. Look, Heck . . . you yourself said there are Nice Guys rackets running in different countries. Interpol strongly suspects that too, and Mike Silver was our only lead. We had to get him to talk.'

'House arrest? For how long?'

'The remainder of his life.'

'And what are we talking . . . some hotel somewhere? Swimming pool? Five-star restaurant?'

'A SOCAR safehouse.'

'Now, don't tell me . . .' Heck couldn't believe what he was thinking, but suddenly it all made sense. The newness of the place, the OTT security. 'It isn't by any chance near the village of Lea down in the Cotswolds?' He could tell from the flush to her cheek that this was true. 'Just out of interest, ma'am . . . did you take a diploma in how to add salt to nasty wounds?'

'Look . . . it was a bit tasteless, I admit that. But you were only sent to the same place because it was ready to receive an occupant.'

'And you couldn't just have told me all this?'

'Not after Rochester's phony escape turned into a real escape. I knew you'd disapprove on principle . . .'

He nodded. 'Well that's one thing you were right about at least.'

'Plus we'd made a hell of an error . . .'

'You can say that again.'

'So the less people who knew about it, the better.' She stood up. 'Heck, think about this . . . can you imagine the

424

impact if the Eurosceptic British public ever learned we'd engineered a prison break for one of our worst killers purely to help the police overseas?'

'Can you imagine the impact if they ever learned you'd been planning to hole him up in a country house in the Cotswolds for the rest of his life?'

'Well, exactly. So you've answered your own question.'

'And you think that by finally revealing all this to me – now that you've no bloody option because I've sussed it anyway, that will keep me on-side?'

She folded her arms. A defensive posture, he noted, and nervous; this was a new experience for her. 'Heck . . . as far as the general public are concerned, this whole disaster has now been resolved. Mike Silver's prison cavalcade was ambushed by his former associates, after which he provided them with a list of all former clients, who they sought to liquidate as a security measure. And we managed to intercept them halfway through. It was a big upset, a big crisis . . . but now it's been resolved. And more to the point, we're going to arrest a lot more people . . . both here in the UK and abroad. It's been a costly battle, but it's won us the war.'

He regarded her for several long moments, during which she flushed an even deeper shade of pink.

'Why are you looking at me like that?' she said.

'I'm just wondering what it's worth to keep *my* version of events out of the newspapers . . . and subsequently prevent you, Frank Tasker, and whoever else was involved in this fiasco facing a public enquiry.'

'You'd really do that?' she wondered.

'I don't actually know. There'd be a furore for sure. On the basis that fall-guys' heads always have to roll, quite a few people would lose their jobs. You, almost certainly. Maybe Tasker, though I'm not certain . . . he probably got his orders direct from the Home Office. Perhaps he'd just get busted down to DI like poor Jim Laycock, for whom I won't forgive myself easily. But ultimately . . . well, that'd be all, wouldn't it?' Heck shrugged wearily. 'The crisis has ended. The bad guys are either dead or in jail. Perhaps to say more would be a pointless exercise . . .'

'Glad you see it that way . . .'

His expression tautened. 'Except that I don't . . . not totally. Because one thing we still haven't accounted for, Gemma, is you deliberately trying to con me.'

'*Con you!*' She looked flabbergasted by this. 'Heck . . . you know we run black ops from time to time, with "need to know" classifications. You also know the fewer bodies in the loop, the better. Plus, as you're well aware, there's a chain of command. I mean who the hell are *you*, anyway? A sergeant! With an attitude! And a well-blotted copybook!'

'You can forget the heavy stuff,' he said dismissively. 'I'm not just any old sergeant. Me and you have been round the track together more times than a pair of shagged-out lurchers. And yet rather than bring me in on this, you bloody well locked me up! And not only that, you tried to guilt-trip me into keeping my nose out. Made me feel like an absolute shithouse who'd made your life a misery.'

'There was more than a bit of truth in that.'

'And now we're square, is that it? You've managed to out-shithouse me?'

'Enough melodrama.' She tilted her chin. 'Let's cut to the chase . . . what do you want?'

He pushed his transfer request across the desk. 'Just this. Straight away. No explanations in writing. No question-and-answer sessions. No fucking about in any shape or form.'

'And where do you want to go?'

'Anywhere . . . so long as it's far away from you. So if that'll be all, ma'am . . .' He turned to the door.

'Heck . . .'

He glanced back.

'This is really stupid. You realise that, don't you?'

'Sorry . . . I don't. I reckon it's high time you guys started solving a few crimes yourselves.' The door banged closed behind him.

Are you #HOOKEDONHECK? Tell us all about it @CrimeFix and @paulfinchauthor.

And if you can't wait for your next Heck fix, read on for a sneak peek of Paul's next book, *Dead Man Walking*, which will hit the shelves in November 2014 . . .

Prologue

The girl was quite content in her state of semi-undress. The boy wasn't concerned by it either. If anything, he seemed to enjoy the interest she attracted as they drove from pub to pub that sultry August evening.

They commenced their Friday night drive-around in Buckfastleigh, then visited the lively villages of Holne and Poundsgate, before penetrating deeper into Dartmoor's vast, grassy wilderness, calling at ever more isolated hamlets: Babeny, Dunstone and finally Widecombe-in-the-Moor, where a posse of legendary beer-swilling reprobates had once ridden Uncle Tom Cobley's grey mare to an early grave.

The girl was first to enter each hostelry, sashaying in through the guffawing hordes, and wiggling comfortably onto the central-most bar stool she could find, while the boy took time to find a place in the car park for his sleek, black and silver Porsche. On each occasion she made an impact. The riot of noise under the low, gnarly roof-beams never actually subsided, but it never needed to. Looking was free.

She wasn't behaving overtly flirtatiously, but she clearly

revelled in the attention she drew. And why not? She had 'all the tools', as they say. A tall, willowy blonde, her shapely form showcased to perfection in a green micro mini-dress and strappy green shoes with killer heels. Her golden mane hung past her shoulders in a glossy wave. She had full lips, a pert nose and delicate, feline cheekbones. When she removed her mirror shades, subtle grey shadow accentuated a pair of startling blue eyes. In each pub she made sure to sit prominently: back arched, boobs thrust forward, smooth tan legs sensually crossed. There was no denying she was playing it up, which was much appreciated by the taproom crowd. For the most part these were beefy locals, countrymen to the last, but there were also visitors here: car-loads of lusty lads openly cruising for girls and beer; or bluff, gruff oldsters in denims and plaid shirts, down in Devon for the sailing, the fishing, or the moorland walking – they might only be away from their wives for a few days, but they too revealed an eye for the girls; in particular an eye for this girl. It wasn't just that she smiled sweetly as they made space for her at the bar, or that she responded with humour to their cheeky quips, but up close it could be seen that she wasn't a girl after all – she was a woman, in her late twenties, closer to their own age therefore, and because of this even more of a taunting presence.

And still the bloke with her seemed oblivious to – or maybe was simply unconcerned by the stir his girlfriend (or perhaps his wife, who knew?) – was causing. He was well dressed – beige Armani slacks, a short-sleeved Yves St Laurent shirt, suede Ted Baker brogues – and of course he drove an impressive motor. But he was plumpish, with pale, pudgy features – 'fucking snail', as one leery bar-fly commented to his mate – and a shock of carroty red hair. And he drank only shandies, which made him seem a little soft to have such a tigress on his arm – at least from the locals' point of

432

iew. And yet by the duo's body-language, the man was the more dominant. He stood while she sat. He bought the drinks while she disported her charms, leaning backward against the bar, her exposed cleavage inviting the most brazen stares.

'Got a right couple, here!' Harold Hopkinson, portly land-lord of The Grouse Beater, said from the side of his mouth. 'Talk about putting his missus on show.'

'She's loving every minute of it,' Doreen, his foursquare wife, replied.

'Bit old to be making an exhibition of themselves like that, aren't they?'

'Bit old? They're just the right age. Where do you think they'll be off to next?'

Harold looked surprised. 'You don't mean Halfpenny Reservoir?'

'Where else?'

'But surely they *know*? I mean . . .' Harold frowned. 'Nah, can't be that. Look, she's a bonnie girl, and he likes showing the world what he's got.'

Doreen pulled another pint of Dartmoor IPA. 'You really believe that?'

Briefly, Harold was lost for words. It all made an unpleasant kind of sense. Halfpenny Reservoir wasn't Devon's number one dogging location – it was a long way from anywhere of consequence – but it was well known locally and it got busy from time to time; at least, it used to get busy before the panic had started. He eyed the fulsome couple again. The woman still perched on her bar stool, sipping a rum and lemonade. Now that he assessed her properly, he saw finger and toenails painted gold, a chain around her left ankle decorated with moons and stars. That was a come-on of sorts, wasn't it? At least, it was according to some of his favourite websites (the ones he only perused after Doreen had gone to bed). Of course, it wouldn't have been unusual at one time, this kind of display. The swinger crowd would occasionally trawl the local boozers en route to Halfpenny Reservoir – somewhat more covertly than this, admittedly, but nonetheless 'displaying their wares', as Doreen liked to call it, looking to pick up the passing rough that seemed to be their stock-in-trade.

Things were markedly different now, of course. Or they should be.

'They must be out-of-towners,' Harold said. 'They obviously don't know.'

'They'd have to be from another planet not to know,' Doreen replied tersely.

'Well . . . shouldn't we tell them?'

'Tell them what?'

'I don't know . . . just advise them it's a bad idea at the present time.'

She gave him her most withering glance. 'It should be a bad idea *any* time.'

Harold's wife had a kind of skewed morality when it came to earthy pleasures. She made her living selling alcohol, and yet she had a real problem with drunks, refusing to serve anyone she suspected of sampling one too many, and was very quick to issue barring orders if there was ever horseplay in the pub. Likewise, though she consciously employed pretty local girls to work behind her bar, she was strongly antagonistic to 'tarts and tramps,' as she called them, and was especially hostile to any women she fingered for members of the swinging crowd who gathered for their midnight revels up at the reservoir – so much so that when 'the Stranger' had first come on the scene, targeting lone couples parked up late at night, she'd almost regarded him with approval.

Until the details had emerged of course.

Because even by the standards of Britain's most heinous murders, these were real shockers. Harold couldn't help shuddering as he recalled some of the details he'd read about in the papers. Though no attack had been reported any closer to The Grouse Beater than a treed-off picnic area near Sourton on the other side of the moor, twenty miles away as the crow flew, the whole of the county had been put on alert. He glanced around the taproom, wondering if the predator might be present at this moment. The pub was full, mainly with men, and not all of the 'shrinking violet' variety. Devon was a holiday idyll, especially in summer – it didn't just attract the New Age crowd and the hippy backpackers, it drew families, honeymooners and the like. But it was a working county too, even up here on the high moor, the local male populace comprising far more than country squire and Colonel Blimp types in tweeds and gaiters; there were farm-labourers, cattlemen, farriers, hedgers, keepers; occupations which by their nature required hardy outdoor characters. And hadn't the police issued some kind of statement about their chief suspect being a local man probably engaged in manual labour, someone tough and physically strong enough to overpower healthy young couples? At the same time, he was someone who knew the back roads so he could creep up on his victims unawares and then make his getaway afterwards.

There were an awful lot of blokes satisfying those criteria right here, right now.

The more Harold thought about it, the more vulnerable the young couple looked in the midst of this rumbustious crowd. Even if the Stranger wasn't present, the woman ought not to be displaying herself like that. The man ought to realise that several of these fellas had already had lots to drink, especially those who were openly ogling; that temptation might get the better of them and that it would be so, so easy just to reach out and place a wandering hand on that smooth, sun-browned thigh. If that happened there might be trouble, swingers or not, and that was the last thing Harold wanted.

'We have to say something,' he said to Doreen.

'What?' she sneered. 'Casually tell them all the local dogging sites are closed? How do you think that'll go down? They might just be show-offs. Might just have come out for a drink.'

'But you said . . .'

'Just leave it, Harold. We don't need you making a fool of yourself. Again.'

'But if they are swingers, and they go up there . . .?'

'They'll be taking a chance. Like they always take chances. Good God, who in their right mind would go looking for sex with strangers in the middle of nowhere?'

'But darling, if they don't know . . .'

'They're adults, aren't they! They should make it their business to know.'

Three minutes later – much to Harold's relief – 'the adults' left, the woman swaying prettily to the pub door, heads again turning to watch, the man digging a packet of cigarettes from his slacks as he idly followed. In some ways it was as if they weren't actually together; as if the man was just some casual acquaintance rather than a partner, which was a bit confusing. Still, it was someone else's problem now.

Harold edged to the diamond-paned window overlooking the pub car park.

The duo stood beside the Porsche, the man smoking, the woman leaning on the car with arms folded, her bag dangling from her shoulder by its strap. They chatted together, in no apparent rush to go anywhere – perhaps they were just a dressy couple out for a few drinks? Harold felt a slow sense of relief. Probably a nice couple too, when you got to know them; it was hardly the woman's fault she was hot as hell.

It was approaching nine o'clock now and the sun was

setting, fiery red stripes lying across the encircling moorland. Maybe they were all set to go home? But then, when the man was only half way through his cigarette, he stubbed it out on the tarmac and placed it in a nearby waste-container. And when they climbed into the Porsche together and drove away, it wasn't along the B3387 to Bovey Tracey, or even back through the village towards Dunstone and ultimately Buckfastleigh, it was along the unnamed road that ran due northwest from here. The next inhabited place it came to was Beardon, some fifteen miles away.

But long before then, it passed Halfpenny Reservoir.

It had been a vintage August day in the West Country, but the heat was finally seeping from the land, the balminess of the evening receding. An indigo dusk now layered the hills and valleys of Dartmoor.

By the time they reached the reservoir it would be near enough pitch-black.

The woman checked their rear-view mirror as they drove. Fleetingly, she thought she'd glimpsed headlights behind, but now there was nothing; only the greyness of nightfall. Ahead, the road sped on hypnotically, the vastness of the encircling moor oppressive in its emptiness. Tens of minutes passed, and they didn't spot a single habitation – neither a cottage, nor another pub – though in truth they were too busy looking for the reservoir turn-off to indulge in any form of sightseeing. Even then, they almost passed it; a narrow, unmade lane, all dry rutted earth in their headlights, branching away between two granite gateposts and arcing off at a slanted angle amongst dense stands of yellow-flowered furze.

They slowed to a halt in the middle of the blacktop.

'This must be it . . .?' the man said. It was more a question than an observation.

The woman nodded.

They ventured left along the rugged route, bouncing and jolting, spiky twigs whispering down the Porsche's flanks, following a shallow V-shaped valley for several hundred yards before star-lit sky broke out ahead; the radiant orb of the moon suspended there, its reflection shimmering on an expansive body of water lying to their right. Like most of the Dartmoor reservoirs, Halfpenny Lake was manmade, its purpose to supply drinking water to the surrounding lowlands. A row of wrought-iron railings flickered past in the glow of their right-side headlamp as they prowled the shoreline road, and the solid, horizontal silhouette of what looked like a dam blocking off the valley at its farthest end, affirmed the mundane purpose of this place.

There were several sheltered parking bays along here, all notoriously a dump site for used condoms, dog-eared porn mags and pairs of semen-stained knickers – though any such debris now would be old and rotted; there was no one present to add new mementoes.

Apart from the man and the woman.

They parked close to the entrance of the second lot, and there, as per the manual, turned the radio down – it was tuned to an 'easy listening' station, so was hardly intrusive in any case – opened all the windows, and climbed into the back seat together. Here, they sat apart – one at either end of the seat, exchanging odd murmurs of anticipation as they waited for their audience.

And so the minutes passed.

The stillness outside was near absolute; a gentle breeze sighing across the heathery moorland tops, groaning amid the granite tors. The couple's eyes roved back and forth along the unlit ridges. The only movement came from tufts of bracken rippling against the stars. It was almost eerie how peaceful it was, how tranquil. A classic English summer's night.

All the more reason why the fierce crackle of electricity jolted them so badly.

Especially the man, who stiffened and fell back against the nearside door.

It happened that fast. He simply froze, his eyes glazed, foam shooting from his rigidly puckered mouth. Then the featureless figure outside who had risen into view from a kneeling posture and reached through the open window with his Taser, now reached through again and unlocked the door.

All this happened too quickly for the woman to take it in. *Almost* too quickly.

As the lifeless shape of her beau dropped backward again, this time out onto the gritty tarmac, which his head struck with a brutal force, she grappled with her handbag, unsnapping it, fumbling inside. It was a quick, fluid motion – she didn't waste time squawking in outrage – but their assailant was quicker still. He lunged in through the open nearside door. In the dull green light of the dashboard facia, she caught a fleeting glimpse of heavy-duty leather: a leather coat, leather face-mask, and a leather glove, as – *POW!* – his flying fist caught her right in the kisser.

She too slumped backward, head swimming, handbag tipping top-down into the foot-well, spilling its contents every which way.

With thoughts fizzled to near-incomprehensibility during what felt like an age of stupor, the woman probed at her two front teeth with her tongue. They appeared to wobble; at the same time her upper lip stung abominably, whilst her mouth rapidly filled with hot, coppery fluid. She coughed on it, choking.

And then awareness surged abruptly back – like a dash of iced water.

She was lying on her back, but the intruder was now in the car with her, on the rear seat in fact, already positioned between her indecently spread-apart legs. With one gloved hand, he kept a tight grip on her exposed upper left thigh; it was so high, his thumb was almost in her crotch. With his other hand, he was slowly, purposefully unfastening his coat.

From some distant place, the woman heard a new song on the radio. A rich American voice poured through the nicely central-heated car.

Wondering in the night what were the chances . . .
We'd be sharing love before the night was through . . .

A beastly chuckle, hideous and pig-like, snorted from the leather-clad face. Still vaguely dazed, the woman strained her eyes through the greenish, pain-hazed gloom. Frank Sinatra, she recalled. One of her father's favourites. Old Blue Eyes, The Voice, the Sultan of Swoon . . .

'Looks like they're playing my tune,' the intruder said, as the final button snapped open and his coat flaps fell apart. If she'd had any doubts before, she had none now.

Something in my heart told me I must have you . . .

He hadn't spoken before. Not a single word – not to her knowledge. But then who would know? The weird sex-murderer who'd been stalking lovers' lanes and dogging spots all over Devon and Somerset this last year had not left a single living witness. All five couples he'd targeted had been eliminated with precision, ruthlessness, and great, great enjoyment; the men with throats cut and skulls crushed, the women sexually mutilated in a ritual that went far beyond everyday sadism.

Strangers in the night . . .
Two lonely people . . .
We were strangers in the night . . .

440

'Definitely my tune.' He chuckled again, using his left hand to fondle the array of gleaming implements in his customised inner lining: the tin-opener, the screwdriver, the mallet, the hacksaw, the razor-edged filleting knife.

The woman could barely move, yet her eyes were now riveted on *his* eyes: moist baubles framed in leather sockets; and on his mouth, the saliva-coated tongue and broken, stained teeth exposed by a drawn-back zipper. But that voice – it could only have been a whisper in truth, a gloating guttural whisper. But she would remember it as long as she lived. At least, she would remember that one previously unknown but oh-so-essential detail.

It was Scottish.

The Stranger was a Scotsman.

The key thing now, of course, was to ensure that she *did* live.

Perhaps he was too busy drawing out that first instrument of torture – the tin-opener, an old-fashioned device with a ghastly hooked blade – to notice her right hand working frantically through the debris littering the foot-well.

As he raised the tin-opener to his right shoulder – not to plunge it down, as much as to tease her with the terror of it – her fingertips found something she recognised.

He kept her pinned in place with his other hand, a grip so hard in that soft, sensitive place that it was now agony, as he crooned along to the tune.

> *Ever since that night we've been together . . .*
> *Lovers at first sight, in love forever . . .*
> *It turned out so right . . .*

'For strangers in the night,' he concluded. They'd first dubbed him 'the Stranger' in the West Country press because of the sex-with-strangers scene he'd so viciously crashed. It now seemed even more appropriate. 'You're a taunting, godless bitch,' he added matter-of-factly, still in that notable accent. 'A whore, an exhibitionist slut, a prick-teasing slag . . .'

'And a police officer,' she said, pointing her snub-nosed Colt Cobra .38 straight at his face. 'Move one muscle, you bastard . . . open that filthy yap of yours one more time, and I'll put a bullet straight through your fucking skull!'

The expression on his face was priceless. At least, it probably would have been had she been able to see it. As it was, she had to be content with his sudden almost comical paralysis, with the whites of his eyes widening in cartoon fashion around his soulless black pupils, with his gammy mouth sagging open between zippered lips.

'Yeah . . . that's right,' she said. 'It's all over. Now drop that sodding blade.'

Of course, it couldn't be over in reality, and her heart pounded harder in her chest as this slowly dawned on her. He couldn't let it end like *this* – so abruptly, so unexpectedly; or in *this* fashion: trapped like a rabbit by one of these frail, sexual creatures he so brutally despised. Warily, she transferred the .38 from her right hand to her left, keeping it levelled at him as she lay there. With her empty right, she again reached into the foot-well. Her radio was down there somewhere, but she was damned if she could find it. All the time, he sat motionless, nailing her with that semi-human gaze, strands of spittle hanging over his leather-covered jaw. And now she saw his mouth slowly closing, those discoloured teeth clamping together in a final, hate-filled grimace. He wasn't frozen with shock anymore, she realised; he was taut with tension – like a spring set to uncoil.

'Don't you do it!' she warned, but it was too late; he arched down with the tin-opener, intent on ripping her wide with its wicked, hooked point.

BANG!

The slug took him in the left side of his upper chest, just beneath the collar bone, flinging him backward out of the car and down onto the tarmac, where he lay silently twisting alongside the prone form of Detective Constable Maxwell.

She found the radio and slammed it to her lips as she threw herself forward through the cordite. 'All units, this is DI Piper! Converge on Halfpenny Reservoir! Repeat, converge on Halfpenny Reservoir . . .'

Her words tailed off as a stocky figure rose awkwardly to its feet outside. For a half-second she tried to kid herself that this was Maxwell, though internally she knew it couldn't be. The DC had struck the tarmac with a hell of a whack.

Without a word, the figure swayed around and blundered across the car park.

'Repeat, this is DI Piper! Decoy unit Alpha. One shot fired. Suspect suffering a chest wound, but on foot and mobile.'

There was a scrabble of static-ridden responses, but even as Piper watched, the lumbering form of the Stranger scrambled over the car park's low perimeter wall, the dark blot of his outline swiftly ascending through the deep furze on the other side. He was hurt badly; that was clear – he lurched from side to side, but kept going in a more or less straight line, uphill and away from her.

'Suspect heading west . . . away from the reservoir, over open ground,' she added, clattering onto the tarmac in her tall, strappy shoes. 'We need an ambulance too.' She dropped to one knee to check the carotid at the side of Maxwell's neck. 'DC Maxwell is severely injured . . . he's received a massive shock from some kind of stun-gun and what looks like a head trauma. Currently in a collapsed state, but breathing, and his pulse feels regular. Get that ambulance here pronto! In the meantime, I'm pursuing the suspect, over.'

She hurried across the car park, but once she was over the

wall into the furze, her heels sank like knife-blades in the soft earth. She kicked the shoes off as she ran uphill, flinching as twigs and sharp-edged stones spiked the soles of her feet, and thorns and thistles raked her naked legs. Very briefly, the Stranger appeared above her – a lopsided silhouette on the night sky. But then he was gone again, over the ridge.

'Get me that back-up now!' she shouted into her radio.

'Ma'am, you need to hold back,' came a semi-coherent response. *'DSU Anderson's orders! Wait for support units, over!'*

'Negative, that!' she replied firmly. 'Not when we're this close.'

She too crested the ridge. The starlit moor unrolled itself: a sweeping georama of grass and boulders, obscured by patches of low-lying mist but rising distantly to soaring, tor-crowned summits. On lower ground now, but a hundred yards ahead of her at least, a dark blot was struggling onward.

The ground sloped steeply as she gave chase, ploughing downhill through soft, springy vegetation, shouting that he was under arrest; that he should give it up.

Perspectives were all askew, of course, so she wasn't quite sure where she lost sight of him. Though he wasn't a vast distance ahead, curtains of mist seemed suddenly to close around him. When she reached that point herself – now hobbling, both feet bruised and bleeding – she found she was on much softer ground, plodding through ankle-deep mud. He ought to have left a recognisable trail, but it was too dark to see and she had no light with which to get down and make a fingertip search.

Further terse orders came crackling over the airwaves.

Again, she ignored them. It occurred to her that maybe the suspect was wearing a vest and therefore not as badly injured as she'd thought. But if that was the case, why had he fled . . . why not use the advantage to go straight on the attack, ripping and mauling her in the car? No – she'd wounded him; she'd seen the pain in his posture. If nothing else, that meant there'd be blood.

Unless the rain came before the forensics teams did.

'We need the lab-rats up here ASAP!' she shouted, cutting across the frantic exchanges of her colleagues. 'At least we'll have his DNA . . .'

There was a choked scream from somewhere ahead.

She slowed to a near-halt. Fleetingly, she couldn't see anything; liquid mist, the colour of purulent milk, ebbed on all sides. But had that cry been for real? Was he finally succumbing to his wound? Or was he trying to lure her?

There was another scream, this one accompanied by a strangled gurgling.

She now halted completely.

This was Dartmoor. A National Park. A green and hazy paradise. Picturesque, famous for its pristine flora and fauna. And notorious for its bottomless mires. The third scream dwindled to a series of choked gasps, and now she heard a deep sploshing too, like a heavy body plunging through slime.

'Update,' she said into her radio, advancing warily. 'I'm perhaps three hundred yards west of the reservoir parking area, over the top of the ridge. Suspect appears to be in trouble. I can't see him, but it's possible he's blundered into a mire.'

There was further insistence that she stop and wait for back-up. Again she ignored this, but only advanced five or six yards before she found herself teetering on the brink of an opaque, black/green morass, its mirror-flat surface stretching in all directions as the mist seemed to furl away across it. She strained her eyes to penetrate the gloom, but nothing stirred out there; there wasn't so much as a ripple, let alone the distinctive outline of a man fighting to keep his head above the surface.

There was no sound either, which was worrying. Dartmoor's mires could suck you down with frightful speed. Their bowels were stuffed with sheep and pony carcasses, not to mention the odd missing hiker or two. But all she could identify now were the twisted husks of sunken trees, their branches protruding here and there like rotted dinosaur bones.

Even Detective Inspector Gemma Piper, of the Metropolitan Police – wilful, fearless and determined – now realised that caution was the better part of valour. Especially as the mist continued to clear on the strengthening wind, revealing, despite the darkness of night, how truly extensive this mire was. It lay everywhere; not just ahead of her but on both sides as well – as though she'd strayed out onto a narrow headland. It was difficult to imagine that even a local man could have lumbered this way, mortally wounded, blinded by vapour, and had somehow avoided this pitfall. And if nothing else, she now knew their suspect was not a local man – but, by origin at least, from the other end of the country.

Voices sounded behind her, torches spearing across the undulating landscape. Within an hour, the Devon & Cornwall Police, with assistance from Scotland Yard, had cordoned off this entire stretch of moor, were searching it with dogs, and had even brought heavy machinery in to start dredging the mire and its various connected waterways.

At the reservoir car park, the conscious but weakened form of DC Maxwell was loaded into the rear of an ambulance. Gemma Piper meanwhile sat side-saddle in the front seat of a police patrol car, sipping coffee and occasionally wincing as a medic knelt and attended to her torn, bloodied feet and swollen face. At the same time, she briefed Detective Superintendent Anderson on the events of the evening.

The hard-headed young female DI, already impressive to every senior manager who'd encountered her, had just assured herself a glowing future in this most challenging and male-dominated of industries. But of the so-called Stranger, the perpetrator of ten loathsome torture-murders – so spoke the *Dartmoor Advertiser*: 'These crimes are abhorrent, utterly loathsome!' – there was no trace.

Nor would there be for some considerable time.

Chapter 1

Present Day

There was no real witchcraft associated with this part of the Lake District. Nor had there ever been, to Heck's knowledge.

The name 'Witch Cradle Tarn' had been applied in times past purely to reflect the small mountain lake's ominous appearance: a long, narrow, very deep body of water high up in the Langdale Pikes, thirteen hundred feet above sea-level to be precise, with sheer, scree-covered cliffs on its eastern shore and mighty, wind-riven fells like Pavey Ark, Harrison Stickle and Great Castle Howe lowering to its north, west and south. It wasn't an especially scary place in modern times. Located in a hanging valley in a relatively remote spot – official title 'Cragstone Vale', unofficial title 'the Cradle' – it was a fearsome prospect on paper. But when you actually got there, the atmosphere was more holiday than horror. Two cheery Lakeland hamlets, Cragstone Keld and Sticklefoot Ho, occupied its southern and northern points respectively, while for much of the year the whole place teemed with climbers, hikers, fell-runners and anglers seeking the famous Witch Cradle trout, while kayakers and white-water rafters were catered for by the Cradle Boat Club, based a mile south of Cragstone Keld, near the head of the Cragstone Race; a furiously twisting river, which poured downhill through natural gullies and steep culverts before finally joining the more sedately flowing Langdale Beck.

The single pub at the heart of Cragstone Keld only added to this homely feel. A rather austere looking building at first glance, all grey Westmorland slate on the outside, it was famous for its smoky beams and handsome oak settles, its range of cask ales, its crackling fires in winter and its pretty lakeside beer garden in summer. Its name – The Witch's Kettle – owed itself entirely to some enterprising landlord of decades past, who hadn't found The Drovers' Rest to his taste, and felt the witch business a tad sexier, especially given that most visitors to the Cradle were always awe-stricken by the deep pinewoods hemming its two villages to the lakeshore, and the rubble-clad slopes and immense granite crags soaring overhead. Its inn-sign, which was regularly repainted and re-framed in black iron, was a landmark in itself, depicting a rusty old kettle with green herbs protruding from under its lid, sitting on a stone inscribed with pagan runes.

It was just possible, visitors supposed, that current land-lady, Hazel Carter, might herself be a witch, but if so she was a far cry from the bent nose and warty lip variety.

At least, that was Heck's feeling.

He'd only been up here three months, but was already certain that whatever magic Hazel wove, it was unlikely to be the sort he'd resist easily. Not that he was thinking along these lines that late November morning, as he entered The Witch's Kettle just before eleven, made a bee-line for the bar and ordered himself a pint of Buttermere Gold. It was early in the day and there were few customers yet. Only Hazel was on duty. Like Heck she was in her late thirties, but with rich auburn hair, which she habitually wore very long. She was doe-eyed, soft-lipped, and buxom in shape, a figure enhanced by her daytime 'uniform' of t-shirt, cardigan and jeans.

They made close eye-contact but only uttered those words necessary for the transaction. However, as she handed him his pint and his change, the landlady inclined her head slightly to the right. Heck pocketed the cash and sipped his beer, before glancing in that direction. Beyond a low arch lay the pub's vault, which contained a darts board and a pool table. One person was present in there: a young lad, no more than sixteen, with tousled blond hair, wearing a grey sweatshirt, grey canvas trousers and white trainers. He looked once, fleetingly, in Heck's direction as he worked his way around the pool table, ignoring him thereafter. All the youth had seen, of course, was a man about six feet in height, of average build, with unruly black hair and faint scars on his face, wearing jeans, a sweater and a rumpled waterproof jacket. But he'd probably have paid more attention had he known that Heck was actually Detective Sergeant Mark Heckenburg of the Cumbria Constabulary, that he was based very near to here, at Cragstone Keld police office, and that he was on duty right at this moment.

To maintain his façade of recreation, Heck found a seat at an empty table, pulled a rolled-up *Westmorland Gazette* from his back pocket and commenced reading. He checked his watch as he turned the pages, though this was more from habit than necessity. He felt he was following a good lead today, but there was no great pressure on him. Ever since being reassigned from Scotland Yard to Cumbria as part of ACPO's new Anti-Rural Crime Initiative, Heck had been well-placed to work hours of his own choosing and at his own pace. Ultimately of course, he was answerable to South Cumbria Crime Command, and in the first instance to the CID office down at Windermere police station; he was only a sergeant when all was said and done. But as the only CID officer in the Langdales – the only CID officer in twenty square miles in fact – he was out here on his own as far as many colleagues were concerned: 'Hey pal, you're the man on the spot', as they'd say. There were advantages to this, without doubt. But it was never a nice feeling that reinforcements were always a good forty minutes away.

His thoughts were distracted as two other people came down the stairs into the taproom. It was a man and a woman, both in their mid-twenties, both carrying bulging backpacks. The woman had short, mouse-brown hair, and wore a red cagoule, blue cord trousers and walking-boots. The man was tall and thin, with short fair hair. He too wore cord trousers and walking-boots, but his blue cagoule was draped over his narrow, t-shirted shoulders. Neither of them looked threatening or in any way unwholesome; in fact they were smiling and chattering brightly. At the foot of the stair, they separated, the man heading to the bar, where he told Hazel he'd like to 'settle up'. The woman turned into the vault and spoke to the youth, who pocketed his last ball and grabbed up a backpack of his own.

The trio left the pub together, still talking animatedly – a family enjoying their holiday. As the door swung closed behind them, Heck glanced over the top of his newspaper at Hazel, who nodded. Leaping to his feet, he crossed the room to the car park window, and watched as the trio approached a metallic green Hyundai Accent. He'd been informed by Hazel beforehand that this was the vehicle they'd arrived in two weeks ago, and had already run a PNC check on it, to discover that its registration number – V513 HNV – actually belonged to a black Volvo estate supposedly sold to a scrap merchant in Grimsby nine months earlier. Without a backward glance, they piled into the Hyundai and pulled out of the car park, heading south out of the village.

Heck hurried outside – it was only noon, but it was a grey day and there was already a deep chill. Thanks to the season, the village was quieter than usual. Beyond the pines, the upward-sweeping moors were bare, brown and stubbled with bracken.

Heck climbed into his white Citroën DS4, starting the engine and hitting the heater switch, but resisted the temptation to jump straight onto the suspects' tail. At this time of year, with traffic more scarce than usual, it would be easy to get spotted. Besides, there was only one way you could enter or leave the Cradle: via the aptly named Cragstone Road, a perilously narrow single-track, which wound downhill over steep, rock-strewn slopes for several hundred feet, sometimes tilting to a gradient of one in three – so it wasn't like the suspects could turn off anywhere, or even drive away at high speed. Of course, once the trio had descended into Great Langdale, the vast glacial valley at the heart of this district, it was another matter. So he couldn't afford to hang back too far.

As such, he gave them a thirty-second start.

It was about three miles from the village to the commencement of the descent, and Heck didn't see a single soul as he traversed it, nor another car, which was comforting – though it was useful to be able to hide among normal vehicles, an open road was reassuring in the event you might need to chase. As he began his descent, he initially couldn't see his target, but he refused to panic. The blacktop meandered wildly on its downward route, arcing around perilous bends and through clumps of shadowy pine. But when he finally did sight the Hyundai, it had got further ahead than he'd expected. It was diminutive; no more than a glinting green toy.

He accelerated, veering dangerously as the road dropped, taking curves with increasingly reckless abandon. As he did, he tried his radio, receiving only dead-air responses. There was minimal reception in the Cradle, the encompassing cliffs interfering so drastically with signals that most communications from Cragstone Keld nick had to be made via landline. But it would improve as he descended into Langdale. In anticipation of this, he was already tuned to a talk-through channel.

'Heckenburg to 1416, over?' he repeated.

He'd descended to six hundred feet before he gleaned a response.

'1416 receiving. Go ahead, sarge.' The voice was shrill, with an Ulster brogue.

'Suspects on the move, M-E . . . heading down Cragstone Road towards the B5343. Where are you, over?'

M-E, or PC 1416 Mary-Ellen O'Rourke, Cragstone Keld nick's only uniformed officer – she was actually resident there, bunking in the flat above the office – took a second or two to respond. *'Heading up Little Langdale from Skelwith Bridge, sarge. They still in that green Hyundai, over?'*

'Affirmative. Still showing the dodgy VRM. I'll give you a shout soon as I know which way they're headed, over?'

'Roger that.'

As Heck now descended towards the junction with the B5343, he had a clear vision both west and east along Great Langdale. This was a vastly more expansive valley than Cragstone Vale, its head encircled by some of Cumbria's most impressive fells; not just the craggy-topped Langdale Pikes, but Great Knott, Crinkle Crags, Bowfell and Long Top – their barren upper reaches ascending to dizzying heights. By contrast, its floor was flat and fertile, and perhaps half a mile across, much of it divided by dry-stone walls and given over to cattle grazing. Down its centre, in a west to east direction, flowed Langdale Beck, a broad, rocky river, normally shallow but running deep at present after a

453

spectacularly soggy October and November. A hundred yards ahead meanwhile, at the end of Cragstone Road, the Hyundai passed straight onto the B5343 without stopping, following the larger route as it swung sharply south, crossing the river by a narrow bridge. Still hoping to avoid detection, Heck dallied at the junction, watching the Hyundai shrink as it ascended the higher ground on the far side. 'Heckenburg to 1416?'

'*Receiving, sarge . . . go ahead.*'

'Suspect vehicle heading south along the upper section of the B5343, over.' He glanced at his sat-nav. 'That means they're coming your way, M-E.'

'*Affirmative, sarge. I'm headed in that direction now. You want me to intercept?*'

'Negative . . . we haven't got enough on them yet.'

There was only one patrol vehicle attached permanently to Cragstone Keld police station: the powerful Land Rover Mary-Ellen was currently driving. Decked in vivid yellow-and-turquoise Battenburg, it was purposely designed to be noticeable on these bleak uplands; it even had a special insignia on its roof so air support could home in on it – but that was less useful on occasions like this, with stealth the order of the day.

'M-E . . . proceed to Little Langdale village, and park up,' Heck said as an afterthought. 'That way, if they reach your position and we still don't want to pull them, you can get out of sight.'

'*Wilco,*' she replied.

He hit the gas as he accelerated onto the B5343 and followed it across the valley bottom, taking the bridge over the beck. The Hyundai was still in sight, but high up now and far away; a green matchbox car. It would dwindle from view altogether shortly. Heck floored the pedal, the dry-stone walls enclosing the paddocks falling behind, to be replaced by swathes of tough, tussocky grass, which sloped steeply upward ahead of him. The fleecy white/grey blobs of Herdwick sheep were dotted all over the valley's eastern sides, several wandering across the road as he accelerated, scattering and bleating in response. Officially, the B5343 no longer bore that title at this point – it was now significantly less than a B-road, but it never rose as high as the Cragstone Road, and in fact levelled out at around seven hundred feet. Once again, it banked and swung, though Heck kept his foot down, managing to close the distance between himself and the Hyundai to about four hundred yards.

The ground on the right had now dropped away into a deep, tree-filled ravine, through the middle of which a smaller beck tumbled noisily, draining excess water from Blea Tarn, the next lake on this route, located about five miles ahead. Before that, approaching on the right, there was another pub, The Three Ravens. In appearance, this was more like a Lakeland cottage, low and squat, built from whitewashed stone. Despite its dramatic perch on the very edge of the ravine, a small car park was attached to one side of it, though only one vehicle was visible there at present: a maroon BMW Coupe.

Heck glanced at his watch – it was lunchtime. This was the time of day the bastards usually pounced. His gaze flirted back to the Hyundai, the tail-lights of which glowed red, its indicator flashing as it veered right into The Three Ravens car park, pulling up almost flush against the pub wall.

Heck smiled to himself. They'd sussed this spot out previously, and knew where the outdoor CCTV was unlikely to catch them.

'Heckenburg to 1416, over?'

The response was semi-audible owing to the higher ground, filtered through noisy static. *'Go ahead, sarge.'*

'We're on, M-E. Suspects have called at The Three Ravens

pub, overlooking Blea Tarn ghyll. If I'm right, they're going to hit their next target somewhere between here and the tarn. It's perfect for them. Five miles of the remotest stretch of road in the Langdales. In fact I think it's a must-hit. They won't want to chance it after that . . . too many cottages.'

'*Received, sarge. How do you want to play it, over?*'

'Bring your Land Rover up the B5343. Wait on Blea Tarn car park. But tuck yourself out of the way in case they carry on past, over.'

'*Roger, received.*'

Heck proceeded past The Three Ravens car park, catching sight of the lad from the Hyundai loitering about, now with his sweatshirt hood drawn up, while the two adults entered the pub, no doubt to size up any potential opposition. Mindful of indoor CCTV, the girl had affected a blonde, shoulder-length wig, while the man had donned a woolly hat with what looked like ginger hair extensions around its rim. Heck could have laughed out loud, except that unsophisticated precautions like these often aided criminals hugely. Though not on this occasion, if he could just get his timings right. Feeling that old tingle of excitement – something in distinct short supply these last three months – he scanned the roadside verges for a lying-up point. A couple of hundred yards further on, he spied a break in the dry-stone wall on his left, a farm track leading through it and dropping out of sight into a hollow. He swung through and swerved down the stony lane, only halting among a thicket of alder, where he threw his Citroën into reverse, made a three-point turn and edged back uphill, halting some forty yards short of the gate. Jumping out, he climbed the rest of the track on foot, dropping to a crouch behind the right-hand gatepost and watching the road.

He wasn't sure how long this would take. If his suppositions were correct, the first thing this crew would do was establish whether or not their potential target was likely to be easy: an elderly couple perhaps or someone travelling alone would be preferable. Under normal circumstances they'd then ascertain which car in the car park belonged to said party. This was more simply done than the average member of the public might imagine, especially at a time of year when there were fewer cars to choose from. Maps and luggage, for example, would indicate visitors rather than locals; an absence of toys would suggest older travellers, which in its turn might be confirmed by evidence of medication or a choice of music or reading material – it was amazing what you could learn from the books and CDs that routinely littered foot-wells. In this case of course it would be even easier than usual – there was only one car. After that, it was a straightforward matter of disabling the car in question – previously this had been done by inflicting small punctures on the tyres with an air pistol – and following until it pulled up by the roadside.

A low rumble indicated the approach of a vehicle. Heck squatted lower. A soft-topped Volkswagen Sport roared past, leaves swirling in its wake. It was running smoothly with no sign that it was suffering any kind of damage.

He relaxed again, ruminating for another fifteen minutes or so, reminding himself that patience and caution weren't just virtues in this kind of work, they were essential. So much of the success enjoyed by professional criminals was down to the fear they created with their efficiency – the way they came and went like ghosts, the way they knew exactly who to victimise, exactly where to find such easy prey, exactly when to catch it at its most vulnerable. It bewildered and terrified the average man and woman; it was as though the felons possessed supernatural instincts. Yet in reality it owed to little more than thorough preparation and a bit of basic cunning, and in the case of distraction-thieves like this particular crew, a quick glance through the windows of a few parked cars. In some ways, that was impressive – you couldn't fail to admire someone who was so good at what they did, even something as nasty and callous as this, that it provided them with a fat living – but it didn't make them the Cosa Nostra.

The radio crackled in his jacket pocket. *'1416 to DS Heckenburg?'*

'Go ahead, M-E,' he replied.

'In position now, sarge.'

'Stay sharp, over.'

'Roger that.'

Another vehicle was approaching, this time minus the low, steady hum of a healthy engine. Instead, Heck heard a repeating metallic rattle – as if something was broken. He tensed as he lowered himself. Two seconds later, the BMW Coupe from The Three Ravens car park chugged past, its driver as yet unaware he had two slow-punctures on his nearside.

Unaware now maybe, though not for long.

Heck tensed again, waiting. The thieves wouldn't have dashed straight out of the pub in pursuit of the BMW's occupants – that might have attracted attention; but they wouldn't want to let them get too far ahead either. And right on cue, only half a minute later, the Hyundai itself came slowly in pursuit.

Heck dashed back to his Citroën, gunned it up the track to the main road and swung left. It was only a matter of distance now. With a single deflating tyre, it was possible an innocent motorist would keep driving, failing to notice, but with two that was highly unlikely. Around the next bend, the road spooled out clearly for about two hundred yards, at the far end of which Heck saw the BMW wallowing to a halt beneath a twisted ash. The Hyundai prowling after it hadn't reached that point yet, but was already decelerating.

Heck hit the brakes too, swinging his Citroën hard up onto the nearside verge, so that it was out of sight. He jumped out, vaulted over the wall, and scrambled forward along undulating pasture, staying parallel to the road but keeping as low as he could.

This was the ideal spot for an ambush, he realised. Brown Howe was a lowering presence on the left, Pike of Blisco performing the same function on the right. Utter silence lay across the deserted, bracken-clad valley lying between them. The dull grey sky tinged everything with an air of wildness and desolation. No tents were visible, no hikers; there wasn't even a shepherd or farm-worker in sight.

Heck advanced sixty yards or so, and moved back to the wall, where a belt of fir trees would screen him. The two cars were still visible, the Hyundai parked directly behind the BMW. Four people now stood by the vehicles' nearside. A dumpy balding man, and a thin white-haired woman, both in matching sweaters, had clearly been the occupants of the BMW. But Heck also saw the girl in the blonde wig, and the lean young man in the woolly cap, who even now was stripping off his cagoule, no doubt offering to change one of the BMW's mangled tyres. Heck could imagine the advice he'd be giving them – mainly because the same spiel had been dealt to those others who'd suffered this fate in the Yorkshire Dales and the Peak District.

'A double blow-out's a bit of a problem,' the Good Samaritan would opine. 'But if you use the spare to replace the front one, you should be able to get down to the nearest town, where a garage can fix the rear one for you.'

Wise advice, delivered in casual, friendly fashion – and all the while, the third member of the trio, the youth, who the victims wouldn't even know was present, would be sliding unobtrusively out of the back of the Hyundai's rear and crawling around to the target vehicle's offside, from where he could open the passenger door and help himself to whatever jackets, coats, handbags and wallets had been dumped on the back seat. A classic distraction-theft, which even now – as Heck watched – had gone into play. The lad, still in his neutral grey clothing, snaked along the tarmac, passing the Hyundai on all fours.

Heck stayed in the field but ran forward at pace, climbing a low barbed wire fence, and hissing into his radio. 'Thieves on, M-E! Thieves on! Move it . . . fast!'

Mary-Ellen responded in the affirmative, but it was Heck who reached the scene of the crime first, zipping up his waterproof jacket as he jumped the wall and emerged on the roadside, coming around the twisted ash before anyone had even noticed.

'Afternoon all,' he said, strolling to the rear of the BMW, where the youth, still on hands and knees, but now with a purse, a wallet, an iPad and a laptop laid on the road surface alongside him, could only gaze up, white-faced. 'This is illegal, isn't it?'

The elderly couple regarded Heck in bemusement, an expression that only changed when he scooped down, caught the lad under his armpit and hoisted him up into view. At once the younger couple reacted, the girl backing away wide-eyed, but the bloke actually turning and sprinting along the road.

He didn't get far before Mary-Ellen's Land Rover, blues and twos flickering, spun into view over the next rise, sliding to a side-on halt, blocking the carriageway. The thief fancied his chances when he saw the figure who emerged from it: a Cumbrian police uniform complete with hi-viz doublet, utility belt loaded with the usual appointments, cuffs, baton, PAVA spray and so forth, but with only a young girl inside it – probably younger than he was in fact, and considerably shorter, no more than five-five. Of course he didn't know PC Mary-Ellen O'Rourke's reputation for being a fitness fanatic and pocket battleship. When she crossed the road to intercept him, he tried to barge his way past, only to be taken around the legs with a flying rugby tackle, which brought him down heavily, slamming his face on the tarmac. He lay there groaning, his fake head-piece hanging off, exposing the fair hair underneath. Mary-Ellen knelt cheerfully on his back and applied the handcuffs.

'Sorry folks,' Heck said to the astonished elderly couple, as he marched past, driving the other two prisoners by the scruffs of their necks. 'DS Heckenburg, Cumbrian Constabulary. We've been after this lot for a little while.'

'We've not done nothing,' the girl protested. 'We were trying to help.'

'Yeah, by lightening these good people's load while they were on their holidays,' Heck replied. 'Well don't worry, now you're going on *your* holidays. At Her Majesty's pleasure. You don't have to say anything, but it may harm your defence if you don't mention when questioned something you later rely on in court. Anything you do say may be given in evidence . . . in case you were wondering, you're all locked up for being a set of thieving little scrotes.'

It was mid-evening when the arresting officers finally returned from Windermere police station, where they'd taken their prisoners for interview and charge. While Mary-Ellen headed to Cragstone Keld nick to sign off and close up for the day, Heck made his first port of call The Witch's Kettle, not least because on a cold and misty autumn night like this – the chill in the air had now turned icy – the warm, ruddy light pouring from its windows was very alluring. Inside, a big fire crackled in the grate, throwing orange phantasms across the *olde worlde* fittings. Though

461

once again, thanks to the time of year, there were only a few customers present: Ted Haveloc, a retired Forestry Commission worker, who now did everyone's gardens for them; and Joe and Mandy Elwell, who ran the Post Office. Hazel was alone behind the bar, reading a paperback. She laid it down as Heck approached.

'And?' she asked, vaguely uneasy.

He took off his jacket and pulled up a stool. 'Couldn't have done it without you.'

'You arrested them?' She looked surprised, but still perhaps a little shaky. Hazel was every inch a local lass – she was well travelled but had never actually lived outside the Lake District, as her soft Cumbrian accent attested – and the thought of serious crime finally visiting this peaceful quarter was something she was still trying to get her head around.

'All three,' he confirmed. 'Caught 'em in the act.'

She served him his usual pint of Buttermere Gold. 'So what was it all about? Or aren't you allowed to tell me?'

'Suppose you've a right to know,' he said. 'Several times in the last fortnight, tourists up here have been waylaid by distraction-thieves. It happened in Borrowdale, near Ullswater and down in Grizedale Forest. The usual form was the visitors stopped for lunch somewhere, but no sooner had they got back on the road than they had to pull over with a couple of flat tyres. A few minutes later, a young bloke and his girlfriend would conveniently stop to assist. Once these two had driven off again, the tourists found valuables missing from their vehicles.'

Hazel looked fascinated, and now maybe a little relieved that the crimes in question weren't anything more violent. 'I've heard about that on the Continent.'

'Well . . . it if works in France and Spain, there's no reason why it shouldn't work here. Especially in rural areas. All we knew was that the suspects were driving either a green or blue motor, which might have been a Hyundai. The victims were never totally sure, and we only got glimpses of it on car park security footage . . . on top of that we only ever had partial VRM numbers, and they never seemed to marry up. You won't be surprised to learn that after we arrested this lot, we found dozens of different plates in the boot, which they changed around regularly.'

'So this was like their full-time job?'

'Their career. The way they made their living. Anyway . . .' He sipped at his beer. 'As the crime-spree only seemed to start around here two weeks ago, I made a few enquiries with other forces covering tourist spots – and I got several similar reports. A young male and female distraction team targeting motorists out in the sticks. It was always the same pattern. The boy offered to help with the tyre-change, while the girl stood around chatting. In no case did the spree last more than two weeks.'

'They only booked in here for two weeks,' Hazel said.

'They never outstay their welcome,' he replied. 'The upshot was I canvassed all the hotels and bed and breakfasts.'

'And that worked?' She looked sceptical. 'I mean, even in the off-season there are thousands of young couples who come up to the Lakes.'

'Yeah, but not so many who've got a gooseberry in tow.'

'I don't get you.'

Heck leaned forward. 'You may recall . . . I didn't ask you if there were any adult couples staying here. I asked if there were any adult trios.'

'Ohhh.' Now Hazel looked impressed. 'Who's a clever boy?'

'It struck me there'd have to be a third thief, someone concealed in the Hyundai. He would do the actual stealing while the others put on their show.'

'And sure enough one such trio was staying here,' she said. 'And they even drove a Hyundai.'

'And the rest is history.' He grinned. 'Mind you, I'm not saying we didn't get lucky that they happened to be rooming right here.'

She continued mopping the bar. 'So long as they're gone. I mean I hope they haven't left anything behind . . . I wouldn't want them coming back here.'

'I wouldn't worry about that. Quite a few forces want to talk to them. They'll be in custody a good while yet.'

Realising he hadn't yet paid for his pint, he pushed some money across the bar-top, but she pushed it back. 'On me. For a job well done.' She shook her head. 'I'll tell you what . . . I'd never have had them pegged for criminals. Didn't seem rough at all. If anything, they came over as a nice young family.'

'Successful crooks are rarely dumb. You want to infiltrate quiet communities, it doesn't make any sense to ride in like a bunch of cowboys. Not in this day and age.'

'Makes you realise how vulnerable we are up here, though.'

'Nahhh,' came a brash, chirpy voice. Mary-Ellen had materialised alongside them, now in a black tracksuit with *Dorset Police* stencilled across the front. She leapt athletically onto the bar stool next to Heck. She was toothy but pretty, with fierce green eyes and short, spiky black hair. A champion swimmer, fell-walker and rock-climber, she radiated energy and enthusiasm – even now, at the end of a long, tough shift. 'You've got us two, haven't you?' she said. 'We're a match for anyone.'

Heck made a modest gesture. 'And here's the other girl of the moment. Wouldn't have been able to do it without her, either.'

'What'll you have, M-E?' Hazel asked.

The Irish lass feigned astonishment. 'You buying, sarge?'

464

'*I'm* buying,' Hazel said. 'You two have taken some nasty people off the streets today. *Our* streets. And with the bad weather due, they could have been stuck around here for God knows how long. Who knew, we could have been murdered in our beds.'

'Don't think they were quite that nasty,' Mary-Ellen replied with her trademark rasping chuckle. 'But I'll have a lager, cheers. I'll tell you what . . . felt good getting our hands on some proper villains for a change, eh?'

'Too true,' Heck said, peeling away from the bar and heading off to the Gents. 'Excuse me, ladies . . . too bloody true.'

Neither of the women chose to comment on that parting shot.

Mary-Ellen was a newcomer to the Lake District herself, having transferred up here only a couple of months ago. Prior to this she'd served in Sherborne, near the South Coast, another semi-rural area, so she lacked Heck's experience of big city policing and major investigations. But given that the most serious crimes they tended to have to deal with up here involved low-level drug dealing, thefts from gardens, and the occasional drunken incidents in pubs – she could understand how he might be feeling a little restless. He'd taken to this distraction-thefts enquiry giddily, like a kiddie in a toy shop, and had almost seemed disappointed he'd closed the suspects down so quickly. But whether Hazel would sympathise with this was another matter. In the real world, the handsome, homely landlady – newly divorced thanks to her beer-bloated rat of a husband running off with one of his barmaids two years ago – should be the apple of every single bloke's eye. The problem was there weren't that many single blokes in the Cradle. As such, it was perhaps no surprise Hazel and Heck had gravitated towards each other.

It had occurred by increments, if Mary-Ellen was honest . . . with near-reluctance, as though both parties were trying to avoid being hurt, or perhaps trying to avoid hurting each other. But though they'd never so much as exchanged a kiss in public, the Irish lass had seen their mutual attraction grow: the furtive looks they'd exchanged, the occasional touching of hands, Heck perched comfortably at the end of the bar where the till and telephone sat, a position of familiarity that wouldn't normally be reserved for everyday customers. In light of all this, it was anyone's guess what kind of confidences he and Hazel shared – and maybe a concern that he was wasting himself out here in the boondocks was one of them. Even if it wasn't, Hazel was surely worldly enough to sense it for herself . . . and yet she was famously proud of this small, successful business she ran, and she adored her tranquil life in Cragstone Keld, this 'haven in the mountains' as she called it. The idea of moving anywhere else was hardly likely to appeal to her. In that respect, Heck's increasing boredom with his current post was a subject probably best left alone.

'Will I have to give evidence?' Hazel asked when he returned to the bar.

Heck pondered. 'Shouldn't think so. I mean, there's nothing they could cross-examine you on. I enquired if you knew anyone matching a certain description. You did and gave me a statement. After that, you had no further involvement. In any case, they've already coughed to the distraction-thefts up here in the Lakes, so the chances are that part of the case won't go to trial.'

'I may need that from you in writing if I'm not going to worry about it,' she said, moving along the bar to serve another customer.

'So what do we think?' Mary-Ellen asked. 'Good day?'

'Very good day,' he confirmed.

466

'Hazel's right about the weather. Forecast's terrible. Freezing fog up here tonight and tomorrow. Maybe even longer. Visibility down to a few feet.'

'Great. Life'll be even quieter.'

'Hey . . .' She elbowed him. 'A few detectives I know'd be glad of that. Catch up on some paperwork.'

'To catch up on paperwork, M-E, you first have to generate it.'

She regarded him appraisingly. As a rule, Heck didn't get morose. But he was leaning towards glum at present. 'Heck, didn't you *volunteer* for this gig?'

'Yeah . . . sort of.' He waved it away. 'Sorry . . . quiet is good. Course it is. Means low levels of crime, people sleeping safe in their beds. How can I complain?'

She chugged on her lager. 'It won't be cakes and ale. There'll be accidents. People'll get lost, get hurt . . . there's always some bell-end who'll come up here alone, whatever the weather man says.'

Heck pondered this. It was true – the fells were no place for inexperienced hikers, especially in bad weather. And yet all winter the amateurs would try their hands, necessitating regular and risky turn-outs for the emergency services. If this coming winter turned particularly nasty, the Cradle itself could face problems. With only Cragstone Road connecting it to the outside world, snow, sleet and even heavy rain had the potential to cut them off. The predicted fog would be even more of a nuisance as it may prevent the Mountain Rescue services deploying their helicopter.

'I think I can safely say,' he concluded, 'that even I would rather be tucked up warm in bed than dealing with that lot.'

'I'm sure that'll be an option,' Mary-Ellen said quietly, as Hazel came back along the bar.

'Looks like there won't be much custom in here for the next few days,' the landlady commented.

'Just what we were saying,' Mary-Ellen agreed, drinking up. 'Anyway, I'm off. Thanks for the beer.'

Heck glanced around. 'Bit early . . .?'

'*True Detective*'s on satellite again tonight. Missed it the first time round.' She sauntered out of the pub. 'See you later.'

'*True Detective* . . .?' Hazel mused. 'Isn't that the one where they were after some kind of satanic killer?'

'Seem to recall it was,' Heck replied.

She recommended mopping the bar-top. 'Not the kind of thing we get up at Witch Cradle . . . despite the name.'

'So I've noticed.'

'These sneaky buggers pinching people's handbags and wallets are about the toughest we're used to up here.'

'Let's hope it stays that way.'

She gave him a warm half-smile. 'Yeah . . . course you do.'

'Hey, I may surprise you.'

'Oh?'

'I'm adaptable. The quiet life has its attractions.'

'Such as?'

He shrugged. 'We're all adults. It's not like we can't find ways to fill these long, uneventful hours.'

She smiled at him again, saucily, as she pulled Ted Haveloc a pint.

Outside meanwhile, as the forecasters had predicted, a front of semi-frozen air forged its way across the mountains and valleys of northwest England, sliding under the milder upper air, gradually forming a dense blanket of leprous-grey fog, which, in a region already famous for having very few street-lamps, reduced visibility to virtually nothing. The scattered towns and villages were shrouded in murk. Cragstone Keld – a hamlet of only twelve buildings – was swamped; one house couldn't see another. And of course it was cold, so terribly cold: billions of frigid water crystals suspended in the gloom; every twig, every tuft of withered vegetation sprouting feathers of frost. By eleven o'clock, as the last few house-lights winked out and the full blackness of night took hold, the polar silence was ethereal, the stillness unearthly.

Nothing stirred out there.

These were foul conditions, they'd say.

It was a foul night all round.

The foulest really.

Abhorrent.

Loathsome.

Want more? Read the rest of
Dead Man Walking
*when it hits the shelves in
November 2014.*

Get back to where it all started
with book one of the series, where Heck
meets the Nice Guys for the first time...

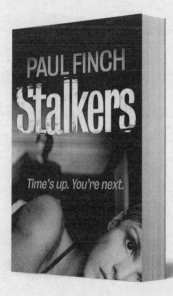

Dark, terrifying and unforgettable.
Stalkers will keep fans of Stuart
MacBride and James Oswald
looking over their shoulder.

A vicious serial killer is holding
the country to ransom, publicly – and
gruesomely – murdering his victims.

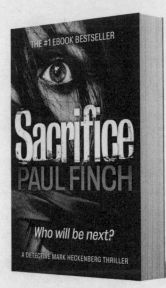

A heart-stopping and unforgettable
thriller that you won't be able to put
down, from bestseller Paul Finch.